The

and the

Redcoat

Lorna Windham

© Lorna Windham, 2017
Published by:
Tyne Bridge Publishing,
City Library, Newcastle upon Tyne, United Kingdom
tynebridgepublishing.org.uk

This edition 2019.

The right of Lorna Windham to be identified as the author of this work has been asserted by her in accordance with Sections 77 and 78 of the Copyright, Design and Patents Act 1988.

All rights reserved. No part of this publication may be reproduced, stored in a retrieval system or transmitted, in any form or by any means, electronic, mechanical, recording or otherwise, in any part of the world, without the prior written permission of the publisher.

This book is sold subject to the condition that it shall not, by way of trade or otherwise, be lent, resold, hired out, or otherwise circulated without the publisher's prior consent in any form of binding or cover other than that in which it is published and without a similar condition, including this condition, being imposed on the subsequent purchaser.

This book is a work of fiction.

For Mam and Dad

I'd like to thank my family, Tyne Bridge Publishing, the Border Reivers' writing group, all my writing friends and David for being David.

CHAPTER One

The last of the sun's rays played on an indigo tapestry in Kerbilly House. Lady Anne Kerr sat in the Needle Room. A pine sea chest overflowed with linen chemises and silk skirts which cascaded over the carpet at Anne's feet. On her lap lay a cream bodice woven with gold thread made for her wedding by French seamstresses

Scents from rose and honeysuckle pervaded the air; Anne had cut and arranged the flowers in a blue and white vase on a table in the centre of the room.

She held the bodice against her breast. *Rob Stewart. Would they get on?* She turned at a knock on the door. 'Yes?'

Her father entered his mouth set in a grim line. In one hand he carried his spectacles and in the other a crumpled sheet of parchment.

'Father, what's wrong? Is it the Rising? Has Prince Charlie landed?'

'My dear...sit and read this.' His breath came in small gasps.

Wide-eyed she took it from him and sat beside the marble fireplace. The letter had been written the week before.

At first Anne couldn't make sense of it. Words such as, *honourable* and *deepest regret* danced then blurred on the page. She took a deep breath, allowed her vision to clear and read again.

Her stomach knotted; blood pounded in her ears. *Lord, he couldn't mean it.*

Braedrumie House,
July 1st, 1745.
Sir,

I feel it is only honourable to inform you that for reasons personal to me, I must leave Scotland. It is, therefore, with the deepest regret that I release your daughter from our betrothal contract. Please offer my sincerest apologies to Lady Anne and my very best wishes for her future.

I remain your obedient servant,

Rob Stewart.

Leave Scotland. Leaving, jilting me. The marriage has been negotiated between our fathers. I've never even met Rob Stewart; I'll be a laughing stock. Invitations have been out for months, gifts starting to arrive. He has to know what I'll endure: the scornful looks, the pitying glances. Her head swam.

A hand patted her shoulder. 'I'll write to his father, he'll no' be happy with this.'

'No.' She tasted metal in her mouth and had bitten her thumb till the blood flowed. She strode towards the window and looked out. The grey surf as restless as her thoughts.

'Young fool,' said her father. He thumped his fist into his palm. 'There's money to be made if they can drag him back.'

'I'll not have a man who's forced.' She watched as spume flew over the rocks.

'But it's only right. We shook hands on it.'

She turned and in five paces stood by the fire. 'I said no. I'll not have him.' She balled the letter in her fist and threw her rejection in the grate. *Pity it isn't Rob Stewart's head.* The flames blazed, but had little effect. She sighed.

Her father put out his hands. 'Anne, be reasonable.'

'No.' She hugged herself. 'I'll not have you beg and shame me even more.'

'I sought references.' He put his thin arm round her. 'Was assured in the highest places he's a gentleman from an honourable family. He's much admired, well thought of by all who spoke of him. As heir to Braedrumie, he's the perfect match.'

'No' for me.' She moved away from him and tucked a stray strand of red-gold hair back in place. 'You thought him honourable. We're well rid of him.'

'But daughter, you dinna understand. With the Stewart's ships added to ours and their trading links in the Americas we'll double our wealth.'

She spun round. 'No Father, you dinna understand. He's played us false and embarrassed and humiliated me to the point of ruin. Who'll have me now?'

'That's why I must write to his father.'

'I'll no' marry Rob Stewart, if he was the last man on earth. I'll never forgive him for this. Marriage to him would mean no joy for either of us.'

Her father's face and shoulders sagged.

Oh, no. The devil with Rob Stewart. 'I'm sorry.' She took him by the hand and led him to her favourite armchair. 'Sit by the fire, Father. You look weary. Would you like some snuff or shall I light your pipe?'

'In the Needle Room? No, thank you my dear.' He sat and laid his grey head on the chair's leather back. 'Your mother would have known what to do in these troubled times.'

He looks pale. Anne settled on her knees beside him and squeezed his hand. 'I'm sure she would.'

'I counted myself the most fortunate of men when we married and the most miserable when she died. God be thanked He gave me you. You have her hair and eyes, you know.' He kissed Anne's forehead. 'Aye and her temper and I love you for it.'

She ran her fingers along new furrows on his forehead as if to erase them. 'I love you too, Father. You seem concerned, is ought else worrying you?'

'Nothing for you to concern your wee head about.' He eased himself out of the chair. 'I'll write to everyone and inform them the wedding's cancelled.' He set off towards the door. 'Why God saw fit to stiffen old men's bones I dinna ken. I'm sorry, my dear.' He shook his head and closed the door behind him.

Anne stared through the window at the gardens and the white flecked sea beyond. Earlier that morning she'd worn her wedding dress newly arrived from France on one of her father's ships. She'd swept up the hair from the nape of her neck and looked in the mirror. A fairy tale image in a cream and gold bodice, skirt and slippers had looked back at her.

Joan's hazel eyes had looked up at her mistress in wonder. The maid stuffed her own bush- brown hair in some semblance of order and with a mouth full of pins, knelt on the carpet.

Anne turned this way and that, pleased with what she saw. If this marriage had to happen then she'd wanted this stranger, this Rob Stewart of Braedrumie, to know that his bride was desirable and wealthy.

Joan removed the pins. 'You look wonderful, milady.' She clutched her thin hands together as if in supplication. 'I canna wait to see all the grand ladies and gentlemen in satins and silks. The weddin' breakfast will be so lovely and you a Jacobite bride with your handsome groom.'

Anne fluttered her fan and paced the room. 'Lord, it's warm.'

The comment earned her a glance from Joan, who'd raised her dark eyebrows as the wind gusted down the chimney.

Anne hadn't been able to stop thinking about Rob Stewart. Her cheeks burned at the thought of the physical intimacies she would have shared with this man. She gave a deep sigh. Her father assured her love would grow, as it had done for him and her dead mother. Anne hadn't known if she could endure a loveless marriage and wished she'd a mother's hand to guide her. It wouldn't be needed now.

A maid came and lit the candles. Anne inhaled the scent of beeswax mixed with that of the flowers. Darkness fell and a pale moon rose. Anne opened the sash window and let the wind stream through her hair.

Something glittered on the sill, caught in a silvery beam. Her fingers brushed the miniature and lingered a moment. She fingered the gold and pearls, admired the workmanship and examined the cameo Rob Stewart had sent her some months ago. A dark fellow with ocean-blue eyes and a strong chin stared back. His portrait held no answers to the questions she wanted to ask. *Impossibly handsome, Stewart must have paid the painter well to flatter him.* Her fingers tapped the miniature, lingered a moment and then grasped it. She leant forward and let it fall from her hand like a shower of iridescent stars to the ground below.

CHAPTER Two

Rob Stewart's conscience pricked him, no doubt about that. He'd spent days in the saddle going over what he'd done. Damn it, he felt guilty. His family and the Kerrs would be shocked, but there'd been no way out. He couldn't confide in anyone in his family. Since he'd returned from France, he'd been at loggerheads with his father about the Jacobites and his mother was unwell. He couldn't approach his brothers. Euan, would have been outraged, Johnnie too inexperienced and Duncan a bairn.

Rob ran his hand through his hair in frustration. He needed to talk over his problems with someone he trusted, like Davie Walker. They'd been students together, covered up their numerous madcap escapades at Glasgow University and kept in touch. Non-judgemental and a good listener, Davie had always understood. Rob decided Davie would be just the man and Lachlan House, nestled in a secluded glen, north west of Aberdeen, just the place.

It had taken Rob several days to ride from Braedrumie in the west Highlands through the rift valley of the Great Glen before he turned east. Days when he thought about the letter he'd written to the Kerrs and nights when he wrestled with images of Morag McColl. His troubles sat like a pack of hard rocks on his back as he passed several lochs and urged his pony south and headed for Davie's home.

Rob had thought to put all his troubles behind him, but they'd tormented him like demons. A thunderstorm hadn't helped. The only time he'd been at peace, was when he'd lain on beds of heather and slept like a dead man.

He arrived at Davie's, soaked and bespattered by mud as he trotted through the Walker's wrought iron gates. He followed the dipping drive and its avenue of oaks towards the house, a two storey, double fronted brick building with a byre, stables and paddocks.

Davie appeared at the front door and shaded his eyes as a watery sun slid from behind a cloud. 'Rob, man is it really you? What are you doing here? We had no word.'

Rob stopped his mare in front of him. 'It's good to see you, Davie.' His friend seemed a few inches taller and broader since he'd seen him last.

'And you.' Davie's fair brows creased in concern as they shook hands.

'My apologies,' said Rob. 'I thought to call in before continuing on to...er Edinburgh.'

'You'll stay a wee while?' Davie's widowed mother stepped out of the house at her son's side. Her grey hair escaped from under a dainty cap.

'Mother, this is Rob Stewart, from Braedrumie, Lady Anne's intended.'

Rob winced at that remark, trust the Walkers to know her. His conscience pricked him again. This could be deuced awkward.

'He's my friend from university,' said Davie.

'You've come a long way. Are you well, Mr. Stewart?' Mrs. Walker eyed him with a shrewd look.

Rob shifted in his saddle and then steadied himself. 'Merely tired, ma'am.'

'You're exhausted, Mr. Stewart, come in before you fall down, Davie will see to your pony and I'll see to a room.'

He'd rest here, talk to Davie and find some sort of peace. No sleeping in the heather tonight. He dismounted, tried not to wince, gave the reins to Davie and limped towards the wink of candlelit windows.

'You're hurt?' said Mrs. Walker.

'My mare shied in a storm and threw me,' said Rob.

'I'll organise a bath to ease your bones,' said Davie's mother and rushed ahead of him.

After a long soak in hot water, Rob rubbed a generous amount of liniment on his right knee which ached and his bruised backside. He assured himself the pungent smell would soon disperse, changed his clothes and glanced in the mirror. The face that stared back looked almost himself.

His stomach growled. The handful of oatcakes he'd grabbed from the scullery at home a distant memory. He sat himself at the table with all the caution of someone about to sit on a hedgehog.

Davie sniffed the air and stared at his friend.

Mrs. Walker coughed. 'There's plenty food, eat your fill.'

In front of them lay an array of cold meats. 'I've a fine syllabub for dessert, sweetened with wine and a hint of nutmeg,' said Mrs. Walker.

Rob demolished both dishes with little effort. 'That's the best I've ever eaten. Please give my regards to the cook.'

Mrs. Walker sat taller in her chair as her lips creased into a smile. 'More dessert, Rob?'

'I canna resist, ma'am,' said Rob helping himself. He ate it in three spoonfuls.

'There's nought wrong with a braw appetite.' She placed the syllabub in front of him again.

'I canna eat more of your fine food, Mrs. Walker, or I'll burst.'

'Janet.' She smiled at him. 'My friends call me Janet.'

Davie grinned at Rob as he kept them entertained with talk of Highland fashion and tales of hunting.

Once the servants cleared the table, Janet eased herself out of her chair. 'I'm away to my bed now. Davie, don't keep Rob from his too long, he looks fit to drop. Good night, gentlemen.'

Rob, restless, limped from window, to fireplace to shelves of books. Davie poured two generous drams of whisky and handed one to Rob. 'To Glasgow: May its university always thrive and its graduates prosper.' Rob raised his drink, gulped it down and welcomed its fiery breath.

Davie saluted Rob with his glass and followed suit. He poured more whisky for them both then settled in an armchair in front of the fire. The silence stretched in front of them like a dark night. 'Well,' said Davie at last, 'this is very fine, very fine indeed, to be drinking a wee dram with an old friend.' He indicated the chair opposite. 'Sit and rest yourself.'

A muscle twitched in Rob's cheek. He lowered himself and sat ramrod straight. He thanked God his backside seemed less tender.

Davie put his tumbler on the table and said, 'Out with it, Rob. Why did you no' send word you were coming?'

'My apologies again, spur of the moment decision.' Rob swigged his whisky.

Davie's eyes narrowed as he refilled the glass yet again. 'The last time we drank like this was after we graduated. To the King,' said Davie his brow furrowed. He quaffed his drink in one and tipped the bottom of his glass towards Rob who knew there'd be no etching of Prince Charlie there.

'It's a fine glass,' said Rob, 'and a fine toast.' He let the whisky flow down his throat and this time savoured the peaty taste. He lowered his voice. 'It seems we still agree we dinna have to go over the water for a fine King.'

Davie leant towards him and whispered, 'They say the Highlands are alive with rumours, Charlie's coming with French backing and promises from some of the clans, that there's another rebellion in the wind. Is that what this is all about?'

'There's always rumours in the Highlands,' said Rob. 'This Jacobite cause is mostly wishful thinking. The French canna be trusted nor some of the clans, if you could only hear them as I did. We've stability and peace under George II. Glasgow and Edinburgh are prosperous, given time wealth will spread to the Highlands. The British government willna stand for another rebellion. They didna with the others and willna now.'

The timbers of the house creaked or perhaps a foot shifted on a floorboard outside. The two men, missed a breath, looked at each other and listened.

Rob motioned Davie to be silent as he grabbed a candle and wrenched open the door. Cold air wrapped round him like a shroud. The flame fluttered and he shielded it with his hand until it spurted into life again. The hall and staircase leapt from darkness to flickers of gloom. No one, not even in the shadows. Closing the door Rob asked, 'Are your servants loyal?'

'Aye, but to whom?' Davie settled in his seat again. 'There's many a man plays both sides or keeps his true loyalties to himself until he knows who the winner will be. And your Father?'

'Still of the same mind, Jacobite to his last breath. He's no' thinking with his head.'

'Another whisky?'

'Aye.'

'But you havena come here to discuss Charlie, have you?' Davie poured the amber liquid into Rob's tumbler.

Rob swirled the whisky in his glass and then swallowed it. He felt his senses dull and the words came in a flood, 'No. I came to tell you, I'm leaving the Highlands, Braedrumie, my family, everybody and everything that I was.'

'You're no' serious? What about Anne and your wedding?'

'Called it off. She should be relieved, we never met you ken? Wouldn't have been much of a husband, her family are Jacobites, Father made sure of that.'

'You're a fool. She's a distant relative and quite lovely. She and Mother write.'

'It wouldna have mattered if she'd been Helen of Troy. I havena told anyone this, but I love someone else. And it's hopeless, quite hopeless.' Rob had a vision of brown hair and laughing eyes. He grimaced.

'Have you lost your senses, man? What about your family?'

'I just left with no word.'

'Ye Gods. Rob, you know how to shock a man. You canna expect me to condone this.'

'Do you remember when you called out MacLeay, because he besmirched the honour of a certain lady and her family?'

Davie fingered the scar on his cheek and groaned.

'And you asked me to be your second?'

'Aye.'

'And I tried to talk you out of it?' said Rob.

'It's no' the same.'

'Hear me out. You said it was a matter of honour. That sometimes a gentleman had to sacrifice himself for others.'

Davie sighed. 'Aye.'

'Well, that's what I'm doing, though the lady and family are unaware of it. And in a way that's what I am asking you to do, be my second.'

Davie half rose in from his chair in alarm, but Rob's outstretched palm stopped him.

'No' in a duel, but to hold my honour and theirs in your hands. If anything befalls me...'

Davie half rose again, Rob waved him back down.

'I want at least one trusted friend to know I acted with the best intentions for all concerned even though it may not seem like it now.

'And your family?'

'They'll think me ungrateful and probably disown me.' Rob shrugged. 'Father will never understand, my brothers perhaps, in time.' Their faces flashed in front of him. Would Euan always eager for battle; bookish Johnnie, or wee, impatient Duncan understand? 'There was nought else I could do.'

'What next?'

'I dinna ken. Go south, to England perhaps or abroad. I've uncles in the fur trade in the Americas who might look kindly on a wayward nephew. I wanted you to know, you're the only one I thought would understand. It's a matter of honour you see. I overheard Morag accept Euan's proposal. I canna possibly go back.'

'Ah. The lovely Morag, of course.' Davie eyed Rob over his glass. 'Bide a wee while with us. It'll give you time to think, work things out.'

'Decent of you,' said Rob and stifled a yawn.

'My apologies, you're tired of course.'

'I'm drunk,' Rob said as his eyes drooped.

'I'll show you to your bed. Perhaps we can talk more about it tomorrow, when you're more rested.'

'I'll no' change my mind.'

Davie's nostrils twitched as he helped Rob out of his chair. 'Well, perhaps you could change your cologne, smells like horse liniment to me.'

CHAPTER Three

Lady Anne leant over her desk as her quill scratched away at a letter.

Joan knocked and opened her mistress's door as she did every morning at nine. 'Good mornin', Milady.'

'Is it?' Anne didn't turn, but pointed in the direction of her wedding dress. It lay crumpled on the floor beside her trousseau which she'd kicked aside the previous night. 'Get rid of these clothes, I never want to see them again.'

'Is there somethin' wrong, Milady?' Joan picked up bodices and skirts and tried to smooth out the creases in the fine silk.

'Better still, you have them.'

'Me?'

You're betrothed to Angus, one of the grooms?'

'Aye.' Joan's gaze wandered to the four poster bed and the pillows on the floor. 'Did you no' sleep well last night?'

Anne blinked back a tear as she stared at Joan.

'Milady, whatever's wrong?' Joan ran to a drawer and handed Anne a newly laundered handkerchief. 'You were so happy yesterday. It's no' weddin' jitters, is it? They say everybody gets them. They'll pass. It's to be expected, you havin' never met the laddie...'

Anne disintegrated inside. *This is the beginning of humiliating explanations, trite remarks, false smiles and gay laughter.* She mopped her eyes, blew her nose and sniffed. 'Joan, stop please. I ken you mean to be kind, and I'm grateful, but you'll find out sooner or later. The marriage...he's...the wedding's been cancelled.' She gulped.

'Cancelled?'

'Yes, it appears Mr. Stewart no longer cares to marry me.'

'But...it's all been arranged. He must know...oh Milady...you poor wee thing...' Joan hugged her in her thin arms. 'It's no' fair, you dinna deserve such treatment.'

Anne broke free and paced the room. 'No, but I have to carry on, despite Mr. Stewart.' She paused, took a deep breath and frowned in concentration. 'The household must be informed. Wedding gifts need to be returned. I've made a list and written a short note of apology to each guest, I've just to hand them to Father's secretary. Once I'm dressed tell Mrs. Scott to come to the drawing room, she can inform the staff and please take those.' She pointed at the garments which littered the floor.

Joan bundled the clothing under her arm, but her gaze didn't leave a fine silk skirt as she did so.

'Now, I have a lot to do to make order out of chaos.' Anne clapped her hands. 'Are those carriage wheels I hear?'

Joan ran to the window. 'It's Lady Charlotte with Lady Jean and Lady Margaret and they're dressed for ridin'.'

'Oh, Lord. I'd forgotten. What time is it? Anne examined her face in the dressing table mirror and groaned. *I have to tell them.*

'Nine-thirty, Milady.' Brisk and business like, Joan moved to the door. 'I'll tell the maids to fetch the water for your toilette; ask Johnstone to seat your friends in the drawin' room and say you've been delayed; see if cook can provide some refreshment for you all and tell Mrs. Scott you want to see her this afternoon.' She paused. 'That Mr. Stewart doesna ken what he's thrown away.'

'No, he doesna,' said Anne and summoned a smile. 'You, are a dear for saying so.'

'Thank you, Milady.' Joan closed the door quietly behind her.

Anne turned and frowned at the mirror. Tired eyes and tangled hair stared back at her. She chewed on her thumb. Rob Stewart's hated face had sneaked behind her eyelids. She'd tossed and turned for hours. Her mind had seethed with explanations and excuses for his behaviour. None satisfied her. Only one man had given her sleepless nights before and she'd given up all ideas of Philippe long ago. She'd made a silent vow then, not to let another affect her like him, but Rob Stewart had piqued her interest. *What had her relations said? 'Devilishly handsome, a leader of men and a man of honour.' Hmmm.*

She caught sight of her tangled hair in the mirror. *Lord, look at me. What will my friends think...what should I say? I must hurry.*

***

Forty-five minutes later, the excited chatter of female voices floated up to her as she descended the staircase. She hesitated on the landing and examined the oil painting which had hung there for as long as she could remember. Her mother's kind eyes and smile offered comfort, but perhaps it was Anne's imagination. She sighed, lifted the yellow folds of her skirt and continued down to the hall as her friends' voices, punctuated by the clink of china, became louder. She made herself move towards the closed doors. Just as she touched the brass handles, she heard Lady Charlotte's voice. 'Everyone who is anyone will be there.'

Lady Jean spoke in a soft undertone. 'Yes and they say he's very handsome and very dashing. Of course he is from one of the leading Jacobite families. Anne's done very well for herself, very well indeed.'

Lady Margaret said, 'I've decided on lilac silk. Mrs. Pattison is worth a visit, she has all the latest French patterns.'

Their voices twittered on.

Ann's stomach seemed hollow. *Lord, I have to tell them.* She chewed at her thumb. *My 'set' have opinions about everything.*

Surely they'll understand and not abandon me, like Rob Stewart, to society's condemnation.

The front door bell rang through the house. Anne watched as Johnstone, their sombre-faced butler, limped along the gloomy hall and opened the main door. A shaft of sunlight illuminated Uncle William and the pastel patterned carpet which rippled at Anne's feet. The draught made Anne pull her cream wrap round her shoulders. Johnstone closed the door and took the light with it.

Uncle William gave his hat and coat to the butler.

'How's the leg, Johnstone?'

'No' the same since the '15, sir,' said Johnstone, 'best weather vane I know.' He lowered his voice, 'Of troubled times.'

'No' if we steer a wise course.'

'And which course do you wish to steer, Uncle?' said Anne. She walked towards him and kissed his cheek.

'A safe one, my dear Anne.' Uncle William's bald head always seemed too large for his body.

'Uncle William, how nice to see you and how's little Florie?'

He bowed and kissed her hand. 'Well, she sends her regards. Came as soon as your father sent word. My condolences.'

Damn.

'Stewart's a rogue you can be sure of that. You didna scare him off?'

Typical, Uncle William. 'No.'

'About to go into the lion's den are you?' He signalled towards the female chatter from the room on her left.

She nodded.

'Dinna let them draw blood.' He chucked her under the chin and strode into her father's study and closed the door behind him.

She took a deep breath and walked into the drawing room.

'Oh, Anne, darling, at last.' Charlotte enveloped her in her arms.

'The blushing bride to be,' cooed Jean.

'Your yellow taffeta, so becoming, but aren't you riding?' Margaret arranged her new grey habit to best effect.

Anne paused. 'I have something to tell you. There will be no wedding. We...we have had second thoughts.' She watched the colour drain out of their faces, saw their mouths gape, form shapes, but no words came.

They'll never understand. She moved to the window and looked out at the well-cut emerald lawns and the apricot-streaked sea and sky beyond. On her left a herring gull wheeled over the tower of St. Paul's. To her right, in the bay, a fishing smack's bow, half-hidden in the swell, streamed with white foam. *Life goes on. One day the hurt will go away and I'll forget he ever existed. Devil take him.*

'Darling girl how awful for you,' said Charlotte.

Ann turned.

'Oh, Anne.' Margaret's hand covered her open mouth.

'He would, I'm sure, have proved a brute, a cad and a cold-hearted monster,' said Jean surprised at her own forcefulness.

Anne joined them. 'Frankly it's a relief. We didna ken each other. How can one have feelings for someone, one has never met? Besides, there are much more interesting things afoot. This means I have no distractions and can put all my energies into helping the Cause.'

'The Cause?' Charlotte's eyes narrowed.

'No distractions?' said Margaret and pursed her thin lips.

'You dinna care?' Jean's mouth gaped.

'No.'

Charlotte started to clap. 'Bravo. How fierce you are, Anne. We're all at the mercy of men. Good for you.'

'But how will you manage in society, Anne?' Jean plucked at the lace at her cuff.

Margaret gave Anne a sideways glance. 'I'm sure I should want to hide away forever with the shame of it.'

'I'll carry on as usual. I've done nothing of which I should be ashamed.'

'But people will talk, they will wonder, well...they'll think...' faltered Margaret.

'I dinna give fig for what they think. And if they dinna like it they can....eat their own wigs.' Anne raised her voice.

They stared at her with big eyes, until Jean put her hand to her mouth. Her shoulders shook.

Charlotte spluttered and then laughed.

Margaret looked down her long nose at Anne. 'Oh dear.'

'Eat their wigs? ' Charlotte repeated. 'You'll be the talk of the country. There'll be some who will despise you, but many will secretly admire your spirit. You sound like the Colonel I remember.'

Colonel, the childhood nickname Philippe gave me. Two years and a day since I saw him. 'Well, I'm no' going to lock myself away like Catrina Mackenzie.' Anne, remembered the tearful-eyed spinster from her childhood. 'I'm going to do all I can to support the Cause.'

'Are you now?' Charlotte's eyes assessed her.

'Aye I want to help. They'll need gold for the campaign.'

'Philippe visited Buick House for a short time last night,' Charlotte said.

Philippe. An image of a handsome boy with brown hair and brown eyes leapt into Anne's head.

'He didna say it in so many words...' Charlotte said in a conspiratorial whisper, 'but I think the Rising will be soon.'

'It canna come too soon for me,' said Anne. *Philippe's been close, but didna' call to see me.* She'd adored those childhood summer months when the St. Etienne's ship sailed into the bay from Calais. Their fathers had discussed business whilst she and her friends had been given the task of entertaining Philippe. In fact, being older by four years, he'd got them into more scrapes than anyone could have imagined. She'd loved him, not that he'd paid much attention to the innocent longings of a young girl. His failure to call upon her hurt.

'I dinna think I'll ever marry,' she said.

'No' marry?' said Margaret, sniffed into her handkerchief and regarded Anne as if she'd said she'd commit murder.

'No. Why would I want to lose my sense of self, be restricted by what my husband said I could or couldna do? Better be an old maid.'

'You canna think that. Remember Philippe?' Charlotte played with a gold ringlet.

'I try not to,' said Anne.

Her friends giggled and nudged each other.

Loup de Mer is anchored off the Needle's Eye,' said Charlotte. 'Didn't you see his signal, Anne?'

'No.' There'd been a time when she'd watched for a signal every night, until she realised its absence was his way of saying goodbye.

Charlotte's words brought Anne back to the present. 'He said there are government ships in the area, but sent his regards to you all.'

The ladies knew that although Philippe and his father were merchants, they also smuggled lace and brandy. The St. Etiennes had evaded the Royal Navy for years.

'How...how did he look?' asked Anne, her finger circled the rim of a tea cup.

The women stared at each other and then her.

She turned saucer-eyes on them. They'd all been a little in love with Philippe.

'Oh, you know Philippe,' Charlotte replied. 'He did seem a little distracted when I talked of your wedding.'

Anne chewed her thumb. 'I dinna want to talk about him. Men have so much freedom. *Unlike me.* I want to do something to help the Prince.'

'We all do.' Charlotte pressed Anne's arm. 'I'll consult with Lord Alan. I'm sure my brother will agree that a soiree with music, gaming and fine food may be just the thing to raise gold for the Cause. We could hold it at Buick House.'

'How is he?' Anne asked, 'I haven't seen him since his illness.'

'Somewhat changed,' said Charlotte and looked away. 'He thanks you for the sweetmeats you left. It is hard when one's brother willna let one help.'

'Always so independent, it will stand him in good stead I'm sure,' said Anne and put her arm round her friend.

Margaret shuddered. 'How awful it must be for one to have had smallpox. Is he terribly disfigured?'

Charlotte stared at her in silence, her lips set in a straight line.

Jean's rounded in alarm. 'Er...Anne, I know my dear cousin, Lord Alistair, will want to be by your side.'

Anne's heart sank. Alistair, Jean's fifty year old bachelor second cousin and a lawyer had regular bouts of gout. 'Thank you.'

'Wonderful.' said Jean. 'We should wear something tartan, to signify our support for the Cause.'

'Oh, that is so romantic and of course the most eligible men in the area must be invited and I'll wear my lilac gown.' Margaret adjusted the lace at her neckline.

'Anne?' asked Charlotte.

'It's a marvellous idea.' *But there'll be gossip, cruel whispers, nasty asides and fingers pointed at me. Easy to say I dinna care.*

Charlotte put a hand on Anne's shoulder. 'You show remarkable courage, and are only to be admired. It could happen to any of us. We're all pawns in the games of men. Dinna doubt we'll stand by you, we always have. Alan will no' brook discourtesy from anyone.'

'Well said, Charlotte.' Jean clapped her hands.

'And you, Margaret?' asked Charlotte. 'Can you no' offer Anne words of comfort?'

Margaret's small bosom heaved as she examined her nails. 'I'm no' a beauty, like you three.' The others protested, but she waved their words away. 'Mother says I'm a disappointment and will be fortunate to receive a proposal. I have to protect my reputation. Anne, I must speak plainly, you can no longer assume we are friends.'

'What are you saying?' Anne stared at her. 'It wasna my fault.'

Margaret rose in a flurry of rustled skirts and put on her gloves. 'My apologies Anne, but it's what society expects. I'll attend the soiree, Charlotte dear, anything to support the Cause. Anne, I'd rather we didna speak again, I dinna want to have to cut you in public.' She didn't look back as she swept out of the room.

In the silence Anne sat down, ashen-faced. She could hardly blame Margaret. Lady Anne Kerr had become a social outcast, a pariah. Anyone who linked themselves to her would commit social suicide. Humiliation washed over her. She straightened her back and waited for what her friends would say.

'Dinna mind her.' Charlotte sat beside Anne and squeezed her hand. 'She's a flibbertijibbet and will probably marry someone as shallow as herself.'

'Yes.' Jean took Anne's other hand. 'My mother may not be too happy, but I dinna care.'

Lord, they're standing by me. 'Thank you, you're true friends.' Anne kissed them on their cheeks. Margaret's words had cut her to the quick. *This is only the beginning, how many others would act in the same way?* The clock chimed eleven. Luncheon. *Damn*

Stewart and damn Margaret and her kind. Anne kept her voice light and carefree. 'I suggest we forgo our ride and plan the soiree.'

CHAPTER Four

Anne stood in her father's wood-panelled study where a fire crackled in the hearth. She hadn't received visitors, cards or invitations for weeks. An icy sheet had descended over Kerbilly and isolated her from the outside world.

That evening, much to her consternation, her father waved away his invitation to the soiree. 'Your Uncle William dines with me tonight. We've important things to discuss.'

'Oh Father, Lord Alan and Lady Charlotte will be so disappointed. Please make an appearance.'

'I think not. My business with your uncle must take precedence. And you, puss, look tired.' He kissed her forehead. 'Cook says you're no' eating. Dinna let this Stewart business distress you.'

Her heart sank like a fishing weight as she kissed his weathered cheek. 'I willna, he's...nought to me.' It plunged even further with the arrival of Lord Alistair, her escort for the evening. His long, lined face did nothing to recommend him, though he'd a kind nature.

Lord Alistair spoke of the weather and the price of corn. She pretended to listen, but her thoughts were of Rob Stewart. *Blast the man.* Last night she'd imagined his arms around her and woke before dawn.

***

Lord Alistair helped Anne out of the carriage. The cool night wrapped itself round her under a sky like a black sheet strung with a silver moon and stars. Buick House glittered before her, a house she'd known and loved since childhood. Its elegant symmetrical frontage shone golden light from every window. The soft drone of musical instruments wafted towards them on the breeze. She shivered inside her cloak and tried not to think about the barbs and stings which awaited her.

As if he sensed her inner turmoil, Alistair squeezed her hand and whispered, 'Courage.' They mounted the stone steps together towards the portico and main door as she prepared to act out the part of a carefree woman. *Rejection hurts like the devil.*

This evening would be about funds for the Cause. She'd waited a long time for the exiled Charles Edward Stuart, grandson of James II, to reach manhood and claim the throne. *Well, not for very much longer.* The thought made her press her lips together in a smile as she reached the door.

A man-servant took their cloaks. Anne caught a glimpse of Charlotte in a crimson gown as she passed the entrance hall. 'Charlotte. Charlotte. Please accept my apologies for our early arrival. I sent Johnstone ahead with the card tables and chairs you requested and wanted to ensure they'd arrived without mishap.'

Charlotte came towards her, all smiles and frills and outstretched hands. 'Darling Anne, how charming. You look most becoming in silver and grey, like a stormy sea and the red tartan sash, just the thing. You're the first. I declare you'll start a fashion for arriving early. Sir Alistair, how delightful to see you again.'

'Your servant, ma'am. May I say, you look particularly radiant tonight?' He bowed and kissed her hand.

'You are too kind, sir.'

'Would you mind if I left you two dear ladies for the moment to inspect the banquet?'

'Not at all. Please do.'

Charlotte linked her arm in Anne's and drew her forward. 'Of course your tables have arrived.' She led Anne to a side room. 'Let me show you them and do tell how you came by your sash?'

'My maid spied a bolt of tartan cloth in the sewing room.'

'Well, I had to practically tear these ribbons out of Mrs Pattison's hands.' Charlotte lifted a bow on her bodice. She lowered her voice. 'What's most interesting is she said there's a rare shortage of tartan and Laird Guthrie's placed an unusually large order with the weavers. Now, what do you make of that?' She looked at Anne.

Anne stopped midstride. 'He wants to clothe a large number of men in the same tartan. Is it the Rising? Has it come at last?'

Charlotte drew Anne to an alcove. 'We canna be too careful. Servants have ears.' She continued in a whisper. 'They say the Hanoverians have arrested suspected Jacobites. When governments are nervous this is what they do. Rebellion's in the wind. I'm sure of it.'

A ripple of excitement ran down Anne's spine as she clutched at Charlotte's arm. 'Then our soiree is well-timed.'

'Yes, but we need to be careful, it's also treason.' Charlotte scanned Anne's face as if she searched for answers.

Anne's stomach lurched. They'd all heard stories of what happened to those involved in the 1715 rebellion, the executions, their land sequestered by the Crown. This hated union with England only served one partner and it wasn't Scotland.

Anne's chin went up. 'Sometimes when a cause is worth fighting for, the risks need to be ignored.'

Charlotte nodded in agreement. 'I see we're of one mind, Anne. Oh, I must apologise, but Alan was called to Edinburgh, some urgent business a few days ago, though he assured me he'd return in time for our soiree. Now, whilst I welcome our guests, would you be a darling and instruct the servants to put the candlesticks and cards on every table? The cards are in there.' She pointed to a porcelain gaming box. 'This is where we will play.' She opened double doors to a blast of cool air. The long room had been set with fifteen gaming tables and four chairs for each. A fire made a feeble attempt to warm the space as the rising wind rattled the window panes. 'I'll leave you to it.'

Anne wrapped her shawl round her as she stepped forward. To her surprise a strong, masculine hand reached out, pulled her behind one of the doors and closed it.

She took in the scent of sea air and Philippe St. Etienne's tanned face and arms. She fought down excitement and said, 'Oh, it's you. What are you doing here?' The slim boy she remembered had become a dark, handsome man dressed in wine red with white lace at his neck and cuffs, his shirt of fine linen and his breeches clung to his lean body. *No wonder I loved him. Well, I've no time for men, not anymore.*

He bowed and let his gaze roam at will over her. 'My apologies, Mademoiselle, I expected a young girl, not a beautiful woman.'

'You didna call.'

'The tide and the British Navy.'

She sniffed.

'I must say I expected a warmer welcome. I 'ave obviously done you great wrong.'

'Not for the first time.'

'That ignorant, ill-mannered youth you knew, is no more. Perhaps we can start again. I have the honour to present before you Philippe...'

'St. Etienne,' Anne said.

She curtsied, 'And I have the honour to present before you Lady Anne of...'

'Kerbilly.' He moved close and looked with wonder at her face.

She became seventeen again in the grounds of his father's chateau at St. Etienne. Had longed for her dare-devil childhood companion, this handsome boy to acknowledge her existence, 'You didna answer my letters.'

'I dared not. I knew you were meant for another. Forgive me.' He put his hand on his heart. He bowed and then moved closer. 'Mon Dieu, Colonel, is it really you?'

She laughed.

'I'd know your tinkling laugh anywhere, but I never imagined you'd become so enchanting.' He twirled her around, kissed her on both cheeks and again she smelt the tang of salt and sea. 'That fierce little urchin who pelted me with apples has finally grown up.'

He held her against his broad chest and she felt safe and warm, too warm. 'I have grown, certainly. ' She tried in vain to disentangle herself.

'Into an irresistible woman if I'm not mistaken.' He smiled, let her go and looked her up and down, admiration in his eyes. 'I have often been sailing off the coast, seen Kerbilly's lights and thought of you. You've become a beauty you know.' He kissed her hand.

She withdrew it. 'You used to say that to Charlotte, Philippe.' She tried not to look into his brown eyes framed by black lashes.

'This time I mean it. You're angry with me.'

'And you said it to Jean and Margaret. You didna call at the house.'

'Cherie, I couldn't. I 'ad business with Alan and the British 'ave stepped up their patrols. You wouldn't want me arrested as a smuggler. Think of my reputation.'

'You're a rogue and deserve to hang for it. There's talk of a rebellion, soon. What will you do?'

'I've a letter de Marque. I'll do what I can for the Cause. And you?'

'Work for the Cause of course.'

They smiled at each other.

'Rob Stewart should be called out. On the other hand, I should be grateful you're free of him.'

Drat. He knows. She fluttered her fan and hoped the cool air would help. 'Thank you. He means nought.' *He'd have been my future and now...now I'm destined to be an old maid.*

A violin and cello tuned up and the chatter of excited voices wafted towards them as more guests arrived. 'May I ask you to save the first dance for me?' he said.

'Yes, if you'll help me organise the servants. I've been most tardy and Charlotte needs the tables set for gaming.'

Within fifteen minutes all was ready and Anne opened the door to find the next room filled with groups of Jacobite ladies and gentlemen. White cockades, tartan ribbons and sashes decorated almost every shoulder, breast and waist of those assembled. Dark-haired Lady Montrose, dazzled in a close-fitting peach satin bodice, overskirts and sleeves with flounces. Lady Brodie clasped at her scarlet tartan wrap draped over a cream, silk gown with no hoop. At her side, son and heir, broad-shouldered, James, scratched under his bag wig. Lord Brodie had a quick word as he strutted like a peacock in his blue knee-length coat and breeches. Florid-faced Lord Galbraith smothered his laughter and brushed an imagined thread from his green plaid. He tugged at the white stock at his throat as if he sought release.

'Welcome. Welcome to you all.' Charlotte stood in front of the windows as the rain beat on them and raised her voice. The room hushed and went silent. 'Sir Alan sends his apologies, unfortunately he's been delayed.' James Brodie groaned. 'But will be joining us later this evening.' Lord Galbraith led the cheers. 'As you know you've been invited to this soiree primarily to make a donation to a worthy cause. Lady Anne and Lady Jean will collect donations throughout the evening.' Anne noticed Lady

Montrose's eyes glint at her and Lord Brodie's lips form a sneer. She raised her chin, straightened her back and stared them out. One after another, their heads turned from her. *Lord, this is awful. I want to run, hide, be anywhere, but here.*

'There's a buffet in the dining room behind you and music, enjoy yourselves,' continued Charlotte to more cheers. 'I wish you luck at Buick House's gaming tables.'

Two stout ladies rushed in a babble of excited shrieks to be near friends; Charlotte helped an elderly gentleman to a seat by the fire, whilst a round-shouldered man lost his spectacles and Anne found them for him. In the hubbub, eager players of Pharaoh and Basset filled the gaming tables.

The orchestra struck up for the allemande. 'My dance, Anne?' Philippe extended his hand, she hesitated for a moment and took it.

I dreamt of this moment when younger. Envious glances came her way as he swirled her round. *He's a head taller than me, handsome, light on his feet and a graceful dancer. Yet...*

'Thank you, cherie.' The music had stopped and he led her off the ballroom floor. 'Regretfully, I must leave. I must get back to my ship before the tide turns. Till we meet again, Colonel.'

'Till we meet again, Philippe.'

He bowed, his eyes never left her face as he kissed her hand and left. *Why do I feel like that hopeful girl again?*

Anne sought out Jean and they started to collect donations on silver platters from the gaming tables. Alistair plodded behind them. Lady Brodie whispered something behind her hand to her husband who gave a shrug of disdain. Anne took a deep breath and set her lips into a smile as she moved from group to group only to be greeted by Lady Montrose's acidic glance before she hid behind her fan.

Anne turned away, but a burst of laughter made her look back to note the smiles of the Brodies and easy manner of Lady

Montrose and Lord Galbraith when they greeted Jean. *So humiliating. I thought them friends. James Brodie and Lord Galbraith have repeatedly asked for my hand in marriage and the ladies begged me to attend their tea parties. Now they treat me like this.* Several strident female voices broke into her thoughts.

'Hussy!' said Lady Montrose.

Lady Brodie sniffed. 'Has she no respect for decency?'

'No wonder he wouldna have her.' said Margaret.

Lady Montrose turned to smirk and Lady Brodie sniggered.

Lord, the remarks are pointed at me. This is torture. Anne's smile widened and she raised her chin another inch.

'Ow,' squeaked Lady Montrose and rubbed her slippered foot.

'My apologies,' murmured Lord Alistair.

'Ooh,' squealed Lady Brodie as he jabbed her in the ribs.

'So sorry, Madam,' he mumbled.

'Aaagh,' shrieked Margaret as she tipped forward in her jolted chair.

'Damned careless of me,' muttered Lord Alistair.

Anne caught Alistair unawares and could have sworn his eyes twinkled. Then he winked at her.

Anne raised her head. *Thank you, Lord Alistair.* She remembered how only months ago these people had anticipated invitations to her wedding. How stupid to think them friends.

With a fixed smile, Anne pretended to enquire after people's health and collected their donations as she went. She approached Margaret who turned her back and signalled the rest of her table who followed suit.

Anne felt a flush of resentment. Before she could stop herself, her hand swept a glass of red wine which gushed onto Margaret's lap. 'Oh dear,' said Anne.

'My gown, you've ruined my beautiful gown.' Margaret's shriek of outrage drowned another as Alistair grazed her shin. 'Ow.'

'Dearie me,' he said and applied his quizzing glass to the situation. Margaret blushed with embarrassment. Fortunately, the string quartet struck up and drowned the rest of her cries.

Anne allowed herself a small smile of satisfaction behind her fan as Margaret scuttled from the room surrounded by clucking friends.

'It was no more than she deserved,' whispered Charlotte at her elbow. 'Hopefully, we'll never see that frightful lilac gown again.'

Jean hurried to Anne's side and linked arms with her. 'She deserved it…I've wanted to do something similar, since we were little.' The pair grinned at each other.

'Pray give the footmen the platters.' Charlotte signalled two with a wave of her hand. 'I'll lock the donations in Alan's study. We appear to have done well, ladies. I think supper calls.'

'May I?' said Lord Alistair and offered his arm to Anne.

Anne allowed herself to be led into supper and viewed the table. It groaned with venison, beef, mutton, jellies, gateaux and syllabubs.

'Let me fetch you something to eat, my dear,' Lord Alistair said.

'Thank you, you are most kind, but I've no appetite.'

'Then pray allow me to escort you to a quiet seat.'

Aware of the hostile stares in her direction, she nodded.

He lowered his voice. 'Charlotte informs me you wish to work for the Cause?'

'Aye, more than anything.'

'Your loyalty is to be admired.' He leaned closer, his usual dull expression animated. 'If such an opportunity arose, what would you say?'

About to tell him, a door opened, candles flared, died and flared again. Anne shivered at the icy blast of air as a figure entered, swept off his hat and stroked his dark hair. A gesture Anne knew well, but this man had a face scarred and pitted by smallpox.

Everyone stared at the apparition. Anne's breath stopped for several heart beats. She felt Lord Alistair's hand on her arm. It steadied her. *Lord, Charlotte's poor brother Alan.*

James Brodie drew back, handkerchief over his mouth, Lady Montrose hid behind her fan and muttered, 'He's cribbaged-faced.'

Anne saw Alan's lips tighten, but he didn't flinch. She released herself from Lord Alistair's grip and walked to Alan's side. She put her lips to his ravaged cheek and said, 'It's so good to see you're restored to health again.'

'Bless you,' he said so quietly no one else heard.

Charlotte gripped his hand. 'Brother, you're cold, come sit by the fire.'

'Thank you dear sister, but I've news of great import from Edinburgh.' He raised his voice and waved several copies of the 'Edinburgh Evening Courant' in the air.

Uproar.

Galbraith shouted, 'Let him speak. Let him speak.'

'The Prince sailed on June 22nd from Nantes on the *Du Teillay* accompanied by the *Elisabeth.*'

'At last,' shouted James Brodie. Uproar again.

Alan silenced them with raised hands and continued, 'They were attacked by HMS *Lion* off Cornwall which so badly damaged the *Elisabeth*, she returned to France.'

'No,' said Lady Montrose and led a chorus of groans.

'But the *Lion* thought the *Du Teillay* bound for the Americas and let her go. Prince Charles Edward Stuart landed in Scotland on July 23rd.'

Shocked silence, then everyone spoke at once.

Anne grabbed the newspaper from Alan and skimmed through it, unaware someone had sidled up beside her. Margaret's familiar voice spat poison in her ear. 'You've no business here, Anne Kerr. Your father's a turncoat; he's been seen meeting Whigs. Everyone knows. No wonder poor Mr. Stewart didna want to marry you. You should be ashamed of yourself.'

Alan intervened. 'Lady Margaret, what you've said is unbecoming and inaccurate.'

Charlotte restrained Anne as she faced Margaret. Anne took a deep breath. 'How dare you insult me by mentioning my father in the same breath as those loathsome creatures. Never address me again. I wouldna like to cut you in public.' The room grew silent. Anne drew herself up, took Lord Alistair's arm and swept out, instead of doing what she longed to do: slap Margaret's smirk off her face.

Anne made her apologies to Charlotte as she left. 'I have to talk to Father and stop this malicious gossip.'

'Of course you must. I find what Margaret said...difficult to believe.'

'Thank you for that.' Anne kissed Charlotte. 'I'm sure once I talk to him there'll be a simple explanation.'

'I am sure this will be the case,' said Charlotte kissing her cheek. 'Remember I'm your dearest friend.'

Anne nodded as she allowed Lord Alistair to assist her into the carriage.

He gave curt instructions to the coachman. 'Kerbilly, and be quick about it.'

She leant back in her seat and closed her eyes. She tried to ignore the dull headache that had begun. Margaret's vile words whirled in Anne's head. *Why would she say that? My darling Father wouldn't dream of associating with Whigs. Outrageous,*

Unbelievable. He fought for the Jacobites in the '15, he's been one all of his life. She needed to tell him the lies she'd heard.

Lord Alistair stared out of the window and a thoughtful silence fell between them as the coach rattled along the country lanes and brought them to a stop in front of Kerbilly's main entrance. He helped her down, escorted her to the front door, bowed and kissed her hand. 'I'm sorry for what was said. I know you're loyal to the Cause, my dear.'

'My thanks, Lord Alistair. Please have a safe journey home.' He returned to the coach as she hurried into Kerbilly's hall, flung her cloak towards Johnstone and her gloves on the table. 'Where's Father?'

'In the study with your Uncle William, Milady,' said Johnstone. 'Would you care for some refreshment?'

'No thank you,' she said and ran towards the study door. She burst in.

'What's wrong, my dear?' Her father sat in an armchair by the banked fire. Uncle William sat opposite. Both men turned worried faces towards her.

'My apologies, I didna mean to disturb you both, but I need to speak to Father.'

'Can't it wait till morning?' he said.

'No.' She chewed her thumb.

'I'm going home anyway.' Uncle William rose. 'You'll remember what I said, brother, it's for the best.' He kissed Anne's cheek. 'I'll see myself out.'

'Sir.' She dipped a curtsey as he left.

'Now Anne, what is it?'

'At the soiree, Margaret accused you of seeing Whigs.'

'Did she now?'

'You're going to refute it of course.'

'No, daughter I am not.'

'But Father, as a Jacobite...'

'Oh, Anne you see everything in black and white. Sometimes there is grey.'

'I dinna understand.'

'Sometimes, a man canna follow his heart, he has to use his head. In the 1715 rebellion, some of my friends were executed, their lands taken and their families made destitute. I was pardoned and fined. You've no idea of the guilt which haunts me every day. I've had a full life and they are gone for a lost Cause. The government won't be so forgiving this time. I'd be executed, Kerbilly and all our assets sold and you'd have nothing.'

'But Father, you talk only of failure. The Prince needs us. Alan says he's in Scotland.'

'Yes.'

She gasped. 'You knew and didna tell me?'

'Uncle William and I have discussed it at great length. He's right. I've disassociated myself from the Cause.'

'Uncle William's a Whig too? He persuaded you to be a turncoat. I canna believe it.' A blind ache throbbed behind her eyes.

'Do not judge us harshly, Anne. As you know, William has a wee daughter.'

'Dinna make me your excuse.'

'Anne, listen.'

'I'm retiring to my room.' Shafts of pain swept across her brow.

'Anne.'

'Good night, Father.'

As she pulled herself up the stairs, her mother's painting reproached her. Anne's headache raged now. She lay on her bed and let her head sink into the goose down and feather stuffed pillow.

I've made a complete fool of myself. Margaret's right and now everyone at Charlotte's soiree kens. I thought father perfect, put him on a pedestal, but he's only human after all. I'm tired, so very tired.

CHAPTER Five

Joan drew back Anne's bedroom curtains, shards of light pierced the gloom. She woke with her cheek on the damp pillow.

'You were sound asleep, but it's gettin' late,' said Joan. 'Them in the kitchen says the Prince's landed in Scotland. It's a lovely day, listen to the birds. Would you like your breakfast tray?'

Only Joan could mention war followed by nonsense and treat them both the same. Her voice grates this morning. 'I'm no' hungry. What time is it?'

'Ten. The Laird's gone to Edinburgh on business. He said to tell you he'd no' be back for some days and that he loved you, as if you didna ken that already. I'll fetch your tray.' Before Anne could answer, Joan shut the door behind her.

Anne threw back the covers and walked to the window. A cock crowed; one of the scullery maids fed the hens and a lad leant on his fork while a pile of manure steamed in front of the stables. Life continued as it always had, yet everything was different. She could have held up her head about being jilted, but her father's treachery ate into the core of her being. *How could he? We'll be vilified.*

She sat at her desk and put her head in her hands. A pile of letters tied with a blue ribbon lay in front of her. She fingered them, and reread the last one. Janet's neat script covered two pages and continued around the margins. Her godmother had sent her deepest sympathy about Anne's broken betrothal. She wrote of domestic affairs, the purchase of a new cow, the weather, news of Davie, her only son, and a sense of peace. Anne craved peace.

She made up her mind, took up her quill as if in a fever, wrote to Janet, then her father and signed the letters with a flourish. She sprinkled them with pounce powder. Her fingers

37

trembled as she shook the papers and folded them. She wrote Father on one and Janet's address on the other, then sealed them. Her lips curved into a smile of satisfaction.

Joan knocked and entered with a tray full of smoked beef, fresh eggs, porridge, currant preserve, fresh bread and coffee. Anne ignored the wonderful aromas whilst Joan helped her dress.

'It's no' true is it, Milady? They say in the scullery the master's a turncoat?'

Anne closed her eyes. *Lord, give me strength.* 'Pack my travelling case and trunk. We leave this morning and will be away for a few weeks.'

'We?' Joan's voice trembled.

'You're going with me to visit my godmother, Mrs. Walker, near Aberdeen.'

'Aberdeen.' Joan said it as if it was a foreign land. 'Milady.' She bobbed and closed the door.

Anne skipped downstairs, notes in hand. 'Johnstone, I want this to be delivered immediately to Mrs. Walker and a carriage made ready. This note put on my father's desk.'

***

An hour later, Anne and Joan set off for Lachlan House. Throughout the journey Anne saw Lady Margaret's accusing face and heard her father admit he'd changed sides. Heard him say it was for her, though he hadn't asked if she'd wanted him to do it. She should have told him she'd rather be destitute than betray everything she believed in.

Some days later when Anne's coach approached the outskirts of her godmother's estate she began to doubt the sense of her actions. Janet might be away, or her visit might not be convenient. Though they'd written weekly, Anne had only met her at a few family occasions such as weddings and funerals. Janet might think her presumptuous and impolite to descend on her with so little notice.

Joan blinked at her, owl-like, as if expecting an explanation for this sudden departure from Kerbilly and everything Anne knew.

The coach turned in the Walker's gates and followed the drive and avenue of oaks. Anne looked up at the hills which surrounded the house as two riders galloped down the slope. She leaned forward as one lost his hat and shouted in dismay. The other yelled back. She couldn't catch what they said. She supposed one might be Davie, the other taller with long limbs looked well on his horse. She lost sight of them as the carriage turned away and she shook off her thoughts as they pulled up in front of Lachlan House.

Joan saw to the baggage as Anne greeted Janet, her face more lined and hair more grey than the last time they'd met some years ago. 'How are you? I hope you dinna mind me arriving with such little warning? It's so good to see you. Have you heard? The Prince has landed. I bought this government rag to prove it.' She thrust the *Edinburgh Evening Courant* at her.

'My dear, girl.' Janet's forehead creased in concern as she took the paper. She offered her cheek for Anne's kiss. 'You bring such news and I've only just received your note. This is all very sudden.' Janet darted an uneasy look at the hills behind Anne. 'Davie...Davie is riding.' Her voice seemed to lose its strength.

'Yes, I saw them,' said Anne.

'You saw them,' Janet squeaked.

'Well, only from a distance.'

Anne could have sworn Janet's knees were about to give way. 'Are you well? I didna realise my visit would put you out so. I just needed to see you. You were close to my mother, I thought you might understand.'

Janet put her arm round her. 'Of course I'm delighted to see you, dear. If only you'd written sooner.' Her brow puckered in thought. 'But we canna' make a better of it, our housekeeper, Mrs. Eddis will organise...something. How are you bearing up? From your last letter I know you've been badly let down by Mr. Stewart.' Janet cast a black glance at the hills. 'I'll...send the newspaper to Davie and er...the servants can deal with your luggage. Come, have you eaten?' She led Anne up the steps and into the hall.

Anne shook her head.

'Well we must feed you up, you're far too thin.' Janet opened a door on the right. 'I'll tell cook to prepare some broth...Make yourself comfortable in the sitting room whilst I see to it. I'll get a fire lit and then you can tell me all your news.'

Oh dear, Janet seems on edge. Anne walked to the sash window and gazed at the sapphire sky and the sage forest beyond. She stretched to ease the ache in her lower back from the rickety coach. Noises from the rest of the house filtered into the room: hushed commands, the sort of voice used when someone is ill and a rush of footsteps up the stairs as if whole armies were on the move. Doors opened and closed and she watched a groom gallop away from the house towards two distant riders.

Anne's eyes wandered round the room, noted a china ornament here, a piano there and some sewing that looked like it had been stabbed to death. The needle pinned it to the arm of a chair. She stroked the man's jacket and enjoyed the sumptuous feel of the blue velvet against her cheek. The sleeve gaped at one seam and looked forlorn. She'd often watched the sewing maid at work and in poorer times, she'd mended clothes herself. She sat, withdrew the needle, sewed four stitches into the fabric and unable to find scissors, cut the thread with her teeth.

She held the jacket against herself. It swamped her. *Whoever wore this had broad shoulders. I can't remember Davie being this* big, but then I haven't seen him for several years. She breathed in a faint tang of heather, peat and whisky which clung to the fabric and tried to visualise the man who wore it. *His chest had to be muscular and by the cut of the fabric, his waist and hips slim. He must be well over six foot. Goodness.*

A maid knocked.

'Yes?'

A young, mouse-haired girl entered carrying a heaped coal scuttle in one hand. She'd a smut on her nose which poked out like a stunted teapot spout. 'The mistress sent me to light the fire, Milady.' She stared at the jacket in Anne's hands.

Anne felt her cheeks burn and put the jacket down.

The maid knelt by the fireplace. 'It belongs to the young master's friend, Milady. The sewin' maid's ill and the mistress was mendin' it when you arrived.'

'It seems my arrival has the whole house in a flutter.'

'Beggin' your pardon, Milady but it's no' you.' She sat back on her heels the fire forgotten. 'It's a certain young gentleman who's captured the heart of every maid in the household. The mistress is at her wit's end, as no chores are bein' done for maids swoonin' over him. He's so tall and handsome and has eyes like a deep loch. When he speaks, you feel weak and your heart pounds.' The maid wafted a sooty hand in front of her face.

Lord, I wish I could meet a man who made me feel like that.

Anne thought of Rob Stewart. *Blast him.*

'He's a very fine figure of a man on horseback,' said the maid. 'He and the master ride every day in the hills.'

'And this gentleman's name?'

'Mr. St-'

'-Gail.' Janet entered the room and wrung her hands. 'That's quite enough. You ken what I think of gossip about your betters. Off with you girl, the top stairs need doing.'

Gail reddened. 'Aye, Mistress.' She bobbed a curtsey and left the room.

Janet dabbed at her face with a handkerchief and turned to Anne. 'One canna get the quality of maid these days.'

'Well, she did say they were all of a dither because of Davie's friend.'

Janet's eyes flickered in alarm as she stared at the jacket over the arm of the chair. 'Mr. Ogilvy.' Janet's voice trembled. 'A brack-faced creature. I do wish the servants would tidy things away.'

'Brack-faced?'

Janet took the jacket and put it on her lap. Her hands folded and refolded it as her eyes darted hither and thither as if she looked for a means of escape.

A light tap sounded on the door.

'Come,' commanded Janet. A maid entered with a tray. 'Ah. Your broth. Now you sit and enjoy it.' Janet pinioned Anne in a chair with the tray on her lap. 'I'll be back once I've…I've seen to…everything.' The jacket went under her arm and with a vague smile Janet left Anne to her meal.

***

'It's kind of your Mother to offer to mend my jacket.' Rob bit a chunk out of an apple. 'I didna think to make work for her. It's good I'm leaving tomorrow.' He fed the rest of the fruit to his brown mare enjoying the rasp of her tongue on his palm and the feel of her velvet nose. 'Is that one of your grooms galloping towards us? He's waving something.'

Davie shaded his eyes. 'So he is.'

The groom pulled up his horse. 'Master Davie, the mistress said you've to read these. ' He thrust a newspaper and note at him. 'The Prince's landed.'

Rob's eyes narrowed. 'So, it's begun again.'

Stunned, Davie accepted both items and they both read the report as the servant galloped off to spread the news.

'It may come to nought.' Davie looked at the horizon.

'I think not.' Rob tapped his boot with his whip. 'I met Prince Charles in Rome. He's impulsive, naive, knows little of the real world. Jacobite exiles told him what he wanted to hear: that the French will support him to regain the Crown. He lapped it up. Father canna wait to send my brothers to war. Johnnie's not convinced; his head's always buried in books. Euan canna' see we have peace and prosperity under the Hanoverians and Duncan's too young, thank God. The Jacobites are going to fight for a pretender whose grandfather lost his right to the throne in 1688 and whose father was defeated in 1715. I have to be true to what I believe; I follow the British Crown and George II.'

'So you're not going to the Americas?'

'No, I'm going to follow the drum.'

'God help you then.' Davie shook his head. 'I pray you never meet your brothers in battle.'

'And you?' asked Rob. 'What will you do?'

'Me? I'm an the only son of a widowed mother. I dinna wish to take sides and will stay out of it. I hope you dinna think less of me for that?'

'Each man must make his own choice. Who am I to judge?'

'Friends.' Davie stretched out his hand.

'Friends.' Rob shook it.

Davie unfolded the note. 'Ye Gods.'

'What now?' Rob groaned.

Davie read the note aloud:

'*The mistress begs to inform you of Lady Anne Kerr's unexpected arrival.* Mother's her godmother and they write. Unfortunate timing in the circumstances.'

'Hell's teeth,' said Rob.

CHAPTER Six

Anne and Janet sat either side of the fire in the Walker's sitting room when Anne became aware of a sudden draught round her ankles, a door which slammed and footsteps in the hall. She wondered what had happened, but as Janet perched on a seat beside her, all rapt attention, she felt she had to continue. '...so there was no hint, no warning, Mr. Stewart's letter was the first we knew...' A door closed upstairs. Anne continued, '...that he wanted to withdraw from the marriage contract.'

Several heavy footsteps pounded up and down the stairs and a small speck of plaster fell from above their heads and dusted the floor.

Anne stared at the ceiling as the chandelier shook, but carried on. 'My father's taken it badly, but I think, perhaps it's for the best.'

'How wise you are, Anne. Very wise for your age I mean.' Janet glanced at the ceiling and then the door.

'Aye and then I hesitate to share this, Janet, as I dinna wish to upset you, but...' she lowered her voice.

Janet looked nervous and leaned in to hear more, but another furtive conversation seemed to be taking place on the other side of the door. Anne tried to ignore it and continued. '...Father has been persuaded by Uncle William, who has far too much influence over him I can assure you, to become a turncoat.'

'A turncoat? Whatever can you mean, Anne?'

'Father has decided to become a Whig.'

'A Whig.' Janet started to laugh. The conversation stopped in the hall. The front door slammed which sent another draught, a horse neighed outside and galloped off.

Anne half rose to look, but Janet's words pulled her back into her seat. 'My dear girl, how sheltered your father has kept you.

Do you no' ken I'm a Whig or Jacobite depending on who asks? It's only sensible. I dinna want to be on the losing side again.'

'And Davie?'

'Davie doesna wish to take sides.'

'Oh,' said Anne. *This is turning into a nightmare.*

The door opened and Davie strode into the room, a little taller than when she'd last seen him. A bag wig covered his fair hair.

'Lady...Anne.' He brushed at his coat and mud-spattered breeches. 'Forgive my...appearance, I've been...riding and heard you'd come to visit. How are you?' He gave an awkward bow and kissed her hand.

'Well, and delighted to see you, Davie. I saw you and your friend earlier, riding in the hills.'

'My friend?' he gulped.

Why so nervous? 'Yes, isn't he with you now?' She looked for a tall, broad shouldered man, with eyes the colour of a loch, but saw no one. She hid her disappointment with a wry smile until she saw Davie's eyes bulge and look at his mother as if for help whilst she stared at the ceiling again.

Davie took a deep breath. 'He's...gone...home, family business. Rather sudden, left his apologies. I'll change shall I, and join you later for dinner?' And he left.

How odd.

Janet sank into her chair with a sigh. 'Well, dear, I'm sure your stay with us will help you forget this...dreadful episode. Mr. Stewart is no' worth thinking about. I'm sure Davie has some eligible young friends. Do you ride?'

After a dinner of family reminiscences, exhausted, Anne excused herself. She needed to sleep, but her bedroom had an air of sudden vacation about it. A wardrobe door stood ajar, she locked it in place; one drawer lay open, she closed it and then straightened a curtain. A half empty glass stood on the windowsill. She sniffed at the amber contents. The smell hit the back of her throat and she coughed. *Whisky dregs.*

As she lit a candle, her elbow knocked a book from the bedside table. A leaf of parchment fluttered to the floor. *A letter...and Rob Stewart's name on the bottom of it. My Rob Stewart? Surely not. Could there be more than one Rob Stewart? I canna read the letter, have no intention of so doing, one did not read another's mail. Drat.* She tore the letter open and her eyes devoured every word:

Lachlan House
Dear Davie,

I cannot thank you or your dear mother enough for making a lost soul so welcome in your home. The fact that I just arrived on your doorstep and was welcomed into the bosom of your family means more than I can say.
You always were a good listener. Having met my family and seen how it was with M, I knew you would understand. The ladies will do for us all in the end. I have trusted you with information I have shared with no other. Use it well and if, perhaps, you meet with Lady Anne Kerr when it is all over with me, tell her I was not the rogue she may think. Of course, I do not expect this moment to come for a long time yet.
Please give my best wishes to your mother. I will forward my address, once I have one.
Your obedient servant,

Rob Stewart

She sat with a thump on the feather mattress. Comprehension came like a lightning bolt. She sprang up again as if scorched.

Lord. My Rob Stewart has just stayed in this house, slept in this bed, laid his head on this pillow. Of course he had to be Davie's riding companion and the Walkers tried to spare me the pain of seeing him. Stewart disturbed the maids and he's disturbing me again. She fingered the letter and skimmed over the words. *He seems...nice, well mannered, gracious even...and Davie must know a lot about him. What did he mean '...seen how it was with M. The ladies will do for us all?' Why am I so interested? He isn't my Rob Stewart any more.*

In the next few days, she waited for Janet or Davie to say they knew Stewart, but they never mentioned him. She rode with Davie every morning, but he said little. His friends regarded her with interest, but made it clear she'd become damaged goods.

Stewart invaded her night, haunted her sleep and made her restless for the next two weeks. She dreamed of eyes the colour of a loch and a man whose presence caused a flutter amongst the maids and stole their breath away. He affected her so much she rode in the mornings and walked in the afternoons. She hoped when her head touched the pillow, sleep would come. *Davie's friends can go to the devil for all I care and so can this woman 'M' and Rob Stewart. He's probably brack-faced like Janet said.*

It was on a hot day that a coach trundled down the dusty glen towards Lachlan House. A heat haze lay over the distant hills and the moors appeared spun with purple and gold. Charlotte clambered out and waved. They met on the dusty track as she sent the coach ahead. Her young maid looked like a lost sparrow.

'Anne, darling girl, how are you?' said Charlotte as they embraced.

'Bored.' Anne laughed and Charlotte joined in.

'Your father told me where you were. I'm on my way to visit an aunt in Aberdeen before staying with two more in Edinburgh. Thought I'd call in on you.' She linked arms with

Anne. 'Shaw, you may follow at a distance.' The lost sparrow nodded.

'How are Alan and Jean?' asked Anne as they walked down the drive.

'Well.' Charlotte glanced at her. 'But we all miss your company of course.'

Anne lowered her voice. 'You must be the only ones who do. I've fallen out with Father and Uncle William. They're both Whigs. Margaret was right, much as it grieves me to say it.'

'I'm sorry to hear it.' Charlotte wrapped an arm round her.

'Let's walk to the house, but I warn you, I discovered my godmother and son Davie are friends of Rob Stewart, the rogue,' said Anne. 'He's been staying with them, we just missed each other.'

'That would have been so embarrassing.' Charlotte put a hand to her cheek. 'They're Jacobites?'

Anne frowned. 'Janet and her son are a disappointment; they change their politics like the wind.'

'And you?' Charlotte's eyes sparked with interest.

'How can you ask? I'd give my life for the Cause.'

'Would you? Put yourself in danger? Become a member of a secret group of Jacobites to gain information from the enemy?' Charlotte held Anne's hands. 'The redcoats wouldna suspect a woman, especially one with Whig relatives. Say yes, Anne. Join us.'

'Us?'

'Alan and I and others of course.'

'You're members of a secret group? Charlotte, I can hardly believe it. How exciting. What about my maid?'

'Send her home. My aunts have plenty of maids.'

Anne thought of her father and how tired he'd looked, but she'd made the decision to work for the Cause long ago. 'What do you want me to do?'

'First we'll tell your godmother you've been invited to stay with relatives of mine, the Mountjoys, at Pennycuik Hall near Edinburgh. Once there you'll receive a visit from a certain lord. He'll give you assignments. You'll inform your father of your change of address and hint at an estrangement because of his beliefs. It's important you write to him at regular intervals. We'll ensure any letters from him get to you. Your former life must be dead to you now, do you ken?'

'Yes. ' Anne knew if she returned to 'Kerbilly' the atmosphere would be strained. She couldn't forgive Uncle William or her father. She had few friends and nothing to lose. This adventure could rid her thoughts of Rob Stewart and his broken promise.

CHAPTER Seven

Rob's pony clattered over the grey cobbles at The Drover. Rob hoped for a good meal and a night's rest, tired of flea-bitten mattresses in ancient inns. A poster tacked to the thick trunk of an oak caught his attention. He studied it for a few minutes:

WANTED
A FEW SMART LADS
FOR THE
15TH ELLIOT'S DRAGOONS

Recruiters seemed everywhere. Rob's muscles ached as he dismounted and noticed black clouds overhead. His brow creased in frustration, he should have arrived hours ago, but his mare had cast a shoe some miles back and cost him valuable time. He and his pony needed rest. Grey smoke spewed out of the The Drover's ruined chimney and a broken shutter clattered against a wall in the wind. It didn't bode well for the inn's interior.

He'd enjoyed his stay at the Walkers, a pity Lady Anne had arrived. Davie spoke well of her as full of spirit and a paragon of virtue. An interesting combination, but his feelings for Morag were still raw. When he'd seen Euan kiss her and they'd told him of their betrothal, he'd thought of nought but leaving and that's what he'd done. He hadn't said goodbye or left a note. They'd have wanted an explanation. He wouldn't have been able to give it. To say he loved her, dreamed about her in his sleep, even though she'd never given him any sign she cared for him, would have bared his soul. He wanted nothing to do with the fair sex for a long time.

The rain which had threatened all day began to fall in earnest. He paid an old ostler to stable his pony and pushed open the inn's door. Centuries of alcoholic fumes and a fug of tobacco attacked the lining of his nose. Thirsty, hungry and in need of a bed for the night, he wasn't in the mood to be denied any of the three.

Three redcoats and a lantern-jawed officer sat at a table in the corner. They looked up as he entered and a brown, curly-coated retriever bared its teeth and growled. 'Quiet Romsey,' commanded the officer and the dog settled.

Sassenachs, by that accent thought Rob. 'Whisky, single malt.' He put his coins on the counter.

The hatchet-faced inn-keeper poured the drink. 'You're not from these parts, sir.'

'No,' said Rob.

'Come far?'

'A distance.'

The inn-keeper retired to his back room and shouted, "Lileas Scott, get your lazy backside out here, now."

A brown-haired serving wench with a bruised cheek sauntered in. She wiped her hands on her grease-spattered apron which covered a blue cotton dress. Navy blue wool stockings and black leather shoes with shiny buckles peeped out at the hem. The girl's hazel eyes widened when she saw Rob. She swayed towards him, hands on hips.

'Here Lil.' The officer put out a hand, but she slapped it away. The soldiers laughed and stopped when the officer stared at them.

'I'd say he's from the Highlands, one of those dirty, thievin' Jacobites,' the burly sergeant said and the privates laughed again The sergeant had his back to Rob.

Four against one not good odds. Rob took his drink to a quiet corner. The soldiers sniggered.

'Would you like some...supper, sir?' Lil's plump lips glistened as she ran the tip of her tongue over them and her hands down her filthy apron.

His stomach growled and his body wanted to rest. He wasn't in the mood for the company of a young lass. 'I thank you, no.'

She played with a thick strand of hair. 'Are you stayin' the night?' She leaned towards him and his vision filled with her breast bone and flat chest.

Damn. 'I'm not. How old are you?'

'Eighteen.'

'Thirteen if you're a day.'

She sat beside him. 'I can make you forget your troubles, sir.' He felt her foot high on his thigh. She grinned at him.

Where had she learned that trick? He reached into a saddle bag, and shoved some coins towards her. A speculative look came into her eyes as her hand reached out to grab them, only to find Rob's long fingers covered hers.

'Here, what's your game?' She struggled to release her hand.

'Buy a night's rest, or passage out of here,' he said. 'I bid you good day.'

She watched him open-mouthed as he doffed his hat at her and strode out.

He could have done with a meal and, tired as he was, to bed a woman, but he saw no pleasure in using little lassies and he'd no time for anyone who did.

He supposed he could make an Edinburgh inn before dark and report to the castle in the morning. The acrid stench of old hay, urine and manure engulfed him as he entered the dark stable. He knocked his head on a hanging lamp. 'Damn it.' His mare whinnied in recognition from a far stall.

He dug deep in his saddlebags till he found an apple and fed it to her. She munched, contented, as he threw a blanket and saddle on her brown back. He held the reins with one hand, whilst the other tickled her behind her ears just the way she always liked. 'Good girl,' he whispered as she nuzzled his palm with her soft nose.

'Bet he treats all his doxies like that,' said the sergeant behind him.

Rob turned as a stream of tobacco juice splattered his boots. He weighed up the sergeant who'd a torn ear, splayed nose and scarred eyebrows. The two privates one with a missing tooth and the other, a pimpled face, grinned and fingered the points of their bayonets. The officer lounged against the door and smoked his pipe. Damnation. He drew his sword and his gaze took in the restrictions of space, stalls and bridles.

The dog bared its teeth. 'Romsey, sit,' ordered the officer. He turned to Rob, 'You've a choice, accept you're being pressed into service for king and country or die fighting.'

'There's no need for this.'

'Which is it to be?"

'I'll no' be pressed, I'll fight,' said Rob. 'But dinna count on me dying.' He'd fought since he was a boy of seven and been sent to another Clan to train. His mother hadn't wanted it, but she'd little say. 'You're the son of a laird and must learn what it means,' his father had said.

Rob had been up before dawn to fight with sword and dirk against boys older than him. It meant he could eat only what he'd hunted and never complain. He endured until his muscles became rock hard. Fearless, he'd honed his skills with the master swordsmen in Scotland and France and could wield a dirk with the best. He'd learned to pick his fights and judge men. When his father sent for him at sixteen, he didn't know who'd been more shocked to discover they'd become strangers.

The officer blew smoke rings. 'I'll watch.'

Bastard. Rob noted his uniform, a lieutenant.

'Go on, Dunston and Widderson, nail the bastard,' snarled the lieutenant.

Two against one. The odds had moved slightly in Rob's favour. Rob circled the stable and the privates rushed him. He knocked their bayonets aside, smashed one on the side of the head with the pommel of his sword, and grabbed the collar of the other. He used the man's momentum to drive his head into a wall. Blood spurted. His mare snorted and reared.

'Your turn, Plaskett.' The lieutenant grinned at the sergeant.

Plaskett looked startled and then smiled and showed two rows of rotted teeth. He tapped Rob's sword with his bayonet. 'Let's see how you feel when you've fourteen inches of cold steel up your arse.'

Rob grinned. 'I'd imagine the same as you when I cut off your balls.'

Plaskett gave a nervous laugh and spat. More brown juice spurted out of his mouth and onto the floor. His eyes darted round the stable and he grabbed a harness suspended from a nail. He lashed out and caught Rob's brow. A flash of pain. A bloody weal trickled blood into Rob's left eye. He wiped it away. Damn.

An animal-like snarl erupted from Plaskett as he moved in for the kill. Each time he lunged Rob's sword parried the blade and then drove him back with sweeping strokes, towards the lieutenant.

The lieutenant dived out of the way as the men burst through the stable door and out into the inn yard. The dog growled, hens squawked and feathers flew. The frightened mare trotted towards the tree and a patch of grass.

'Down Romsey, down I say,' snarled the lieutenant.

Plaskett's chest heaved and beads of sweat stood out on his seamed brow. Rob increased the intensity of his strokes and forced the sergeant on the defensive again. He lost ground all the time and Rob lunged forward. The sergeant tottered backwards into a dung heap.

Rob grabbed his mare's reins and leapt into the saddle.

The lieutenant brushed straw off his sleeve.

'If you had asked I'd have told you I've a king's commission in my pocket,' said Rob.

'Rank?'

'Lieutenant. I've to report to Edinburgh Castle tomorrow.'

'Name?'

'Stewart. Yours?'

'Lieutenant Hartlass, at your service.' He gave a slight bow, clicked his fingers at the dog and strode off. 'Plaskett you stink. You're for the Hole.'

Rob made a mental note of their names as the sergeant's face darkened into a scowl.

'Sergeant, tell the men to fall in at the double and keep your stench downwind of me.' Hartlass raised a silk handkerchief to his nose. 'Call yourselves redcoats, you're dregs from the gutter. Come, Romsey.' He tossed a coin at Lil. 'There'll be more where that came from if you leave with me now.'

A grin like a crooked line lit up her face. She held the coin in a tight fist, winked at Rob and followed Hartlass.

Rob looked heavenward and groaned. To think he'd joined the British army to serve with men like this? What had he done?

CHAPTER Eight

August 1745

Pennycuik Hall lay to the north of Edinburgh hidden behind high walls and a stout gate. The Mountjoys, Charlotte and Alan's aged aunts, Mciver and McFee never left their bedrooms. When introduced to Anne the former used a hearing trumpet and shouted, 'Eh?' and the latter whispered, 'There's a veil over my eyes.'

'They're my father's dear widowed sisters,' said Charlotte.

Alan added, 'As you can see there'll be no interference in the business we're about to undertake.'

The house, quiet except for the tick of the hall clock, seemed to wait along with its young inhabitants for something auspicious to happen.

'I'm sick to death of embroidery,' said Anne.

'And if I pay another game of cards, I think I'll die,' said Charlotte.

Alan burst into the room. Anne spun around and Charlotte stood.

'It's begun,' he said. 'The Prince has raised the Standard at Glenfinnan on the shores of Loch Shiel.' That evening the three of them celebrated with a banquet and a toast to Prince Charlie.

A few days later, a tall, thin-faced gentleman called. The butler introduced him as, 'Lord Glenroy.'

'My dear fellow,' said Alan and shook his hand.

Once the butler left the room, Glenroy whispered in Alan's ear.

Alan nodded. 'The weather is very clement, perhaps a walk in the grounds?'

Whilst Alan and Charlotte held back, Glenroy strolled beside Anne. He rubbed his forefingers and thumbs together as he spoke. 'You'll have gathered Glenroy is no' my real name. Lord Alan assures me you can be trusted. I hope so, lives are at stake. I want you in Perth, disguised as a merchant's daughter visiting relatives. There's a coffee house, Ruffles where officers converse. I need information about troop movements. Will you do it?'

Anne's hand went to her throat. 'Yes.'

He patted her shoulder. 'Good girl.'

'What about Charlotte and Alan?'

He put a finger to his lips. 'They have their missions, you have yours. I'll say no more.'

'I understand,' she said. Her heart beat too fast as she thought of the dangers ahead for them all.

***

Once in Perth and settled in a lodging house with a bowed roof and tiny windows, she visited Ruffles every day. Situated at the junction of two busy roads, it had a corner position. The pungent aroma of coffee beans made her nose twitch each time she opened the door. Inside, a wench served from behind a wooden counter to row after row of customers seated at crowded tables and benches. Men discussed, argued and fought over the latest news. A wart-faced man rubbed his knees by the fire and a ginger cat slept in the hearth.

Anne watched shopkeepers, tradesmen, farmers and housewives, come and go. She heard only grumbles about the weather and how this latest rebellion would affect people's purses.

One blustery morning two redcoat captains arrived, caught in a downpour. Newspapers fluttered to the floor as they closed the door and ordered coffees. Her heart beat a faster rhythm. They strode to the fire to dry their cloaks, close to where Anne sat on a settle.

Water dripped at her feet as she laid her head on the oak and closed her eyes as if asleep. *Better they can't see how much I loathe them and their uniform.*

One, a Lowlander by his accent said, 'Never known such poor recruits, must have dredged the gaols for this lot.'

'They'll learn,' said the other, the southerner. 'Always do. Once they've witnessed a flogging it's enough for most, even the hardest. Need to whip 'em into shape now the Pretender's landed.'

The Lowlander lowered his voice. 'Scouts say he's moving fast in this direction.'

His friend whispered, 'Cope's been ordered north to cut them off at Corrieairack Pass. It'll all be over before it's begun.'

Sir John Cope, Commander in Chief of British forces in Scotland. Anne passed the news on to Glenroy.

Some days later she learned the Jacobites had raced to the Pass and arrived first. They'd held the coveted high ground and waited for the redcoats, only for Cope to think better of it and retreat to Inverness.

September arrived and once the Jacobites took Perth, Glenroy returned to Pennycuik Hall he needed information about Edinburgh.

Excitement bubbled up inside her when Glenroy explained what he wanted her to do. 'We need details about Edinburgh's defences any way you can get them. You're to pretend you're a young widow. We've arranged employment for you as a serving wench at the Old Soldier near the castle.'

'A serving wench!'

'It's no' work for a lady, but these are no' ordinary times.' His grey eyes pierced hers. 'A lot of redcoats drink there. The landlord, Ned Boyle's expecting you. Lady Anne, will you do it?'

Glenroy rested one foot on a chair and leaned towards her in an earnest manner.

'Of course, how can you doubt it?' she said. The thought of the dangers made her blood race. Instead of silly tea parties, not that she'd any invitations since she'd been jilted, she'd be doing something useful for the Cause, just like a man.

Anne arrived at the Old Soldier, a building whose top storey overhung others at the foot of the castle. She knocked on the weathered oak door. It opened. The smell of damp and decay assaulted her senses. The landlord, Mr. Boyle, his lank grey hair adrift from his bald spot, looked up at her. Anne, though impressed by his muscular shoulders and chest, realised the rest of his body appeared out of proportion. His legs bowed as if they the weight of the rest of him had become too much. *Rickets.* His head barely reached the top of her chest. *Poor man.*

'What do you want?' His brown teeth snarled at her and the stink of his breath almost knocked her backwards.

She managed to say the code word she'd been given. 'Thistle'.

He scanned the empty street then indicated she could enter with a quick movement of his head. She did so and he slammed the door behind her. They stood in a tiny hall with little light.

'I'm delighted to make your acquaintance, Mr. Boyle,' she said and extended her hand.

He looked her up and down. 'I canna believe they sent a lady.' he said. 'Forget the bloody fancy airs and graces learned at your Papa's knee. This is an inn, not a bloody parlour. You're to be a servin' wench they said, so you need to bloody look and act like one. My lassie'll help. Aileas. Aileas.'

What an ungracious little man. As a fellow Jacobite he could at least be civil.

'Da?' Aileas stood at the door, all bosom and hips.

'This is the lady I told you about. Do somethin' with her.'

Makes me sound like a sack of oats.

Aileas scratched her curly hair and laughed. 'I'll try me best. You're Ena Salmon. Got it?'

'Aye.' *I'll have to eat, drink and sleep it - be Ena.*

The other wenches are still asleep. Come on, we'll go to my room. You're sharin' with me.' They climbed a staircase which creaked at every step, to a room which consisted of two beds and a dirty window with cracked panes.

Aileas rummaged through a pile of dirty linen, then handed Ena a filthy cap.

Ena stared at her in shock. She put it on and prayed no lice had made their home in it. She tucked her red hair inside. *Lord, what I do for the Cause.*

Alileas gave her a soiled bodice, skirt and apron.

'Is there nought clean?' Ena said.

'Dinna be daft woman. Why would ye have clean clothes, they'll only get dirty again,' said Mr. Boyle at the door. He spoke to Alileas. 'Bring her down once she's dressed.'

Ena shook her head and grimaced as Alileas wrapped the coarse material round her skin like a greasy blanket. The smell of stale sweat, smoke, and alcohol meant she struggled to breathe.

Alileas led her down another staircase to a large room with a bar at one end, an unlit fire in a stone fireplace at the other and wooden tables and benches on a flagstone floor. The only light came from an un-shuttered window.

At the sight of Ena, Mr. Boyle slapped his huge palm against his forehead in despair. 'Still looks too bloody good for round here. Wait a moment.' He went to the fireplace and came back with a handful of soot and blew it in her face.

Ena sneezed and coughed which sent the black dust over Boyle and his daughter.

'That's better, Da, she's one of us now,' said Aileas.

'Aye, but can you get her to bloody behave and sound like one of you? You've only got an hour before the wenches are up.' He gave a knowing look at the stained ceiling.

'Right, Ena, you need to show 'em what you've got.' Aileas swayed her hips as she walked and placed her hands on them.

Lord. Dressed in rags, Ena looked the part, but could she act it? She'd never been in an inn and never served anyone before. She copied Aileas. *Oh, the shame of it.*

'No' bad,' said Aileas. 'You have the walk. Now, a lot of men will want to talk to you and others will want to touch. Those that get too bold need to be slapped down fast, like this, 'Keep your bloody hands to yourselves or I'll turn your prick into a purse - see?'

Ena's eyes widened and her mouth formed an o.

'It's the only language some understand,' said Aileas and shrugged her shoulders. 'Now you have a go.'

Ena tried to remember what she'd overheard heard from Kerbilly stable hands and workmen. She took a deep breath and mimicked Aileas's voice. 'Bastard. Whoreson. Keep your filthy paws to yourself, you little prick!' *Well, now that wasn't too difficult, quite liberating in fact.*

Aileas stared at her. 'You'll do.'

When the other wenches arrived sleepy-eyed they filled the room with loud, coarse voices and raucous laughter. The noise doubled when their customers strode in. Ena, found it hard to be so free and easy around men, to listen to their oaths and not be shocked, to accept a stranger's arm around her waist or worse, slap away hands which fondled her backside. Her father and uncle had shielded her from such lewd behaviour and she could see why.

These wenches thought little of a bare of bosom or leg if a man paid coin to look. They leaned over customers, put their arms around them and made free with their kisses. But if a man overstepped the mark, they rounded on him with such foul language Ena thought the air should crackle with fire and brimstone. And now she'd joined them.

'Keep your bloody hands to yourself, you mongrel,' she yelled as fingers travelled over her buttocks. 'I'll have your bollocks for breakfast.' *Lord, I really said that.* The fellow's hands jerked back to his lap as friends jeered and jostled him whilst Mr. Boyle, nodded his head and smiled at her.

***

Ena had been on her feet all night. She'd carried tankards, full to the brim, to hordes of thirsty redcoats who filled the low-ceilinged room. She wanted to hate them as devils, but when they shared a joke with her and the other wenches, she realised they were just boys and men. She wiped sweat from her brow. *So this is how women like this have to live.*

Mr. Boyle tapped her shoulder 'Get some fresh air out back. Don't want you faintin' on me.'

Ena squeezed between customers to reach the scullery. A blast of cool air met her and she took deep breaths.

'What?' Aelias stood at the open door, her back to Ena and hands on hips. She glared at a

girl of about thirteen who stood in a shaft of light in the yard. Her narrow fox-face sat beneath a lopsided loaf of brown hair. She wiped her hands on her faded blue dress and sucked in her cheeks. Two spots of rouge and her scarlet mouth made her look even younger.

'Name's Lil Scott. I'm lookin' for work.'

'You're wastin' your time, there's none 'ere,' said Aelias and started to shut the door.

Lil put her boot in the way, fluttered her eyelashes and pressed up her small bosom with two hands. 'I can do more than wait on tables.'

Aelias snapped. 'Told you before, there's no work 'ere for the likes of you. This is an honest establishment.'

'What do you mean?' the girl screeched. 'I'm honest and want to pay my way.'

'Not behavin' like that.'

'I'm 'ungry. Hartlass doesna' feed me unless I give him me earnin's.'

'Ere.' Aelias thrust a chunk of bread at her. 'Now bugger off.'

The girl's dull eyes lit up as she tore at the bread and Aileas slammed the oak door in her face.

'She's just a bairn,' said Ena.

'A street whore,' said Aileas. 'Can't encourage 'em or the place will be swarmin'.'

She's too young to be on the streets. She must have family. Who's Hartlass?

'Where's Ena? Ena!' yelled Mr. Boyle. 'I've an inn to run no' a home for the idle. Get servin'.'

Lil Scott's face stayed with Ena as she waited at tables again and listened for useful information to pass on to Glenroy. She put a hand to the ache in her lower back and wished she could take off her shoes. She wondered how the other lassies managed with their constant smiles and small talk. Then she realised they had to, or become like poor Lil Scott. *Poor things, at least I've a choice.*

She copied the girls' false smiles and memorised names, ranks, regiments. Her head buzzed with facts and figures, for the Cause. She put three tankards on the table for a sergeant and two privates, avoided their hands and wiped the ale spills from tables nearby as she listened.

'They've got townsfolk guardin' all the gates. Not like real soldiers. Take the Nether Bow Port,' said a private with a missing tooth. 'They dunno wot they're doin', let anybody in.'

'Stands to reason the Jacobites'll try to take Edinburgh. Good thing we hold the castle. Heard we've a load of ammunition arrivin' by ship this week,' said the burly sergeant. He blew his splayed nose into a filthy handkerchief. 'We'll need it if there's a fight.'

'Ere, sarg, that big fella at The Drover could fight, couldn't he?' The private scratched his pimples. 'Must 'ave been over six foot. Pleased he's joined up. Knocked me senseless.' He fingered a livid bruise on the side of his face. 'Still 'urts.'

'Need your muvver do you, Dunston?'

'No sarge.' Dunston flushed and drank from his tankard.

'He's Lieutenant Rob Stewart now, saw him in the castle. Showed spirit, I'll give him that. If I 'adn't tripped...'

Rob Stewart. Ena started. *It couldn't be him.*

'Tripped?'

'Aye, tripped. Got something to say about it, Dunston?' He put his huge fist under Dunston's nose.

'No, sarge. Just thought he's a leader wot you could follow. I mean he took on three of us an' didn't turn a 'air. Wot do you fink, Widderson?'

"E's a fighter. I still get 'eadaches,' said the pimply-faced private. He gulped down his ale.

'He'd beat that bastard, 'artlass. Disgustin' how he's treats poor Lil. Gave me a month in the 'Ole. I won't forget,' said the sergeant. 'Plaskett never forgets. Drink up lads, we're on duty in an hour.'

Ena moved away. *Rob Stewart. I'm haunted by his name. So, took on three of them and didn't turn a hair. A lieutenant in the British Army. A redcoat! It couldna be him. He's from a staunch Jacobite family. This isna **my** Rob Stewart.* She thumped her tray on the bar. *Wait a minute, he isna mine, I dinna give a fig about the man or 'M'; I despise him. Now, what was that about the Nether Bow Port, one of the gates into Edinburgh?*

She took a letter to the Retrieving Office near Greyfriars Kirk. At some point, she knew, an agent would collect it.

A few days later a sealed note instructed her to: *Return to Hall.*

CHAPTER Nine

September 1745

Anne, dressed as tavern wench, Ena Salmon, returned to Pennycuik Hall in a torrent of rain and used the tradesman's entrance. She'd left the inn the day before the Jacobite attack. Her report about Edinburgh and its lax defences meant the Jacobite army took it on September 16th.

The weathered door opened and a whippet-thin footman looked down his nose at her. 'Be about your business.'

She shivered and wafted Lord Glenroy's pass in front of him. He read it three times, searched her face and said, 'Sorry, Miss.'

Anne couldn't blame him. Soot and grease clung to her skin, hair and clothing. She raised an armpit and breathed in. *Lord.*

She ordered the maids to prepare a bath and bring up buckets of hot water. Their flushed faces and frail bodies made Anne call a halt before the bath had been half-filled. Then she used perfumed soap and scrubbed every inch of soot and grease off her.

Some hours later in the sitting room Charlotte greeted her with a hug and said, 'I'm so pleased you're back. I willna ask what you've been doing. Alan's upstairs and I only returned an hour ago. It's so exciting, helping the Cause and now these have arrived.' She gave Anne a letter written in her father's hand and an invitation from Prince Charles to a ball at the Palace of Holyroodhouse.

'As you can see we're all invited,' said Lady Charlotte.

Oh no. To have faces staring at me, overhear snide comments, not again. 'Charlotte, I'd prefer to stay here.'

'But I must introduce you to Lord Archibald, he's so handsome. Our fathers are old friends.' Charlotte's cheeks flushed. 'They, well...have an agreement. He may ask for my hand tonight. Alan has agreed to escort us. You must come or the Prince will be insulted.'

Anne sighed. 'Very well.' She retreated to her bedroom, sat at a desk near the window, hesitated, broke the seal on her letter and read it.

Kerbilly
September, 1745
My dearest daughter Anne,

I find it difficult to express my anxiety on your behalf. This estrangement is not of my making and I wish it to end. Can we not agree to disagree?

You have always been dutiful, if a little headstrong. Please return home to Kerbilly and me. In these bad times I am concerned for your safety and well-being.

Your mother would not have wanted this and neither do I. It hurts me more than I can say that you prefer to stay in a stranger's house than with me. I should not need to remind you of my love, but I do so in the dearest hope that you will return.

Father.

Guilt swept over her. *He begs for reconciliation, but our estrangement provides perfect cover and no one pries or asks leading questions about my comings and goings. I have to help the Cause.* She took a quill, dipped it in the ink pot, steeled herself and replied:

September, 1745

Dear Father,

Thank you for your letter. I am safe and well. Please do not concern yourself. I think it better if I reside where I am for some time. I remain as always your daughter.

Anne.

Every word she wrote sounded the death knell of their relationship in her head. As she dressed for the ball, she sighed at the chasm which had opened between them, but she had to work for the Cause.

***

She tried to put her father's letter behind her, took a deep breath and left the safety of the carriage. Alan led her into Holyrood where the candelabra glittered and mirrors sparkled.

James Mackintosh, a former neighbour of Anne's noticed her entrance and nudged his wife, Hanna, who shimmered in crimson satin. She whispered behind her fan to Charles MacNeil of Barra who elbowed his daughter, Isla, in chocolate silk.

Heads used to turn because of her beauty and now they turned because of her notoriety. A pity, Anne thought, as Holyrood's grandeur and meeting the Prince should have been enjoyable.

She'd chosen to wear a purple gown, tartan sash, gold earbobs, necklace, cream stockings and satin slippers. Her hair un-powdered as she disliked the fashion for wigs. Alan tugged at the lace cuffs of his ebony jacket. He showed a good leg in cream stockings and black shoes with silver buckles.

Anne stood by Alan at the top of the grand staircase as they waited to be announced. Music swirled up to them along with the scent of festoons of wild, white roses which decorated every table. A cascade of chandeliers swept along the centre of the cream and gold ballroom.

Lady Montrose's peacock gown and Lord Galbraith's silver jacket glimmered amongst hundreds of others in mirrors which lined the walls. Lady Montrose deep in conversation with Lady Brodie, in pea-green, froze.

'Lady Anne Kerr of Kerbilly...'

At her name, Lady Brodie's eyes flicked towards her and away.

Anne's stomach churned.

Alan pressed her hand and whispered in her ear. 'You are the most beautiful woman in the room and risk your life for the Cause. It doesna matter what people think. I've learned that since this.' He pointed at his ruined face.

'Oh, Alan.' *I thought only of me, not you.*

'If you look to the right, you'll see the Stewarts,' he said.

'Rob Stewart's here?' Her heart did a mad dance.

'No, but his brothers are.'

Two tall Highlanders glowered at her. *They'll have heard the gossip.* The tallest brother had his arm round a striking young woman. They stood out, because like Anne, they didn't wear wigs. Their hair, his auburn and hers dark shone with coppery lights under the chandeliers. The other brother, shorter by an inch perhaps, had hair like bracken and a broad face.

Lord, what a handsome group. Anne stuck out her chin and allowed herself to be led to the Prince. Her thoughts unsettled her. *Stewart probably resembles his brothers with their proud bearing and commanding looks. And 'M' would of course be breathtakingly beautiful.* Her breath quickened and she fought to bring it back to its normal rhythm.

'First I'll fetch us some refreshments.' Alan pushed his way round the Brodies and disappeared into an adjoining room. Lady Montrose turned her back.

Anne held down a need to run as fast and far away as she could. She stuck out her chin, determined not to give these false friends the satisfaction.

'Colonel.'

She whirled.

'You look exquisite, but what are you doing 'ere? Philippe waved his hand. 'These people hate you, look at their faces.' He motioned towards the Brodies.

'I dinna need to look. The Prince invited me. And you?'

Loup de Mer is moored in Leith, so I too received an invitation. I was sorry to 'ear you're estranged from your father.'

Drat. 'You've heard my father and uncle are Whigs no doubt?'

'I heard, but you've remained loyal to the Cause, 'aven't you?'

'Yes.' She gave him a half smile.

He waved a lace handkerchief in the direction of the Brodies. 'I suppose these wretches think you a Whig and 'ave ostracised you because of the broken betrothal.'

'Yes.'

'You poor girl.'

'Dinna feel sorry for me...'

'I love it when your eyes flash like emeralds, Colonel.' The musicians struck up a minuet 'You'll allow me the next dance?'

Love? 'Of course.' She held out her hand and he grasped it in his. A fire ignited within her. She tried to concentrate on his white necktie, but a glance told her he regarded her with an amused smile. *He has such long, sooty black lashes and deep brown eyes I followed him as a child and longed for a moment like this, but he ignored me, let me take the blame for his mishaps or left without a glance.*

The violins stopped and he escorted her off the floor. 'I think in my youth, I must 'ave been a fool.'

Lord, what's he saying?

'Philippe, it's good to see you.' Alan put a hand on his shoulder.

She heard Philippe's sharp intake of breath. He searched his friend's ravaged face for some semblance of the man he knew.

'I missed you at the ball in July,' said Alan. His voice filled the silence as he shook Philippe's hand. 'How is it with you?'

Philippe recovered his composure. 'Well, my friend. Business is good. Let me know if you want some brandy. I 'ave the best.'

The men talked and Anne sipped wine and sat on a chair. She avoided Lady Montrose's spiteful eyes. *I shouldna have come.*

'I 'ave to leave, the tide...'

'The tide, again?' She arched a brow at him.

'My ship.' He bowed to Alan and lingered as he kissed her hand. 'Till we meet again, Cherie.'

She watched his tall figure stride away. *He used the word love, said he must have been a fool.*

'Anne, was that Philippe I saw you talking to?' Charlotte stood at her shoulder.

'Yes.'

'You do know he's married?'

Anne's heart stopped beating. 'No.'

'I thought you knew,' said Alan and shook his head.

Charlotte put her arm round Anne's waist. 'Married an heiress of course, some weeks ago, the Comtesse Marie de Lyon.'

Anne stared at her. *I'm the fool to think that self-serving, arrogant man might have changed.* She chewed her thumb.

'You poor, darling,' said Charlotte. 'You really must forget him. He's a rogue not to have told you. Come and sit, I have important news.' She patted a seat furbished in gold silk beside her. 'Lady Margaret and Lord Ross have an understanding. He canna ken her true character. Oh and I must introduce you to Archie, he's the most dear...' She signalled to a heavy-set, fair-haired young man who elbowed his way to join her. 'Archie, meet my dearest friend, Lady Anne from Kerbilly. Lady Anne, may I present Mr. Archibald Cameron.' Archie had sandy hair, freckles and a ready smile. Charlotte held Anne's hands. 'You can be the first to know. Alan has agreed. Archie and I are to be married once we've won. What do you think of that?'

Anne's jaw dropped. *I'll be the only single woman left in Scotland.* She managed a strangled, 'I'm pleased for you both.'

'Thank you, most kind,' said Archie and bowed.

'Thank you,' said Charlotte and leaned towards Anne. She whispered behind her fan, 'I'm sure you'll find someone you love, one day.'

Anne tried not to wince. *Charlotte means no harm, but that wound hasna healed.* She watched as Charlotte wandered off with Archie.

'Anne, let me introduce you to the Prince,' said Alan.

The Prince. Lord.

Alan took her across the room to an alcove. An unseen hand drew back the cream velvet curtain to reveal Lord Alistair, in black. He stood beside Prince Charles and looked elegant in his blue jacket, embroidered waistcoat and black breeches.

'Your Majesty,' she said and performed a low curtsey.

The Prince allowed her to kiss his hand, then bowed.

'Lady Anne, it is a pleasure to meet you at last. Lord Alistair has told me of your exploits, but failed to mention your beauty. Thank you for your efforts on my behalf.'

He has a slight accent. 'Thank you sir and, may I congratulate you on your success so far.'

'You may, victory is close at hand. I will not forget those who have supported my Cause.' He kissed her hand, presented her with a fan, then started the whole process again with Lady Brodie.

Anne flicked open the fan and examined the carved ivory handle and exquisite paintings of Prince Charles as a classical figure. *The real man's charming, but not as handsome as some said. I've seen taller and broader men, but has he got it in him to win back the throne for the Stuarts?* She wafted her face, grateful for the flutter of cooler air.

Lady Anne,' said Lord Alistair. 'May I introduce Lord Sinclair?'

The man's hooded eyes raked her from head to toe before he bowed and his cold lips kissed her hand. 'I'd heard of your beauty, they lied, words cannot paint the picture you make tonight.'

'You flatter me, sir.'

'Lord Alistair tells me you have brains too, deuced rare in a woman. Not to be encouraged in times other than these, of course.'

She snapped her fan at him. *A viper if I've ever met one.* 'Alan, would you have our coach made ready? You must excuse me gentlemen, I find I'm suddenly tired. I'm sure you understand?'

'Of course Lady Anne,' said Lord Alistair.

Sinclair bowed.

Did I imagine it, or did Sinclair's eyes, like a snake's, snap back at me? Pompous, poisonous man. So, women should return to their 'place' once danger has subsided? Odious creature.

She allowed Alan to help her into the carriage. He settled opposite her as they left the golden lights of Holyrood behind them and rattled down dark wynds lit by torches which flickered and flared in the dark. She leant her head on the leather upholstery. The carriage swayed from side to side as she and Alan travelled back to Pennycuik Hall. She found her thoughts wandered to Philippe, more handsome and dangerous than ever. *He didn't tell me. He's a law unto himself and married to the* Loup de Mer. *Poor Comtesse Marie de Lyon.*

Lorna Windham

CHAPTER Ten

November 1745

Grey clouds had threatened rain all morning. Drops pattered on the cobblestones and formed puddles as Rob left his billet at The Three Bells in Spitalfield. He thought about how his regiment had been ordered to London not long after the Jacobites left Edinburgh and wondered if Johnnie and Euan had been amongst them. His father would have ensured they'd be part of this rebellion. If he'd stayed, as his father's heir, he'd have been expected to do the same, thank God he'd left.

He served under Wolfe, he'd enough of drills and exercises and longed for a distraction. It came in the form of the Duchess of Carstairs' lavish ball at Grosvenor Mansion. Cumberland, his commander would be there and Rob would be able to forget about parades and punishments, not to mention Braedrumie and all he'd left behind.

'You've only to visit the duchess for an invitation.' Percy Newton, a young naval officer and new friend smirked.

Rob understood when he met her.

She sat on an overstuffed sofa, clutched at his jacket and pulled him down beside her. 'We can always do with a few dashing soldiers in uniform to make up the numbers.' The Duchess of Carstairs patted her powdered hair with one plump hand and fondled Rob's thigh with the other.

He did his best not to flinch, but moved his leg away from her, sure that under her white makeup, she had to be at least seventy.

Her carmine mouth became a slit. 'Mind your manners, young man, a Scottish accent may not be welcome at the moment. Cumberland and his set will be here of course.'

He stared at her eyebrows, mouse fur came to mind. He eased himself away from her fingers and false brows, thanked her for the invitation card, made his apologies and left. He fancied her eyes stabbed him in the back as he made his escape and hoped God would save him from lascivious ladies.

On his way back to barracks he pondered being in Cumberland's illustrious company at the ball and that soon his regiment could be marched north to contend with the Jacobite problem. He just prayed Euan and Johnnie had stayed at home. He didn't want to meet his brothers or any of the Stewart clan in battle.

***

A few nights later Rob stood in front of Grosvenor Mansion, the facade illuminated by torches on either side of the great doors. Chandeliers within cast light onto the ground. In front of him coaches and sedan chairs stopped and deposited passengers at the bottom of the marble steps. Rob followed their chatter into the hall as a grey-coated servants accepted cloaks, hats and gloves flung at them by party goers eager to enter the sumptuous inner rooms. Lieutenant Hartlass stood opposite and gave Rob a sardonic grin. He saluted Rob with a glass of champagne and swallowed it in one gulp.

Rob determined to stay away from him and skirted the edges of the ballroom. He observed a parent bowed with the burden of a dowdy daughter. Some distance away, an eager opportunist scanned a plump woman's face and jewellery. Perhaps he sought a pretty young widow or spinster, preferably with a large dowry. An ensemble played a minuet which filtered towards Rob as young couple took to the floor.

Rob had no interest in one lady's white-lead stare that followed him wherever he went. He still thought of Morag's face and her smile which was for his brother Euan. No, the marriage market was not for him. Besides, a soldier's life could be short and precarious. If he were to fall in battle, he didn't want to leave a widow or any offspring to grieve after him. He'd seen too much of that in the Highlands.

He moved on to stand near the royal party and noted Lieutenant Wolfe amongst a crowd who listened to the Duke of Cumberland.

'We live at a momentous point in history,' the Duke said. He helped himself to a sugared plum from a silver salver. 'Damn Prince Charles Edward Stuart. His grandfather gave up his right to the throne when he fled the country. Why should his grandson pretend this wasn't so? Had to bring ten regiments back from Brussels to deal with him. Damn the man.' He turned his attention to his game of Faro as a plump gentleman bowed, whispered something and hid Cumberland.

A dandy dressed in purple and black led a beautiful woman in ochre beside Rob. She stood on tiptoe and pouted. Rob gave her a wry grin, even with his height he couldn't see over the heads round Cumberland. The plump gentleman moved and Rob's view cleared.

'Go on, sir, bet higher,' said another gentleman with jowls. His ivory dentures clicked as he spoke.

'You're reckless with my money, Kingston,' said Cumberland and eyed him with a cold stare.

The plump waistcoat moved back in front of the Prince. To his irritation, Rob could hear, but see very little.

'And the French, sir, what do you think of them?' asked a woman with a low, seductive voice.

Rob strained his neck to catch sight of her, but as everyone else did the same, to no avail. Damn.

'I do not think of them at all,' said Cumberland to roars of laughter.

A tall man drifted away and allowing Rob to see Kingston. 'But surely, sir, after Fontenoy, ain't the French a force to be reckoned with?'

'Kingston's said the wrong thing there,' a male voice hissed at Rob's ear.

Rob agreed, Cumberland wouldn't want to be reminded of his defeat by the French. A hushed silence fell as Kingston looked like a stranded seal in a multi-coloured ocean.

'I do not think of the French or Fontenoy, only of future victories over our enemies.'

Rob noted Cumberland clench his jaw as if his wound from the battle at Dettingen still pained him.

Light hand-claps started at Cumberland's words and a bald-headed man shouted, 'Well said, sir.'

'It's getting late, Kingston,' continued Cumberland. He regarded him with steely eyes. 'Perhaps you'd better retire early. I hear your young wife don't like being left on her own for too long.' A heavy-browed gentleman's guffaw became a cough whilst one of the ladies lowered her eyes and hid behind the flutter of her fan.

Kingston coloured, bowed, made his excuses and left. Scarlet faced, he pushed his way past a man with a quizzing glass and a sea of smirks, sneers and sniggers.

Rob felt for Kingston who had no form of redress. Cumberland had made an enemy and for what?

'He's no sense of honour.' The Highland accent alerted Rob and he turned. The speaker's rat-like look of concentrated hatred aimed at Cumberland, held Rob's attention. Lots of Scots lived in London, all of them loyal or so Rob thought.

The man, aware he'd been overheard, pointed a bony finger at his knee. 'Makes one tetchy.'

Rob's eyes narrowed as he watched him limp away with his friends. He'd only spoken what Rob thought.

The clock on the ornate mantelpiece struck twelve. A major went to dance, a colonel to partake of the sumptuous buffet of: lobster, beef, lamb, jellies and sorbets.

'Madam,' cried a petulant Cumberland. He flung his cards on the table, 'you have the luck of the devil.'

Rob turned back to the crowded gaming tables.

'And you, sir, are the devil.'

Her voice had a rich, velvet sound, but Rob still could not see her over the rows of be-wigged heads.

Shocked silence followed her riposte, then Cumberland roared with laughter. A dandy in black and purple threw back his head and joined in. Rob again strained every sinew to see this woman who dared to speak to Cumberland in such a way, but waves of redcoats, ladies and gentlemen had flocked to the table, drawn by Cumberland's presence and the riotous noise. She must be seated and he wanted to see her.

A slim arm held a black pouch aloft by its silver strings. 'I shall take my 'Princely' winnings whilst I'm ahead.'

The Prince laughed again.

All Rob could see: a shapely arm.

She disappeared behind a bull headed, silver-haired gentleman.

Rob used his elbows to force his way through. He glimpsed the woman's powdered wig, a turn of an alabaster shoulder and heard the swish of her silk petticoats as she disappeared into the garden.

Rob followed her at a distance. So self-assured, with a voice that made his senses reel. He wanted to see her face.

She led him into the vast gardens which lay behind Grosvenor Mansion, lit by bands of light from the huge windows and the flare torches. Shadows flitted down paths and behind trees.

Rob waited for his eyes to become accustomed to the semi-darkness. She'd her back turned to him as the rat-like fellow talked to her. Rob watched with envy as the man took something from her, bowed, kissed her hand and limped off. A lovers' assignation?

Rob cursed his luck and headed back to the ballroom, hot after the cool night air. He drank, ate and cut short conversations. For the first time since Morag, he'd been intrigued by another woman, her voice, a shoulder and the whisper of her petticoats. *Madness.*

With a decisive gesture he placed his champagne flute on a table and made to go. His thoughts full of how Cumberland hadn't acted in a princely manner towards poor, bloody Kingston. Rob couldn't understand it; the Prince could afford to be generous towards others.

Rob turned to go, but caught someone's arm.

'Clumsy loon,' snarled the rat-like fellow as objects dropped from his hands and littered the floor.

A card, swept by a lady's pink skirts, lay still at Rob's feet. He bent to retrieve it and realised several muscular legs and stout shoes surrounded him. Rob stood upright and scanned the rat-like fellow's comrades. A man with no neck scowled at him, the second showed wolfish teeth and the last looked like a dog held back by a leash. One by one their hands dropped to where their swords should have been. Rob, recognised their murderous intentions and wondered again about them. The rat-like fellow held out his palm.

'Yours, I believe, sir,' Rob said. He bowed and offered the card to him.

The rat-like fellow's mouth creased into a ragged smile as he took the card. He gave a short bow. 'My thanks, Lieutenant.'

Rob's ears thrummed with the man's Highland accent.

The rat-like fellow left with his companions, whilst his friend, with no neck, didn't turn his back on Rob until he reached the safety of the main door.

Rob stared after them. Some Highlanders fought for King George, but not all. Had he witnessed a lovers meeting, or something else? He pushed his way back into the garden. No one there. He quizzed those who'd stood round Cumberland and got a name.

'Oh, that's Lady Jane Forsythe,' said an aide. 'From the Surrey Forsythe's, so I believe. She said they kept her very close, only came out this season.'

Forsythe? Rob remembered her voice low and soft, with a slight burr perhaps? He'd swear she came from the Highlands too.

A small object rolled towards his feet, courtesy of one of the dancers' skirts. Picking it up, he examined a white, satin rose, a potent symbol of the Jacobite cause. What other proof did he need? They'd Jacobites at a ball with Cumberland present. And the card? He'd made a mental note of the ten of hearts surrounded by rows of letters and numbers.

He rushed to tell the only officer he could find, Wolfe, who stood at one side of the ballroom. He'd one hand behind his back and the other held a full glass of champagne 'Pity you didn't hold onto the card, Stewart,' he said. 'Good show all the same. I like my officers to be alert.' He tapped his lips with his forefinger. 'We'll increase the guard round Cumberland and I'll send some men to look for them. Probably long gone by now.'

'Sir.' Rob decided to leave. The woman and the Highlanders had turned the ball sour. He collected his sword. As he stepped out of Mansion House he paused at the top of the steps and stood in the shadows. He let his sight adjust before he left the building. A middle-aged gentleman and lady spilled out of the ball. The former laughed and the latter chattered as they stepped into their coach.

Rob scanned the darkness and thought of the Highlanders. A horse neighed in the darkness. He coiled himself ready to spring and checked all the dark alleys and lanes for movement. This would be too public, any attack would be on his route when he least expected it.

A dog barked and a raised voice alerted him to a confrontation a hundred yards down the street to his left.

'Damn it. You little slut. You work for me. What I say goes.' A man stood with a clenched fist over a bundle on the ground.

Rob recognised the voice.

Without warning Hartlass kicked the bundle which shrieked and shrunk from him. 'Dinna, I'll do what you want.'

To his dismay, Rob recognised Lil Scott. She must have joined the baggage train and trudged all the way with Hartlass to London. The brute had hold of her hair. The dog's barks became more frantic.

Blast that dog Rob thought as he strode towards them and then broke into a run. His insides twisted at the relentless assault he could see before him.

Each time Hartlass' boot landed, Lil whimpered. 'You're drunk. Please, no more. I'll do it, dinna. Aaagh.'

'Hartlass, stop I say.' Rob sprinted towards the dreadful scene. The dog growled, the man kicked and the girl squirmed to get away. 'Hartless.'

The dog bared its teeth and Hartlass looked round. The light caught the whites of his eyes and for a second Rob thought he looked like a madman.

"Lieutenant?" said Rob.

Hartlass stared through Rob for a few minutes then gathered his wits. 'Yes?'

'You'll kill her or the dog will, sir. Call him off.'

'Romsey.' The dog sat. 'Just teaching the little slut a lesson. That's right, Lil, isn't it?'

'Aye. It were my fault.' Lil put a hand on Rob's arm and looked at him with big eyes in a pinched, pale face.

Rob clenched his teeth. Her patched dress, darned stockings and worn shoes the same she'd worn at The Drover weeks ago. 'Tell you what, sir,' he said to Hartlass. 'I know a place where's there's lots of doxies will pay us attention. Let's leave this ungrateful drab and find those more grateful for our favours.'

Hartlass stared at Rob and then Lil who cowered against a wall. He wrapped his arm round Rob's neck. 'Lead on.'

As they staggered off, the dog padded behind them. Rob winked at Lil and threw her a shilling which she caught with one hand.

She gave him the thumbs up and danced a little jig.

Rob's eyes narrowed at the man he half-carried at his side, the bastard had to be stopped.

He dumped Hartlass at a whore house round the corner and returned to barracks.

***

Some days later Rob received a report from Wolfe about Lady Jane Forsythe. She hadn't been seen nor heard of since the ball and the Forsythes of Surrey said they'd only sons, so who the hell was she? That question filled his days and nights.

CHAPTER Eleven

November 1745

The thwack of a butcher's cleaver in Newcastle's Flesh Market made Anne jump. She watched as the man's huge hands ripped the pig's ribs from the carcase with ease and then started on the shoulder.

Glenroy had arranged for Anne and Alan to stay in rooms in Sandgate, near the Tyne and the poorest part of Newcastle. He instructed them to meet him in a higher part of the town, opposite St. Nicholas', amongst the smells of fresh and rancid meat and cries of 'Best rabbit here', 'Tripe for sale' and 'Lamb's liver'.

Anne would have ignored the stooped figure who sniffed at a slice of black pudding, but Alan tugged at her sleeve. They stopped at the covered stall beside him. Glenroy glanced at them and Anne took in his sunken eyes, skin stretched over cheek bones and skeletal frame. The effects of his work for the Cause, she supposed. *Poor man.* He signalled them with a slight movement of his head. Alan then Anne followed him as he threaded his way round a woman who wrestled with a ragged child and entered a dark alley. Anne wrinkled her nose. Drains.

'Alan, check we're not being followed,' said Glenroy.

Alan scanned the market for a few minutes. He shook his head.

Glenroy hissed at them from the shadows, 'Redcoat regiments are gathered here. We need information about the town's defences and troop movements, soon as you can get it.

Alan, you're a sutler and Anne you're his sister. Names: Edward and Annie Bryce. You'll sell provisions to the redcoats. Get yourself settled, trusted and copy the accent. We've organised a wagon and horses. They're at a premium. The army's commandeered the best. Collect them a week today from Arthur Newson, a corn merchant in the Hay Market, north of the town. Camp with the army on the moor.'

Annie and Edward Bryce. Anne longed for the silks and satins in London, but Glenroy had insisted he needed her and Alan in Newcastle. *No. I must remember we're Annie and Edward.*

'Follow me, but no' too close,' said Glenroy. He left the chare at a pace and weaved his way through the bustle of the market.

So, Anne became Annie who loitered at stalls. Alan, now Edward walked some distance behind and to one side. Glenroy trudged ahead towards Newcastle's Black Gate and its bleak tenements four storeys high.

Glenroy paused and scanned a keelman in his blue bonnet, jacket, yellow waistcoat and bell bottomed trousers, scrutinised a wealthy merchant with a silver cane and examined a ragged woman with a basket of fish under her arm.

'Canna be too careful', Glenroy said. 'Just a little way now.' He stopped under the castle walls. Below, the grey Tyne rushed to the coast and verdant pasture carpeted the hills to the south. 'See,' he whispered. 'This town's of strategic importance to Jacobite and British forces. The castle, guards the bridge and river. Town's got good roads in all directions. Hold Newcastle and you control this part of England right to the Scottish border. It's vital we receive accurate information from you. One of my men will make himself known. I wish you luck, you'll no' see me here again.'

Annie watched his bowed back as he scuttled down the steep Castle Steps, past several clog shops. He disappeared round the turn which led to the Close and its merchants' houses far below.

***

Annie and Edward left their Sandgate lodgings a week later. Edward collected the laden cart and met Annie on the Town Moor where they made camp and became sutlers. She'd listened to keelmens' families and worked hard to master the guttural, sing-song Geordie accent. She'd even joined howls of derision directed at a lowland Scot, who'd been gaoled by the militia. Anyone with a strange accent was treated with suspicion in this place. Annie understood why, when a plump baker's wife informed her, 'Newcastle's been besieged by the Scots, but the walls have only been breached once.' She shuddered and added, 'The tales I've heard. Never again'.

Annie shared this revelation with Edward whilst she agreed to investigate the quayside and he assessed the strength and weakness of the town's medieval walls. They would meet in the Queen Bess at Sand Hill. He took himself off dressed in a simple shirt and brown breeches.

A few minutes later, she tamed her hair under a cap and looked at her dove-grey bodice and skirt. The colour reminded her of drab streets, but she'd merge into the background with rest of the local women. She picked up a wickerwork basket, opened the tent flap and shivered as her cloak swirled round her ankles. Soldiers everywhere. She wended her way through rows of tents which rippled in the breeze.

Anne walked through New Gate, past the White Cross and sauntered through the Groat Market. A trader shouted in her ear, 'Buy your oats here'. But she bought six red apples from a pasty-faced urchin. On she went past hymns sung in St. Nicholas' Cathedral. The castle loomed ahead of her. She turned down into The Side, a steep street which led to Sand Hill where the Scale Cross stood in the centre of a higgledy-piggledy fish market. The clamour of hundreds of voices filled her ears. She sniffed the air and the tang of salmon, cod and plaice wafted towards her from the numerous carts and stalls.

To her right a moon-faced boy held up fish from his basket and yelled, 'Fresh herrin'. A stout man shouldered him aside. He carried a tray round his neck and shouted, 'Pie, pies, damn your eyes'. Behind him a middle-aged woman, covered in flour, cried, 'Fresh, baked bread' as she held up a loaf.

To Annie's left a frayed-cuffed young man gossiped with another who wore a fine frock-coat. A raddled whore displayed her bosom. In front of her a ragamuffin child bumped into a one-armed sailor who kicked the urchin's backside. The child howled as a plump woman sold butter, eggs and milk from a hand- cart.

A goose honked and made Annie jump. A hen which clucked at her feet. She steered clear of the cattle which grazed on a scrap of grass and walked past the Queen Bess, which seeped alcohol into the air and leant in all directions. Once through Sand Gate she memorised the number of ships, regiments and cannon being unloaded. She also noted Dutch coasting barges and trading brigantines lined up to take their turn at the busy quay.

She traced her way back to the Queen Bess, sidestepped groups of redcoats, and stepped into the tavern's gloom. Her throat erupted into a cough at the smoke from clay pipes and the coal fire. She took in the room at a glance. Men stood shoulder to shoulder in deep discussion. Others rested their elbows on a long plank of wood supported by two beer barrels. Edward sat hunched in a corner seat.

Annie, put her basket on the flagstone floor and plumped down beside him. He adjusted his hat low over his brow and put his pockmarks in shade. She rubbed her sleeve on the smut-covered window and wondered at the lines of masts above the town wall and soldiers who poured by.

Edward nudged her and whispered, 'There's workmen strengthening the ramparts and hundreds of cannon being hoisted into position. Two-hundred county militia arrived yesterday, they look fit, well-fed and armed.'

She replied, 'And the quay's heaving with redcoats, they're transporting them here by ship, they've piles of munitions, provisions...can we defeat them?'

'We have to.' He put a hand on her shoulder. 'I'll get you an ale shall I?'

She nodded and tried to shrug off her fears as she turned her attention back to the scene in the window.

A sailor lugged a bale of hemp. Another rolled a barrel of spirits into a cellar. A captain and lieutenant haggled over a box of munitions which had fallen from a cart whilst black-faced kittiwakes swooped on an open barrel of fish.

Annie needed fresh air. She opened the window and the first notes of a sea shanty played on a fiddle drifted towards her from Sand Hill. She breathed in and wished she hadn't. The wind had changed and the smell of damp from Sandgate's tenements and the stench from the Tyne made her cover her nose. The odour seeped into the streets and chares and mixed with the stink of piles of dung and human waste where the poor scrabbled for a living. Annie had seen the same desperation in faces in Edinburgh, London and now Newcastle.

Opposite, on the other side of the street, a painted girl stopped and lounged against the town's sandstone wall. Her dull eyes searched men's faces...Annie started. *Surely it couldn't be her?* The waif from Edinburgh...Lil, looked thinner and paler. Her fox-like features unmistakeable, even though she'd dyed her hair bright red. *A young lass alone is easy prey.*

As Annie watched, the girl ran her fingers through her greasy hair and thrust out her flat bosom. A sailor strolled by and laughed. Her ragged dress hung on her thin frame and a naked toe peeped out of her muddy shoes.

My God, this isn't right. Lil's a child, should be protected. I must do something. Annie started to rise, but Edward's arm held her in her seat. He nodded in the direction of a redcoat who'd eyes only for Lil. Edward thrust a tankard in front of her. 'Sup up, bonny lass.'

Annie drank and watched.

The lieutenant, his lantern-jawed face tight and controlled, loomed over Lil and rubbed his thumb against his fingers. His dog sat beside her. Lil shrunk back, looked at the ground and shook her head. He thrust his fist under her nose and made her cower. The dog growled and bared its teeth.

'Dinna Hartlass,' she said and shielded her face with her thin arms.

'Romsey.' The dog whimpered. 'Next time I'll not call him off. I'll be back. Make sure you've earned your keep.' He clicked his fingers. 'Come, Romsey.' The dog padded after him.

My God, the bairn works for him. Anne had heard of such scoundrels. She wanted to kick him round Newcastle and into the Tyne. How could men use children in such a way?

Lil tossed her head, put a hand on her hip and called out to an aged man who passed, 'Want a good time, Mister?'

In the inn, Edward took a final swig of ale from his tankard and wiped his hand across his mouth. Annie joined him. He kept his voice low and spoke with a northern inflection. 'Ready, bonny lass?'

She nodded. The scene she'd watched had made her morning turn sour. She stepped out of the inn and shaded her eyes to see Hartlass stride off with his dog towards Sand Gate.

'Let's go back to the moor,' Annie said. She slipped a few coins into Lil's hands as she passed.

'Thanks Miss,' shouted Lil.

Annie only hoped the money would take the child off the streets, buy her a bed for the night and some food. The sound of barks made Annie turn, Lil forgotten. Sand Gate. Curious, she walked towards it, parallel to the town wall.

Hartlass' had a hand on his dog's collar as it snarled at a mongrel held in the grip of an elderly, wispy-haired man.

'No.' The man retreated as Hartlass crowded him into a corner. 'No.'

Hartlass seized his hand and shook it. 'It's agreed, Twyzzell, can't back out now.' Then he crooked his forefinger and a private came at the run and saluted. Hartlass put coins on the private's palm and elbowed Twyzzell to do the same. A gentleman in a velvet-coat paused and joined in, followed by a one-eyed sailor and a sweep who sent his apprentice 'at the double' to the Ship Inn. Within minutes a tight circle formed round Hartlass and Twyzzell.

What are they doing? Annie pushed her way through cattle, sheep and pigs to stand behind the velvet-coated gentleman who urged someone or something on. Annie stood on tiptoe and watched.

'I'll give you five to one on the lieutenant's hound,' cried the velvet-coated man.

'Done,' said the one-eyed sailor.

The two dogs circled each other. Eyes locked, fangs showed. The larger, brown dog leapt and nipped the other's foreleg. The smaller animal howled.

'I'm beggin' you, Hartlass, call him off. I don't want this,' Twyzzell pleaded.

Hartlass threw the man's hand off his arm. With a look of disdain said, 'It appears your dog's losing, Twyzzell, and I'll win my bet. Go on, Romsey. Teach him a lesson.'

The brown dog, his jaw foam-flecked, leapt at the other, his teeth grabbed an ear. The injured victim squealed as he tried to shake off his opponent. Crimson drops spattered the ground.

'Go on.' A huge man with muscles clenched his fists.

'Kill the bugger,' yelled a tall fellow. He wiped hands the size of dinner plates on his bloody apron.

'Treat him like a dirty Scot,' shrieked a neat little woman. She shook her handful of ribbons in the air.

The larger dog showed the whites of his eyes and tightened its grip.

'Kill!' screamed the little woman.

'Kill!' shouted the man in the bloody apron.

'Kill!' yelled the gentleman in the velvet-coat.

Annie's gorge rose, but she fought the vomit down. 'Stop,' she shouted. 'Stop.'

'Annie.' Edward grabbed her arm and tried to pull her away.

'Stop it, call him off.' Twyzzell shrieked.

A smirk flitted across Hartlass' face. 'Go for his throat, Romsey. Good boy.'

Blood speckled Romsey's coat. It streamed down the mongrel's head as he yowled, tore free and left his tattered ear behind. He dived through a pair of legs, shot under several bulls and into The Side.

Romsey's pink tongue licked his wounds as Hartlass smiled and counted his winnings.

The man's a monster.

The snort of beasts and the pound of hooves made Anne whip round.

'Watch out!' came a shout from the sailor. Edward froze as several runaway cattle headed for him and he dived to the left. He disappeared in a cloud of dust as the bulls headed for Sand Gate and the quay.

'Alan,' Annie yelled. *They'll be on me at any second, I've my back to the river with nowhere to run.*

A strong arm wrapped itself round her waist and held her to a muscular chest. The man twisted, took the brunt of the fall and grunted as they hit the cobblestones. They fell to the ground as one. Annie's basket overturned and her apples rolled in all directions. She lay stunned, cushioned by the man's body as the cattle charged towards two dyers. One jumped and the other fell over the quay with a splash.

'Oh,' said Annie as she watched a distraught young man in a farmer's smock, stumble to the quay just as his last bull fell into the Tyne.

Annie's cap slipped over her eyes. Her nose lay buried in the man's crimson jacket which smelt of the outdoors, of a clean, healthy male. He released her. She pushed up her cap to see two ocean-blue eyes which stared into hers. 'Are you hurt, lassie?'

She blinked at him. His voice had a deep, rich Scottish burr. It reminded her of fine whisky full of notes of heather, peat and wood smoke. Her backbone tingled. *Lord, his voice would melt chocolate.* She could only stare at his shock of raven hair, straight nose, full mouth and firm chin. She sensed a frisson. That she'd known this man for a long time and she'd been waiting for him. Something collapsed inside, her head swam and she couldn't speak or move.

His brow wrinkled. 'Is anything broken?' He felt her arms with his long, fingers. She watched his mouth form a wide smile. 'You've strong, wee limbs. I'll check your legs.'

'I'll thank you to keep your hands to yourself.' *I'm supposed to be a Geordie.* She pushed his hands away and felt her cheeks redden as strands of hair fell over her face. 'I'm always being told off for apin' me betters.'

He looked puzzled. 'My apologies, I only meant to help.'

My hair. She stuffed red waves under her cap, wanted to look anywhere, but at him, but then he stood up. He towered over her in his uniform, she'd be lucky if her head reached his chest. *A damned redcoat.* She grabbed her wicker basket and started to collect her apples.

He handed her some. 'Well, you havena lost your voice at any rate.' A boyish grin lit his face as he gathered more fruit opposite her.

'Nor anything else,' said Edward as he dusted his torn jacket and examined his bloody knee.

Lord, I forgot all about him. 'Are you alright?' she said.

'I'll live.' He turned to the redcoat. 'Edward Bryce.' He put out his hand and the soldier took it. 'Thanks, Lieutenant. Annie's me sister. If you hadn't acted so quickly, she'd have ended up in the Tyne like them.' He pointed to an unconscious dyer who'd been hauled onto the quayside, the other one lay still.

Annie gave Edward a startled look. She'd forgotten the danger she'd been in, those poor people.

'Lieutenant Stewart at your service,' the redcoat said. 'Any idea what started it?'

Edward stared at him for a second.

Annie blinked. *Stewart. That name again and I'd just forgotten about him and 'M'. It can't be him.*

'A dog fight involvin' a lieutenant whose dog was winnin' and refused to call him off,' said Edward. 'The losin' dog escaped, poor beast, and frightened the cattle.'

She blinked again. *This Adonis is called Stewart? He couldna possibly be my Rob Stewart, there are lots of Stewarts. But he's no **my** Stewart because this Stewart is a redcoat.* She admonished herself whilst she wracked her brains to remember the face on her miniature.

'I'll have a word with the Mayor. One day there'll be a law against dog fights.'

Annie's breath caught somewhere between her lungs and her mouth. 'He threatened a bairn, over there by the wall.'

Lieutenant Stewart's blue eyes held hers for one beat of her heart. Then he turned towards Lil who sat with her back against the wall. 'Sometimes, men dinna act with honour. I apologise on his behalf, it willna happen again.'

'How can you be so sure?' snapped Annie. *What's a British soldier doing, talking about honour?*

'Thank you, Lieutenant, it's good to be aware some of his Majesty's officers know how to behave,' said Edward. 'I'm a sutler on the Town Moor. If there's anything you need in the way of provisions, bonny lad, I'll see you alright...'

Annie dug an elbow into his side.

'Ow,' said Edward and gave her a look as he felt his ribs.

'You ought to get a sawbones to look at them. You had a hard fall,' said Stewart.

'Thank you, I'm fine,' said Edward.

Stewart grinned at Annie and showed strong white teeth. He bowed and kissed her hand. 'It's strange, we've never met, but I'm sure I've heard your voice before, just canna place where. Miss Bryce, Mr. Bryce.' He saluted and strode off.

The merest touch of his lips on her skin burned like a brand. *Does he know the effect he had on me?* 'Lord, what did you say that for?' said Annie to Edward. 'Now he'll be nosing around, making life difficult.'

Edward grabbed her arm a walked her away. 'Unless there's two Rob Stewarts, he's your ex-suitor and knows your voice. Also you called me *Alan* when the cattle stampeded. I want him close.'

CHAPTER Twelve

A few nights later the full moon glowed in a sapphire sky as the cold October wind whistled down the quay. Vessels bobbed up and down on the Tyne as the tide surged upstream. Lanterns swung as masts creaked, rigging clinked and the river lapped against moored ships and boats.

Annie met Edward in the shadow of a cart which waited for the next day's load on the quay. 'I've got what we need, you?' Her eyes searched the quayside behind them for movement.

Edward nodded, his brow creased. 'Let's go back to the moor.' They walked east towards Sand Gate.

'There's more of everything,' she said. 'I'm worried.'

Edward grimaced. He whispered, 'Glenroy needs to know. A sailor told me there's extra cannons at Tynemouth and he saw a French ship off the coast. Mentioned smuggling.'

Annie's heart missed a beat. *Philippe.*

They re-entered the town through the gate and kept to the shadows of the wall. Occasionally there'd be the cry of, 'Thief' and feet pounded into the labyrinth of alleys. Annie noted a whore and her younger pupil lounged against an inn as a man stopped to try their wares. *Poor Lil.* Annie shivered and pushed the child to the back of her mind. She needed to concentrate on the Cause.

She knew Edward used more than one Jacobite sympathiser to pass messages to Prince Charlie and General Murray in Edinburgh. They'd now know Newcastle was well-garrisoned with a formidable wall and gates. If Prince Charlie meant to take the town, he'd have a fight on his hands.

Annie jumped and Edward froze as the door of The Mermaid Inn banged open and a shard of light streaked across the pavement opposite. Three soldiers appeared. Two supported a man whose head lolled. They stumbled along for a few steps as a dog padded behind them. The group turned into Lean Chare. She watched two dark figures dump the third on the cobbles, heard a curse, the clatter of boots and the dog's bark.

'What's happening?' she said.

Edward put up a hand. 'Don't move,' he hissed.

He shrank in the shadows of the wall, she hardly dared to breathe as a large cloaked figure stepped out of a doorway and another, squatter, detached himself from the gloom of an arch. The first wielded a club which he smashed down on the drunken man's skull. The second threw stones at the dog which whimpered and ran off. It howled like a banshee as it fled up The Side.

Annie put her hand to her mouth to stop the scream in her throat.

'That'll teach you, you bastard for sendin' me to the Black Hole." The large figure booted the helpless man in the ribs whilst the squatter fellow pummelled his face. At a signal from the man with the club, they stopped and ran. Their boots hammered the cobbles as they sped towards Sand Hill.

Annie gasped as Rob Stewart stepped from Broad Chare. He led several redcoats with bayonets at the ready. 'Officer being attacked. At the double,' he shouted. Soldiers raced round the corner into Lean Chare where the prone figure sprawled on the ground.

'Corporal, help that officer to his tent,' said Stewart. Four men grabbed the man's arms and legs and carried him off.

'Should we go after those ruffians, sir?' asked a private.

'Long gone, better no' make a fuss; dinna want the lieutenant on a charge for being drunk.'

***

Annie stared at Edward, she couldn't take in what she'd seen.

He tugged at her sleeve, his voice urgent. 'We have to get back. No telling what they'd do if we're discovered. We'll follow the wall, head east and then north, it's longer, but Stewart will want to return to camp as soon as possible, cover his tracks. We'll steer well clear.' He pulled her back towards Sand Gate and the way they'd come.

'So, you think Rob Stewart organised that attack on a redcoat officer?'

'Don't you?'

'But why would he do that?'

Edward shrugged and hastened his steps.

***

Rob owed Plaskett and his men a jug of ale for this night's work as Hartless would be out of action for weeks and gain Lil some respite.

The previous evening Rob had found the sergeant propped up the bar in the Dog and Duck just off The Side and they'd talked deep into the night.

'My pleasure to organise it, sir, some of the lads need exercise,' Plaskett had said. 'Bastard deserves what's comin' to him. I've watched him, know where he meets Lil. Just ensure you're there to pick up the pieces, sir.'

CHAPTER Thirteen

Rob breathed in the scent of autumn and looked out over an ocean of tents. In the last week of October Newcastle's Town Moor rang with the sounds of a blacksmith's hammer, the jangle of reins and shouts of men. Grey wreaths from hundreds of campfires curled up into the cloudless sky. A warm wind rippled through tawny foliage and flurries of leaves fell to the ground.

He searched for Annie Bryce amidst rows of tents, found an expanse of green and strolled along the line of sutlers. Pity about her brother's ruined face.

A magpie flew off with a worm in its beak as Rob scanned the carts. Only one had customers. At the front of the queue, Private Dunston picked at his teeth. Widderson, stood alongside him and used his fingers to comb his lank fringe over a volcanic spot on his forehead. Annie Bryce stood pink-faced and arms akimbo behind a wooden bench and a canvas awning crammed with barrels of wine, rum, boxes of tea and sacks of sugar. One burly sutler folded his arms and glowered from a distance. Another lowered his brows and clamped his teeth round the stem of his clay pipe.

Rob hadn't been able to erase the memory of the woman's eyes, the beauty spot above the swell of her top lip and the feel of her in his arms. Dunston's word brought Rob back to the present.

'What's a lovely lass like you doin' 'ere?' said Private Dunston who showed the gaps between his teeth.

'Should be in bed. Mine,' said Private Widderson and licked his lips.

'What you chargin'?' asked Dunston. He counted the coins in his hand.

Robs's eyes narrowed as she flushed deep crimson. He stepped forward, about to intervene when she hurled a bag of nails at Dunston. It bounced off his head and split. Mini arrows spun in the air.

'Take cover,' yelled Widderson and dived under a cart.

'Enemy fire,' cried Dunston from behind a cart. He peeked out from behind the wheel and rubbed his head. 'No need for that Miss, we was just jokin'.'

'Not unless you'd like your balls sliced and fried with onions.' She swiped at the air with a lethal-looking knife.

Rob blinked at her colourful language and then grinned. He liked the way her cheeks flushed when angry.

A corporal with a misaligned jaw hooted with laughter. Dunston looked sheepish and Widderson stared at his boots whilst a fresh-faced private slapped him on the back. Annie threw back her head and laughed and revealed two perfect rows of white teeth.

Rob drew in a breath, this woman had something about her. Not just her beauty, but a charisma that attracted men.

Dunston nudged Widderson and turned to a thickset private. 'No pushin' in now, there's a lady present.'

'That's right,' said Widderson. 'Deserves respect, she does.'

The corporal with the misaligned jaw ushered the soldiers into a line.

'Just an ounce of baccy, please Miss,' said Dunston. 'Thank you.'

'A bottle of rum, please,' said Widderson. 'Thanks'

'Have you a pipe?' asked the corporal. 'Broke the stem of this one.'

As she served him she looked up, saw Rob and her cheeks flamed as she took the corporal's money.

She'd remembered him. 'Good morning, Miss Bryce.' He gave a slight bow.

'Mornin, Lieutenant Stewart, what brings you here, bonny lad?' She gave change to the corporal and received his thanks with a smile.

She remembered his name, even more good news. "I dinna' require anything frying, just a bottle of-'

She put her hands to her cheeks. '-You heard.'

'I particularly liked the idea of onions. A nice touch, I thought.'

Her eyes widened and her mouth pursed into an, 'Oh.'

Her beauty spot drew his eyes towards that very kissable top lip.

Sergeant Plaskett's chest heaved as he came to a full stop in front of Rob and saluted. 'Sir, you're...needed...at the castle.'

Rob damned the man. 'A problem?'

'Think I've caught a spy, sir.'

'No,' she said.

They both turned to look at her.

'You're quite safe, Miss Bryce,' said Rob. 'Duty calls. My apologies.' he said. 'Plaskett come with me.'

CHAPTER Fourteen

Annie thought of Edward. He'd left just after dawn that morning to meet someone at one of Newcastle's gates. *He couldn't have been caught.*

A cold breeze wafted over the grass and billowed through the redcoat tents. Annie drew her shawl round her as two customers she knew well appeared at the front of the queue. A grizzled sergeant and his little daughter. 'Morning Sergeant Meadows and Miss Hattie. What was all the excitement earlier?' she asked.

The sergeant held his little girl's hand. 'Saw it mesel', just come off duty. We've captured a spy. Farthin's worth of chocolate, please, Miss.'

Annie turned from him. Her mind raced a she put the block of chocolate on a wooden board and tried to steady her hands as she cut it and released its wonderful aroma. *Edward went to one of the towers...He's always so careful, the prisoner couldna be him.* She put two pieces of chocolate in a twist of paper.

Annie composed her face into a smile and knelt beside fair haired Hattie. 'As she's been so good, I think this bairn deserves more than one piece, don't you, Sergeant?'

'That's kind, Miss. What do you say, Hattie?'

'Thank you, Miss Bryce.'

Annie patted Hattie's head before Sergeant Meadows led her away.

'Two ounces of baccy, Miss,' said a corporal.

'Heard about the spy?' she said as she weighed the golden leaves and the pungent smell hit the back of her throat.

'He were caught at Andrew Tower.'

Andrew Tower. That's it. She meant to pour the leaves onto paper, but her hand missed the square. Tobacco sprinkled onto the ground. *Lord, not Edward.*

The corporal pointed with his clay pipe at her feet. 'Careful Miss or you won't 'ave any baccy left. Your brother won't like that nor will we.'

She took a deep breath.

He leant across the table and lowered his voice. 'They say this spy had information on him.'

Edward.

'Can't trust no one these days. 'artless has 'im. He'll talk. Shipped to London tomorrow.'

She forced a smile, scooped more tobacco onto the paper, pulled the ends together and twisted it. She tried to still her hands as she accepted the corporal's coins. *They've caught, Edward, I'm sure of it.*

She served a few others, tried to appear calm and unhurried on the surface, when all the time she needed to think. 'If you'll excuse me gentlemen, I must close now,' she said. ' We've run out of baccy. I'm sure the other sutlers will be pleased to have your custom.' She tugged at the ropes on the awning.

'Oh, Annie, they're not as bonny as you,' said a disgruntled soldier as the queue moved on.

Poor Edward might talk, most people would if tortured. Nought I can do for him and the redcoats could be coming for me now. I'll leave the cart, take some supplies and a horse and head north. Her mind churned. *No they'd expect me to do that. I'll go north-west.* She stuffed a leather bag with bread, rum, sausage and smoked bacon she'd bought in the Flesh Market.

***

Rob listened as Plaskett said, 'Landlady of the Green Tree reported 'im. Gave 'er the name Cuthbert Smith, but she reckons 'e's a Scot, new in town and askin' lots of questions. His accent comes and goes. Keeps strange hours too, creeps out before dawn, returns late at night. I caught him sneakin' through Andrew Tower Gate. He'd a plan of Newcastle's defences, lists of regiments, senior officers movin' in and out and ships. Best you're quick sir, Lieutenant 'artlass 'as 'im.'

'We'll ride, it'll be faster,' said Rob as he strode toward the picket line. God only knew what Hartlass would do to him.

'Me and 'osses don't get on, sir,' said Plaskett, his mouth downturned.

'Better learn then,' said Rob and saddled a stallion. Before he galloped off, he looked back.

Plaskett had his meat-cleaver hands on his mount's bridle. 'Now look 'ere I 'aint done nuthin' to you, let's be friends.' The horse's eyes rolled, its ears pricked up and hooves struck the ground.

Rob grinned, Plaskett could handle most men, but not horses. Rob wondered who'd win. He wound his way through the encampment on the town Moor and into the town through New Gate. His thoughts ran riot. Who'd been caught? A poor beggar misled by Prince Charles Stuart, a Pretender with no hope of victory, like his family, like Euan and Johnnie. They'd have more sense, surely, and stay at home.

Grey smoke snaked upward from chimneys as he cantered along Newgate Street to its junction with Low Friar Street. He slowed at the White Cross and its stocks where a limp crone, covered in mud and excrement, stared at him through hollow eyes. Hell's teeth. He dismounted, took his canteen, poured water into his palm and let her lap it like an unkempt cat.

A shrunken woman hung out a petticoat on a line and shrieked, 'She's a thief, let her suffer.'

He ignored her.

'Thank you,' mumbled the crone.

'That's alright, Mother. Have you long?'

'An hour or so.'

'Soon be over, then. May it give you strength.' He wished he could have released her, but he'd done what he could for the poor soul.

He re-mounted his horse and trotted towards the crowd in the Bigg and Groat Markets. He took a left and smelt barley and oatmeal as he passed coaching inns and low dilapidated dwellings on either side. Black Gate loomed ahead as he trotted into the shadow of the castle. Built on a mound to defend the bridge over the Tyne, the castle, had a bloody reputation. Forlorn prisoners sat shackled in the yard.

A sentry came to attention.

'The spy?' Rob asked.

'Dungeons, sir. First on the left.' The sentry saluted.

Rob turned into a doorway, along a passage and down well-worn keystone steps lit by the flare of torches. The walls dripped green slime. No outside light infiltrated here, but moans and groans filtered upward. He tried not to breathe, the air pungent. This, how he imagined Hell.

Whimpers. Rob sighed as he followed the sound of fists as they pulverised bone. He stopped at a cell where two burly privates held up a man who sagged between them. Another private panted hard, his shirt flecked with blood and his sleeves rolled up.

Rob stared at the prisoner. He gritted his teeth. 'Saw him in London, sir, at the Duchess of Carstair's ball.'

Hartlass limped into the light. His face mottled yellow and green from the beating he'd received some weeks before. With a snarl he yanked up the prisoner's head by his greasy hair. 'A ball you say?' The rat-like man's eyelids looked purple and bulbous, nose flattened to one side and lips like raw meat.

'Who are you working for? Where are the rest of you Jacobite scum?' asked Hartlass. He spat flecks of saliva onto his victim's face.

The man remained silent.

'Give him another dose.' Hartlass let go of the man's hair and used the owner's jacket, to wipe his hand.

'But sir...' said the private.

'Do it.'

The private looked at Rob before he pummelled the man's ribs.

Hartlass stared at Rob. 'Ah Lieutenant Stewart, now what makes a Scot come to watch a Jacobite spy being interrogated.'

'He willna give in, I ken the type, sir,' said Rob who saw no point in this. Even if the man talked he'd say anything to stop the beating.

'No? He's going to London tomorrow. He'll learn what it means to be a traitor there.'

'Aaagh.'

Rob heard the man's rib crack and winced. 'London might prefer it if the man can speak, sir.'

Hartlass threw Rob a look that could have pinned a lesser man against the wall.

The private paused. His chest heaved and he wiped beads of perspiration from his forehead with his sleeve. He glanced from Rob to Hartlass.

'Just so,' Hartlass said. 'You can stop.'

'Sir.' The private came to attention and gave Rob a grateful look as he picked up his jacket and his burly friends let the prisoner slump to the ground.

'Lieutenant.' Hartlass beckoned Rob over and hissed in his ear. 'The next time you wish to give me advice, not in front of the men. Understand?'

'Sir.'

'You're in charge.' Hartlass strode out of the cell.

Rob waited until Hartlass' steps receded. 'Get him water, food and some fresh straw. Tell the surgeon to have a look at him. He might have a broken jaw.'

'But, sir...'

'He's no use to us if he canna talk.'

Rob, sucked in lungfuls of fresh air once he'd escaped from the dungeons. The sound of hooves made him turn to the Black Gate as Plaskett jogged through like a sack of vegetables on horseback.

Rob held his horse's rein. 'What kept you, sergeant?'

'A bit of a disagreement with this 'oss, sir.'

Rob grinned.

'Is the prisoner still alive, sir?'

'Just. Well done, by the way. He's off to London tomorrow.' Rob thought about the poor bastard, with only a traitor's death to look forward to. Better he died before he got there.

***

'Annie, what are you doing, pet?' Edward stood beside her as he took great bites out of a pear. He'd a bag under one arm.

She dropped her voice. 'I thought...haven't you heard? They've caught a spy at Andrew Tower.' She lowered her voice, 'I thought he was you.'

He went ashen and took her aside. 'It'll be J, poor soul, never saw his face, nor he mine. Just as well, if he talks he canna say much. Thank God he doesna ken my name.'

She grabbed his arm. 'You're sure?'

He nodded.

'They'll know there's others,' she said.

'Dinna worry. I went straight to the orchards after we met, to get these.' He dumped the pears on top of a rum barrel. 'I wasna followed. God help him and damn those redcoats.' He placed an acorn and a twig of oak leaves beside the apples. 'Reminded me why we're doing this.'

She hissed at him. 'Best not be seen with them.' Annie's hand swept the Jacobite symbols on the ground and trampled on them. 'They could get us hanged.'

He pulled under the awning. 'We've instructions from J.'

'The note's not on you is it?'

'Swallowed it on the way back,' he said.

'They're no' thinking of attacking the town, not after the information we've given them?' We're to spread the information there's a thousand Scots seventeen miles from Newcastle.'

Annie's eyes lit up.

***

The following cloudy morning Annie and Edward stood helpless, squashed between a fishmonger, his shirt smeared with guts and a butcher with a knife, part of the impatient crowd at Black Gate. Finally, a redcoat guard formed a line outside. A roar followed by jeers. A cart appeared which carried a prone man in a cage. His rags bloodied and any skin to be seen black and blue. A broad-shouldered farmer pelted the captive with refuse. The prisoner didn't stir.

The cart creaked onward then slowed to turn into The Side. More jeers as a young woman leant out of a high window and emptied a chamber pot on him. The contents splattered the driver and escort with excrement and a yellow stream of urine. One surly private waved a fist at her. Another, large with sweat on his brow, urged the horse on. The cart trundled down to Sand Gate. A market trader spat on the cobbles and a leather worker shook a harness at the unconscious prisoner. Once on the quay, a sailor hurled fish guts, missed and hit a sergeant. Gulls squawked and wheeled overhead

'You stupid bugger,' the sergeant snarled as slime streamed down his uniform.

An order rang out. 'Fix bayonets.'

A gaunt man, dropped an axe. A tavern wench, who stank of ale slunk into an inn. A young, muscular man, his shirt and breeches covered in a fine layer of sawdust, hid a hammer inside his shirt. Silence.

Annie held Edward's arm as two soldiers carried the unconscious man up the gangplank and onto the *George*. A sunburnt sailor slipped the mooring ropes and leapt aboard as the sails unfurled. They billowed as the wind caught them and the ship headed for the mouth of the Tyne and the open sea.

Annie whispered, 'Go with God.'

Edward squeezed her arm. 'Pray he dies on the voyage.' Then he turned to an old fishwife as she gutted cod. He jerked a thumb at a plump man in the crowd. 'He's just said the Jacobites have an army of a thousand and they're seventeen miles from Newcastle.'

'Never. Bloody hell.' She turned to her friend. ''Ere, Peg, listen to what I've just 'eard.'

CHAPTER Fifteen

The next day, Rob stood on the town wall above New Gate. An icy wind stung his face. He scanned the snow-covered hills to the north, imagined the Jacobite force as it poured over Newcastle's rebuilt walls. Since they'd caught the spy, the redcoats had installed new cannon and doubled the guards. That thought gave him comfort.

Huge clouds gathered in the sky above him. Rob's cloak flapped open and the cold air settled round his bones.

Lieutenant Wolfe joined him. He blew on his hands and stamped his boots. 'Damned cold day. Well, Lieutenant, what do you think of this rumour? Are there thousands of rebel troops several miles north of here? Think they mean to attack us? Lieutenant Hartlass is convinced of it.'

Rob thought and said, 'The coastal plain means they can move fast, sir, but I listened to some farmers in the Flesh Market this morning. They complained about Jacobites stealing horses from them at Wooler. Said the road from there to Whittingham's impassable in bad weather and they had snow when they left. Also, if the Scots travel down the east coast they'll be caught between two armies, one in Berwick and the other here, with every castle and Pele Tower between in communication.' Should he tell Wolfe what he really thought? He'd be a laughing stock if proved wrong. He blurted it out. 'I think it's a feint, sir.'

'A feint?' Wolfe studied him.

'To draw all our forces to this area, sir.'

Wolfe tapped his forefinger on his lips. 'You think they're making for the west and Carlisle?'

'It's what I'd do, sir.'

Wolfe's forefinger stopped. 'By God, you could be onto to something.'

They both looked up at the gun-metal sky as the first snowflakes fell.

'I'd bet my life on it, sir,' said Rob and stared north.

'You may have to. I'm going to put it to General Wade.'

***

That afternoon, as the sky darkened, Annie and Edward packed their dry goods on the wagon beneath a tarpaulin. Edward tightened the guy ropes as the wind rose to a gale. He blew on his fingers as the tent shook, but stayed fastened to the ground. Large snowflakes swirled and coated the Town Moor in white. Trees bent, iced branches cupped as if in supplication to the sky.

Annie watched and listened in trepidation as Rob and other officers barked orders to soldiers dusted in snow. 'Form columns.'

Edward pointed at an older man on horseback. 'That's General Wade leading them west. Damn it, they know.'

'Towards Carlisle? Our ruse didn't work then,' said Annie.

Edward looked at the sky. 'Weather's closing in. It's over fifty miles by road to Carlisle.'

'Do you think they'll cut off our men?'

'In this?' He jerked a thumb at the leaden sky. 'It's nothing to Highlanders. I'd put my money on the Prince.'

As the soldiers marched out, one private with a tuneful voice sang out and others joined:

Lord, grant that Marshall Wade
May by thy mighty act
Victory bring.
May he sedition hush and like a

Torrent rush
Rebellious Scots to crush
God save the King.

Annie watched until one tall figure disappeared into the murk and out of sight. *Forget him.*

***

Rob couldn't believe it. Seventy-two year old Wade had ordered them to march over fifty miles to Carlisle in conditions which worsened at every step, in an attempt to cut off the rebels. Bar that, they only had three pounders which wouldn't damage the castle walls and how would they manage the cannon in snow?

Nevertheless, the columns set off along the Tyne Valley and the old highway towards Hexham and Carlisle. Gun carriages followed behind pulled by teams of horses as soldiers threw straw under hooves and wheels to gain purchase. The wind rose to a howl and hailstones beat into faces. Men put their heads down against the fury and ice of the storm and tracked others by their boots' imprints in the snow. Even if Rob had known the road, landmarks had long since disappeared, lost in the storm's fury. The snow deepened and began to drift.

Within an hour they had difficulties. The straw ran out and the cannon slowed. The columns marched on and left the cannon to catch up. Rob wiped the snowflakes from his eyelashes and tried to see through the blizzard as the snow deepened every minute.

Soldiers struggled through drifts which rose from their boots, to their knees then mid-thigh. Cannon stuck in snowdrifts and horses strained. Ice formed on eyebrows, lashes, moustaches and clothing as the march slowed. Icy air snaked inside collars, curled inside cuffs, nestled under jackets, seeped through breeches and soaked socks. Faces, noses, lips and fingers changed colour to blue. The men and horses inhaled cold and exhaled ice-breaths. A ghost army.

Rob knew as the cold intensified and the weather worsened, they'd never reach Carlisle, never mind stop the Jacobites. Highlanders rose before dawn, long before the British army, and marched until dusk. Apart from that they would shake off this weather, like dogs with fleas.

The columns gave a collective sigh when ordered into Hexham at midnight. The bedraggled army arrived in groups and carried comrades to places with shelter and rest. The officers used lodgings, the men, tents and those sick or just too weary, lay in snow drifts. The teams which dragged the cannon arrived twenty four hours later with men and horses at the point of collapse. As if sculpted from ice, soldiers and animals staggered from their exertions.

On November 19th, Rob and other junior officers waited as Wade held a Council of War in the Red Lion. A blizzard raged outside and a torrent flooded nearby tenements. Details of the meeting were issued to the junior officers some hours later and Rob agreed with the decisions made.

Intelligence suggested their force in Hexham wasn't large enough. The rebels had taken or destroyed forage and provisions for fifteen miles to the west of Carlisle. There'd be no wood or straw if Wade advanced further. Worse, difficulties with carts meant the biscuit ration would have to be cut from eight to three per man and they'd have little cover from the awful conditions. Also, Wade couldn't follow the rebels if they went north or south because of the barren and mountainous terrain and if the enemy decided to attack, he had little defence against them. Wade decided to rest his forces in Hexham. He'd wait for the snowstorm to cease then march back to Newcastle.

Very wise thought Rob as he trudged to the stables through the hailstones.

Hartlass' face loomed in front of him. 'I hear this damned expedition was your idea, Stewart. You should be bloody court-martialled.'

'I thought the rebels would head for Carlisle, but I didna suggest we march there in this weather, sir.'

'Best keep your thoughts to yourself next time, Lieutenant,' Hartlass spat at him. 'Some of us want to live to fight against this rebellion.'

Rob's eyes narrowed as he watched the man stomp off into the snow. He hoped the lieutenant would never discover who organised his beating. At least with Hartlass in Hexham, Lil would be free of him for a time.

CHAPTER Sixteen

Annie wore every item of clothing she possessed, poked her head out of her tent and wished she hadn't. Her face stung as if pricked by icy needles. A grey sheet of sky lay over the Town Moor, the town walls lost to sight as snowflakes fluttered and spun to form a crisp, bleached cloth over everything. The sky lowered and hailstones pelted the ground. Trees became iced statues as the air froze and sound muffled itself.

What must the weather be like in the open countryside? No. Be honest with yourself. What must it be like for Rob Stewart? Why do I care, he didn't with 'M'?

The encampment deserted. No doubt some men shivered, swathed in army blankets and huddled in groups for warmth in their tents. The last remnants of camp fires lay buried under mounds of snow.

She stamped on the ground, blew on her numb hands then put on woollen mittens. Edward had gone to town earlier, to seek any information he could glean. She prayed he'd be careful as she trudged to gather firewood, a daily task. Each footstep an effort as the snow closed over her boots before she heaved them out ready for the next step.

Woodland lay close by, but every day she had to trudge a little further as townsfolk, soldiers and the baggage train cut down trees. Frosty breaths rose like mist to the dull thud of axes and shh...shh of saws.

Annie hugged her thick woollen cloak closer to her. Light filtered into a thicket as she placed a shawl on the snowy ground and rooted around for twigs to pile in a heap.

She stumbled and stubbed her toe on a forgotten log hidden by a snow drift. *If I can get this back, it will keep us warm for hours.* She grasped it with both hands, and tugged, but it didn't budge. She put her feet apart and pulled with all her strength, but it still didn't move. A grotesque face like an annoyed fox peered at her from the other side of the brambles, holly and tangled undergrowth. One hazel eye spat sparks at her, the other half-closed, was a swollen mass of purple.

Annie stared at her. 'Lil?'

'It's bloody mine and how do you ken my name?' Lil clung onto the log with both hands.

'We could share it, pet.'

'It's mine. Let go, I saw it first.' Lil's face looked gaunt and blue.

Annie folded her arms. 'You can have it.'

Lil stared at her. 'I ken your face. You gave me money on the quay. Why?'

Annie paused and then said, 'Thought you needed it more than me.'

'That's a good 'un. And this wood, why you lettin' me have it?'

'Same reason,' said Annie.

Lil shook her head and hauled the log towards her. 'What you after?'

Annie stared at her. 'Nowt.'

'Thanks.' Lil gave the log a big heave. 'Never got somethin' for nothin' since I was a bairn. '

'You still are', said Annie. 'Please stay away from Hartlass, go back to Scotland.'

'How do you ken Hartlass? He looks after me,' said Lil.

'And your eye?'

'My business.' Lil fastened a rope round one end of the log.

'But...' began Annie.

'It's nothin' to do with you,' said Lil. 'Leave me alone. I'm doin' alright.'

Annie watched her as she dragged the log through the clearing. She left a trail behind her. It seemed to Annie, at that moment, Lil's life was that log.

***

Some days later Annie spotted movement in the flurry of snow to the west, silver figures in ones twos and threes, a sorry column of soldiers. Their heads hung and feet dragged.

Hartlass led them. Men supported comrades. Their uniforms hung as they sagged into a scarecrow line. Once dismissed, others came and wrapped the men in blankets and loaded them onto carts headed for warm lodgings in Newcastle.

'Have you seen Lieutenant Stewart, bonny lad?' Annie tugged at one soldier's sleeve.

He peered at her with dead eyes. 'No.'

'Did you get to Carlisle?'

The private's cheekbones gave his face a skeletal look. His lashes, whiskers and hair encased in ice. 'Hexham,' his blue lips mumbled. 'We made it to Hexham.'

She watched him stumble off towards a cart.

Edward arrived beside her, his nose blue with cold. He whispered in her ear, 'Thank God. Carlisle's ours then.'

'Yes.' His words didn't seem to enter her brain. In the maelstrom her eyes searched for a lieutenant with blue eyes who stood head and shoulders above the rest. Surely he should have arrived before now. Young, fit, from the Highlands and used to weather like this, he should have been first. Yet something nagged at her. Men lost their bearings or succumbed to the biting cold. Many a one had been found frozen to death within yards of home. She knew all this, yet peered into the swirl of greyness and wished him to appear.

Why do I care? Remember 'M'. He's a redcoat. One less is all the better, isn't it? She'd been so sure about spying for the Cause, but now it didn't seem right, not honourable somehow.

Stewart, one of the last to arrive, carried an unconscious man over his shoulder. Each step he took sank into the snow and it took longer each time before he moved forward. At the end of his strength, redcoats ran to take his burden and carried the frozen man to a cart.

'They need hot food,' she said.

'Good, it might teach them a little about Highlanders.' Edward turned and went into the tent. She watched as Stewart waved away the men who came to help him.

'Lieutenant, do you need a lift to town and warm lodgings?' asked a private.

Stewart waved him away too.

A provision cart arrived full of hot beef broth in canisters packed inside layers of straw. *Well, if the man willna help himself I'll do it for him.* She grabbed a mess tin and joined the queue. She told herself it was her Christian duty.

'It's for Lieutenant Stewart,' she explained to the corporal.

'Fourth row on left, first tent, Miss,' he said giving her a knowing wink. 'Can't miss it.'

Damp wood from fires shrouded the limp tents which stretched across most of the moor. She trudged down the rows, until she found Stewart's. He'd a sleeping sack and a chest. She placed the tin on top of his bed and hoped it would warm him. *Why do such a thing? He's the enemy.* She watched him from a distance as he saw to his men and stumbled through the forest of tents to find his own.

Hopefully, he'll be so exhausted he'll forget someone left him hot food.

CHAPTER Seventeen

Rob woke. Hailstones pelted his tent and he inhaled the aroma of last night's beef broth. The empty tin lay where he'd left it.

He rubbed his cold hands together and his breath frosted when he said, 'Plaskett, thanks for the broth.'

'Wasn't me, sir. By the time I got 'ere, you was asleep.'

'Who the hell was it then?'

'Don't know, sir.'

'That's all.' It perplexed Rob for a few days. He decided that Wade had been right to return to Newcastle as the bad weather continued for some time. At least they had bread and ammunition in good supply here. Wolfe said he'd received more intelligence from Penrith, that the rebel quarter master had asked for billets for 2,000 foot and two squadrons of horse. To Rob's chagrin, Wade headed for Barnard Castle two days later and left him and his company behind.

***

Annie tramped into town, through the Flesh Market, past the castle, the clog shops and down the Castle Steps to the Tyne. She did this every day and memorised the movement of regiments and ships. A layer of ice sparkled on the quayside and vessels. Everything appeared as if carved from diamonds

'Have you summat to spare, Miss?' A man's breath shimmered in the cold air. A beggar's filthy fingers held out a battered tin can. He wore rags, a wide brimmed hat and leant on a crutch.

Annie had seen many like him as wounded sailors haunted the quaysides of every port. Her penny clinked into the can. Newcastle teamed with beggars: men, women, children and the sick. *Pitiful, especially in this weather. The army makes it worse. They need provisions which creates shortages for locals and drives up prices.*

She hadn't looked at the man's face. Didn't want to see wounded pride in his eyes. She made to move on.

'Generous as always...Colonel?' The last word hissed at her through his teeth.

Annie started. Only a few knew her by that soubriquet. His tattered clothes hung over a strong, lithe body. He raised his head so his face wasn't in the shadow of his hat's brim.

Her heart thudded against her ribs as she stared into familiar brown eyes. 'Lord, Philippe.'

'Philip.' He corrected her and glanced around him at a couple of redcoat sentries chatted at the foot of a gangplank.

She surveyed the busy quayside and hissed. 'Are you mad? If they catch you, you'll be arrested and worse. What are you doing here?'

'This and that. Glenroy told me you and Alan were in Newcastle, I 'ad to see you.'

'Sssh. They've already caught one spy. This town doesna like strangers.'

'Don't worry, I've a little business to do 'ere, then we're off.' He indicated a rough group of men who sat on coils of rope on the quay. 'We'll row down the Tyne. *Loup de Mer's* moored off the coast and we'll sail tonight. You know, you look more ravishing each time I see you, Anne, even dressed like this.'

'It's Annie,' she hissed, 'this is not the time.'

'For a letter from your father?'

'Father?' She took it and clasped it to her breast. 'It's been months. Thank you.'

'You'll destroy it after you've read it?'

'Of course.'

He brushed a strand of hair from her cheek. 'Each night I wonder if you're safe.'

'And your wife?'

A flicker of exasperation crossed his face.

'Is this rogue annoying you, Miss Bryce?'

They both jumped. Stewart looked as if he'd like to pin Philippe by his ears to the stocks.

'No, no, Lieutenant,' said Annie. 'He's starvin', can't afford to feed himself or his family. I thought to help. That's all.'

'Ah.'

At least Stewart had the grace to look discomfited.

He flipped a shilling into Philippe's tin cup. 'Perhaps I can help too.'

'Thank you, bonny lad.' Philippe held the coin between his teeth and bit down. 'It's the real thing alreet, should feed me and the bairns for a week.' He tipped his hat at them both and hobbled off as he leant on his crutch.

Annie struggled for control. *Typical of Philippe, living life on the edge of danger, always thinking he'll never be caught. Isn't this his attraction?*

'May I walk with you and carry your basket?'

Lord, Rob Stewart. 'Aye.' She walked in the opposite direction to Philippe. She couldn't bear the thought of him being caught like the Jacobite spy in the cart.

'You've received a letter I see.'

'Aye.' She clasped it tighter in her hand.

'I envy you.'

'Your family doesn't write?' *He's from ardent Jacobites, must be difficult.*

'I'm...estranged from them. We dinna agree over...certain things and then...Well, and then there was someone...'

'Ahah.'

'Someone I have...had to forget.'

'Oh.' *The mysterious 'M'?*

'Who...?' She spoke to the air. Stewart, sprinted towards the bridge and flung off his jacket as he did so. *What's he doing?*

'Help!' A pale face bobbed above the grey waters of the Tyne. *A child. Stewart isn't going to dive in? Not in this weather.*

'Save him, sir. Please save me son.' A young woman clung to his arm a she stood at the quay. 'Told the little beggar not to play near the edge.'

Rob climbed down one of the wooden timbers and held out his hand. Philippe skidded to a stop at his side and did the same.

A crowd of sailors, merchants, soldiers and hawkers gathered and shouted advice.

'Water's too cold. He's a gonna.'

'The current's pushing 'im towards us.'

'Wait for him to pass.'

Stewart grabbed the boy's shirt and Philippe an arm as he floated towards them.

'Got him,' the men said in unison as they lifted the boy onto the quay. His teeth chattered.

His tearful mother covered him with her thin shawl. 'Eeeh, our Joe, I thought I'd lost ye.' Tears fell as he shivered. She rubbed his body and tried to dry him.

'Oh ma..m, divn't bu ..bble.' Joe turned to his rescuers. 'Th...an...k you.' The child's blue lips formed a grin and showed a gap between his front teeth. 'It...were...perish...in'...in...there.' His body shook.

'Best get him beside a fire.' Stewart looked for his jacket and Annie held it out for him. He eased himself into it.

Philippe walked off.

Stewart stared after him and his eyes narrowed. 'Thought he had a crutch and hobbled.'

Oh no.

The boy's mother tugged at his sleeve. 'We lost our lodgin' last week, been on the streets since then.'

Stewart took in the woman's pinched face, bony figure and bare feet. 'Take this,' he said and pressed a coin into her hand. 'Should buy you a warm fire and something to eat.'

She looked at him in wonderment. 'Thank you kindly, sir.'

'Miss Bryce, your basket. Now where were we?'

'Your...family, tell me...about them,' Annie said. Her tongue stumbled over the words as she wished him to forget Philippe. By the time they'd walked back to camp she'd learnt about his childhood escapades with his brothers. How Johnnie loved books, Euan a claymore and how the youngest, Duncan couldn't wait to fight and Dougie, their father's tacksman kept them all in order. He also talked about Braedrumie, Loch Linnhe and how much he missed his home, but he didn't say a word about the mysterious 'M'.

She experienced the raw emotion Stewart had caused once again. They would have been her family. The hurt twisted her insides. *Well, he didn't want me and I certainly didn't...want him. Do I? He's much more handsome than the miniature suggested and kind. Impossible.* Her head buzzed with questions. *Aren't we enemies fighting for different causes? Is 'M' his sweetheart? If so, why did he have to forget her? Is she the reason he cast me aside and became a redcoat? Lord, I could drown in his eyes.*

'It was you who left the broth, wasn't it?'

She started.

'Private Dunston saw you leaving my tent. I want to thank you.'

'It was nowt, an act of kindness anyone would do.'

'Nevertheless, you did it for me and I'm grateful. And you, Miss Bryce? You've been very patient listening to me. What about your family?'

'Well, I never knew my mam, died when I was born. *Lie*. Da...died last year. I was born in...Shields.'

'And what did he do?'

'Do? He was a...cabinet maker. Look you must excuse me, Lieutenant Stewart, but Alan will wonder where I am.' She tramped back to the Town Moor with a cold wind in her face and ignored the yells of a stall holder who dangled a couple of thin rabbits in front of her. She hid her face in her hood as she passed soldiers and made her way through the tents on the moor until she came to an empty space. No sutler's wagon.

'Alan...I mean Edward.' She put a hand to her mouth as she stood aghast. Had she said 'Alan' to Stewart?

Her tent looked forlorn on its own. Barrels of ale, boxes of tobacco, a musket and ammunition had been stacked inside which left just enough room for her bed. A note with *Annie Bryce* scrawled in black ink lay on her pillow

Dear Annie,
I have left to visit friends. I'll purchase more provisions in the south where prices are not as high. Do not worry about me.
Fondest regards,
Edward.

Oh Lord, he's gone to join the Jacobite army, I'm sure of it. She lay down on her bed and fingered the letter from her father. She sighed and broke the seal.

Kerbilly,
October, 1745
My dearest Anne,
I hope this letter finds you well as I have heard little from you for months. I cannot help, but think you are being very hard on your

poor old Father who loves you dearly. Staying in Edinburgh and refusing to allow me to visit you increases our estrangement. Can't you agree to accept our political differences?

Your Uncle William sends you his and little Florie's regards, but shares my feelings: come home where you belong. These are dangerous times and this year or the next may seal Scotland's fate and the Jacobite Cause.

*You are in my prayers every night as I hope I am in yours.
My love always,*

Father.

I'm torn in two. She memorised the words, then screwed the letters into a ball. She'd bury them.

CHAPTER Eighteen

Rob looked out from his tent at the December landscape and the Town Moor which had been churned into mud by thousands of boots. Snow lay on the hills to the north. He hadn't seen much of Annie or her sutler brother. The wagon had disappeared. It had been the second time she called her brother Alan, a pet name perhaps. Rob pondered about the man with the crutch and made a mental note. Did he have a French accent? Damn Edward Bryce. How could he leave his defenceless sister alone in an army camp? He went to find her.

'Your brother's left I see.'

'Gone for supplies,' she said and didn't look at him.

'I'll help you collect firewood.'

'There's no need, man.'

He ignored her and chopped wood with an axe for an hour. He left a huge pile of wood by her tent. It had taken him longer than he thought as he'd had to walk further past stumps which had once been woodland.

He hurried towards the command tent. It wouldn't do to be late. General Hawley, gruff and surly, had taken over from Wade and officers had been ordered to attend his briefing:

'Gentlemen, good news,' said Hawley. 'The rebels aren't heading for London as feared, they turned back at Derby.'

'Good show.' An officer patted another on the back.

'Does that mean we miss a fight, sir?' asked one.

'Cumberland's linked up with Ligonier's Midland army to pursue the rebels. An advanced group has been repulsed at Clifton Moor near Penrith. Carlisle's been retaken, but now Cumberland's been recalled to London over fears of a French invasion.'

Rob thought about the French, and hoped they'd stay out of it.

'Our orders are to leave Newcastle tomorrow and march towards Scotland. Barrel and Pulteney's regiments will remain behind with several other companies.'

Rob thought of his Jacobite brothers. They'd curse if they'd marched all that way and London so close. And now...? Rob's gut twisted, this wouldn't end well.

He joined several of his fellow officers in the Queen Bess that night to celebrate their march north. When he left he felt light headed, cursed the local ale and took some deep breaths. He walked along The Close, candlelight streamed through windows of several Tudor houses. He turned right up Castle Stairs and into darkness with shuttered clog shops on either side. Under a lantern, a bundle or rags stirred at the turn of the worn stone steps. A few shops squatted here and paint peeled from their rotten woodwork.

His jaw tightened as his hand moved to his sword. A single figure, slight – a young girl got up as if she carried a burden. He'd almost forgotten Lil. He couldn't stop two thoughts which leapt into his head. Why in Hades did she stay with Hartlass? Who'd be a female without family or friends?

'What is it, Lil?' His voice barked at her as if on the parade ground.

'Hartlass's leavin' Newcastle with you lot, says he's tired of me, likes 'em young. ' Her head seemed too large, eyes lifeless and her limbs like twigs. She stood in rags and clasped a darned shawl around her. She shifted from bare foot to bare foot.

He took in her matted hair and sunken cheeks. A thin dress swamped her skeletal frame. His voice softened. 'What a mess he's made of you, lassie.'

'I love him, Lieutenant Stewart.'

He groaned, a pity he couldn't kill the bastard. 'We'll be heading north soon. Why don't you hide in the baggage train and I'll spread the word you've run off. You should be in Scotland, with your own folk.'

'Bless you sir.' Her thin face shone at him. 'I'm goin' home. I just came to say goodbye. You've shown me kindness and I wanted to thank you for it.' She stood on her toes and grasped his shoulders. Rob bent towards her and allowed what seemed the cold wings of butterfly to brush his cheek. She gave him a tremulous smile and hurried away down the steep steps.

He watched her small figure until she was lost in the darkness. Now he wouldn't feel responsible for her. He climbed the steps, bent under a stone arch and reached the foot of the castle and the shadow of Black Gate. He halted. Something wasn't right about Lil; the way she held her shawl in front of her; the way she walked and carried her weight on her heels. Hell's teeth. A thought exploded in his brain: she was expecting a bairn and needed help. Which way did she go? The river. No. Sure of his suspicions, he sprinted after her into the dark.

Later, he went over and over the sequence of events. His shout, her balanced on the stone parapet, the sad look she gave him and how she flung her arms out when she jumped. There'd been no sign of her by the time he got to the bridge, just the black water which flowed beneath.

Every night since, her ghost-face appeared and her words *I'm going home* tormented him. He should have realised, poor Lil. Hartlass had a lot to answer for.

CHAPTER Nineteen

Annie went north with the redcoats and rode the horse Edward had left her. She'd tied the tent and provisions to her saddle. It took about six days for the redcoats to march to Edinburgh, slowed down by artillery, the baggage train and constant rain. She'd seen Stewart, most days, if she hadn't known better she'd have thought him a friend.

One cold morning when she'd just made some broth, shouted orders rang round the camp. A private told her Stirling Castle was surrounded by Jacobites and Hawley had decided to march to Falkirk, his intention: to raise the siege.

Edward, pale, exhausted, but full of news, arrived as she struck camp.

'I've broth,' she said.

He gulped it down. 'We were so close, just a hundred miles from London,' he said as he pulled a guy rope.

'Close? What happened?' Her brow creased.

'The Prince held a Council of War. An English Jacobite, Dudley Bradstreet, arrived, told them an army under either General Hawley or Lieutenant General Ligonier was north of London with 90,000 soldiers.'

'No. So many?'

'I didn't believe him. The Prince and several others professed confidence in the English Jacobites who'd come out if we marched on London. The Prince feared if we retreated we'd be caught between Cumberland and Wade. He argued that Lord Drummond's letter proved the French would land in Essex or Kent and support us.'

'Of course the French will support us,' said Annie and clenched her fists.

'Murray shook his head, said we couldn't defeat three armies and even if we captured London we'd be besieged. Lord Elcho agreed and wasn't convinced the English would rise with us.'

'How could they?' said Annie.

'Cameron of Lochiel and Cluny MacDonald of Keppoch said if we retreated we could out march Cumberland and defeat Wade if he tried to attack us. The Council of War voted to retreat. Damn them.'

'Oh, Edward,' said Annie. 'What do we do now?'

'I've orders for you. General Murray wants you to pretend you're Lady Falkirk and invite General Hawley to dinner this week on the evening of December 17th. You're to keep him well entertained, get him drunk and ensure he stays at Falkirk House for a long as possible.'

Some days later, Annie escorted the middle-aged Lady Falkirk out of her house and into her coach. 'Dinna concern yourself about me, Lady Falkirk,' Annie said. 'Just ensure you're safe at Bilairy Castle. I'm sure your mother will be pleased to see you.' Annie looked at the clouds which hung over them like huge bunches of black grapes. 'I wish you a safe journey before the storm breaks.'

'You're so brave, so brave,' said Lady Falkirk, as she sniffed into a handkerchief. 'My nerves, you know, are not the best.'

Annie waved her off.

***

It was late afternoon and it drizzled all day. Rob had forgotten what dry clothes felt like as he spurred towards Hawley. 'Sir, there's a large Jacobite army marching towards us. We need to assemble in battle order.'

General Hawley stared at him. 'Nonsense, Lieutenant, it's nothing but a few Jacobites here to scrutinise our position.

Haven't marched this far to be misled. Their main army's besieging Blakeney in Stirling Castle which we'll relieve.'

'But, sir, I've seen them myself. They're marching in force towards the moor south west of Falkirk. There's thousands of Jacobites under General George Murray and Archibald Primrose of Dunipace, moving from Plean, swarming over the rivers Carron and Bonny and heading towards Falkirk.'

'Heard enough. Keep an eye on 'em. Off to dine at Falkirk House.' Hawley looked at the banks of clouds. 'Hope the weather doesn't break.'

Rob could have shaken Hawley till his teeth fell out. It took an iron will to stop himself. Hawley was a fool. Incapable. Incompetent. He needed to act. Rumour had it, illiterate. Rob didn't envy him his nickname amongst the men, 'Hangman Hawley'. God help any deserters.

Thunderation, if the Jacobites got on the moor, they'd have the advantage of high ground. Surely Hawley could understand that? Government troops would face a Highland charge, the speed and force the like of which they'd never experienced before. It would chill the blood of the bravest.

'Sergeant, with me.' Rob's voice sounded low and guttural. As they mounted, Rob remembered soldiers' gossip that General Cope, beaten at Prestonpans, had wagered £10,000 Hawley would also be defeated by the Jacobites. As he urged his horse into action, Rob thought Cope could become a wealthy man.

Plaskett shook his head as he and Rob inspected the Jacobites again from behind a line of trees. The rebels looked strong and ready for battle. All Rob could do now was watch and wait. If only Hawley had acted. Too late now. The Jacobites would be on the moor soon. Rob grimaced. In the valley, behind Dunipace, rode his brothers, Euan lean and tall, Johnnie broad-shouldered and an inch shorter and their Stewart tacksman, Dougie, wiry, grey-haired and stoic.

Rob had dreaded this moment. He felt the first pricks of guilt. What had he done when he'd left Braedrumie in a pique over Morag? He fought against an urge to join his brothers and reminded himself as a commissioned officer, he'd given an oath of allegiance to king and country. Anyway, the British army hanged deserters and if the Jacobites caught him, his life wouldn't be worth a farthing. Better stay.

***

Annie read Hawley's acceptance of her invitation. She'd ensured he'd have a fine dinner and taste the best wine in Falkirk House's cellars.

She dressed for the occasion in the real Lady Falkirk's blue silk gown and wig. She trusted Hawley never noticed the women in his baggage train.

Hawley arrived half an hour late, by which time Annie had paced the floor and started as the bell jangled throughout the house.

He mopped his face, bowed and kissed Annie's hand. 'My dear, Lady Falkirk, please accept my apologies. My duties, you understand.'

'No apologies needed, General, welcome to Falkirk House. I'm delighted to meet you having heard so much about you.' *What an ignorant bully you are.* Annie made her lips curve into a smile, curtsied and fluttered her fan. The last month or so had been difficult. When Stewart had apologised for his morose looks, he'd told her about Lil. Annie cursed herself. *I saw the state she was in and should have got her out of Hartlass' clutches.* Lil's death had shocked her and been the talk of the camp. It had been painful to watch Hartlass carry on untouched by the tragedy. *Is he really unaware of whispered comments and turned backs? Poor*

Lil, I was too engrossed in the Cause to spare you more than a thought. I'll never forgive myself.

'Call me Henry, my dear.' Hawley's grey eyes regarded her. He'd a long face with a high brow, strong nose and pronounced chin. She decided his character suited his brutal features exactly. She'd heard about the hangings.

'Some wine, Henry? Our finest.'

'Thank you, my dear.'

She filled his glass and he swigged the French wine back like ale, then smacked his lips.

'More, General?' She beckoned a servant.

His large hand with its spatula fingers covered his glass. 'I think not. A general needs to keep his wits about him at all times.'

Curse him.

She led him into the candle-lit dining room and realised, with relief, the light outside had faded. Hawley eased her chair out for her, sat and tucked his napkin under his chin. *He looks like a stuffed pig waiting at a trough.* She didn't mind. The longer he stayed with her, the more likely their victory at Falkirk.

***

The clouds hung lower and dusk wasn't far off when Rob decided to act. He'd no doubt the rebels were close to the moor as their first riders arrived. 'Sergeant, warn the camp to ready themselves for battle. I'm off to see General Hawley.' Rob turned his horse and cursed a system which allowed useless men to buy their commissions.

Falkirk House lay on a crag surrounded by a defensive wall. The sentries had their muskets at the ready as he galloped towards them. One relaxed and the other beckoned him forward when they saw his uniform and rank. They knew him.

'Let me through, I've an important message for General Hawley.'

'Sir.'

He interrupted Hawley, spoon in mouth, in the middle of his dessert. Lady Falkirk snapped open her fan. He remembered himself and saluted. 'My apologies, Ma'am. Sir, the rebels are on the moor. I've alerted the camp.'

Lady Falkirk's fan stopped and then continued apace.

Hawley's eyes bulged as he struggled to his feet. His stained napkin lay over his chest and paunch. 'By God, are they? Insolent curs. What are you waiting for, man? We must return at once.'

***

Rob and Hawley galloped back to their encampment at break neck speed. The light had faded and rain hammered into the ground like bayonets. Hawley reined in his horse and almost fell out of his saddle. His napkin still tucked under his chin as he ducked inside the command tent. Officers stood ready. 'Get our troops onto the damn moor,' he growled. 'Rebels will never stand against cavalry, saw it in 1715. I want three regiments of dragoons in place now and our artillery, tell Cunningham to make haste.' Men ran in all directions to follow his orders.

Rob raced to his horse, mounted and swept a glance around him. Too little too late, he wrestled with the thought. Deserted tents flailed in the wind. It tore at heather and gorse and made them bow to its mournful tune. The rain thrummed down. It turned grass into mud which sucked at Cunningham's cannon where men and horses strained to get them up the hill to the moor. Rob didn't spare his steed as he galloped past. He'd visions of the Carlisle debacle in his head.

On the moor the troops stood in line, but the artillery? Rob sped back through the rain to the crown of the hill and went cold. Cunningham had managed to wheel the cannon to the bottom of the incline, but it had stuck axle deep in mud. Worse, even if they got the eighteen pounders onto the moor he could hear Cunningham calls for shot. The cannon couldn't be fired.

Rob swore under his breath at Hawley, then stared aghast as the man ordered the dragoons to charge straight at the Jacobites. Rob watched as if in slow motion. Saw the gallant horses race towards the rebel lines, watched the dragoons, swords high in the air and heard the volley that hit them. One, still alive and his horse untouched, dragged to the ground by a prone Highlander who ripped at him and the animal's belly. Slaughter. A maddened and maimed, wild-eyed, horse returned, followed by a wounded man charged down by a Jacobite. The government troops wavered and broke, streamed down the hill and passed the cannon as if chased by the devil.

Rob hauled his horse to a halt and flung himself out of his saddle. 'Stand! If you stand and fight we've a chance.' Rob grabbed at sleeves and collars as men fled with only one thought: safety. 'I'll shoot the next bastard who runs past me.' Rob raised his pistol, a private slid to an undignified halt and others followed.

Rob formed them into three defensive lines, bayonets bristled in front of the cannon. Ligonier's, Barrel's and Price's regiments held and retreated in an ordered manner. Once they'd passed, Rob's troops fired continuous volleys at the enemy. Barrel ordered a group of his men to tie their traces to the cannon, drag them back to safety and fired the encampment to prevent it falling into Jacobite hands. Flames streamed from tents as a horse ploughed round them and another charged into the darkness. Men ran, flung their weapons aside and all the time the rain beat down and added to the cacophony.

Rob's rear guard managed to withdraw and later, at roll call, Rob discovered they'd 350 men, dead, wounded or missing. Rob could only presume their main force hadn't been harried because of the dark, the rain and the rebels were so spread out that they'd no idea who'd won. Guilt swept over him about his brothers. He'd no time to think of them during the battle. He prayed they survived.

That night, as the disheartened troops retreated to Edinburgh, Rob massaged his neck muscles. His frustrations came boiling to the surface. The battle had only lasted about twenty minutes. Twenty bloody minutes. Hawley, of course, didn't regard it as a defeat. Well, he wouldn't, too busy protecting his own skin. He'd already had poor Cunningham arrested for incompetence in the field. As if Hawley was a good judge of that. Rob took a swig of cold water from his canteen, it eased his dry throat, but not his sense of disillusionment.

The British high command needed to respect the rebel forces. Murray had out thought them in every battle so far. Highlanders fought with targe and broad sword, bloody difficult to stop. He blinked, but there was a weakness...why hadn't he thought of it before? He hoped to God, Wolfe would listen. A dull ache started behind his eyes.

***

Annie's mouth creased into a smile. *Another battle won.* Stewart would never have the chance to compare the sutler's sister and Lady Falkirk alongside each other. Even if he did, he hadn't seen the latter's face. She ran to the stables at Falkirk House, where Edward waited for her. She climbed aboard the sutler's wagon and joined the redcoat retreat to Edinburgh. *I bet 'M' wouldn't have dared leave her sewing.*

CHAPTER Twenty

In late January, under clouds which scudded past, the pudding-faced Duke of Cumberland, arrived in Edinburgh and took command from Hawley. His orders sent troops out of the gates in search of his cousin, Charles Edward Stuart, the young Pretender. They returned weeks later, weary, disconsolate and without the Prince.

Cumberland, undeterred, led his troops along to wild east coast and Aberdeen. There he and his army stayed.

Rob asked Wolfe to listen to his idea as they sat on two rocks by a beck. 'You see, sir, high ground is perfect for a fighting Highlander. He comes down at you cursing and yelling, fires, then throws his musket away. Before you ken, he's at you with his targe knocking your weapon to one side and killing you with one sweep of his broadsword, like this.' Rob sprang up and demonstrated with his captured weapons.

'This is not new. We're all veterans at fighting Highlanders,' said Wolfe as he cast a stone into the water.

'With respect, sir, we've lost every time. We're no' learning how to win. Look there's a weakness in how a Highlander fights when he raises his right arm.' He demonstrated. 'See, he's vulnerable. His targe is over to one side, his right arm and armpit unprotected.'

'Let me see.' Wolfe took the targe and broad sword. Rob lunged as Wolfe attacked. Wolfe looked at the point of Rob's sword touching his side. 'Damn me, it works. By God, you may have something here. What are you suggesting?'

'I think we should spend time training our soldiers so they fire a volley when the Highlanders are in range and then bayonet the Highlander on their right under their sword arm.'

'Right,' said Wolfe. 'I'm off to see Cumberland, let's hope he can see the sense of it. Don't look so downhearted man. Well done, Stewart, well done.'

Rob's conscience seethed with the sting of treachery towards his family, clan, friends and brothers and all because of their bloody hopeless Cause. He didn't dare think of those in Braedrumie. His father's face came unwanted into his head. Rob blanked it out as he rubbed his palm on his forehead.

***

Wolfe called his officers to his tent. He stopped the tap of his forefinger on his lips. 'I've reports about a house north west of here where they're said to store muskets and ammunition for the rebels. A French ship's moored off the coast, just north of us. There's talk of smuggling, but also of weapons. Stewart, take some men, search the house and see what you can find.'

'Sir!'

Hartlass stepped forward. 'I think I'd be better suited to do it, sir, I'm senior to Stewart after all and more experienced.'

Wolfe, stoney-faced regarded Hartlass for a few seconds. 'And Stewart needs to gain that experience. You'll get your chance, Hartlass, meanwhile you're drilling men. Dismissed.'

Wolfe waited for Hartlass to leave before he handed Rob his orders. 'Don't mind him, just champing at the bit, wants to get his sword bloodied. The house and directions are written here. Good hunting.'

'Sir. Rob returned to his tent, read and re-read the orders. He tried to take in what they said. No. Not Lachlan House. Not the Walkers. Davie, always cautious, thought ahead, wouldn't take sides. He'd agreed the Cause was hopeless. Rob ran a hand through his hair. Bloody hell, he hoped his friend had nought to hide. At least it would be him in a red coat, not bloody Hartlass.

Rob and his men rode along the drive to Lachlan House and passed the bare oak trees. Bar the season, it looked as it had all those months before with the double fronted house nestled in the valley. The sun rose like a gold coin and set the snow-topped hills on fire. A cock crowed, a shutter clattered open and smoke curled from the chimney.

Rob dismounted and gave his reins to Plaskett. What reception would he get here?

He met Davie as he came out of the scullery door. He carried a wooden bucket in one hand and tugged on his waistcoat with the other. His jaw dropped as he took in the redcoat uniform and Rob's face.

Rob gave him a look and shook his head.

'What do you want?' said Davie.

'Mr. Walker?'

'You...Aye.'

'Let's go inside.' Rob led the way into the warm scullery. An empty dish and spoon lay on the well-scrubbed table and porridge bubbled in a pot over the fire.

'We've had reports you're hiding arms for the rebels.'

A frown creased Davie's forehead. 'My God, Rob. No.'

'Don't let my men see you know me. You'll no' mind if they check?'

'I do mind, of course I mind.' Davie stared at him.

Rob stared back and assessed his friend. 'The truth: have you any weapons here?'

Davie shook his head. 'Only my musket.'

'Then let us search. I'll ensure my men do no damage. We'd reports of a French cargo...'

Davie stared open mouthed at him.

Rob's stomach churned. 'God, you're no' involved?'

'No.' Davie looked at the flagstone floor.

'If you're lying...I have to do my duty.' Rob shouted through the doorway, 'Plaskett, Mr. Walker's agreed to us searching the house. Dinna' forget the stables and the byre.'

'Sir.'

Rob watched men scatter over the yard and tramp into the scullery.

Davie tugged at his sleeve. 'Mother's abed, ill.'

'Your word we'd find nought in her bedroom.'

Davie gave a slight nod and turned to the fire.

Rob directed orders at his men. 'Be thorough, but no damage. Mrs. Walker is indisposed, her bedroom is no' to be searched. These people are to be treated with respect and allowed to carry on as normal. We'll be staying the night.'

Davie picked up his bucket. 'Cow needs milking.' He headed for the byre.

Rob watched him go.

***

That night Annie and Edward crawled through tangled undergrowth. Annie winced as a stone dug into her knee. 'Edward, are you sure what you overheard?' she hissed and rubbed the fierce nettle rash on her legs and arms. She lifted her head above the dunes and marram grass. Saw the sea and smelt the tang of salt and seaweed.

Edward raised his head too. 'A French ship smuggling weapons. That's what Wolfe said. Fortunate I was passing his tent. Look.' He pointed out across the sea at the silhouette of a ship. A sliver of moonlight shimmered like a silver net on the calm sea. A dark shape scurried from behind a rock on the beach, another dashed through the surf to a loaded rowing boat. One took off bundles and the other tied them on a waiting pony's back. 'Smugglers.'

'No,' said Annie after a few minutes. 'That's *Loup de Mer,* I'd recognise her anywhere.' She scrambled down a steep path to a sandy beach as Edward stumbled behind her. The sea slurped and slapped as the tide went out. A cold breeze swept over them and sand swirled.

'Get down,' said Edward. 'I'll talk to them. They might shoot first.' He walked forwards and waved his hands. 'Philippe.'

She followed him.

'Who's that?' called a voice as dark shapes raised weapons or dove into the shingle. 'Who's there?'

'Friends who know Philippe.'

'Alan, is it you?' A figure rose and walked forwards. 'And Anne? This is dangerous my friends, what are you doing 'ere?' The breeze tossed strands of Philippe's hair across his face. He brushed them aside.

'Better call us Annie and Edward. We've news of redcoats. They've been sent to search Lachlan House,' said Edward.

'Merde.' He scanned the dunes. 'We'll make other arrangements. My thanks.' Philippe shook Edward's hand and kissed Annie's.

His lips made her skin tingle in response. His eyes twinkled at hers for a second. Then his voice was full of urgent commands to his men as they led the ponies off the beach. He turned back to Edward and Annie as if to say something.

Annie looked at *Loup de Mer* and then him. 'I know, the tide.'

Philippe smiled, embraced them both and raced for the boat as it nosed into the silver-speckled sea.

***

Rob and his men found nothing hidden and spent the night camped out in Lachlan House, its stables and byre.

Davie's eyes darted everywhere, he walked from room to room and went to the byre several times escorted by a vigilant Plaskett. He wiped his hands, looked at the door and started at the least sound.

Rob sighed, he hadn't signed up to hang friends. He didn't know whether Davie was more relieved or him when the cock crowed at first light and the house and area round it remained undisturbed.

Plaskett and his men yawned. They brushed straw off uniforms, wiped dung from their boots and assembled in the yard.

Davie managed to whisper to Rob as he left, 'They threatened to burn us out.'

Rob nodded, he'd heard such tales. Civil war forced men to take sides. He thanked God nothing happened last night. 'Goodbye, Davie, I'd leave if I were you. Safer for you both.' He held out his hand, but Davie turned away.

Davie's action left a sour taste in Rob's mouth. They'd been good friends. A curtain on the first floor twitched as Davie's mother shook her fist at Rob from her bedroom window. At least, he thought, it wasn't a musket. Rob pondered on Davie's words as he and his men mounted and trotted off to Aberdeen. Had his friend told the truth? Rob massaged his neck muscles with one hand and damned the ache in his head.

CHAPTER Twenty-one

Rob watched with mixed emotions as Prince Frederick of Hesse led several thousand Hessian troops to Aberdeen. The Jacobites would have their work cut out to win against such a force. Though Rob agreed with the decision to position the Hessians to the south, so they cut off any Jacobite retreat.

Cumberland said he expected his soldiers to trust the new tactic and carry it out without thought. The Duke viewed them in action, resumed the campaign and marched to Cullen.

Rob leant on his sword and wiped the sweat from his brow with his sleeve. Ready. After months of training, Wolfe informed Rob their forces were to be joined by six battalions and two cavalry regiments.

Days later Rob's troop approached the River Spey guarded by a couple of thousand Jacobites. Rob spotted a taller Johnnie and a leaner and broader Euan, but saw no flash of recognition from them. The last thing they'd expect would be to see him dressed in the enemy's uniform. Rob had dreaded this. His neck muscles strained as he led his men towards them. Yells. The pound of claymore on targe. Curses. A Highlander in brown tartan rose from a dip in the ground and grabbed at Rob's reins. Rob used the pommel of his sword on the man's dark head. Blood spurted from his crown as Rob lunged with his boot and shoved him backwards.

Another, with fair hair and the beginnings of a beard, sprang from a spot hidden by the river bank. Rob's horse reared as he fought for control. The man circled him with claymore and targe raised. Rob spurred his horse straight at his opponent and slashed downwards. The man shrieked as blood poured from his throat and he keeled over in the river.

A Jacobite who bristled with red hair, charged at Rob from behind a knot of gorse. Rob turned to meet him, twisted in the saddle to avoid a dagger thrust and cut across the man's chest. His red hair disappeared under the horse's hooves and the bloody water.

Rob became aware of the ebb and flow of individual battles taking place all around him. He lost sight of his brothers in the melee. A Jacobite gave a shout and Rob watched as one after another Highlanders disengaged and ran behind their lines. The rebels formed a walking retreat to the far bank.

One young Jacobite waved his blue bonnet and taunted Rob from a distance, 'You've still no' beaten us.' The rear guard protected his back whilst he and the rest of his band fled north in the direction of Elgin and Nairn.

Rob watched them go. This had been a skirmish, the deciding battle to come. He thought of his brothers and wished them far from the river.

***

By April 14th after the Jacobites evacuated Nairn, Cumberland led his troops to Balbair and camped, just west of the town. Wolfe received reports of the Jacobites near Drummossie Moor, a few miles away. Rob had to stop a couple of fights, a sure sign his men needed a battle.

Cumberland ordered the issue of two gallons of brandy and extra rations to each regiment on April 15th, his birthday. That night Rob sat amongst men who clinked their tin cups together, sang and danced round campfires. He'd looked for Annie and the sutler's wagon, but found no sign. They'd slipped away, probably frightened at the thought of a battle. A pity. He wouldn't have blamed her. Though he'd have liked her company tonight. He thought of her Scottish burr, though born in Shields. How she sometimes talked like a lady, at others like a street slut. He decided her family must have fallen on hard times, like the Jacobites who hadn't recovered from the rebellion of 1715. But Annie was a Whig and part of the government baggage train. If honest, he wanted her.

Rob circled the encampment twice. If he'd been the Jacobite commander, this would be the night to take Cumberland unawares.

Stars twinkled in the black canopy overhead, but nothing stirred in the wilderness beyond the sentries. The notes from a tin whistle and fiddle rose and fell behind Rob. He stroked a horse's nose and thought of Johnnie and Euan. The British army camp had been illuminated by hundreds of campfires. Rob scanned the darkness beyond the sentries. This was the night, he could feel it. Where were the Jacobites?

He made sure the sentries remained alert and returned to his tent after midnight, lay on his bed and closed his eyes to try to still the thump of his head.

The next morning he found a dirk. The blade pierced a piece of parchment on the ground by his bed. The words danced a jig in front of his eyes. *To Rob Stewart, your mother's dead. D.* His mother's silver brooch, with its painted picture of the Pretender, lay beside it. His heart plummeted as his fingers curled over the cold metal and held it to his chest. Mother had been ill when he'd left; he hadn't thought...How the hell did Dougie find him? He'd have to have a word with the sentries. Rob put his head in his hands. Mother.

CHAPTER Twenty-two

APRIL 16th

Just before first light Edward came to Annie's tent and woke her. 'There's to be an attack,' Edward had hissed. 'We need to leave.'

'Leave Nairn?' Annie had stared at him hollowed eyed. The last drunken redcoat had fallen asleep hours ago. 'Where we going?'

'Sssh. Drumossie Moor. Come on.'

Lord, what about Stewart? She'd no chance to warn him. *Madness. He'd rouse the redcoat army.* Edward didn't leave her side. They'd left the baggage train on foot and led their horse and cart through the redcoat lines.

'Halt,' said a sentry. He yawned,

'Need more supplies,' lied Edward.

The sentry waved them through. Annie strained to hear sounds of a fight behind them. 'Can you hear anything, Edward?'

Grim faced he shook his head. 'Read our orders.' He handed her a note.

Lord.

Several hours later, Edward hobbled the horse in a wood and Annie and Edward crept closer to the moor near Culloden.

Daylight. Edward held her back with an outstretched arm. 'No further or we risk being shot by our own men.' Mist swept across the ground. The main Jacobite army huddled in disconsolate groups under a sombre sky.

'They look bone weary,' Annie said. She didn't add *and in no fit state to fight a battle.* Annie's anxiety mounted as she watched a trail of Highlanders stagger onto the moor from the direction of Nairn and collapse. 'I dinna think they've been in a fight.'

One by one men drifted off.

'They'll be back, they're scavenging for food,' Edward reassured her. 'I should be with them,' he said and motioned to the men on the moor.

Annie's put a hand on his arm. 'Remember your orders. If the redcoats win this battle, I stay to track their movements. You have to protect the Prince at all costs.'

'It's hard to stand back and watch everything for which we've worked, played out in a battle,' said Edward.

'I know,' said Annie and chewed her thumb. 'We women do it all the time, then mend or bury you when you return.'

Edward stared at her. 'I hadna considered that.'

The first drops of rain pattered down from the gloomy sky as a young dark-haired Highlander rose from the heather in front of them, and made them start. Annie's hand went to her dirk, Edward's to his sword as they stood.

'You Jacobites?' The lad rubbed his bony arms.

They nodded.

'Thought so. Come to watch the battle?'

They nodded.

He put a hand to his stomach as it growled. 'Any food?' he asked. 'My belly's bloody empty.'

Annie rummaged in her pack and gave him their bread and cheese.

'Thank you.' He tore a bite out of both and rolled the morsel round his mouth. He tucked the rest in his plaid. 'For my brothers,' he said. He gestured at his chest with his dirty thumb. 'I'm Duncan Stewart.'

Stewart? No' one of Rob Stewart's brothers, surely? He looks so young. 'We're...friends. You need to be careful, we could have been Whigs.'

He stared at her and shook his head. 'No. Not with that fiery hair.'

Drat. Annie pulled her hat further down her head.

'Johnnie says I'm to guard our army's rear,' said Duncan.

Johnnie and there's another brother Euan. Of course the Stewarts are here.

'It's boring. They wouldna let me go on that useless night march to Nairn.'

*Nairn? So they **had** tried to surprise the redcoats. If our men are starving and tired, what hope have we against Cumberland? We know the redcoats are well fed and rested.* She attacked her thumb again. No one had been allowed to watch their new training drill, but she'd seen the soldiers' smug faces. *And what about Stewart? He'd dread this, meeting his brothers in battle.*

A shout came from a tall Jacobite who waved his arm in Duncan's direction. Another shook friends awake, whilst a third mounted his horse as pipes started up and drums beat.

'I have to go,' Duncan said. 'We'll meet again after our victory.'

'Good luck,' Annie shouted and waved as they watched him race back to the Jacobite lines.

He grinned and waved back at them.

'He's so young,' she said.

'A laddie doing men's work. I should be with them,' said Edward. He pounded his fist in his palm.

Two women tramped up the hill behind them. One struggled with laden baskets, the other with armfuls of linen. 'Morning,' puffed the older of the two. 'I'm Mrs. Leith from Inverness and this is Eppy, my maid. Didn't expect to find another woman here.'

Snub-nosed Eppy bobbed her curly head at them while Mrs. Leith arms akimbo, looked out over the moor.

'Annie and Edward,' said Annie. 'Have you come to watch?'

'To help the injured and dying once the battle's over, look.' Mrs. Leith showed them bundles of rolled linen and jars of salves in the baskets. 'We've come prepared.'

What about redcoat Stewart and his Jacobite brothers? Someone has to win and the other side lose.

Several of Prince Charlie's men dragged cannon into position. Annie thought some Jacobites would struggle to return to the battlefield from their hunt for food.

At noon, the rain beat down. Cumberland's troops marched into battle positions as he arrived on horseback, surrounded by aides.

The Jacobites sprang up and raced to their leaders, to find men and load cannon. Rank after rank faced their enemy.

The redcoats formed three lines, like streams of blood, with cannons to the front, mortars behind the first and second ranks and dragoons on either wing.

Rob Stewart could die on this moor, so many from both sides will die here. Annie chewed her thumb as the Jacobite pipes skirled and the redcoats advanced to the rat-a tat of drums with colours flying. *She'd never see him again. Fool. You don't want to see him again. Lord, if it's possible, let him survive and the Jacobites win. I don't care about 'M'.*

The Jacobite cannon boomed first, followed by Cumberland's. Jacobite bodies, earth and fire exploded in a scream of air. Holes appeared amongst their ranks and grapeshot scythed down even more. Those left formed ragged lines with empty spaces. The redcoat lines untouched, their guns pounded the Jacobites until men, unable to stand the sight of friends' deaths and wounds, broke rank. They charged, yelled war cries at the redcoats and forced the rest to follow.

Annie watched in horror as those on the left slowed and obstructed by the uneven, marshy ground, crushed those on the right funnelled towards a small section of the redcoat line.

She made herself look as cannon roared and clouds of grey and yellow smoke swept across the battlefield. Mortars shrieked and the reek of gunpowder caught at the back of her throat. Few of the Jacobites had time to fire before, with a mighty roar, the two lines clashed and a large group of Highlanders hacked their way through Barrell's front line and on towards Wolfe's regiment and Rob Stewart.

Annie put her hands to her mouth. She couldn't spot Stewart. *Surely the Jacobites will win.* Desperate figures on both sides rocked backwards and forwards. Wolfe's men held their ground. A redcoat private knocked a Highlander's targe aside whilst a sergeant thrust his bayonet through the man's unprotected right side.

Shouts made the Highlanders turn. Dragoons on horseback jumped over a walled enclosure and shots came at the Jacobites from behind a stone wall.

With dead and wounded all around them the Highlanders pulled away, it started with one or two and then became a rout.

Lord, no.

The redcoats let out a great cheer and pursued them across the battlefield.

Annie grabbed Edward's sleeve as they watched the battle come to its grim conclusion. Occasionally, solitary groups would make a stand and fight. They'd either be cut down by dragoons or escape for the moment to be harried again on another part of the moor. *No. Lord, no.*

A man reeled, his hand clutched a crimson stain on his chest, a boy shrieked as a bayonet plunged up and into his rib cage. Blood flowed from a wounded Highlander's head, shoulder and thigh as he fell to his knees. A redcoat bayonet flashed and the soldier ran on. The bodies of the dead and wounded littered the moor like broken toys. A man's moans and a boy's cries rippled across the battlefield.

'Water.'

Annie couldn't stop herself. She broke from Edward's grasp and grabbed a leather water bag in her headlong rush to help.

'Annie, for God's sake, Annie. You'll be killed.'

She didn't hear Edward's shout, her attention fixed on bodies, half hidden by marsh grass and heather. She knelt beside a Highlander who struggled to rise. He'd a hole in his stomach. She forced back the vomit in her throat and lifted the man's head onto her lap. His green eyes opened as he sipped the drink from the flask. He looked about eighteen. Annie held his hand as his eyelids fluttered and closed for the last time. *Oh, Lord.*

Edward crouched by her side. He whispered in her ear, 'My duty is to help the Prince.'

'Do it,' said Annie. 'I'll rejoin the redcoat lines. It isna over yet.'

Edward pressed her shoulder with his hand and sped away through the heather.

Annie turned to see Mrs. Leith her face set as she bound a Jacobite's chest. His ribcage stilled. Mrs. Leith shook her head in defeat and moved on to the next man. Nothing in Annie's life had prepared her for this. Too many on both sides needed medical attention and she had so little knowledge.

'Miss, 'ere, Miss.'

A redcoat's bloody fingers gripped Eppy's hand.

'It's me leg. Me leg. So cold. So cold.' Blood spurted from the stump of his shredded limb.

Annie tore strips from her muddy petticoat to staunch the red river. She felt her stomach lift up to her throat and vomited whilst Eppy moved on.

'Help.'

'Someone 'elp me.'

'Water.'

Annie didn't know where to turn. A few women who'd ventured onto the moor gave comfort where they could. Occasionally one stopped and with a pitiful cry fell down beside the body of a loved one.

A tattered figure rose from behind the yellow gorse followed by others who flocked like birds of prey over the bodies. Annie froze in shock.

'No. It's all I've got.' A bloody hand clawed at a wrist to be brushed away.

The thief slipped a gold signet ring onto his finger and held up his hand to admire it.

'Leave him alone,' Annie shouted. 'Have you no feelings?'

'Dinna fash Missus, he's no need of it now.'

One of the rogues held a sovereign between finger and thumb as he danced on the spot.

Annie could do little for the wounded and dying except give care and comfort as she went from one body to another. Her skull ached as her senses reeled. Screams and random shots sounded in the distance as redcoats pursued their enemy.

From the corner of her eye she caught a flash of scarlet and watched as a familiar redcoat officer and his horse criss-crossed the battlefield. *He's survived, thank you, Lord. What's he doing?* Curious, she sank down to watch.

'No. Oh, brother. No.' Rob Stewart leapt from his horse and she lost him in a dip in the marshy ground. Annie crept forward. Her eyes widened as she saw a Highlander spread-eagled on his back, his face covered in blood.

***

Stewart knelt beside him. 'Euan? By God it is you. During the fighting I wasna sure. It's Rob, do you understand? Rob.'

Euan shook his head as if to clear his vision. He mumbled, 'You're a redcoat bastard. Good...Jacobites died...because...of...you.'

Stewart ignored his feeble efforts to fend him off. 'Let me bind that head wound.'

Euan's bloody hand held Rob's in a vice-like grip. 'Mother died because you left.'

Stewart swatted Euan's hand away. He hung his head and snarled between clenched teeth, 'She'd been ill for months. I didn' ken it was serious.'

'Why did you leave?' Blood dripped from Euan's head onto his shirt

Stewart ignored the question and ripped a dead redcoat's shirt, tied it tight over his brother's forehead and left eye to staunch the flow of blood. 'You've got to get away.' His eyes searched the field of dying men and all the time came the sound of single shots in the distance. He sprang up to strip a dead body.

***

Annie ducked and hugged the ground above them. Stewart knelt Euan lay in a patch of low boggy ground. Stewart's mare shielded the men from prying eyes. Blood ran from Euan's ears and he passed out.

Annie averted her gaze as Stewart ripped Euan's green plaid and bloody shirt from him and replaced it with the dead redcoat's uniform.

***

Stewart fastened the last button.

Euan moaned. 'Rob?'

'Euan, listen we havena much time. You're Private John Maxwell. The poor sod took a claymore in the face and you're wearing his uniform. Tell them you're with Wolfe and I'm your lieutenant. Let's get you up. Can you walk, if you lean on me?'

'I'll never...lean...on...you,' Euan mumbled.

Stewart grappled with him, and tried to stand him upright. 'I'm putting you on the cart with our wounded. It's going to Inverness. They'll look after you there. It's the best I can do. Your damn Jacobite Cause was lost from the start.'

'But...no'...my...soul.' Euan's hand went to the empty space round his neck, a sudden urgency in his voice. 'Cross? Where's Morag's...cross?'

Stewart half pulled, half carried him towards a cart and its driver. 'Halt, private. I've a wounded soldier for Inverness,' he commanded, then whispered something in Euan's ear.

'Go to hell,' mumbled Euan.

'Head wound, doesna ken what he's saying.' Stewart laid him beside the redcoats on the cart. 'Look after him, he's a good man. That's an order.'

'Sir.'

***

Annie saw Stewart turn and continue to search the battlefield. *Lord, he's looking for his brothers.* Her heart ached for him and for all those involved in the battle. She moved away to help those she could, but stopped when she saw a gleam of gold where the cart had churned up mud. A gold cross.

CHAPTER Twenty-three

Rob sent Euan off and when the last cart with Hanoverian wounded rolled off, he walked the awful ground in search of Johnnie and Dougie. He found childhood friends who'd defended each other to the last and died together. Tight lipped he said a silent prayer and set a sentry to guard their bodies. At least they'd have dignity in death as they had in life. His mind twisted with thoughts of his mother. She'd want him to help his brothers even if the British army would regard it as treason.

By mid-afternoon Rob had scoured the battlefield. He hadn't found Johnnie or Dougie and assumed they'd escaped. For how long though? He strode towards Wolfe who stood on his own and looked over the moors.

'Sir. Have you orders?'

Wolfe turned. He tapped a playing card and flicked it at Rob.

'What's this, sir?' asked Rob.

'Cumberland's order,' said Wolfe. 'Read it.'

Rob read the fine, spidery writing between the nine of diamonds. *No quarter.* He stared at the words. 'I canna believe this, it goes against all codes of honour.'

Wolfe raised his eyebrows and pressed his forefinger against pursed lips.

Bile rose in Rob's throat. 'Permission to be excused from duties, sir,' said Rob. 'I've news my mother passed away.' He showed Wolfe Dougie's note.

'Sorry to hear it,' said Wolfe. 'Please accept my felicitations. Permission granted, but report to me tomorrow.' He gave back Rob's note. 'Rather terse, isn't it?'

Rob left Wolfe and summoned men to carry out Cumberland's orders. Could Cumberland do this? Rob hoped to God he hadn't missed Johnnie, Dougie or any Stewart wounded lying on the moor. He lay on his bedsack and listened to the distant screams and shots. He took the brooch from his saddlebags, closed his eyes and willed memories of his mother to step forward.

***

The rain turned to sleet and soaked Mrs. Leith, Eppy and Annie as they helped the wounded. By dusk a wind sprang up on the battlefield. Hartlass and a group of redcoats appeared out of the gloom with their bloody swords drawn.

'Sergeant Plaskett,' ordered Hartlass. 'Get these bitches away from those Highland curs. Shoot any thieves and strip the enemy wounded.'

'But sir...'

'Do it.'

'No.' Annie stepped forward with Mrs. Leith and Eppy, but bayonets stopped them. 'You can't, it's inhuman,' said Annie.

'It's war,' Hartlass snarled back at her. 'Sergeant, get these whores out of here.'

How dare he.

Plaskett and his men pushed back the women.

Hartlass threw a piece of dried meat to his dog which sniffed the ground round his horse. His voice softened, 'Good boy, Romsey. Eat, sir.' The dog gave a loud barked and gobbled up the titbit.

Plaskett drew Annie to one side, lowered his voice and spat on the boggy ground. 'And a bigger bastard you're never likely to meet. Get out of 'ere, Miss before he realises you're alone, if you get my meanin'.'

CHAPTER Twenty-four

April 16th, 1746

Rob sat in his tent. Sleep had deserted him. The canvas rose and fell with gusts of wind. Isolated shots sounded in the distance. He watched the silver-grey light turn to ebony as darkness engulfed the moor. His duty done, he re-read Dougie's note. *Your mother's dead. D.*

Worms gnawed at Rob's brain. He'd left his family. Didn't explain, say goodbye. Mother – He'd never see her again, never hear her voice or feel the touch of her hand. He reached for the brooch in his saddlebags. If he'd stayed at home, he might have been a voice of reason. Made sure his brothers didn't join the Prince. On the other hand, Father wouldn't have stood for it. Rob folded the note and put it in his saddlebags. He'd also broken his oath to King George when he'd saved Euan's life. He ran his fingers through his hair as a private's voice cut through his thoughts.

'Sir, may we have a word?' Two sandy-haired men, Ian and Gavin Glennie stood to attention in front of him.

Had he been seen with Euan? These men were Lowland Scots and brothers. He slid the brooch under his blanket.

'Well?'

Ian, the eldest said, 'Our youngest brother was a Jacobite, didna ken...any better. The dead are being stripped. We dinna want anyone to touch him, sir, no' till we bury him.'

Rob looked at the ground. He found it difficult to focus on them and couldn't swallow. He could have been in their position. Where were Johnnie and Dougie? His voice rasped. 'You'll stand guard over him all night. That's an order.'

'Sir.' They saluted and marched off.

Rob watched them go. These were the sort of men he wanted to fight alongside, not bloody Cumberland. He saw the brothers pick their way through the dead and dying on the moor and stand back to back at attention silhouetted against the crimson sky in the rain.

Rob lay on his bed. Had Dougie told his brothers he was a redcoat? If so, they must have wondered, as he had, what they'd do if they met in battle. He settled his head on the pillow and closed his eyes. His headache had gone, but he still couldn't sleep. The night air, full of the death agonies and voices of the enemy wounded left stripped and untended on the battlefield. To hell with Cumberland.

CHAPTER Twenty-five

Next morning Sergeant Plaskett snapped to attention and saluted a bleary-eyed Rob. 'Sir, Captain Wolfe's compliments, wants to see you at Culloden House.'

If someone had seen him help Euan, it would mean the firing squad. 'Thank you, Sergeant.' Rob ducked his head into a bucket of cold water. Captain? Wolfe had been promoted.

'Sir,' said Plaskett as Rob towelled his head dry. 'Thought you ought to know, Private Widderson died in the night, shrapnel wound to the head.'

'That's sombre news, Sergeant. See he's properly buried.' Poor laddie, he thought. How many more?

Rob trudged across the windswept moor, sidestepped boggy ground and leapt over a muddy stream. He wrestled with dark thoughts of being court-martialled and then hanged. His steps slowed, he'd no wish to hurry his last moments of freedom. He avoided provision carts, lines of horses and heaps of dead and headed for the park which abutted the moor. After a half mile he came to a low estate wall which he scrambled over. He strode towards the Georgian house he could see through the oak trees. He hadn't expected the grounds to be strewn with Jacobite bodies like rotten fruit. The burial parties had dealt with their own dead first. Rob increased his pace down the drive, kept his eyes on the house and tried not to breathe.

Wolfe had told him that Culloden House, owned by Duncan Forbes, a staunch Hanoverian, had been used by the Pretender as his headquarters before the battle. Cumberland had now installed his own officers including Wolfe.

Rob made his way along the facade. He noted the broken glass in the windows and shattered frames. A scuffle at a side door made him stop. Several soldiers dragged wounded, draped in torn tartan, up stone steps. Rob heaved a sigh.

'Sergeant?'

'Sir.'

'What are you doing?'

'Clearing out scum, sir.' The sergeant had a Lowland Scot's accent.

Rob examined the faces of the figures on the ground. He thanked God Johnnie and Dougie weren't amongst them.

'Skulking in the cellars, sir. Orders to bayonet the buggers.'

The buggers seemed in a sorry state, almost dead with from their wounds. Rob's stomach lurched.

'Permission to carry on, sir?'

'Make it quick, bullet to the brain.' He could do no more.

'Sir.'

It was hard to see his own countrymen shot instead of having their hurts tended. A familiar ache tugged Rob in two directions. What right-thinking government treated enemy wounded in this manner?

He sped up the steps as he heard the first shots ring out and forced himself not to flinch.

Hartlass leant against a pillar. 'Lieutenant Stewart, did you countermand my order?' Hartlass' lantern jaw looked larger than ever. His brown retriever sniffed at his heels. 'Sit.' The dog obeyed.

'Your order, sir?' Rob noticed a new captain's metallic lace epaulette on Hartlass' right shoulder and forced his voice not to betray his disgust.

'My kill, ordered bayonets.' Hartlass patted his dog and arched his back as if something irritated him. 'Saves the cost of musket balls.' He tapped Rob's chest. 'You'll remember, next time?'

'Sir.' Rob made a mental note to avoid him at all costs.

'And you're here because…?'

'Orders from Captain Wolfe, sir.'

'You're dismissed.'

'Sir,' said Rob. He wouldn't have put Hartlass in charge of stables. Rob ran his hand through his hair. Not that promotion was on the cards for him. Wolfe. A noose tightened round his neck.

He forced himself to enter the battered front door. A young private gathered the broken remains of fine furniture in his arms. Another, low-browed, picked up empty wine bottles from the ruined carpet. He tipped back his head and drank the dregs. A constant stream of soldiers hurried up and down the staircase.

'Captain Wolfe?' Rob asked.

The privates sprang to attention and saluted.

'That door there, sir.' The low-browed private pointed to the right of the grand doorway.

'You'll have been ordered to dispose of those,' said Rob. 'No' drink out of them where officers might see you?'

'Sir.' The soldier grinned.

'Carry on.' The men had been through a lot. A sly drink wouldn't hurt and Rob had more important things to think about. Rob paused before he knocked.

'Come.'

Rob stood to attention and saluted. He searched Wolfe's face for a hint that he knew about Euan. Wolfe sat expressionless in a small, wood-panelled room at a fine desk, his finger on a map of the Highlands. A table beneath the sash window overflowed with documents and unfolded maps.

His priority to find the Pretender no doubt. Since Wade built his roads, the Highlands were much more accessible than in 1715. What about Braedrumie?

Wolfe looked pale, but Rob suspected he'd slept in a feather bed while Rob's brain had insisted on a replay of battle scenes.

When Rob had fallen into a restless sleep he'd dreamt of Braedrumie and home.

'Sir, you sent for me.' A firing squad would be a dishonourable end for any man thought Rob. He drew himself up and expected the worst.

Wolfe coughed and covered his mouth with a handkerchief. 'Captain, your orders are to go to Inverness.'

'Captain?' Rob's brow wrinkled.

'You've been promoted, Captain Stewart, on merit. If I'd known about Hartlass' commission, I'd have promoted you sooner.'

Rob relaxed his shoulders and felt all the tension seep out of him. Well, well, he couldn't believe it. 'Thank you, sir.'

'We need to ensure the civilians in Inverness are under our control. This has been a wretched business. Worse for you, yes much worse for you. They're your damned countrymen after all, but you and I are made from the same coin, Rob. Just make sure your demons don't do for you. Don't want you racked with guilt. You're a promising officer.' He coughed again.

'Sir.'

Someone tapped at the door.

'Come.'

Annie's cheeky grin peeked out from above the pile of clean shirts in her arms. 'Brought your washin' back, sir.'

Rob stared at her. A washer woman? What had happened to her brother, the sutler?

'Thank you, Miss Bryce. Give it to my sergeant would you? Down the hall.'

'Thank you, Captain.' She bobbed a curtsy, flashed a smile at Rob and closed the door.

Wolfe turned. 'Don't suppose you've had time to organise such things since the battle. Tell you what, I'll send Annie over.

She's one of the camp followers, lost her brother so she tells me and needs the work. She's not like the others, got a bit of...class.'

'Thank you sir, I've already made Miss Bryce's acquaintance...I'll do that.'

'Ah.' Wolfe gave a speculative look at the door and then at Rob. 'I see.' Wolfe put the tip of his finger over his bottom lip and smiled. 'Well, off you go.' He went back to his map and used a finger to trace a line west.

'Sir.' He'd been promoted on merit. Rob beamed and thought of his lost years with another clan, how they'd made a man of him and how it had all led to this. Wolfe had promoted him. That was all that mattered. He'd stay in the army, do his duty as far as he could and he'd become a respected officer like Wolfe. Then he thought about Annie in an army camp without a man to protect her

CHAPTER Twenty-six

Rob took a detachment of men on the four miles downhill to Inverness. Four miles of dead and wounded, who, out of compassion, they shot. He tried to close his nose to the familiar stink. Flies droned in hordes, landed and settled. He hoped he wouldn't find Johnnie. One body had been left by the roadside covered in a bloody plaid. It looked so small, only a young lad. Rob thought of Duncan, and hoped his father had kept him safe at home. A couple of black crows circled overhead.

As they neared Inverness they came across groups of dead women, children and the elderly. Rob paled. They'd have been no threat to anyone. What about his uncle and aunt Munro and cousin Jack? They lived here. His uncle a Whig, his aunt an ardent Jacobite and poor Jack, the peacemaker, stuck in the middle. Had they left, or decided to stay?

Rob could see the town seethed with unrest. He knew it had been a Jacobite stronghold until they'd blown up the castle. Most of the houses were hovels with stone walls and thatched roofs. An old crone and a young girl leaned out of a window. The crone cried, 'We're for Geordie, have mercy.'

Rob sent his soldiers on whilst he questioned her. 'The Munros, Mr. Ian and Ciara Munro do you know them?'

'He's in London they say, and she's in gaol. Serves her right, she's a bloody Jacobite.' The crone shook her fist.

Rob gaped at her. Gaol. Oh, God, no.

A young maid with a squint pointed in front of him. 'There's Jacobites in the next street.'

Rob watched soldiers bang their rifle butts on doors and rip off window shutters. One corporal snarled, 'Open up.'

Women shrieked and wailed as soldiers threw furniture into the street to be squabbled over by all and sundry. Shackled

Jacobite prisoners shuffled down the street between lines of redcoats. Rob sniffed the air: wood smoke. He followed the pungent scent and brought his troop into the market square. Redcoats gathered round a huge bonfire which spewed out grey smoke into the air. A group fed the hungry flames with ransacked settles and chairs.

A drum beat a fast rat-a-tat-tat. Hens clucked, cattle bellowed and dogs barked. Jubilant soldiers waved captured clan banners above their heads, like blood-spotted sheets after a wedding night. The drum went silent and so did the soldiers. A black-hooded figure, the public hangman, took the banners. The torn remnants fluttered for the last time before he flung them, one after another into the fire. A roar went up from the regiments as ravenous tongues of flame spat and sparked. Each flag devoured along with the Pretender's hopes.

Rob had marched his men into bedlam. His orders from Wolfe: to ensure government troops had full military control over the civilian population.

A musket fired. Everyone turned to see the direction it had come from.

Rob's heart leapt and then sank. A battered figure appeared from a side street and thrust his way into the crowd. His face looked bruised and blood spattered his shirt. Johnnie, impossible to miss as his head and shoulders loomed above others around him.

A group of soldiers broke from the shadows of the same street, spotted Johnnie and raised their muskets. One shouted, 'You there, in the name of the King stop.'

Johnnie used his bulk to push people out of his way.

Odd, Rob thought, the blood looked fresh and his brother wore newly pressed waistcoat and breeches. Had someone taken him in? Rob wouldn't have been be surprised if it had been Aunt Munro, but what the hell did he do now?

Redcoats drew their bayonets and raced to cut Johnnie off.

Rob ran and yelled, 'Halt.' He cursed himself as Johnnie stopped in his tracks. He'd recognised the voice. One of his soldiers aimed as if to fire. Rob yanked the musket down. Soldiers and a retriever which showed its fangs closed in.

'Dinna fire.' Rob shouted above the melee. 'Dinna fire. I'll deal with this.'

'I think not, Stewart,' said Hartlass. 'My men have captured him.'

'Sir, my orders are to have full military control over...'

'The civilian population. Mine, to deal with escaping Jacobites. This man attacked and knocked out one of my men. Until I know who he is, he'll be locked up with the other wounded prisoners. Do you understand - Captain? I believe I still have seniority.' His hand hovered round his waistband as if at an itch he couldn't scratch.

Had Hartlass picked up a louse, thought Rob? Half the British army had them. 'Sir.'

'Take him.'

Johnnie's snarled, 'Bastard.' They dragged him away.

Rob wondered if the insult had been aimed at him. Johnnie always had a short temper. Blast Hartlass.

The crowd cried out and surged. Rob turned to his troops and ordered, 'Form line.' The soldiers moved into position and faced the angry mob.

'Fix bayonets.' Muskets stood on the ground as soldiers rammed blades over metal barrels.

'Port arms.' The soldiers lifted the muskets across their chests.

The mob seethed, quietened and stared at the soldiers.

Rob addressed the mob, 'You have fifteen minutes to clear the square and streets. Return to your homes or be shot.'

No one moved.

Rob lowered his voice. 'Sergeant Plaskett, on my command, get your platoon to fire a volley over their heads.' Plaskett raced down the line.

Rob raised his voice. 'Number one platoon. Present. Fire!'

The mob quivered as one man ducked and another dived. The shots resounded and formed a cloud of smoke in the square.

'Reload!' roared Rob.

A shudder ran through the mob which rippled backward and forward before they fled.

Rob allowed a smile to form as he looked at his powder-burnt soldiers. 'Well done, men. Plaskett, organise patrols to ensure the streets stay clear and find me lodgings. If you need me, I'll be at the gaol.'

'Sir.'

CHAPTER Twenty-seven

The gaoler led Rob down stone steps to the bowels of the earth, or so it seemed. The stone walls glistened with water and a stench, which made him gasp, rose from the earth floor.

Rob lifted the lantern beside his face. Aunt Munro looked dishevelled and weary in the flickering light. She clung to the bars of her cell. 'Rob. Thank God, dear boy. I thought I'd been forgotten.'

'Leave us,' he said to the hare-lipped gaoler and handed him some coins. The man took them, but remained with his palm open.

Rob's aunt tugged at his sleeve. 'I owe the gaoler two sovereigns for posting my letter to your uncle in London,' said Aunt Munro. 'Can you pay the scoundrel, Rob?'

Rob eyed the man. 'Take it and be damned.'

'Thank you kindly, Captain.' The gaoler doffed his filthy cap as he pocketed the money.

He tramped back up the steps and the door clanged shut behind him.

'The rogue, whether he posted my letter, I ken not,' said Aunt Munro. 'Soldiers took poor Johnnie.' She paused. 'You're wearing a redcoat uniform. You were at the battle.'

'Aunt, you're in no position to concern yourself about me and for whom I fought. When someone comes at you with a musket and sharp blade, you fight back. Look, I'm sorry to see you in this position. Dear God, what can I do?'

She pressed herself against the bars. 'Get me out and if you canna do it fast, a better cell and food, I willna last long in this one, I havena eaten.'

'Consider it done. I'll also write to my uncle. Dinna' worry, we'll get you out of here.'

She took his hand and laid it across her cheek. 'I dinna care for your uniform, dear boy, but I have always loved you as if you were my own. Jack's dead, did you ken? Fever, some months ago. God's will. Your cousin will be in Heaven now.'

Damn. 'Please accept my sincere condolences, he was a fine man.'

His aunt took Rob's hand. 'Have you heard about Duncan?'

'Duncan- what do you mean?'

'Johnnie told me. I'm so sorry, Rob. He's dead, killed at the battle.'

'No. I thought Father and my brothers would keep him away.' Rob shook his head.

'And Johnnie and Euan?' asked his Aunt. 'What of them?'

'Aunt.' Rob lowered his voice and tried to sound firm. 'My God, I'm pleased to see you, but you need to be more cautious in what you say for all our sakes. This is a close run thing.' He managed to rescue his hand and held her at arms' length. Tears formed in her eyes. He had to tell her what he knew about his brothers. He whispered in her ear.

She sniffed. 'I'll pray they get away.'

'Dear Aunt, be assured I will try to help them and get you out of here, but it may take time. I'll visit when my duties permit. Can you be brave till then?'

She patted his hand. 'We women are stronger than we look.'

CHAPTER Twenty-eight

April 18th, 1746

Rob parted with a lot more coins and the promise of a month's pay before he left the gaol.

Plaskett found him on his way back to the square. 'There's lodgings at the Wee Dram, but they need scrubbin' out, sir. You'll have to spend another night on the moor till they're ready.'

Before he tried to sleep, Rob's conscience spurred him to write two letters by lantern light. One to his uncle and one to the Gaol.

Culloden
April 1746
Dear Uncle,

I hope you are well. Though I do not wish to be the harbinger of bad news, you need to know that Aunt Munro has been incarcerated in Inverness Gaol and your house ransacked.

I am a commissioned officer in the British army and loyal to the British Crown. I know that you, as a Whig working for the government, can approach powerful men to request clemency and a warrant for your wife's release.

Please also accept my commiserations about Jack. I know what a blow this must have been. I will remember him in my prayers. This war makes all communication extremely difficult.

It is with a heavy heart I also have to inform you that Duncan is dead, though the others are well. I can say no more

I am, most affectionately yours,

Captain Rob Stewart.

Culloden,
April 1746
To whom it may concern,

I believe my aunt, Ciara Munro, wife to Mr. Ian Munro of Inverness, servant of His Majesty's government, to have been wilfully arrested and incarcerated in Inverness Gaol. Her husband is returning to Inverness post haste from London with papers for her release.

Her family will expect to find she has been well treated or questions will be asked of the highest authorities in England.

I am, sir,
Captain Rob Stewart.

Rob spent another restless night in his wind-flapped tent on Drumossie Moor. A ghostly mist rose from the ground and formed wraiths which Rob thought could be taken for men, if his imagination so inclined. He thought of his mother, Duncan, Euan, Johnnie and Aunt Munro.

What about Johnnie? Rob had already committed treason when he helped Euan. He'd be damned if he'd let Johnnie die to satisfy Cumberland's blood lust, but how the hell would he get him out of one gaol and his aunt out of another? He needed to find Johnnie.

Just before light flooded over the land, Rob held his bloody uniform jacket against him. It stank of death. Had he been in his right senses when he joined the army? A pile of blood-smeared, naked bodies lay fifty yards away as soldiers, stripped to the waist, shovelled earth and heather into heaps as they dug a communal grave. Their oaths and jokes split the air as their implements hacked into the dark soil.

He turned as a slight figure stopped at the entrance to his tent and tapped on the pole.

'Ere, Captain, bonny lad, do you want any washin' done?'

Annie Bryce's face peered at him like a goddess in a midden with a bundle of dirty clothing on her hip.

'It's a farthin' an item,' she said.

Rob looked at her, no more than twenty, dressed in a ragged skirt and bodice of indiscriminate colour. A strand of red hair blazed at him from under a grubby hat. Where the hell had she sprung from?

She mistook his look and covered herself with a patched shawl.

'Annie, this is no place for a woman.' He indicated the bodies.

'My brother passed away, fever.' She looked at the ground. 'All I've got left is a cart and horse and a few supplies. I've gotta make a livin', sir.'

'I'm sorry to hear it.' He looked at her and tried disguise his admiration. She was on her own amongst all these men, but had held up despite her brother's death. He played with the coin in his hand. 'You've not joined the others robbing the dead?' He indicated the women, busy at their grizzly work on the battlefield.

She followed his glance and shivered. 'Let the dead rest in peace is what I say.'

He bundled up his uniform and handed her it. 'As good as new mind. I'll pay you half now and half when I've checked it.'

She clinked the coins in her palm. 'You're a careful man, Captain. Suppose you'll be movin' on?' A musket cracked far out on the battlefield. She gave him a fierce look. 'Is it hard to fight against your own, Captain, and you newly promoted?'

She had voiced his thoughts and he bridled. 'More Scots on our side than theirs. We fought against the French, Irish, English, aye and Scots, but most of all against the Pretender.'

Her body tightened, she pursed her mouth to reply and then her shoulders loosened. 'I must go,' she said and whistled as she strolled off.

He watched her. Not many women with a figure like hers and all their own teeth, followed the army. He wanted her in his arms. Hell's teeth. He wanted her in his bed, but first he had to report to Wolfe and then find Johnnie.

**

Wolfe put a hand on Rob's shoulder. 'Sorry, old chap but we all have to be seen to do our bit. Take some men onto the moor and finish off the last of them. Think of it as a mercy.'

'Sir.' Rob had a dry mouth, his brain worked out scenarios as he and his men strode to each huddled body. Damn Cumberland and his order. What if he found Dougie or any of the Stewarts? And what about Johnnie?

Some officers allowed their men to use a bayonet, but Rob insisted on giving the man a quick death. Each single shot had a harsh metallic ring followed by a wisp of smoke in the crisp April air. For most of the wounded he knew it was a blessing, for others it felt like murder. Every death seemed to chip at Rob's humanity.

His troop trudged behind him as if each man carried the burden of death with them. Then they came across a fair-haired Highlander, perhaps no more than seventeen years of age. Musket balls had broken both legs. The lad managed to raise the upper part of his body. 'Mercy,' he pleaded and put out a hand. Rob's men glanced sideways at each other and then the ground.

Rob didn't want to shoot him either.

Cumberland arrived on a brown stallion, with Wolfe, a colonel now, and several men on foot. They stopped beside Rob's group.

'Finish the bugger off,' Cumberland directed. His heavy lidded eyes showed no sign of compassion as he sat squat and fat on his brown stallion.

'His legs could be set...' Rob began.

'Show him how it's done, Wolfe.' Cumberland pulled out a large silk handkerchief and blew his nose.

The wounded lad raised his head, his jaw set and stared with unflinching eyes at Wolfe.

Wolfe studied the wounded lad, then said, 'My apologies, sir, my commission is at your disposal, but not my honour.'

Good for him thought Rob and gave Wolfe a slight nod of approval. But what the hell would Cumberland say?

Cumberland's plump lips formed a sneer. 'Private.'

'Sir.' Dunston snapped to attention.

'It seems two of my officers don't wish to get their hands dirty. Do it.'

Wolfe joined Rob and turned away. Rob's mouth went dry as he imagined the boy stoic in acceptance of his fate. Dunston fired his musket and whimpered.

Cumberland kicked his stallion on and they watched him wind his way across the battlefield.

Wolfe shook his head. 'Carry on, Captain Stewart.'

Rob signalled to his men to move on. The soldiers' shoulders sagged. Rob guessed they hadn't the heart for this filthy business either. What Cumberland had done, dishonoured him. Rob's brain seethed as he wondered whether the butchery would ever end. To kill in self-defence for a cause was one thing, but this...had no purpose, it would only make those left hate the redcoats more.

When Rob had first bought his commission, he never believed he'd witness mindless acts of brutality towards his own people. He stopped. Local scavengers worked on the bodies with their knives. They cut and hacked at gold and silver trophies. To be sold as honest goods at markets and fairs, he presumed. Officers had left them to it, unless they came near the Hanoverian dead. Sickened, Rob sent out Sergeant Plaskett and his men to see them off.

Rob thanked God for officers like Wolfe. Annie had made him question why he'd joined up. Now he knew the answer: to fight for a just cause and to rise to the highest rank. He and his men would follow a strict code of honour, but he had to find Johnnie first.

CHAPTER Twenty-nine

April 25th, 1746

Rob moved to his lodgings in Inverness. More comfortable than a tent and he'd be closer to Johnnie. He'd found the Wee Dram. It leaned between a ramshackle warehouse and a blacksmith's forge. He spent most of his nights there and gleaned news of Jacobite prisoners and Johnnie.

One fellow officer with a large moustache had confided, 'Transports at the quay are full; the last of the prisoners are in the old church.'

'What'll we do with them, do you think?' asked Rob.

'Spare us a lot of trouble if they die. Another whisky?'

Rob fell into bed determined to find Johnnie and set him free.

Someone rapped on his door and woke him with a start. He'd slept like a dead man. He drew back his thin blanket. No morning light filtered through the shutters. So, before dawn then. He opened the door.

'Tut-tut, Captain Stewart, you'll miss reveille and you just promoted. Is Inverness to your likin'?'

Rob regarded Annie through tired eyes and rubbed his hand against the stubble on his chin. 'It beats sleeping on a windswept moor.' Not quite true, he still heard the voices of the dying. They'd pursued him and made his head throb. He remembered Johnnie. 'I'm in a hurry,' he said. 'Have you my washing, Annie Bryce?'

She smiled and he noticed that small black beauty spot again, just above the curve of her very kissable top lip.

'Worth the money you agreed'...atishoo.'

'You've a cold I see.'

'It's nowt, Captain, I've had worse. Are you 'appy with your washin' or not?' She thrust his neatly folded uniform at him.

Rob breathed in the smell of freshly laundered cloth, rummaged in his saddlebags and handed her the coins.

'Thanks, have you more, bonny lad?' She stood hands on hips and almost dared him to say no.

'Aye.' He thrust some breeches at her. 'Same deal?'

Her eyes twinkled and she grinned as if she hid a secret joke. 'Same deal.' She hurried down the stairs as Sergeant Plaskett pushed his way up. He crushed her against the wall.

Annie bridled. 'How dare you...'

Plaskett's jaw dropped and Rob stared at her nonplussed as she sounded like she'd been high born, like the first time he met her in Newcastle.

'You ain't no lady, even if you can mimic one.' Sergeant Plaskett sneered.

Annie opened her mouth and shut it again.

'Plaskett, apologise.'

'Sorry, Miss,' said Plaskett.

Rob watched Annie's eyes blaze and the spark leave them as she slipped past Plaskett. A good mimic. For one moment he'd thought – He shook his head. 'What's your business here?' He snapped at the sergeant. He had to think of a plan to save Johnnie.

Plaskett hurried forward. He wheezed as he advanced. 'Colonel Wolfe wants to see you sir, prompt like, at Culloden House. I'm to escort you, can't be too careful with all these bleedin' rebels about.'

Hell fire, thought Rob. What about Johnnie? Did Wolfe know about Euan? 'Get something for your chest. I'll dress, you saddle the horses.' His visit to Aunt Munro would have to wait.

'Osses and me don't get on, sir, if you remembers?'

'Plaskett.'

'I'll saddle 'em, sir.'

Rob washed, shaved and put on his clean uniform. If he was going to be shot, he'd look like an officer and a gentleman.

It was a fine spring day with a blue sky, little breeze. Rob cantered and Plaskett held on for grim life as they rode out of Inverness. Rob stopped to look back at Loch Ness and the Moray Firth which gleamed like sapphires. Off the coast, Royal Navy ships bobbed up and down like toy boats.

Rob spurred his horse on. It should have been an enjoyable ride. Rob pulled up again. Something irritated his right arm. He took off his jacket and felt along the seam. A pin nestled in the material. Rob pulled the sleeve inside out and withdrew the sharp object. He rubbed the livid marks all over his arm.

'Scratched you somethin' awful, sir.' Plaskett pointed at the drops of blood on Rob's shirt. 'Tailor oughta be shot.'

The vision of a firing squad fixed itself in Rob's brain. 'Let's get on,' he said.

The horses jinked a bit as they rode past the sad mounds of earth. Graves stretched one after another along the side of the road and in haphazard places up and across the moor, for at least three of the four mile ride. He thanked God someone had buried the bodies.

The main entrance to Culloden House had a well-crafted iron gate. Unfortunately one was missing and the other askew. The grounds had been littered with the dead less than twenty-four hours before. Only the discarded carts and items of military equipment strewn along its length gave clues a battle had happened here.

Rob's horse trotted as Plaskett's took off along the long drive. The horse flew by the oaks that lined the way, reared in front of the entrance and deposited the sergeant, with a thud, on the ground.

'Alright?' said Rob.

'Sir,' said Plaskett. He got up and rubbed his backside. 'Thought we was friends,' he said to the horse.

Rob grinned, gave his reins to his disgruntled sergeant and mounted the stone steps to the front door. The hall looked neat and tidy as serious-faced soldiers moved between rooms. Rob paused before he knocked on Wolfe's door. *This could be my last moment of freedom.*

'Come.'

Rob entered a room. Wolfe's desk had been moved beneath the window. A long dining table with even more papers and maps now dominated the room. He scanned Wolfe's face which gave no indication of his thoughts. *Damn.*

'At ease. Well, Captain Stewart, how was Inverness?' Wolfe remained seated a finger over his lips.

'Arrived as they burned the captured banners, sir. I have to report that the civilian population have accepted our presence.'

Wolfe's finger dropped to the table. 'I see. Good.' He shuffled some papers. 'I hear a prisoner escaped some days ago?'

Oh, God, Rob thought, *Johnnie.* 'Captain Hartlass had him in irons almost immediately, sir.'

'Good. Good. So why do you think I've sent for you?'

'I dinna ken, sir.' His shoulders tightened. He hoped to God, Wolfe didn't know he'd helped Euan escape.

'We've orders from Cumberland.' Wolfe leant forward and whispered, 'I've to send a patrol to scour the Highlands for Charlie, his friends and any known Jacobites.'

Rob breathed again.

'I've an important question for you. You're from these parts, you know the people. Where is Charlie, Captain? Where's our princely fox gone to ground? Remember, there's a £30,000 reward on his head.'

Rob had no qualms as he poured over the map.

Wolfe stabbed at an area with his forefinger. 'Reports say he escaped and headed west straight after the battle. Crossed the Nairn by way of the bridge at Faillie about five miles from here. My troops think they almost caught him at Gortuleg House in Stratherick not long ago. That treacherous dog Lord Lovat was there. He's for the axe.

Can you believe the rogues had just dined? The food warm, wine still in glasses on a table with overturned chairs. The servants and owners of the house seemed flustered. An upstairs window had been left open on an icy evening with a bitter wind and men could be seen riding at break-neck speed into the distance. Jacobites. But was it him, Captain? What are your thoughts? Was it our Prince?'

'Sounds like it, sir. If we disturbed him, he'll be exhausted and hungry. He'll need somewhere fairly close to bed down. Somewhere he knows is loyal, where he's been before perhaps, feels safe...'

'Well man, out with it? Where?'

'Creagan An Fhetich...I wonder.'

'Where?'

'The castle I'm thinking of stands on Creagan An Fhetich, the Raven's Rock at Invergarry. It's owned by the Glengarrys, staunch Jacobites and Roman Catholics. They've instigated several insurrections in the past and even entertained Charlie on his way south. Raven's Rock might be worth a look. It's about seven miles from Fort Augustus.' Rob found the place on the map. 'See.' He stabbed at it with his forefinger.

They turned at a crash from in front of the half-open sash window behind them. A light breeze wafted the cream and blue curtains. A vase had fallen off the desk and rolled onto the carpet alongside sheets of fluttering paper. Shards lay on the floor.

Wolfe gathered up the documents. Then he fully opened the window and looked out. 'Miss Bryce,' he shouted. 'Did you stumble, my dear?'

'Bloody hell. Beggin' your pardon, sir, but all my lovely clean washin' will 'ave to be done again.' Annie stuffed clothes into a wicker basket on the cinder path outside the window. 'Just look at the muck. It'll take me hours of scrubbin' to get these clean.'

'Never mind, I can wait another day.'

'Thank you, sir'. She curtsied to both of them and turned to go.

'Miss Bryce.' Rob handed her a cream stocking which hung on a holly bush just to the left of the window.

She flushed. 'Thank you, Captain,' she said and hurried off.

Wolfe shut the window. 'A pretty gal, a damn pretty gal. Pity she's not of the first order. Now where were we? Ah yes, what else do you know of this Invergarry Castle?'

Rob closed his mind to the sight of a small waist and hips which swayed in the distance and considered Wolfe's question. 'It's in good repair, built in an L shape, with a round tower. Five or six floors I think.'

'Good man. Invergarry it is. How far from here?'

'About forty miles.'

'Right, we leave at once. Get provisions and what you think we'll need to take the castle and catch our royal fox. Tell your men, I want us ready to leave within the hour.'

Damn, thought Rob, what about Johnnie and Aunt Munro? 'Sir, may I ask a favour?'

'Yes.' He studied Rob. 'It's not Miss Bryce is it?'

'No, no...it's my aunt, sir, Mrs. Munro....'

'Ah.'

'She's been arrested by our troops and is in Inverness Gaol. Fancies she's a Jacobite, but her husband, my uncle's, a staunch Whig. Would you help, sir?'

'I'll send a request to the crown for clemency, but it'll be buried amongst thousands of others. Do you have family who are close to the government who may speak for her?'

'Her husband, Ian Munro.'

'He's in London. Heard his name mentioned in the officers' mess. Write to him.'

'I've already done that, sir.'

'Not a lot more I can do, Captain. Be careful.' His finger tapped against his lip. 'It wouldn't do if it became known that one of his Majesty's officers had a Jacobite for an aunt.'

Rob's gut twisted, bloody hell and damnation. 'Sir.'

'Remember, catching the Pretender is of paramount importance, not freeing a relative.'

'Sir.' Rob didn't dare mention Johnnie had also been arrested, nor that he'd tried to escape.

Rob hoped his uncle had influence and comforted himself with the fact that he'd done as much as he could

Back in Inverness, Rob packed. He'd catch the Prince. He just hoped he'd be back in time to help Johnnie.

CHAPTER Thirty

April 25th, 1746

A blustery wind swept across the moor as Annie rushed from Culloden House. She dumped her washing in a ditch and raced back to the encampment. The sun streamed down and grass sparkled underfoot. She threaded her way through prickly gorse and marsh grasses as muddy water oozed over her shoes and headed for the picket line. Two sentries leant on their rifles and chatted to each other. She slunk behind them towards the horses which cropped grass. She picked a fine mare, patted its neck and whispered in its ear. 'You'll be fast.'

'Ere, Miss what do you think you're doin'?' asked a thin-faced sentry.

She started. *I know him.*

'Oh, it's you, Annie. What ya up to?'

'Just fancied a ride, just to those hills and back. Don't mind do you, Private Runkin?' She fluttered her lashes at him.

'Oh, Annie, I'll be up on a charge.'

'Not if no one knows. I'll be back in a few minutes, bonny lad.'

Runkin scanned the deserted area. 'Alright then, just this once. But be quick do you hear?'

'Course.'

Several saddles hung over a low bough nearby. She took one, put it on the horse, unhitched the reins and stole down through pines and across a burn. She didn't want to get Runkin into trouble, but she had to warn the Prince.

Within a few hundred yards she mounted. Sure she couldn't be seen, she crouched low over the horse's neck as she sped west towards Invergarry Castle.

She raced past the first shoots of green in fields as blackbirds sang. Mile after mile, she raced round bogs and used drovers' trails which wound over cobalt hills like skeins of wool. She paused at a break in the gorse. Far below she saw a line of carts, guarded by redcoats, which trundled towards Inverness

On the hillside opposite she spied stark, stone ramparts through the green foliage of trees. Her mare checked at a beck, but she spurred her on through the ferns as they plunged down a track into a verdant glen. After many twists and turns she rode across a stone bridge towards the castle. It towered above the landscape and cast shadows on the moss covered cobbles below. Her horse's hooves echoed in the empty courtyard.

'Hello!' she called raising her voice. 'Is anyone there?'

'There? There? There?' The word echoed. Ravens cawed and flew out of a circular tower. Their black shapes wheeled overhead.

'I've come to warn you,' she shouted.

'Warn you. Warn you. Warn you. '

'What do you want?' A short, wiry man peered down at her from an arrow slit.

She lowered her voice. 'Redcoats, they suspect the Prince is here. There's little time. Tell him...'

'You've a password?'

'White cockade.'

'Tell him what?' A tall man with regal bearing showed his face. His fair hair tied back from a high forehead. 'Ah, what have we here? A fair damsel in distress? By God, it's Lady Anne.'

'Sire, you're in danger. Redcoats will be here any minute from Inverness. You must flee this place and I must go.' She turned her mount, but men grabbed the sweating horse's bridle and surrounded her.

'Not so quickly, miss.' The short wiry man addressed the Prince. 'She could be leading you into a trap.'

'She's known to me and loyal. You'll never meet a braver woman. Let her go.'

The men scowled and muttered as they did so.

'It seems a long time since the Edinburgh Ball. Then I had hope,' said the Prince.

'I wish you safe from this place, Sire. You must act quickly.

'My thanks, you've risked much for me.'

'If you value your life, sire, leave at once, as I must.' Annie spurred her mare which leapt into the sunlight. She passed under the portcullis, across the bridge and back up onto the track in the hills.

***

Wolfe insisted he'd join Rob and Hartlass. 'Prince Charlie will be quite a prize if we catch him.'

Rob's respect for Wolfe rose as he led his troops west at breakneck speed, along the road with moorland on one side and Loch Ness on the other. Then Hartlass' dog stopped and barked by a golden belt of gorse. Hartlass checked to see what had disturbed the animal, but his horse shied. With a wave of his arm he signalled to the others to join him.

Hartlass' face had set in hard lines as he snarled at his dog. 'Back, Romsey, back I say. Sit, sir.'

Wolfe hauled his lathered horse to a stop, followed by Rob. A young boy, lay face upward, his throat cut, an older man floated in a bog, his skull staved in. 'Sergeant.' yelled Wolfe.

Rob got down from his horse. He'd noted a bloody trail and tracked it across moor and heather until he saw a redcoat's tunic flutter in the breeze, caught on the spiky gorse. It marked the spot where men lay in a bloody heap on the ground. They'd been stripped, bound and mutilated.

Bile gathered in Rob's throat and his heart dropped like a stone. The repercussions would be dreadful after this.

Hartlass stood beside him and said, 'We're dealing with animals.'

Rob stared at Hartlass and thought of Lil, the battlefield and of what men are capable when they have nought to lose.

Behind them a pasty-faced private retched in the heather.

'Sergeant, burial detail, follow us when you're finished.' ordered Wolfe. 'We go on, gentlemen,' he said with grim determination. He mounted, followed by Hartlass and Rob and made for the road.

After an hour the detachment came across a slow line of carts, guarded by redcoats, headed towards them. Hartlass spurred his horse to the front and left Wolfe and Rob in his wake.

'Whoa.' The carters shielded their eyes from the sun and heaved on their reins. The leather creaked as the wheels ground to a halt.

Hartlass hauled his horse to a stop. 'Anyone seen riders?'

Rob pulled up beside him, his hair prickled as if eyes bored into the side of his head. He turned. Dougie, the Stewart's tacksman glowered at him and Morag McColl sat speechless and wide-eyed on a cart opposite. What the hell were they doing here? Rob quickly remembered himself. His face became a mask of unconcern. Why were Jacobites in army carts with supplies bound for the garrison at Inverness? They could be hanged. He sat as if turned to stone, but his insides churned. Morag was just as beautiful as he remembered and once again he was involved in a situation over which he had little control. He swept a hand through his hair in frustration.

Hartlass pointed up to the blue hills. 'Look.' A lone rider galloped on a track which led from a castle.

'That's Raven's Rock, sir,' said Rob.

'Captain Hartlass, I want that rider alive,' ordered Wolfe.

Hartlass and a group of cavalry broke off from the main body and set off in pursuit of the lone rider. Wolfe, Rob and his soldiers continued towards the castle.

***

Annie watched the troop of redcoats stop the carts down in the valley and one group wheel off in her direction. *I'll draw them away. Lord, I hope I can buy the Prince time.*

The wind lashed her face as mile after mile, she urged her mount up and down steep hillsides. She turned onto a drovers' trail, thinking to lose the riders, but they closed on her.

She bent low over the horse's lathered neck. The mare stumbled, picked herself up and stumbled again. Annie looked back. The redcoats gained on her at every stride. A fallen tree trunk lay in front of her. Her mount shuddered to a halt and threw her. Her cap flew off and her hair, loosened from its pins, streamed over her face and back. She lay stunned and winded in the heather as a dog snarled and snapped at her legs. A redcoat private grabbed her by her hair and dragged her in front of an officer on his horse. *Hartlass.* She didn't recognise any of the others.

He stared down at her, his mouth wrinkled in a sneer. 'A woman. You've led us a mad dance. What the hell do you think you're doing?'

She kept her head low. *He hasn't recognised me.* 'Just riding.'

He leant from his saddle, back-handed her. She sprawled on the ground.

She shook her head to clear her vision. 'How dare you,' she said.

The dog rushed at her. Its eyes wild and jaws which showed a vicious array of teeth.

'Captain Hartlass at your service. Sit, Romsey.' The dog sat on its haunches and looked at his master. Hartlass wiped his face with his sleeve. He threw a titbit to the dog which it swallowed in one gulp. 'Take her.' Hartlass ordered.

Two privates yanked Annie to her feet. Her cheek throbbed and eyes watered.

Hartlass squinted. 'Wait. Do I know you?'

Lord, what a foul man you are. Poor Lil. 'No. I've only gentlemen in my acquaintance. I couldna possibly be on speaking terms with a brute such as you.'

His eyes flashed.

Please don't remember me. She'd always hidden her hair under a cap in camp and knew his reputation. She'd stayed well away from him, though she'd been friends with his washer woman.

He squirmed in his saddle and one hand eased the seam of his britches from his inner thigh. She hid her smirk at his discomfort.

He snapped, 'You dress like a drab and speak like a Jacobite lady.'

Drat. I lost my wits when he hit me.

'We'll see what a walk to Inverness and time in gaol does to loosen your fine tongue. Sergeant, take her back to the carts. Tie her to the last one. Don't let the bitch out of your sight.'

'Sir.'

Lord, help me.

The sergeant threw her over his saddle and after an uncomfortable ride hurled her to the ground. With sniggers and jeers, he looped a rope round her neck, attached it to a cart and tied her hands behind her back. The carters watched silent and tight lipped. Though one woman took pity on her and gave her bread and water. In a daze, Anne stared at the woman's face. *I'm sure she's something to do with the Stewarts.*

A sergeant, in a muddy uniform made Annie walk in the dust swirled up by the carts.

***

'The Prince was here, sir, and left in a hurry.' Rob's boot kicked over fine velvet jackets, silk breeches and stockings which covered the floorboards. 'He's travelling light, left some of his baggage behind.' Rob pointed at the open pig-skin cases.

'Damn.' Wolfe paced up and down the great hall. 'I can smell him.' He paused and rested his arm on the mantel of the great fireplace. The heat of thousands of log fires had cracked the horizontal plinth. He held his palm over the burnt peat, then tapped his lips with his forefinger. 'The embers are warm, we may catch him yet. Give orders for half the men to look for tracks on the loch's path, the rest send to the mountain passes.'

He put his handkerchief to his mouth.

'Sergeant, see to it,' said Rob.

'Sir,' said Plaskett.

Wolfe doubled over in a paroxysm of coughs. Rob looked at him with concern. Wolfe's cough had been persistent. It started as a minor irritation and now seemed to have developed into something more serious. Rob looked round and saw a decanter full of amber liquid on a sideboard

'Some of the Prince's whisky, sir, it might ease your throat?'

Wolfe gave him a wry smile and nodded.

Rob poured the whisky into a glass etched with rose buds and handed it to him. Rob recognised the irony. It would have been last used to toast the Prince.

Wolfe breathed in the fumes and his eyes watered. 'Thank you.' He threw it down in one gulp and spluttered. 'Damned...fine...stuff, Captain, nothing but the best for the Prince.' He muffled his mouth with his handkerchief. 'Who knows it might cure this wretched cough, nothing else has,' he grimaced. 'We almost had him, almost. A damned good guess of yours. Someone warned him, I hope Hartlass caught that cursed rider. Any ideas where our royal fox might have gone from here?'

'He'll try to put as many miles between us as possible. Then he'll go to ground. The people idolise him. They willna betray him.'

'So is it over or do you think he'll rally those left?'

'I think he'll wait for a ship to take him back to France. With luck the navy will catch him if we dinna.'

'We'll see. By God this place is well-named. Listen to the ravens.' He pointed out of a window at the whirl of shadows in the sky. 'Let's give them something to caw about and frighten Charlie so he knows we mean business. This castle's been a nest for Jacobite rebels for too long.' He waved his hand. 'Follow me.'

Rob did as he was told, but not before he saw the livid spots of blood on Wolfe's handkerchief. Rob had been a student in Glasgow University the last time he'd seen stains like that. One of the professors, Alistair McFarlane, had coughed his way through every classics lecture and died three years later. The thought sobered Rob. Wolfe had proved to be a brilliant field officer as his regiment held the line at Culloden. They couldna afford to lose him.

Wolfe led him back down the keystone staircase, into the light and the courtyard below. 'Get me gunpowder, Captain, lots of it.'

'Sir?'

'We're going to blow this castle to kingdom come.'

'I'll send a rider to Fort Augustus sir, for the powder,' said Rob. The sound of horses and a dog's barks made them turn. 'It's Captain Hartlass and his men, sir.'

Hartlass hauled his horse to a vicious halt in front of Wolfe. Foam covered his mount's neck and blood smeared its flanks where Hartlass's spurs had cut into the flesh. 'Quiet Romsey.' The dog whined. 'Caught the rider.' Hartlass leapt from his mount. His face took on a pained expression as he saluted.

'You all right, Captain?' asked a concerned Wolfe.

'Of course, sir.' Hartlass recovered his composure and turned to his dog. 'Quiet Romsey, quiet I say.' He scratched the silent dog behind one ear.

'Did you capture the Pretender, sir?' asked Hartlass.

'No. He was warned, probably by your rider. Tell me about him.'

'Her, sir.'

'Her?'

'Tied her to one of the carts. She's walking all the way back to Inverness, should be ready to talk once she's spent time in gaol.'

Rob knew the poor woman wouldn't last very long on gaol slops.

'And the Prince, sir?' asked Hartlass.

'I've sent out patrols, we might get lucky.'

'In my experience, sir, luck doesn't come into it. Sheer bloody mindedness does. We need to teach these rebels a lesson they'll never forget.' Hartlass set his mouth in a thin line.

'What do you mean?' asked Wolfe.

'At first light tomorrow I suggest we show these Highlanders what we think of them.'

Wolfe and Rob looked at each other and back to him.

Rob couldn't believe it. Hadn't Hartlass had his fill of butchery?

'Our orders are to return to Inverness,' snapped Wolfe.

CHAPTER Thirty-one

April 25th-26th 1746

The sun had set when Rob rode back to Inverness with two thoughts on his mind: to free Johnnie and check on his aunt. Jacobite prisoners tended to have a short life span. He waited till dusk then buried himself deep in his cloak and visited several taverns. Alcohol loosened soldier's tongues. He sat in the shadows.

At the third inn, the Cross Keys the stink of tallow candles, ale and old food hung in the air like a thick blanket. Tobacco stained walls and ceiling clung together and crouched over customers. A meagre light spluttered from a dozen wicks and lit the centre of the room. Soldiers stood packed together and others sprawled over tables. Their talk came in waves.

A short private with a swollen jaw warmed his hands at the blackened fireplace. His tall friend did the same to his bony backside.

'They're rebels, just shoot 'em.' The short private pointed at his injuries. 'Look what one done to me, Danny. Some are wounded anyway and traitors to the crown. 'Twas the same in the '15 with their bastard fathers – load of treacherous dogs.'

The tall private sucked at his clay pipe. 'Should use steel on 'em, Mat. I've got a few scores to settle – old Bill Smethwick and Harry Wilkes 'aint goin' to see the light of day again. Harry 'ad five nippers 'nd Bill ten.'

'They say them in the church is for the firing squad tomorrow,' said Mat. He hawked and spat in the hearth.

Rob's stomach lurched.

'Not soon enough if you ask me,' replied Danny. 'What a waste of bleedin' time guardin' men too weak to walk.'

'Ere that villain we caught the other day weren't weak' said Mat. 'Gave me a shiner didn't he? Fought us all the way to the bloody church. Made sure that Munro woman got put in Gaol, didn't I? What a bitch, near burned me ears with her screeching. Better sup up, change of guard in an hour.'

Bloody hell. Rob calculated he'd just enough time to call at Aunt Munro's house, get some provisions for Johnnie then make for the church. He purchased several bottles of best quality whisky and left by the back door.

The difference between the heat of the tavern and the cold outside took his breath away. The earth and buildings sparkled with a hoar frost lit by candles in windows. He wrapped his cloak around him and made for his aunt's.

The front of the house had closed shutters, the door locked. He slunk into the darkness of the wynd or alley that led to the back and tensed. Had someone followed him? He stopped and listened. No, not a footfall, but the sound of a repetitive tap as the back door swung on its hinges.

He drew his dirk, stepped inside and waited for his eyes to grow accustomed to the darkness of the interior. He listened. Faint scuttles and scratches came from behind the wainscoting. The beams groaned as they adjusted to the cold night air and the wind whispered under the doors, round the windows and into cracks. His boot crunched on broken glass and china. He didn't dare light a lamp. Once he'd helped Johnnie, he had to get his aunt out of gaol. He made a mental note then peered through gaps in the shutters. Nothing stirred in the street. He turned.

A dark staircase stood before him. He sped up it and felt his way to the linen press at the foot of his aunt's bed. He'd apologise when he saw her next. Sheets. He tore a few into strips and stuffed them in the top of his breeches. He grabbed some crumbs of mouldy cheese and stale bread from the back of a pantry shelf. A tablecloth on an upturned clothes-horse. He grabbed it. He laid out the cloth, placed the food in the centre, tied the four corners in a knot and swung the bundle over his shoulder.

As Rob left, he barricaded the door with a broken settle and four upended chairs. The barrier wouldn't stop a determined man, but it might slow him down a bit.

He headed for the church. His breath exhaled in a silver mist. The temperature dropped as ice formed on water butts. He used dark wynds. Stopped. Checked he'd not been followed. Moved on. A shriek of laughter. He jerked back and hid in the blackness beneath an overhanging building. A drunken soldier stumbled past, his arms wrapped around a wench. Rob slunk along a narrow lane. Church Street. He peered through the frosted iron bars of the church gate.

Two figures stood a couple of yards away, huddled together under the flame of a lantern suspended in the doorway of the church. The short private, Mat, from the inn, blew a frosted breath onto his hands. His tall friend, Danny, stamped his boots on the frozen ground. Their voices funnelled towards Rob in icy streams off the River Ness.

'Damn that Hartlass,' Matt said. 'E's 'ad it in for us ever since we joined. Only been 'ere half an hour and I'm bleedin' freezing.'

Danny scratched his backside. 'He won't be 'appy till we bloody freeze to death. Mind you we're in the right place for it.' He pointed at the gravestones. 'Fair gives me the spooks.'

Matt wiped his nose on his sleeve. 'Only a few hours to go 'nd I'll treat you to a victory pint.'

Rob wrapped his cloak round him and staggered into the middle of Church Street. He stumbled into the churchyard making sure the gate clanged back against the wall.

'Who goes there?' Danny challenged. He peered into the gloom, musket at the ready, whilst Mat's fingers fumbled along the church wall and connected with his weapon. It clattered to the ground. 'Bloody hell!' He picked it up and aimed the barrel at Rob.

'Jus' an 'onest citizen of Inverness,' Rob slurred, 'celebratin' the Jacobite dead. 'Ave a drink with John Rob lads.' He thrust the whisky at them and glanced at the church tower and the stout door beneath. Was Johnnie on the other side? If so, could he hear him?

'Bugger off.' Mat menaced him with his bayonet.

'Now tha's no way to trea' a friend who's offerin' you some 'ospitality.' Rob let the bottle clink against the soldier's blade. 'Go on 'ave some.' He wafted the open bottle beneath their noses.

'Keep your bloody voice down.' Danny licked his lips. 'It's enough to wake the bleedin' dead. Give us it…'

'I dunno…' Mat kept Rob at bay with his musket. 'Hartlass…'

'Is asleep in 'is bed,' said Danny. 'I know 'is bloody type. 'E won't check on us on a bleedin' night like this. Give it 'ere, mate, I'll drink with you. Death to Charlie and all those who bloody follow 'im.' With that he drank his fill from the bottle and offered it to his friend. 'Go on.'

'In for a penny…' said Mat, he tilted the bottle to his lips, took a swig and then another.

'Good stuff.' He wiped his mouth with his sleeve. 'Death to all traitors.' He waved the bottle in the air and lowered it to his mouth again.

They drank to the death of everybody. The worst two soldiers Rob had come across in his military career were drunk on duty. Danny, then Matt allowed him to remove their muskets so they could sleep.

Rob searched the gloom for some hint he was being watched – nothing, not even the faintest movement. He had to wrestle with Mat and knock out Danny. Then he tied up and gagged the sentries with the ripped strips from Aunt Munro's sheets. A large key hung from the belt at Mat's waist. Rob took it. He pulled Mat by his leg, then Danny by his arm away from the lantern and into the shadows of the church wall. He listened – again nothing, but the drunken voices of others in the inns. Rob took a deep breath. Now, to rescue Johnnie.

Mens' rough voices erupted in song from Church Street. 'They call me hanging Johnnie, Hooray. Hooray!'

Hell's bells.

'They call me hanging Johnnie, Hang, boys. Hang.'

Bloody hell. Rob dived beside his captives until the figures opposite lurched into the nearest tavern. He waited a second then sprang to the church door. 'Johnnie,' he hissed. 'Johnnie, are you there?'

'I'm here.'

'I'm opening the door. Tell the others to be quiet - we havena long.' The iron key grated in the lock, the hinges squeaked and the acrid stench of stale urine and shit hit Rob like a wall. A tall figure, blinked and stepped out of the interior of the church.

'It *is* you.' Johnnie's eyes searched the velvet-black night as if he suspected a trick.

'Aye. What about the rest?' Rob stared behind him at the open door.

Johnnie shook his head. 'They're wounded, too weak.'

'Take this.' Rob handed him his cloak.

Johnnie stared open-mouthed at Rob's uniform. 'Bloody hell, you *are* a redcoat.' Johnnie leapt for his brother's throat. 'Duncan...died in the battle. I...'

Rob gasped for breath as he seized Johnnie's hands and pushed him away. Johnnie staggered back. Pricks of guilt pierced Rob's brain. A redcoat. Dougie, the Stewart's grizzled tacksman, had kept that to himself then. Loyal to Rob as always. He stared at Johnnie. 'We havena time for this.' Rob massaged his bruised throat. 'Do you want to escape or no'?'

'Aye...but Duncan...'

'What the hell were you doing allowing Duncan on the moor?' Rob had an image of a little boy fishing by Loch Linnhe.

Johnnie looked at the ground. 'You know I tried...he ran away from home.'

'God's teeth,' said Rob. 'Poor little beggar...Euan's alive, should be on his way home.'

'Alive.' Johnnie jerked upright. 'That's good news.'

'Dougie?'

'Fine, heading for Braedrumie.'

Rob let out his breath. He'd always thought Dougie immortal. 'Good.'

'Cousin Jack's dead, fever some time ago, and your damned redcoats arrested Aunt Munro.' Johnnie's eyes blazed at him.

'I ken, damn it. I'm trying to help her.'

Johnnie stared into the dark. 'War is bloody awful isn't it, sets brother against brother. Someone once said, 'We make war so that we can live in peace.' He stared at Rob. 'Do you think King George will let us live to see a peace?'

Rob shook his head. 'You're wanted men, what do you ken?'

''Tis as I thought.'

A muffled cough came from outside the churchyard.

'What's that?' asked Johnnie his body tense, crouched and ready to run.

Rob scanned the street. Nothing stirred. 'You'd better go,' he hissed. 'There's no quarter, even now. They mean to shoot you all tomorrow.' He put a hand on Johnnie's shoulder.

Johnnie winced.

'You wounded?' If he was, Rob knew his brother's chances of escape had just reduced.

'It's nought, a damned redcoat winged me.'

'Are you sure we can't help the others?' Rob signalled at the prisoners inside.

Johnnie shook his head. 'They're in a bad way, havena eaten or drunk since they were locked in here.'

'They need to go now or take their chances.' Rob's eyes raked the area for movement. He and his brother had to get as far away from this place as possible.

Johnnie shook his head and lowered his voice. 'They're dying.'

An old man's voice, thin like a reed came from the pitch darkness of the church, 'God speed, lad. None of us has the strength. Get home, get home for all of us.' Then silence.

Rob stared at Johnnie and clutched his sleeve. 'Tell the family, tell them...about Mother...'

Johnnie shook him off. 'A bit late to care.'

'I care.' Rob threw away the key and thrust his bundle at Johnnie. 'It's a little food, all I could find. Now go.' He put out his hand, but Johnnie ignored it. He wrapped Rob's cloak around him and slipped into the undergrowth.

Rob close the church door and headed in the opposite direction, out of the gate. After a quick examination of Church Street, he sprinted past weak pools of light which cascaded from shuttered windows. He had to get back to the Wee Dram before any alarm. The sky released hailstones which fell like bullets and he thought of Duncan's death, Johnnie's escape, Euan and the Munros.

CHAPTER Thirty-two

The way back to the Wee Dram seemed further, the night darker until the silver moon slipped from behind a cloud. Rob slewed to a halt. A cloaked figure, on the opposite side of the street, bowed his head against the blizzard. A retriever padded at his heels. The pair headed towards the Old Church. The dog barked and ran towards Rob, but stopped when his owner growled, 'Heel, Romsey.'

Damnation. Rob turned into the nearest wynd and raced away. He expected shouts or Romsey's jaws at his heels. Nothing. Hartlass had shown no signs of recognition, but Rob needed to get to his lodgings as quickly as possible.

Rob drew his sword and dirk and sprinted into utter darkness as he took a shortcut through a wynd. He had to reach the inn before Hartlass discovered the tied-up sentries. A man's deep throated-yell and a woman's shrill laugh followed him into the next street.

He stopped. Footsteps behind him? He ran on. In the flicker torchlight a rat scuttled in front of his boots. He stumbled. Damn. His heart pounded and his breath became ragged as shadows loomed from doorways. He got to his feet and the shadows receded. Dangerous times to be out alone at night.

Beads of sweat formed on his brow. Trust it to be Hartlass. Within minutes the escape would be discovered. He needed to be in bed, sound asleep. Had Johnnie enough time to get away?

Drunken songs spilled out of chinks in the inn's shutters and doors. Rob checked the back door. No one. He sped up the stairs and heard a distant pistol shot as he closed his bedroom door. The voices stilled below. A second shot, musket this time. Then the shouts began. He heard tables and settles overturn as soldiers sped into the street. Voices bellowed orders. He stripped off and pulled the covers over himself.

Several minutes later, he pretended to be woken by the sounds of urgent footsteps on the stairs and a fist which beat a loud tattoo on his door.

'Come in.' He yawned as the door opened. 'This better be good, Plaskett. You've woken me from the first sleep I've had in days.'

'Sorry sir, but you'd best get up. One of them bleedin' Jacobites 'as escaped.' Red-faced he wheezed. 'It's the big fella what we captured in the market. Don't think much of 'is chances. Tied up the bloody sentries like meat parcels. You could smell drink on 'em. They'll be up on a charge. Deserve a good floggin' the pair of 'em. Do it meself if I'd a mind.'

A volley of shots sounded. 'What in damnation?' said Rob a he pulled on his breeches.

'That'll be the firing squad, Captain Hartlass' orders. He'll have finished off the wounded in the church. Captain's as mad as Hell, wants to see you sharpish, sir. That's what he said, sharpish by the old bridge.'

Rob's mouth went dry. 'Get my jacket, damn you. We can't keep the Captain waiting.' If Hartlass had recognised him, he was done for.

He thought of Johnnie. He wouldn't try to cross the bridge, too many sentries, though he could swim like a fish. With that wound, the Ness could carry him out to sea or drag him down. Surely to God he couldn't be in the Ness? Rob sweated as he forced himself to act out the role of an innocent.

The Ness Bridge stretched out like a frosted arm across the river. Sentries stood lit by torches, at either end. The night, black as tar, pressed in on all sides.

Despite the cold, Rob felt perspiration run down his back when he heard Hartlass' dog bark as it pulled at its lead.

'Quiet, Romsey.' The dog sat still. 'Ah, Stewart, my soldiers reported seeing something in the Ness.' He bawled at the poor privates who guarded the bridge. 'God blast this damn night, get those torches over here.' The men rushed to carry out his order.

Rob looked down through a veil of sleet at the swirls in the river. The tide on the turn, the inky water flowed towards the sea.

'See there, there.' Hartlass yelled and pointed.

'It's debris.' Rob hoped to God it was.

'Use your eyes man, it's a head. It's someone's head I tell you.' Hartlass seemed hypnotised by the object below. 'Sergeant, tell your men to shoot.'

'Sir.' He bellowed the order and the night filled with the metallic sounds of men as they loaded their weapons.

Rob peered into the ebony river. The sleet came at him in all directions now. He saw something. A round shape, the glint of light from an eye perhaps. He shivered. No man could last long in the Ness.

'Permission to speak, sir?' asked a corporal.

'Yes?'

'Shall I take some men, sir? Wait on the other side in case he surfaces there?'

'Do it.' Hartlass searched the murky water below. 'Damn this blasted weather. I can't see a thing. Do it and we've got him.'

'Sir.'

'Captain...' Rob began, but Hartlass ignored him.

'Fire at will, lads,' the sergeant shouted.

An explosion of noise; the river seethed with rounds. Then silence.

'Bring those torches closer, damn you,' yelled Hartlass. 'We've got him, we've got him. Look, see.' The men cheered at the limp form below.

'The current's pushed him towards us. Sergeant, send your men to the water's edge and drag him to the shore.' Hartlass grabbed a torch. It made his face devilish as the yellow and blue flames danced in the wind. 'Let's see what kind of strange fish we've netted. Go on Romsey, seek.' He unleashed the dog who rushed off in a flurry of excitement, leapt into the water and grabbed his prey.

Two privates cursed as they went up to their waists and dragged the body out of the black river and laid the sodden, bloody mess on the shore.

Romsey circled in a frenzy of barks.

'Sit.' Hartlass ordered him and patted his head. He lowering his torch, kicked the body with his boot and turned away in disgust.

A seal.

A private snorted.

'Attention!' Hartlass glowered and stomped back up the bank with a disconsolate Romsey behind him.

Rob knew it hadn't been Johnnie. When he'd raced down a wynd, he'd tripped over a naked corpse. Johnnie was on the other side of the Ness by now, dressed as a corporal who'd looked for an escaped Jacobite washed up on the tide.

***

The following morning Wolfe said, 'They tell me a prisoner escaped, the same one who got away earlier?'

'Er, yes, from the church I believe,' said Rob. 'Captain Hartlass thought he had him, turned out to be a seal.'

'A seal you say.' Wolfe slapped his knee and guffawed which brought on a bad bout of coughs. He dabbed at his mouth with a handkerchief. 'My, I'd like to have seen the look on Hartlass' face, must have been a picture.'

Rob's muscles relaxed. 'Well, he wasna pleased, sir.'

'No, by God he wouldn't have been. It'll be the talk of the men for weeks. He's been hanging deserters, found them amongst some wounded Jacobites. A bad business, but we can't be made to look fools, can we?'

A muscle twitched in Rob's cheek. He hoped Johnnie had got well away. 'No, sir.'

'Double the patrols, we'll soon reel in our prisoner.'

'Sir.'

Now he had to free Aunt Munro.

CHAPTER Thirty-three

April 26th, 1746

Annie had been woken by distant shots in the early hours of the morning. They reminded her of the aftermath of Culloden and images she couldn't erase from her head.

Later she'd listened to the cries of the Inverness street hawkers and the barks of stray dogs and meows of cats. She watched a succession of dirty, bare feet, shoes with and without buckles and muddy hems of all hues trot past her barred window.

She'd been entombed in dank darkness lit only by the high window through which stripes of weak sunlight and a cold wind shuffled. Rivulets of green slime ran down the stone walls. The building sighed and wheezed when the air shifted as the gaoler clanked his way along passages and unlocked and locked doors.

The sound of grating metal filled her ears. Her life had been frozen in a stone rectangle six foot by four, slightly larger than a grave where cockroaches and rats strolled at leisure over foul straw strewn across the stone floor.

She wrapped her arms tighter around her thin frame. The cold trapped itself in her bones. She'd only the clothes she stood in when arrested: a thin underskirt beneath a filthy dress which had once had a light green check; holed grey woollen stockings and black leather shoes worn through on her forced walk back to Inverness. By the time she'd arrived she had blistered and bleeding feet. *Was this what it had been like for poor Lil? And where's Rob Stewart? He'd not want to know me now. I'll never find out who 'M' is...*

Annie spat on the hem of her petticoat, wiped her face and pinned her lank hair into a bun high up on her head, determined to retain some semblance of dignity. She slumped down on the filthy straw. *I could die in here and no one would know.*

Her memory sought its way back to her mother's portrait at Kerbilly and her father's arms. Her mind snatched at cobweb-memories and dusted them.

Her childhood had been full of blue skies and laughter. *What of Alan, Charlotte and Jean? As known Jacobites, they'd receive little mercy from the British government. Thank goodness my father and uncle steered a safer course, not that I agree with it.*

Annie closed her eyes and thought of walks over the hills smothered in purple heather and yellow gorse above Kerbilly. She took a deep breath, inhaled and imagined the scent of waist high meadows full of thistle and wild flowers. She ran into Kerbilly's walled garden full of sweet-scented orchard fruits. A twist in a path led her past fresh hay and the acrid stench of manure from the stables.

To her left she saw Kerbilly House and the wrought iron balustrade either side of eight stone steps to the front door. If there'd been any more her father said, they'd be too grand, any less, too poor for the local gentry.

In her mind she stepped down onto drive and saw again the deep green lawn which overlooked the crescent bay.

A key scraped in a lock and the metallic clank of a distant door and the sound of footsteps came towards her. She strained to listen at her cell door. *One light footstep and the other a heavier tread – a prisoner with the gaoler?* The gaoler inserted a key in the lock of a cell several yards away. The door squeaked open and clanged shut. She held her breath. The pad of a single pair of shoes retreated. Crash. A distant door locked. Silence.

She paced round and round and tried to rub warmth into her arms. An icy wind whirled through the barred window. Better to sit. She hugged her knees to her torso, but the wall froze her back and the floor her feet. She shuffled forward and massaged her toes.

'Hello...anyone...there?' A woman's voice came from the left. It penetrated the shrouded darkness and cut through the loneliness and cold air.

Annie jerked upright. 'Yes.' *Another poor soul's here.* Relief flooded through her as she ran to the grill of her cell door and peered through, but couldn't see who'd shouted. She hadn't spoken to anyone other than the gaoler, since she'd been incarcerated. This woman must be in the cell at the end of corridor. 'Who are you?'

'Ciara Ross, married to Ian Munro from Inverness.'

'Munro, what are you doing in here? Isna' your husband a Whig?'

'Aye, God love him.'

Annie knew Inverness gossips viewed the marriage as unconventional as Mrs. Munro was a fervent Jacobite.

'It's the only thing we've fallen out about in thirty years of marriage,' Mrs. Munro said.

Surely he should have been able to protect her?

Ciara shared her tale of woe with Annie and ended it when she said, 'The damned gaoler's taken his time moving me to a better cell. Munro's been informed. He'll get me out, mark my words.'

A better cell? Annie shivered. *Dear Lord, there's worse? At least Mrs. Munro has hope. What about my father? He'll be ruined if anyone discovers what I've done.* She put a hand to her throat. *He warned me and I haven't heard from him for months.*

'What's your name, my dear?' said Ciara.

'Rona, Rona MacLean.' The lie slipped off Annie's tongue as it had when she'd been admitted to gaol.

'Perhaps I can help you, Miss MacLean. Why are you here?'

'For questioning.' Annie chewed at her thumb. 'I willna say more.' She didn't know Ciara Munro or who else could hear.

'I understand. You sound young. How old are you?'

Can I trust her? 'Twenty.'

'Can you sleep?'

'Not with the rats and the cold.'

'I hardly closed my eyes in my old cell, at least there's light here.' Mrs. Munro's voice quivered.

Annie tried to reassure her. 'We must be strong.'

'Have you no family that might help?' asked Ciara.

'No.' *Poor Father, the news will kill him.*

'Take heart lass.' Ciara lowered her voice to a whisper, 'I've a nephew in Inverness who kens I'm here. He may be able to help both of us.'

Annie's spirits lifted. *Freedom.* She closed her eyes. *How I long to breathe fresh air, roam the hills and walk along the shore to the Needle's Eye, but are my father and friends safe? The redcoats showed little mercy in the battle's aftermath.*

CHAPTER Thirty-four

April 26th, 1746

Rob had been up most of the night. He'd written a report about Johnnie's escape, decided there'd be no point in going to bed and had been called into meetings all morning. He'd returned to his quarters at the Wee Dram later that afternoon.

The neat bed, table, single chair and unlit fire stared at him. He dumped his saddlebags on the floorboards and ran a hand through his hair. God, he'd chosen a lonely life. He thought of his family in Braedrumie and Aunt Munro. He must visit her. He needed a bath and sleep.

A knock at door made him turn. 'Come in.'

'Sir.' Sergeant Plaskett saluted. 'Thought you'd want this sharpish like. Arrived with the London mail.'

'My thanks. Dismissed.'

'Sir.'

Rob yawned and examined the seal: Uncle Munro. He broke the hardened wax and found the letter enclosed another document. He sat on his bed.

Westminster Square,
London
April, 1746

Dear Rob,

Please find enclosed a warrant for my wife's release. I would be most grateful if you would see her safely installed in her own home, assure her of my love and inform her, God willing, I will join her soon.

My thanks for your letter. I had no knowledge of her arrest or the house being ransacked. Possessions can be replaced, but your dear Aunt cannot. I have the ears of powerful men who know how hard I have worked for the government. Heads have rolled, I have seen to that.

Thank you for your kind words about our dearest boy Jack. A fever took him before we could even say goodbye. Please also accept my earnest commiserations about Duncan. They were both too young to be taken, but we must accept God's will. I will pray for them both. It is good to hear others are well.

I have business of great import to complete and once I free myself of it, will catch the first coach to Inverness. I feel assured of my wife's safety, knowing you are close at hand.

The rebellion has been the most dreadful business and I have witnessed executions of men in their prime. I can say no more.

I am most obliged, most grateful and affectionately yours,

Uncle Munro

Rob placed the letter and warrant in his saddlebags. He needed to get to Inverness Gaol and free his aunt.

***

Annie was startled by the harsh jangle of keys in a lock and the guttural voice of the gaoler at the cell next door, 'Looks like you was right, Mrs. Munro, you've got friends in high places. The Captain's waiting upstairs with your release warrant.'

A captain. Will Ciara remember me?

'Take heart, Rona.' Ciara pressed Annie's fingers as she passed. She followed the warder, up a stone staircase and was lost behind a wooden door at the top.

Annie clung to the cell bars, full of hope. *If I can persuade the Captain I was an innocent riding in the hills and have somehow been arrested as a spy, then he might just obtain my release.*

***

'Here she is, sir, safe and sound, just as I promised,' said the gaoler. His hare lip lifted in a broken impression of a smile.

'Rob, bless you my boy.' His aunt rushed forward, faltered then kissed him on both cheeks. 'You look tired.' She whispered in his ear and sniffed. 'Pity about the uniform.'

Her grey hair fell in disorder about her face above a dirty and torn bodice and skirt. She swayed. He stepped forward full of concern and put an arm round her. 'Are you well, have you been mistreated?'

'This place is a hell hole.' She patted his hand. 'But, there's many worse than me.'

Rob squeezed her hand shocked at how cold it was. 'Uncle Munro sent a release warrant for you as soon as he could. He told me to assure you of his abiding love and that he'll be in Inverness as soon as possible.'

Her face creased into a wry smile. 'It's as I thought. Those responsible for my arrest and mistreatment will have to look to themselves. Dear Ian, when his temper's up, there's no stopping him.'

'Leave us,' Rob ordered the gaoler and he shuffled from the room.

'Aunt, they wanted to take you to Carlisle and put you on trial for treason. I must ask you to stay at home from now on and stay out of politics or it may be the worse for all of us.'

'Hmph. Very well, but there's another in this place you could help if you've a mind.'

'Aunt.' Damn her generous heart. 'I've risked...'

'Do it for me nephew. It's a young girl...Rona MacLean.'

He groaned. 'What did she do?'

'She said she was taken for questioning and wouldna' say more.'

Oh God, he thought. Another fervent, bloody Jacobite, but she's young and a lassie. He thought of poor Lil and softened. 'If she's been treated the same as you, I'd best see her. I'll escort you to the coach outside. See if you can keep out of trouble till I return.'

CHAPTER Thirty-five

A cloud must have covered the sun as the weak square of light in Annie's cell faded. She smoothed her hair with her hands and retied it with a scrap of material from her underskirt. *Not enough.* She used another strip to scrub at her face, hands and bruised feet with icy water from a battered tin mug. Her dress hung in grimy rags, nothing she could do about that.

Surely the Captain will see me? What if he refuses? She let her forefinger trace over indentations on the walls. *What's this?* She examined a scaffold with the date 1715 and the name RORY McPHERSON scratched under it. *The last rebellion. Had he been executed?* A shiver raced down her spine. *Ciara must help me.* Minutes went by, each seemed like hours.

The stale air shifted as doors rattled and two sets of boots trudged down the stone stairs. A spot of light illuminated the passage.

The gaoler lifted his lantern. The shadows retreated. His mis-shapen lip made worse in the glow of the candle's flicker. ' 'Ere's Rona, Captain, right as rain, just as I said, she's been well looked after.'

'You lying toad.' Annie peered into the shadows, but could only see the Captain's dark outline. 'I've seen cleaner pig sties.'

'Leave the lantern.'

The Captain has a vaguely familiar voice with a low Scottish burr. Lord, Rob Stewart. The gaoler shrugged his shoulders and put it on the ground.

Annie watched the Captain turn and wait for the sound of the gaoler's feet to fade and the clang of the door as it closed behind him. *Why doesn't he move into the light?*

'Miss Bryce, I'm sorry to see you here, but I admit I'm confused. The gaoler and my aunt think you're name is Rona

MacLean.' He lifted the lantern. Rob Stewart's features looked ghoulish under its yellow light. His blue eyes like ice-chips glowered at her.

Lord. Her world tilted. *Why him?* She peered through the bars. *I'd forgotten how the cut of his uniform suits him...He towers over me, overpowering, unstoppable.* She noticed how his dark brows knitted together and formed a seductive crease above his eyes. Her breath tightened and her bodice seemed restrictive somehow. *Would I want him to stop? What am I thinking?*

She looked up and fluttered her eyelashes. It seemed to disconcert him and he blinked at her. *Good, now if I can just persuade him to get me released.*

He fingered his cravat as if it was too tight. 'My aunt said you wanted to see me?'

'Oh yes, Captain, I want to see you.'

***

Rob was shocked to see Annie Bryce, but even in this wretched state, her beauty shone through the dirt.

She rested her head on the inside of her cell door and played with a strand of hair. 'So, Captain, can you tell me why I'm in gaol? Weren't yer washin' up to standard?'

'My washin'...washing has nothing...I didn't imprison you as you well know, Miss Bryce, Captain Hartlass did. I've seen the admission book and it must be obvious to you this has nothing to do with the standard of your washing.'

'Really?'

'Miss Bryce, dinna make this more awkward that it need be.'

'Do you feel awkward, Captain? Dearie me.'

He rifled through the papers he'd requested from the gaoler and summoned up all his patience. He said, 'Miss Bryce, we know several women have acted against the crown, some overtly,

Isabel Haldane of Ardsheal for instance and others...covertly.' He let the last word linger in the fetid air.

'You do? How terribly brave of them, but what 'as this gotta do with me, bonny lad?'

'Why have you called yourself Rona MacLean?'

Her eyes flicked away from him. 'There 'isn't no law 'gainst a person changin' their name is there?'

'What were you doing prowling outside Captain Wolfe's window at Culloden House?'

'I were pickin' up your breeches which I'd dropped on the lawn, pet. They had terrible grass stains, I had to scrub 'em again. My poor fingers is scraped raw.'

'This report states you were arrested in the hills above Invergarry Castle and its nest of traitors. Rather an odd place for a washer woman using a false name, wouldna you say? I must tell you now as an officer of the crown, I canna interfere...perhaps if you tell the truth, everything you know...I might be able to...' God, she looked frightened.

She lifted her head, set her jaw and stared at him. 'I was ridin', enjoyin' the scenery.'

'A simple washer girl enjoying scenery? Really, Miss Bryce.' He leant forward, 'Who are you and why did you visit Invergarry Castle?'

She laughed at that, a light, musical laugh.

He'd heard it before, but where? He searched his memory. The London ball. No. This wretch couldn't possibly be a lady.

Then she leant forward and whispered, 'I'd rather ken who you are, Captain?'

'What?'

'That surprised you didn't it?'

Shocked, he realised she'd spoken with an educated Scottish voice.

She hissed, 'Oh, I ken you're a government officer, but why would you save a Highlander's life on the battlefield by dressing him in a redcoat uniform, unless he was your brother?'

Rob stared at her aghast. Who the hell was she? She knew enough to get him hanged. How?

'You've become a little pale, Captain. Are you ill? Should I call the gaoler?'

He began, 'I think you're mistaken...you have no proof.'

'Oh, it's amazing what one can find in officers' baggage. Sometimes money, sometimes a love letter and sometimes a white, silk rose and a brooch with a portrait of Prince Charles Edward Stuart in saddlebags. Treason I think they call it, Captain, a capital offence I believe.'

He gaped at her. Hell and damnation. His mother's brooch.

They stared at each other, Rob in horror and her in delight.

'You have them?'

She nodded, leant towards the bars and whispered, 'It would be highly amusing, Captain, if you and I were found to be on the same side, now wouldn't it?'

My God she'd spied on him and gone through his baggage. His words came from behind clenched teeth. 'I'm no' a Jacobite. Who...**are**...you?' His eyes narrowed. He knew most of the Scottish gentry in the Highlands, but he didn't know her.

Her words scorched his ears. 'Get me out of here, Captain. Use your charm, lie, steal, but get me out of this gaol. Once you've done that and only when you've done that...I might, just might, reveal my identity to you. Dinna betray me, for I willna think twice about paying you in kind. I'm relying on you. After all, you've proved how helpful you can be to enemies of the crown. I think this interview is over, don't you?'

By God, she'd dismissed him. 'Gaoler!' he bawled, 'Gaoler!'

He listened to the clang and crash of unlocked doors followed by hurried feet.

'Is the little whore provin' difficult, sir? Give me five minutes alone with 'er and I'll 'ave her singin' like a little bird.' The gaoler's ham fist came within an inch of Annie's nose behind the bars. His ruined lips broke into a smile when she didn't pull back.

'She's to be released,' Rob snapped.

'But sir, she's 'ere under Captain Hartlass' orders, to be 'eld until 'e returns.'

'After questioning this woman, 'tis obvious this is a clear case of mistaken identity. Release her.'

'I 'ave to follow the regulations. There's papers that needs signin'.'

'Fetch your bloody papers. I'll sign 'em.'

The disconcerted gaoler shambled off and muttered as he went.

'Thank you,' she said.

He looked at her and his jaw tightened. 'I'm taking you to my aunt's. You'll stay out of sight. You're to see no one, speak to no one. Do you understand?'

'I...yes. Captain, what do you...?'

Rob put a finger to his lips. He'd heard padded footsteps and the creak of locks. 'He's coming back.'

The gaoler returned with the papers and opened her cell door. 'This is a rum do, Captain,' he scratched his head. 'She's said nothin' but 'er name since she came 'ere.'

'You have to have a way with women,' said Rob. Damn it he'd do what he'd ached to do since Newcastle and to hell with the gaoler. He held her face in his hands and kissed her. She'd taken him for a fool, but she'd soon learn that he wasn't to be duped. God, her lips were warm and her body all curves. Time became suspended in that kiss. He wanted her.

***

Annie froze in shock, tried to resist, but he would have none of it. Her lips parted of their own accord under the tip of Stewart's tongue. Wave after wave of wantonness scorched through her and overpowered her senses. She fell, spun, drowned in his arms and wanted to respond...*but didn't he have someone he wanted to forget – 'M'?* He released her.

Stewart sucked in a breath and said with some authority, 'You see she just needed...'

'Tamin'?' suggested the gaoler, 'like my old dog. You kick 'er and she'll turn on ye teeth bared, but feed and pat 'er, pick the fleas off 'er and she's yours.'

Annie glared at both of them. She didn't feel sorry for Stewart, nor for any redcoat after Culloden. Blood didn't flow in his veins, iced water more like - he'd jilted her after all.

The gaoler's tongue curled over his harelip. 'We're all friends 'ere perhaps if I...?' He lunged towards her.

She stood her ground, her hands formed claws.

'No, my friend.' Stewart put his arm round the gaoler and smiled as he walked him to the door and pulled Annie behind him. 'This wild cat's mine.'

Wild cat? How dare he.

'Take these coins.' He rattled them in his palm. 'Find yourself an obligin' doxy of your own. Rona MacLean's dead. Scratch her name off the list.'

The gaoler took the gold and tested one on a broken tooth. His lip formed a semblance of a smile. 'I'll do that. Thank you kindly, Captain.'

'All the pleasure's in the 'breaking in' if you see what I mean.' Stewart winked at the gaoler.

Breaking in?

The gaoler winked back, 'I do sir, oh I do.' He licked his lips and they roared with laughter at Annie's expense as he opened the door to the ground floor.

Men. She kicked Stewart's booted leg with her foot making her hobble and him curse. Stewart pulled and pushed her up the stairs and through several doors until they were outside and she blinked in the last of the daylight. He then hauled her into a coach where he seated her beside his aunt. He glowered opposite her as he tapped on the coach's roof and the horses set off.

CHAPTER Thirty-six

Rob watched his aunt smile and pat Annie Bryce's hand as they sat side by side. The coach swayed. 'You see, I knew Rob would help. He's the kindest, dearest boy.'

Rob studied Annie's grim expression.

Between tight lips she managed, 'Thank you.'

He sensed a conflict of emotions as they flitted over Annie's face: relief at being out of gaol and a determination to be free of him? He stopped the coach and through the window bought what food he could at exorbitant prices from market stall holders.

Annie glared at him as he issued curt instructions to the driver. Then she stared out of the window.

His mind wouldn't let the question drop. Who was this Annie Bryce, this Rona MacLean? He'd get to the bottom of it, or die in the attempt. He stopped the coach in front of battered Munro House. Two redcoats stood on guard either side of the battered door.

'Oh,' said his aunt. He held out a hand to help her down.

'Dinna worry, we'll soon make it habitable,' said Rob. He shouted an order. 'Remove the rubbish from the street.' The soldiers saluted and did so. 'When Uncle Munro returns, he'll make it right again, Aunt.'

His aunt gave a weak smile and pressed his hand. 'Dear boy,' she said and walked inside.

Rob had a quiet word with the sentries, then realised Annie had disappeared round the side of the coach.

She kicked his ankle.

'Ouch.' His legs would be black and blue. He grabbed her arm and bundled her up the steps, through Aunt Munro's front door and slammed it behind them.

'You are no gentleman,' she hissed at him in the hall.

'And you no lady,' he replied. He dragged her through ground floor rooms full of torn curtains, broken furniture and into the empty scullery.

She side-stepped a copper pan and stumbled over one of several broken wine bottles. It rolled into a trail of flour and shattered glass on the flagstone floor.

'You'll note those guards outside will be here for the duration of your stay with my aunt.' He watched the colour drain from her face. 'Now sit.' He righted a chair for her.

She sat.

'Those redcoat devils have even ransacked upstairs, at least they've left us beds to sleep in,' said Aunt Munro as she sailed through a door and wiped dust off her hands.

'I'll look into it, Aunt,' said Rob. He knew there wasn't a hope in hell. The culprits, long gone.

'Hmm. Come Rona, we'll make our ablutions upstairs and find you something to wear. I'll put you in...Jack's room. Rob, if you'd be so kind as to boil water and bring it to us, we'd be grateful.' His aunt put her arm round Annie's waist and guided her out of the scullery.

Rob drew water from the well in the back garden. Who was Annie Bryce? He dumped the full buckets on the scullery flagstones, shaved some wood and used a flint to start fires under the set pot and in the hearth. The leg of a broken stool and a splintered drawer, he soon had flames.

He poured the water into the set pot and then a copper pan over the fire, swept the floor free of debris, pushed the kitchen table into the middle of the room and arranged the chairs in some semblance of order. When the pan of water bubbled, he threw chunks of mutton, a few root vegetables and grains of barley into it. Who was she?

He filled two jugs with boiling water from the set pot and carried them upstairs. He put one jug on the floor and tapped on his aunt's bedroom door.

'Thank you, Nephew.' He then tapped on Annie's door and thought of poor Jack.

'Yes?'

'I've hot water.'

The door opened a little wider. 'Thank you.' Her shawl slipped as she took it from him and revealed a bare, alabaster shoulder.

Something pricked his memory. London. Lady Jane Forsythe. She couldn't be. He managed to say, 'Once you've washed, there's broth downstairs. It'll take some time.'

She placed the bowl on a dressing table and pulled the ends of the shawl up to her neck. 'Thank you.'

He closed the door. Who was she?

His aunt came down half an hour later, face washed, hair combed, but still in ragged clothes. 'The looters didn't leave very much.' She sighed and fingered her skirt's worn material. 'I should be grateful they left some cast offs.'

She seated her rump on a chair by the fire and spoke in whispers. 'Johnnie came to me after Culloden seeking his fiancé, Kirsty Lorne, what a hoyden she is. If you'd heard her and her mother. All talk of fine clothes and their rightful place in society. Kirsty's wrong for him, Rob. Poor Johnnie. Then some nasty redcoats arrested me, there was nought I could do.' She dabbed at her eyes with the hem of her dress.

Rob made up his mind as to his course of action. 'Aunt, I must leave you and Miss B...Rona for a while. I've...something I must...sort out.'

'Oh, Rob.'

'Now, you're not to worry, Uncle Munro will be here very soon. Till then I've detailed guards to stay outside the house and

Sergeant Plaskett will bring you daily provisions. Keep an eye on Rona. There's more to her than you and I ken. I'll be back in a few weeks.' He took his aunt's hands in his. 'No news of this must get out. Our lives depend on it. Understand?'

'Aye.'

'Farewell.' He kissed her on her plump cheek. A slight movement behind him made him turn to see a clean Annie Bryce, at the door, her red hair tamed. 'I've ordered my sentries to shoot if you step out of the house,' he lied.

His aunt gasped and put a hand to her throat. 'Rob.'

The colour fled from Annie's face.

Good, he thought. It's the first time Annie Bryce has realised I'm not a man to be played for a fool.

CHAPTER Thirty-seven

Annie stamped her foot as the front door closed on Stewart's back. *Where's he going? Can I trust him?* She sniffed the air as her stomach growled. She rushed to Ciara Munro's scullery and the fire. 'What's that wonderful smell?'

'Rob's made us some broth.' Ciara stirred the kettle and didn't look at Annie. 'It willna be ready for a while yet.'

'Oh.' Ciara seemed distant, more reserved. Annie didn't want to eat anything he'd cooked, but her stomach cramped with the thought of the meat juices. She dabbed at her lip. *Lord, I'm drooling.*

'Blasted redcoats.' Ciara surveyed her damaged home. 'Sheer vindictiveness. But I'll no' weep. There's lots worse off than me.' She scratched a series of bites on her arm. 'I'm sure I've got fleas.'

Annie felt itchy too. She had an overwhelming urge to get rid of the stink of mouldy straw, damp walls and drains.

'Come my dear,' said Ciara. 'Let's use some of this hot water.' Annie helped her haul a tin bath from the back yard and carry it through to the scullery. Then she let the older woman rest and filled the tub with buckets of boiling water,

'You first.' Ciara placed a rickety clothes horse round the bath and hung a torn tablecloth on it. 'At least we have privacy. I'll find something clean for us to wear and put fresh linen on the beds. If I can find any. Rogues even took my sheets. You'll want this.' She handed Annie a scrubbing brush and a bar of pale soap. 'Thank God the looters didn't raid all my stores. They were more interested in food.'

Annie sniffed at the soap – lye. *Oh, well.*

'Burn your clothes when you're done.'

Annie watched Ciara's backside wobble upstairs. She filled a chipped earthenware jug and stood it next to the bath.

Behind the half screen Annie peeled off the filthy dress and let it fall at her feet. Her arms were thin, she traced the indentations of her ribs and sniffed an armpit. *Goodness knows what Rob Stewart thought.* She looked like a drab and stank of her cell.

Annie hadn't luxuriated in a tub for months. She sank beneath the water, determined that any vermin would die in the scum and washed her lank hair first. Once she'd worked up a fine lather and rinsed her hair, she twisted the strands into a knot. Then she set to work with soap and the brush. She scoured her skin till it bloomed pink.

Lord, how glorious to be clean and smell sweet, though perfumed soap would have been my choice.

Ciara produced a towel and a patched dress for her. *At least it's clean even if it's a bilious yellow.* Annie towelled herself dry and Ciara tied her bodice's ribbons. Then Annie and Ciara used buckets to empty and re-fill the bath.

Ciara rubbed a plump fist over her lower spine. 'My poor back. First thing tomorrow I'll hire a scullery maid and servant and have my house scrubbed from top to bottom. I willna rest easy in my bed, until everywhere's clean.'

Annie fed the fire with her old dress and set up the jugs by the bath again.

Ciara disappeared behind the makeshift screen and groaned. 'Thank God for hot water and soap.'

Annie hummed to herself as she ran her fingers through her hair and listened to the sounds of Ciara as she worked soap into her scalp and bristles on her skin. Half an hour later, water splashed from the jugs and the sound of something large rose from the depths. Ciara had finished her ablutions.

Annie pulled the ties of the faded apple-green dress as tight as Ciara's waist would allow and sat at the hearth.

'Goodness, what beautiful hair you have, my dear, it's as if it's on fire.' Ciara produced ebony and tortoiseshell combs from the dresser drawer and gave one to Annie.

'Thank you.' Annie eased the comb through knots and long tangles.

'I'll fetch a mirror. Ciara returned and set it at a drunken angle above the fireplace. 'My hair was chestnut in my youth.' She stared at herself and ran the comb through the thin strands. 'It was much admired, I see it's white now. What will Munro say about his old wife.'

'He'll be grateful you're home and well.' Annie stood beside her and stared at herself looking back. She'd changed, matured and had a worldly look in her eyes. *Where's the naive girl gone?*

'That's kind of you, my dear.' Ciara put down her comb and dished out the broth. 'Careful now, the bowl's hot.'

They sat opposite each other by the fire, cradled bowls in their hands and dipped into the hot liquid with spoons. Warmth radiated throughout Annie's body. She'd forgotten what it was like not to be cold or hungry. *Stewart could cook. An odd skill for a man who seemed made for the outdoors and too large for confined spaces. On the other hand, he's lived most of his life in the Highlands in the worst winters God could throw at man. He's a survivor. Well, so was she.* She went to bed with that thought in her head.

***

Next morning Annie tried to bribe the sentries outside Ciara's house.

A shaggy-browed private laughed at her. 'More than my life's worth, Miss. Captain said you'd have a go at catchin' us out.'

She could have cried with frustration. *I've exchanged one gaol for another. Where has Stewart gone?*

CHAPTER Thirty-eight

August, 1746

Annie endured months of tense waiting and bitten fingernails. Sleep had been difficult as the cries of Culloden's wounded and dying turned dreams into nightmares.

She tried to find out more about Stewart, but his aunt refused to be drawn. 'He'll tell you himself when he returns, if he's a mind and I ken no one called 'M'. Folk I know have proper names.'

Then Ciara's husband, grey-haired Ian, arrived. He'd kissed his wife, enquired who their visitor was and closed his ears to Annie's entreaties to be set free.

'The sentries are here for a reason. We'll wait until Rob returns, as I dinna ken you and I trust his judgement,' Ian Munro muttered. Much to Annie's frustration he tutted at the state of the house and settled back into the household as if he hadn't been away. A series of handymen worked had hard to restore Munro House to its former glory and a cook and servant increased their comfort.

It wasn't until the late evening August sun cast long shadows on the ground that Stewart knocked on the door. She watched his tall figure from the shadows of the hallway. His gaze swept over his aunt and uncle as if he searched for someone. *Her?*

'She's still here,' said his aunt.

'I'm pleased to know it.' He pecked his aunt on the cheek. 'Good evening, Aunt. I'm relieved to see you, Uncle.'

'And I, you, Rob.' His uncle peered at him over his spectacles as they shook hands. 'I canna' thank you enough for all you've done. You've been away for some time.'

'Duty called, I'm sorry I sent no letter.'

'Where've you been?' His aunt dabbed at her eyes with the corner of her apron.

'Dry your tears, Aunt.' He lowered his voice. 'I was ordered to Fort William.'

'And?'

He took them into the sitting room and closed the door. Annie only heard the murmur of their voices. She jumped back when the door opened some minutes later and Ciara led the men out.

Stewart said, 'Both sides have done some terrible things, Aunt.

'Why did you join up, Rob, why?'

'Personal reasons, Aunt. I canna discuss it.'

She put her hand on his arm. 'I'm sorry you're estranged from all you love. I want you to know that we love you.' She looked at her husband. 'Your poor, sweet mother wrote to me. She knew she was dying. She didna blame you for her death, no matter what Johnnie said. Oh yes, he shared his feelings with me.' She kissed him again. 'Johnnie missed you, Rob, and your mother loved you and wanted you to know that.'

Stewart coughed, sighed and kissed her on the forehead. His eyes met Annie's as she moved into the light. His voice sounded steely. 'Get packed, we're leaving.'

'I'm no' one of your soldiers,' said Annie.

'Do it, or I'll have you tied, gagged and carried out.'

Lord he means it. Did I ever know this man?

'Rob,' said his uncle aghast. 'Rona's our guest.'

Guest? She stared at the Munros. *We don't even trust each other. All these months and I've told you nothing. I have to escape.*

'Rob?' His aunt stared in horror at him.

'My apologies, but Miss...Rona and I have much to discuss.'

'Where am I going?' Annie asked as his aunt fussed over her and handed her a warm cloak and hat.

'With me,' he said.

'But Rob...' pleaded his aunt.

'Aunt, allow me to know best.'

'Very well, but there's nought for her to wear, but rags.'

'They'll do.'

'As you wish, Nephew.' His aunt rushed to and fro as she stuffed items in a bundle for Annie and handed it to her.

Annie watched Stewart take his aunt and uncle to one side. 'She's under my protection now, but it's important you never mention her name again or ill might befall us all. Do you understand?'

'But, Rob...' began his aunt.

'Ciara,' said her husband. He stared at her till her gaze dropped.

'I'll curb my tongue, husband.' Ciara kissed Stewart's cheek and hugged Annie. She whispered, 'My nephew will make sure no harm comes to you.' Then his aunt raised her voice, 'Take care my dears,' she said. 'Till we meet again.' She opened the door with one hand, whilst the other grasped the corner of her apron and mopped her eyes.

Stewart hissed in Annie's ear. 'It'll be best if you're silent. I want the guards to think you're a maid. Understand?'

She nodded. *Where's he taking me?*

CHAPTER Thirty-nine

Stewart led her outside. 'Stay alert,' he said to the sentries as he thrust her into a small carriage and four. The horses champed at their bits and pawed the ground. He lowered his voice, gave instructions to the driver, jumped in opposite her and slammed the door. The horses plunged forwards and the coach lurched as they set off at a pace.

Annie found herself thrown from side to side much to the amusement of her fellow passenger. He sat opposite, his long legs set apart and looked at her as if at a withered wallflower.

'You could sit beside me,' Stewart said. He grinned and patted the empty seat beside him.

He's a little too self-assured for my liking. She shook her head. *I haven't forgotten that kiss in gaol, it burned like a brand.* 'Where are we going?' The coach rocked to and fro as they descended a hill.

'To the quayside.'

'Why?'

'All will be revealed in good time.'

'You're infuriating. Why won't you let me go?' Her voice went to a whisper, 'You've done things for the Cause...'

He interrupted, 'I'd be grateful if you dinna repeat that.'

'If you stop the coach and let me out you willna have to listen to me anymore.'

'And you'll do what precisely? Tell all you know and then run back into the precious arms of Charlie and his Cause? It's over, don't you understand? Nought but a Prince's dream. Once the reality of war sunk in he was off. If Charlie's any sense he'll be on the first French ship that dares collect him from these shores.'

'Who are you to speak so disparagingly of a brave man who fought for his rightful crown?'

'Who are you to defend him?' Their voices reached a crescendo as they glared at each other.

He's the most disagreeable and hateful man I've ever come across. She sneaked a look at him. He stared out of the window, his arms folded across his chest, jaw set, mouth in a firm line. *I mustn't think about his mouth or that kiss. He's playing with me, after all, there's 'M'. He probably thinks me opinionated and difficult. I don't care.*

The coach hit the flat again and pitched her forwards into his arms. Each time she tried to release herself, the motion of the coach thrust her against his chest, as the vehicle tipped and bumped its way round corners. Her bonnet dipped over one eye, blue ribbons in disarray.

'There's no need to throw yourself at me,' he said. 'I dare say there'll be time for that in the future.'

'Throw myself?' She shoved the straw bonnet to the top of her head. 'Why you insufferable prig! Do you honestly think I'd - what future?' she asked in alarm.

He laughed at that and refused to say more except to mime that her hat didn't look right. She threw it off in fury and refused to meet his eye. The coach flung her back into her seat again and she hung onto the grip at the side with all her strength. *I don't want to be anywhere near this man, he's too unsettling.* Closing her eyes she planned her escape. *The coach will stop, he'll help me out and I'll run.* Then she looked at Ciara's worn leather shoes which cramped her toes. Perhaps not.

The coach stopped. He attempted to help her out, but she brushed his hand aside and her foot landed in a puddle. The dirty water wet her woollen stockings, shoes and streaked the hem of her dress. She pretended not to notice. He seemed to have a bad fit of coughing at this moment. *I hope he chokes.*

'Well,' said Annie and stared about her. 'Why have you brought me here?' She raised her voice above the hubbub and ducked as a gull swooped overhead. Sailors carried mysterious crates, boxes and bundles on and off ships; merchants talked business and females of the worst kind plied their trade. One, a tiny creature, her dark hair in disarray, stopped in front of Stewart and made a great play as she adjusted her grubby red hose. Shocked to the core, two pink spots flared on Annie's cheeks. Then she remembered Lil.

'Wanna a good time dearie?' The girl elbowed Annie out of the way as she sidled closer to Stewart.

A bairn. Her face a pantomime mask of sooty eyes, chalk cheeks and scarlet lips. *She can't be more than ten years old.*

'On your way before I call the Watch.' A muscle in Stewart's cheek tightened.

'No need to be like that mister, a girl's gotta make a livin.' She gave him a flash of her thigh above a grubby garter and sauntered off.

Stewart took a sudden interest in a lobster pot as Annie watched her thin back disappear into the crowds.

She could be a younger version of Lil. 'Couldn't you...?' Annie started.

'What? Help her in some way? She wouldna thank me for it. See those fellows over there?' Stewart inclined his head towards them.

Annie looked at two broad-shouldered men, dressed in the finest materials. They leaned against a stone wall near a dark wynd which led off the quay. Their watchful eyes scanned the crowds. One stooped to dust the silver buckles on his shoes.

'Yes.'

'They wouldna thank me either.'

'Why ever not?'

Stewart peered at the ships anchored at the quay.

Realisation dawned, 'You mean they...? No. She's a bairn. Well...someone should do something.'

'This isna the time or the place.' Stewart put a firm hand under her elbow and steered her towards the gang plank of a ship. When she held back he smiled and extended his arm to assist her to board. 'You'll come to no harm I assure you, she's called *Virtuous*.'

'*Virtuous*'. Annie tried to evade him, but he reacted too fast for her and lifted her up and ignored her cries. She struggled in his arms. 'Best stop or we'll end up in the drink,' he said and indicated the rush of water below. 'I dinna suppose you can swim. You'd be hauled out like a landed fish.'

She stared at him. *I've been allowed to do many things, but swim in the sea wasn't one of them. I'd have had to undress or be naked. I'd never do that.* She peeped a look at him. *He wouldn't have balked at being naked. Oh no, he'd have rejoiced in it.* She let her imagination strip off his red jacket. Reveal bare shoulders wide enough to overpower her, muscular arms strong enough to hold her with ease as he did now and his breeches...*Goodness, I mustn't think about them.*

He'd crossed the plank and dumped her on the ship's deck.

'So Rob, you've made it, and this must be...?' A tall, thin man in a splendid blue uniform and hat smiled down at her.

'Darling, let me introduce you to Captain Percy Newton, my friend from London I told you about.' Stewart kept one arm round her waist as she squirmed and another on his friend's shoulder.

'Darling? I'm not your d...,' said Annie.

Stewart cut her short. 'Anne's tired. We'll talk later, Percy, if we may? Has my guest arrived?'

Anne? What guest?

'He has. He's below in my cabin with a bottle of my good French brandy for company.' He looked at her stormy face. 'Is all well?'

Stewart dragged her away.

'No second thoughts I hope?' Percy shouted after them.

'Second...?' she began.

Stewart shouted back, 'Not at all, we'll go down and meet with him without delay.' He left his puzzled friend, ignored her questions and half-carried her down some narrow wooden steps to the captain's cabin. He opened the door, ushered her in and closed it behind her.

In front of her stood the plump back of a gentleman who drained the last dregs of brandy from a glass. When he turned, she almost fainted. 'Uncle William.'

'Anne, so what have we here eh?' His brow creased. 'A pretty kettle of fish.' He set his glass on the table. She knew that serious look.

'I can explain...'

'No explanation's necessary my dear, I understand, of course. Captain Stewart's filled me in. You've been working for the Cause.'

Stewart's met with Uncle William? What's been said?

'Take a seat, do. This is difficult, but must be done. Brace yourself my dear, I've sad news. There's no easy way to say this, your father, my dear brother, passed away over a month ago.'

'No. Oh God. No,' she said and sank into the leather chair.

'His heart.'

She remembered how tired he'd been and how loving. Instead of staying by his side in his last years, she'd put the Cause first. Her letters had been cruel. Now she'd never see him again. She'd never forgive herself.

'Tried to contact you at the Mountjoy's, when told you weren't there, in fact had not been there for over a year, the family were out of their minds with worry.'

Distant aunts and cousins who'd never visited for years.

'Can you imagine our joy and horror when Captain Stewart informed us of your whereabouts and gave us his news about your...doings? Understood of course, your father lost so much in the 1715 rebellion, but this charade canna go on. You do realise that don't you?' He lowered his voice. 'Any hint of treachery or scandal could mean ruin for the whole family. You must extricate us at once.'

'But, Uncle...'

He hammered his fist on the table and his glass quivered. 'You will listen.' He softened his tone. 'I loved your father Anne, he was my youngest brother, but far too lax, gave you unseemly ideas for a woman and titled lady.'

'Uncle...'

'I will have my say.' He silenced her with a raised hand. 'You said you were staying with the Mountjoys. Your father even received letters for months as if from there. If Stewart hadn't alerted me to your deceit...' He lowered his voice to a whisper,' How could you fall for Lord Alistair's plans? The man's a fool and will meet his just reward from the English Crown when they catch him, it'll mean the axe.'

Shocked, Anne said nothing. Her father's death began to sink in, the first tear fell.

His voice softened. 'Obvious to me you're in need of a man's guidance.'

'What?' Anne started to protest.

He wagged a ringed finger at her. 'It's a man's world Anne, and you're but twenty, too young to know the wiles of men. As your legal guardian I've made a decision and willna be swayed from it, not by tears or hysterics.' He wagged his forefinger at her. 'I've agreed to Stewart's suggestion. You'll be married to him tonight on board this ship.'

'What?' She shrieked. 'Are you mad? This man *jilted* me. There's someone he...'M.'

'Put it out of your mind. Stewart has explained there were difficult circumstances. He's quite prepared to marry you now. I've accepted his apologies for you.'

'You...? Uncle, I canna marry him. Father would have...'

'Realised there's no alternative. The family canna' have you running around the country like a hoyden consorting with...rebels. Stewart's on the winning side. Marry him or, much as it pains me to do it, I'll cut you off.'

'You dinna mean it?' *I've never thought about money, Father looked after that. I haven't a penny to my name. Uncle William can do as he likes, but many in my set have already treated me as ruined because of Stewart's rejection and believe me a Whig. And Stewart only wants to marry me now to save his neck, so I can't betray him.*

'I can and will,' said Uncle William. 'Take the sensible course my dear. He's young, handsome and willing to take you on.'

'Take me on?' Her voice rose to an outraged shriek. *I want Rob Stewart's head on a pike.* 'I hate the man.'

There was a light tap at the door and it swung open. 'Excuse me for disturbing you, I think perhaps if I...?'

Stewart. What a conniving, scheming, redcoat he is.

'Good idea sir,' said her uncle. 'I'm sure she'll see sense.' He swept out of the cabin and left her and Stewart alone.

She turned from him and stared out of the porthole at the silver-net sea. *Sense?*

Behind her the silence went on and on.

CHAPTER Forty

'Ow.' Rob rubbed his forehead. He'd only taken one step into the cabin. Damn the low beam. He coughed. 'May I offer you my sincere condolences, Lady Anne?' Disconcerted she forced him to speak to her back.

Her slender frame became rigid. She didn't turn. 'How did you find out who I am?'

'Easy enough. I asked some fellow Scottish officers. They told me of a beautiful young, Jacobite lady they'd heard about, who lived in the north-east Highlands and had become estranged from her father. It didna take them long to come up with your description and name. Your real speech gave you away of course. I willna deny it was a...shock.'

She whirled round and glared at him. Her hair seemed on fire, her green eyes sparked a warning.

He thought those eyes could drive a man to ruination. 'After Fort William, I visited Kerbilly. Your uncle, very...civil, showed me round.'

'Oh.' Her fingers tapped on the desk.

'The painting on the staircase is a very good likeness if I may say so, though it does not do you justice.'

'She's my mother.' Her face clouded.

'Ah.' He knew he had to tread carefully, after all, she was newly bereaved.

'So you've been visiting Uncle William for the last week?'

'Yes, I introduced myself to him. I'm pleased to say we're of one mind.'

Her fingers stopped. 'That we should marry?'

'That you're in grave danger and urgent need of protection.'

'And you need my silence about your...activities.' Her eyes sparked at him again.

'As you need mine about yours.' He paused. 'We should marry.'

She gave him a wry smile. 'I'm obliged to you for your *second* offer of marriage sir, but this time I'm the one saying, I think not.'

'You're not still upset over...?'

'Being jilted? Of course I'm...' She bit her lip. 'Good God why would you think that?'

'There were extenuating circumstances.'

'Really?' She raised her eyebrows.

'Annie, Lady Anne, you really have no choice. Do you see the redcoats on the quay?' Her eyes followed his outstretched hand and looked out of the porthole. Several soldiers stood on guard.

He steeled himself for the lie. 'They're there to ensure you dinna escape. If you refuse to become my wife, I'll simply order them to arrest you. They'll be informed you've gone mad. Any ravings about me will be dismissed out of hand.' He paused to let his words register. 'Have you visited an asylum? Inverness gaol doesna compare.'

She stared round-eyed at him, then strode forwards her hands clenched. 'You swine, you wouldna. Uncle William...'

'Is of the same mind. He understands what's at stake here.'

'Villain. How can you do this?'

'Easily. Now what's your answer?'

'I...I...Damn you, Stewart.' She whirled round and stared out of the window.

'I'll take that as a yes shall I? The ceremony takes place this evening. I took it upon myself to bring some of your clothes from Kerbilly. They're in the trunks by the desk. I'll leave you to make yourself ready.'

He hesitated before he left, noted the beam and ducked.

***

She collapsed into the Captain's chair as he closed the door. *How has it come to this? My poor father, gentle and as mild a man one could care to meet - dead.* She buried her head in her hands as tears pricked at her eyes. *Dead. The word seems hollow, full of emptiness and no laughter. Dead. Some called him misguided over the 1715, others steadfast in the face of adversity. He almost beggared himself because of the Jacobite Cause, then he turned his back on it. Had he been right? After all, the Jacobites had lost again.*

She remembered weekend invitations, hunting parties and grand balls full of rich, eligible young men. *I spurned all offers of marriage. Then Father said I'd forced his hand; that we'd be ruined unless I made a good marriage. Told me he'd agreed to my union with Stewart, a man I'd never met. Father announced it despite my protests. By the time I reconciled myself to it, Stewart's letter had arrived.*

Now I'm caught in a skein of my own making; forced once again into a marriage with the same man who has proved himself utterly despicable. He hasn't even explained why he jilted me or about 'M'. It's too much. I've been free of any restraints for the past year, made my own decisions and done what I've wanted. Hot tears formed, but she brushed them away. *There's nothing I can do. Or is there?* She rushed to the window, opened it and looked out. The rush of cold air and the lap of the water against the ship warned her of the dangers of the river.

Sometime later, someone rapped on the door. 'Come in.' She sniffed.

***

'Ow. Blast these low ceilings.' Stewart put his hand to his forehead.

Anne smiled. 'Do mind the beam, Captain.'

He scowled at her. This marriage wouldn't work, they loathed each other, but what choice did he have?

'Bring her in,' he ordered those behind him. Something had ticked away at the back of his skull ever since he'd seen the bairn on the quay. He couldn't rid himself of her image or the fact she reminded him of poor Lil.

Two redcoats, one with crooked teeth, the other with jug ears pulled and pushed the child into the room. The private with crooked teeth had his hand over her mouth. She bit him.

'Ow.'

She aimed her boot at Jug Ear's knee.

'Aagh.'

They both released her.

'Grab the brat,' yelled Crooked Teeth.

'You little b...beggin' you pardon Miss, sir,' said Jug Ears in the scuffle.

The child howled and ran to Anne. 'Save me, please save me from the horrible soldiers.' She peered out from behind Anne's skirts.

'It's the bairn from the quayside.' Anne's colour flared as she turned on Stewart. 'Is this a favourite pastime of yours, Captain Stewart? You burst into a lady's chamber unannounced and manhandle bairns?' She patted the tearful child's thin shoulder blades as she clung to her.

Thunderation.

Crooked Teeth grinned and Jug Ears chuckled.

Hell's teeth, couldn't he do anything right for this damned woman? 'Attention!' he roared. In an instant the privates became upright. He turned to Anne. 'This is your...er, our...ward, she'll help you to get ready.'

'Ward? But she...she's...' Anne flashed him a look of horror.

'Just say the word and I'll throw her back to those b.......men,' he snapped.

'But...'

'Ere don't I 'ave a say?' asked the girl as she tugged his sleeve.

'She cost me a month's pay,' said Rob. 'Now do you want her or no?'

Anne's eyes widened in shock. 'I want her.'

'Leave us,' he ordered the privates.

He waited till the door closed behind the soldiers and indicated the open window. 'And don't you two get any damn silly ideas about swimming ashore. I've men on deck with orders to shoot strange fish in the river. Anne, I expect you ready for our wedding by eight tonight. Your servant.' He ducked his head a little more than he needed to before he closed the door.

CHAPTER Forty-one

He's cold and boorish and given me little choice. Damned if I'll go to my wedding looking like a fish wife. If I have to marry Stewart, then I should look my best, but how? And then there's this little bairn, staring at me with large, trusting eyes. As if I know what to do with her. Never had a mother, just a series of nannies. What can I say to the child when we're strangers to each other? Not only that, this girl's been in bad company. Why did Stewart rescue her from the life of a drab? Anne had always regarded him as insensitive because of that damned letter. Then she remembered how he'd rescued her on Newcastle quay, the first time they'd met and how he'd been kind to Lil. *Of course, he probably regarded Annie as a lower class woman, someone to seduce and forget.*

The little girl tugged at her hand. 'I'm hungry.'

'Are you darling? Then you shall have this.' She offered her a rosy apple from a bowl. The girl grabbed and bit into it with no pause until her cheeks ballooned like pouches. She wiped her lips with a grubby sleeve. 'Luvely.'

Goodness, she's starving. 'Sweetheart, I'm Lady Anne, what's your name?'

'They calls me Duch, short for Duchess.' She hiccupped and her brown eyes overflowed.

'Oh, dear. I see. Well, dry your tears. I think, perhaps in your new position with me...us, you ought to be called...Dulcie. What do you think?'

The girl lifted her torn hem and swept it across her face. Dunno. I've always been called Duch.'

Oh dear. 'Well, shall we try Dulcie and see how we get on?'

'Alright.'

'Good, girl and as you're now my ward, I need your help get ready for my wedding.'

'Who you marryin'?'
'The Captain, the man that...brought you to me.'
'He's a temper on him.'
'Mmm. Will you help me?'
'Aye.'
'Yes, Lady Anne.'
'Yes, Lady Anne,' the girl repeated wide-eyed.
'Let's wash. We'll help each other, you first.' Anne poured water from a china jug into a basin. As the grime and makeup came off she realised that Dulcie had bruises from head to toe. 'Darling, how did you hurt yourself so badly?'
'A man on the quay beat me.'
Anne stared at her. *This bairn needs a loving home.* She kissed her cheek and held the girl's thin face in her hands. 'No one will ever beat you again. I promise. Now let me wash your hair.' As she towelled it dry, she realised what she'd thought brown, flaxen. She plaited the thick strands so it lay down Dulcie's back.
'You sit and I'll see what I can find in my trunks,' said Anne.
She flung them open and gasped as Dulcie's eyes shone at the colourful array of silks, satins and French lace from her original wedding trousseau. She'd given them to Joan, her maid, who must have packed them away. *Dear Joan.* She'd tucked Anne's blue jewel case which contained her mother's pearl necklace, ear bobs and bracelet underneath the finery.
Anne hugged the case to her. *I'd such hopes before Rob Stewart jilted me. Do I want to be harnessed to a man who carelessly threw me aside with no thought to the consequences? Has he any idea of my humiliation? Does he even care?*
She'd never forget how neighbours and so-called friends had nudged each other and spoken behind their hands or how invitations to balls and supper parties had faded away. It was as if she'd done something wrong, something of which she should be ashamed. Society had turned its back on her and she'd become a

pariah. *That's why the offer to work for the Cause came as a sweet release. Has Stewart any idea what he did? Does he even think of it?* Anne remembered the frustrations and bitter tears she'd wept at that time. She wondered if Stewart realised he had been the catalyst, the reason she'd agreed to spy for Glenroy. *Lord, there'll be no joy in this marriage and who's the mysterious 'M'?* Time ticked away.

She caught sight of a wild creature in the mirror. Sunlight streamed through the porthole, informed her of what Mrs. Munro's dim light and candles had not. She shrieked, 'My hair.' The moisture in the air had turned it into a red fur ball. Not only that, but she'd lived in the open air for months. She'd freckles and a tanned skin like a crofter's daughter.

'Don't worry I'm used to turnin' bird's nest into silk strands,' said Dulcie. 'Maggie taught me how.'

'Maggie?' Anne sat and handed Dulcie a brush.

'Looked after all the girls, she'd a heavy hand, but were alright with me. I used to do this for all the doxies, even the ugly ones, till Maggie...left. ' The child teased out tangles and pinned up Anne's hair, she left just a few curls lying on Anne's shoulder. Dulcie surveyed her work hands on slight hips. 'What do you think?'

Anne turned her head this way and that. The style suited her. *This bairn's more dextrous than I thought.* 'Thank you, it's lovely.'

'That's alright then.' Dulcie sat on a chair and swung her legs.

How will I civilize this child so she'll be accepted in friends' drawing rooms? Anne decided she didn't care what supposed friends thought. Her true friends would be kind. 'Light the lanterns would you?'

Dulcie took a spill and did so.

'Help me, will you, darling?' said Anne as she climbed into the cream and gold gown designed to give just a hint of decolletage. The sleeves lay low on the shoulders. Dulcie tied her laces. The silk clung to every curve, cut by a French couturier to seduce the man she married. *If only my parents were alive.* Tears formed, but she pushed her emotions back where they'd come from. *I'll have time to grieve after this mockery of a wedding.* The pearl earbobs and necklace twinkled in the lanterns' flames.

Dulcie stared, her large brown eyes fringed with long eyelashes. 'You looks bootiful, better than any of the trollops on the quay. Can I come to your weddin' too?'

Trollops? Oh, dear. The bairn needs to be educated. How to begin?

A fist knocked at the door, a pause and a male voice, 'Captain Stewart sends his regards, Lady Anne, and asks if you're ready to be escorted on deck?'

'Wait.' She knelt beside Dulcie. 'Darling, I'd like you to be a bridesmaid at my wedding, you can wear this.' Anne held up a silver gown. 'It's too big, but I'm sure we can make the necessary adjustments.'

'What me? It's...luvely.'

Now what would Joan do?

Anne stood Dulcie in front of a mirror which hung on the back of the wardrobe.

To Dulcie's delight, Anne pinned and tucked the dress into soft, folds. 'I looks like a princess and you looks like a queen.'

Anne had not chosen the setting and was as far from the place she'd planned to marry as Inverness was to Arabia, or so it seemed. She'd wanted to be married in her local church with her father, relatives and friends in attendance.

She lifted her head and led Dulcie out of the cabin and up the wooden steps to *Virtuous'* deck. Night dropped like a black curtain with studded diamonds. Lanterns swayed and illuminated groups of marines and sailors who wore shirts, short-waisted jackets and rolled up trousers. Anne held back in the shadows, though she sensed the impatience of the private behind her. She willed herself to enter the small circle of men who stood by the mast.

Perhaps the moon lit the gold threads on Anne's dress. One bearded sailor noticed Anne and Dulcie, he nudged another and they all sprang to attention. Anne supposed the leather buckets at their feet, were filled with sand in case of fire. The salt-laden breeze caressed Anne's cheeks as she listened to the repetitive slap and gurgle of water on the hull and the gentle tap-tap-tapping of wind-song in the rigging.

Men stared at her as an expectant hush fell over the deck.

Captain Newton stood centre deck and tapped his watch. Stewart on his left, had his back turned in deep discussion with her uncle.

The private who lead Anne and Dulcie on deck coughed. Captain Newton smiled and her uncle beamed as he came towards her. *Well, he's more than eager to get rid of his troublesome niece linked to the recent rebellion against the crown.* Stewart stared, though his face gave nothing away as Anne's uncle led her to stand beside him. She noticed, with some satisfaction a red mark on Stewart's forehead from his recent brush with the beam in her cabin. *I really need to be less childish.*

Captain Newton began, 'Dearly beloved we are gathered together in the sight of God to join this man and this woman in holy matrimony...' The ceremony droned on.

'Do you take this woman...?'

Stewart stared at her for a long time. 'I do,' he said a last.

'Do you take this man...?' Anne turned to look at Uncle William who'd found something interesting on the quay to look at. She stared at Stewart even longer and then said, 'I do.'

When Stewart placed the gold wedding band on the tip of her finger, he held it there as if undecided. Anne felt a tremor of fear. *Not again.* The watching audience held their collective breath. She stared at him, willed him to look at her. *You want this sham of a wedding, don't you? Or are you thinking of 'M'?* His blue eyes met hers for a few seconds, just long enough for her to note the sweep and curl of each black lash, then seconds later he pushed the ring into place.

'You may kiss the bride.'

Stewart drew her to him. The strength in his arms gave her no opportunity to pull away. His mouth, hot, seared hers in search of a response. She acted out her role. She'd decided she didn't love him, so how could she respond like a sweetheart would? He must have sensed her reticence as he let her go without a look.

'That were a smacker,' said Dulcie with relish.

The sailors roared, stamped their feet and hats flew high in the air.

'Well done. Well done.' Her uncle briskly kissed her and shook Stewart's hand.

'May I propose a toast?' said Captain Newton, 'To the bride and groom.' They all raised their tankards and drained the watered rum in one. Food came on wooden trays. Dulcie piled mutton, cheese and bread in her arms and found a corner of the deck to stuff food in her mouth.

Anne shook her head. *What am I going to do with the bairn?*

Flutes, whistles and accordions appeared and the sailors demanded that they stayed a while and watched their hornpipes. In truth, Anne was grateful. Her mind closed down, numbed by the unexpected news of Father's death and this sham of a wedding. Her father, always there to pick her up when she fell, but she hadn't been there for him.

A handsome man in his youth, he'd kept his slim physique, but before she'd left his clothes had hung on him and he'd been breathless. She hadn't realised he'd been ill. Invincible, is how she'd thought of him. Perhaps she hadn't wanted to notice the lines of pain etched on his face. She'd passed them off as signs of old age. He'd swept her concerns aside with a firm, 'I'll be better soon.' She'd believed him and now he was gone. Tears pricked at the corner of her eyes. She'd miss him and his beloved pipe as familiar as the smell of Virginia tobacco.

'Come.' Stewart, put his hand on her arm. 'You appear weary. You, girl, come with us.'

'My name's Duch...er Dulcie.' She swayed her slight hips from side to side and gripped Anne's hand.

'A good night, to the newly-weds,' shouted a drunken sailor. The cry rang out all over the deck and cheers followed them below deck.

The men on deck shouted ribald comments as they went below.

Dear Lord, I have to be intimate with this man. Would he be demanding, hurt me?

'My apologies.' Stewart stood at their cabin door. 'I meant for us to leave quietly and without fuss. I'll retire to your uncle's cabin. I think it best that we ken each other before we begin our life together as...er...husband and wife. I wish you both a good night.' He kissed Anne's hand, bowed and left them at the door.

What kind of man have I married? Is it 'M', will she always lie between us? Anne cried herself to sleep. Whether it was for the loss of her father or her marriage, she didn't know. At some time in the night Dulcie moved closer and snuggled into the circle of her arms. They slept like new born babes.

Anne woke at first light. The first sound: the drum of bare feet on the deck above The second: a sea shanty, *'Heave away, haul away...'* and the third? The grate of a metal chain dragged across the deck. Dulcie stirred, and her eyelids fluttered. Perhaps she thought it a dream as the ship rocked a little. Anne tucked the child's arm beneath the covers and fell asleep again beside her.

***

Bright sunlight streamed through the porthole and onto Anne's face. Excited shouts of men on deck came to her. The cabin tipped up and down as Dulcie lay flushed and asleep.

Anne scrambled out of the bunk to look out of the porthole – they were at sea and bound for Lord knows where.

She washed and dressed, grabbing for hand holds as the ship tipped and swayed. She put the last brush stroke to her hair when a light knock sounded at the door.

CHAPTER Forty-two

'Come in.'

Rob started to walk forward into the room, eyed the beam, gave a wry smile and ducked his head. He'd noted a red weal on his forehead when he shaved that morning. He wasn't a vain man, but wanted to be presentable to his new wife. 'Good morning...Anne, I've brought you both some food. I thought you might be hungry.' He lurched his way across the room. No mean feat when he considered the angle of the cabin and the swell of the sea. 'Duch...Dulcie is still asleep I see,' he whispered and indicated the child and her snores.

Their eyes met as she nodded, then her face reddened and she turned away.

Hell's teeth, what had he said? 'Her name...Duch...makes it seem like see she aspires to better things?'

'The darling has been...misused, beaten.'

'The men on the quayside.'

'I suppose so. It will take time and care...'

'And love.' He studied her green eyes and enjoyed the animation in her face and that generous mouth with the beauty spot above.

She seemed flustered. 'Yes and love, of course love. She needs to become accustomed to the gentler ways of society. What time is it, Captain?'

'Midday, your uncle disembarked, business in Inverness.'

She ignored him and followed the heaped tray as if tied to it by a rope.

He placed it on a table with a lip which ran round it. 'I thought it best no one should disturb you. Was I correct in that assumption?'

She sat at the table fixated by the thick slices of ham and fried eggs. 'Yes.' She tore a fresh baked loaf in two and sniffed at it. 'Mmmm.' The aroma made her stomach growl. She looked shamefaced. 'I'm ravenous.' She buttered the bread and popped it into her mouth.

'I've noticed. The sea air perhaps?' He poured red wine from a broad decanter into a glass and smiled.

'Where are we going? You didna mention a journey by sea.'

'It's a surprise and one I hope you'll like.'

'Mmm. We'll see,' she said.

'Perhaps you'll come up on deck once you've finished your repast.' Was this her way to make the most of our bad bargain? He left.

The deck teamed with sailors. One sat cross-legged and mended sails, another spliced hemp ropes and a third scrubbed the deck. White sails billowed with the wind and pushed *Virtuous* like an elegant swan through the blue sea. Rob counted twenty-two. Perched high in the rigging sailors followed the shouts of the captain and either hauled in sails or let them out. The three oak masts creaked and groaned as the decks heaved from side to side in the swell and salt-spray flew in the air. Herring gulls circled above, rode on air currents and squawked as the cook tipped a basin of slops overboard. The birds dived to collect a tasty delicacy and then rested on the waves.

Rob stood alongside Captain Newton on the fore deck and rode the swell of the sea. 'Congratulations on your first command, Percy.'

'Thank you. She's smaller and faster than the ships-of-the-line. We're used for patrolling, messenger and escort duties. Caught some smugglers on the west coast and of course we're looking for Frenchies who might have the Pretender aboard. They won't be able to outrace us...Suppose you had a bad time of it at Culloden.'

'It wasna the battle, so much as what we did to them afterwards,' said Rob looking out to sea.

'They're rebels, Rob.'

'They fought for a cause.' Rob turned to look at Percy. He'd never understand. 'At Prestonpans they looked after our wounded, we butchered theirs at Culloden.'

'Dear God.' Percy strained his neck to check no one overheard. 'Keep your voice down. You're not feeling sorry for them, are you?'

Rob stared out to sea. He'd been right, his friend would never understand. 'When will we arrive, Percy?'

'In a couple of hours.' Percy looked around him. 'Excuse me, I must check our course.'

Rob nodded.

**

Anne, hidden by rigging, overheard the men's conversation. It felt as if the whole world searched for the Prince and she was no longer in a position to help him. She also thought of Philippe and the danger he might be in. *Did Stewart feel sorry for the Jacobite wounded at Culloden?* Not wishing to disturb the two men she made a drunken crossing to a handrail and held on for dear life.

Gusts of wind whipped at her hat and threatened to untie the green ribbons and carry it off. She pressed her hand to its silken crown to keep it in place. As if thwarted, the wild flurries unpinned her hair so it streamed like a red banner behind her. A clean smell of salt lay on the wind which buffeted her face.

'So, what do you think of *Virtuous?*' Stewart's tall figure stood beside her.

'I love her,' she admitted. 'I never realised one could feel so free. It's as if we've taken flight.'

'Yes.' he agreed. 'Anne I...'

'Land, land ho!' The shout came from a small boy perched in the crow's nest. They followed the line of his outstretched arm.

'Where are we?' She squinted at the misty haze which covered the land.

'I'm surprised you dinna recognise it.'

She looked again and narrowed her eyes. The mist thinned and cleared. She saw a headland with its church on the point, the soft round curve of a sandy bay and above it, nestled in the green glen, she saw Kerbilly House.

The feather touch of a child's hand sought hers. Dulcie pushed in between Stewart and her. The child stared up at them with large brown eyes.

'Good morning, darling,' said Anne.

'Morning, poppet,' said Stewart.

They spoke in unison. He looked startled and she blushed.

'Mornin',' said Dulcie.

'Anne, I thought, perhaps you might like to spend the first weeks of our marriage in the place that you feel most secure and comfortable,' he said.

'I...' tears pricked her eyes and something choked off her voice. She stared ahead. His thoughtfulness made her speechless. *If only he'd be more open with me, explain...*

CHAPTER Forty-three

Rob breathed in the warm air from the land. It smelt of rich loam and cattle. Had he done the right thing? Should he have brought Anne home with all its childhood memories and her father only recently buried? She'd said little to let him know her feelings. He sighed.

The anchor chain clanked its release as it plunged into the waves froth below.

'See,' said Anne. She stood behind Dulcie and pointed to the land. 'How the path jinks its way up the cliffs and parts at the top, how the right branch leads to St. Cuthbert's church and the left to that house, well that's our home Kerbilly.'

'Our home?' Dulcie looked at her in wonderment.

'Yes, darling, home.' Anne squeezed Dulcie's hand. 'I want you to love it as much as I do.'

Rob stood alone. He didn't know how to draw closer to them both. If only he'd managed to tell her about Morag, but the moment had been lost.

The servants must have been warned of their arrival, for smoke curled from the chimneys in welcome. Rob blessed Uncle William for his forethought, it had to be him who'd made arrangements for them. At least the rooms would be warm and the beds aired.

'All ashore, who's going ashore.' Percy grinned as he held out his hand.

Rob shook it.

'I wish you both well in your marriage.' Percy kissed Anne's fingers.

'Thank you,' she said with a quick smile, then watched the land.

Percy turned to Dulcie and tipped his hat. 'And as for you, little Miss, a fair wind and safe destination.'

Dulcie giggled. 'Thank you, Captain. I wish you as many doxies as you can handle when you're in port.'

Rob gulped and Anne's eyes became white lily pads.

Percy's ears went pink, then red. 'Right. Ahem. I think I'll see to my ship. A few repairs, a ripped sail, ropes that sort of thing.'

Rob intervened as if Dulcie's words had not been spoken. 'I canna thank you enough Percy, if there's any good turn I can do you, you've only to ask.' He made a mental note, to begin Dulcie's education at once.

Percy recovered his composure. 'My pleasure.'

'Where do you sail now?'

'North and then west seeking the Pretender.'

Rob saw Anne's back become rigid and then relax as if she'd accepted there was little she could do for the Cause now.

Rob guided his new family down a rope ladder into an unstable longboat. He went first before Ann and Dulcie. He readied himself for any faints or hysteria that might occur. Much to his amazement Anne looked over the side once and shook off the poor sailor who tried to assist her as she climbed over the rail. With a great flurry of white petticoats, she grabbed the ladder and descended at such a rapid rate of knots, he had to hurry into the long boat. He steadied himself and glimpsed a pair of slim ankles and long, slender legs. The sailors let out a cheer and Anne smiled and waved at them.

She sat, ignored Rob and waited for an excited Dulcie to arrive in the arms of a sailor. Rob couldn't see Anne's face as she looked towards the land. He wondered what she thought as they rowed towards the shore. Had she regrets about spying for the Cause? She whispered a few words to Dulcie who nodded her head.

The tide came in which helped the prow beach. He didn't ask Anne if he could lift her, light as a feather through the surf, he just did it. Took it as his right. She seemed outraged, but Rob pretended to stumble. Her arms flew round his neck and brought her face close to his. He studied her wide eyes, freckled nose and the beauty spot at his leisure.

Anne's words brought him back to his senses. She said, 'We're on dry land unless you intend carrying me up the cliff path, Captain?'

He gave her a wry smile, deposited her on the sand and turned to collect Dulcie. He waded back through the surf as Anne raced up the cliff path. Damn. 'Take the child and our bags to the house,' he said and sprinted after Anne, embarrassed to have lost his bride so early in their marriage.

She didn't make her way to the house as he expected. She hurried along a well-worn path, to the only building on the headland, a church with a bell tower enclosed by a low stone wall. Of course her father's grave. She'd had no time to say goodbye or grieve. Good she did it now. He thought it best to let her pay her last respects alone. He left her and turned to Kerbilly to lead Dulcie to her new home. A handful of sailors tramped behind and carried their trunks up the cliff path.

The house still had a worn out look to it, as if it had seen too many years without proper care and attention. Johnstone, his thin face, dour, leaned on a stick at the front door as Rob marched along the drive.

The Butler bowed. 'Captain Stewart, on behalf of the servants, may I offer you our best wishes on your marriage and a welcome to your new home.'

'Thank you, Johnstone, it's good to see you again. I hope, despite all that has happened, the household will carry on as before.'

Johnstone's face creased into a smile. 'Thank you, sir. There may be a few difficulties, some lost their men, but I've briefed everyone. In times like these one has to be pragmatic.'

'Just so,' said Rob. 'Your leg?'

Johnstone rubbed his thigh. 'An old wound from the...' He stared at Rob. 'Just tells me when the weather's turning bad.'

Rob nodded. Better not to ask questions. 'I know you got on well with Lord Kerbilly, I hope we also can work together to ensure the happiness of the household?'

'I'm sure we can, sir. And Lady Anne, sir? May I enquire as to how she's bearing up?'

'As you'd expect, with fortitude. She's at the churchyard, send her maid to escort her home when she's finished, will you?'

'Of course, sir.'

'You'll show these sailors where to stow our baggage?'

'Of course, sir. And this is...' He indicated Dulcie with a wave of his hand.

'Our...ward, Duch...er Dulcie'

'Ward sir?' Johnstone looked at the child as if he'd just found a spider in the pantry.

'Aye, ward. Ensure a bedroom's made ready.'

'Certainly, sir. I've of course had the master bedroom prepared for you and Lady Anne. It has the finest views of the sea.'

'My thanks.' Oh God, they weren't...hadn't...as man and wife yet. Rob looked round the hall a little lost.

'May I suggest the library, sir and some tea? We have a little left, precious as it is.' Johnstone pointed to the right. 'At this time in the morning the light is particularly restful, and the chairs the most comfortable in the house. It was Lord Kerbilly's favourite room and faces east.' Johnstone's movement revealed a split under the arm of his moth-eaten uniform and made Rob decide he'd replace it.

As Johnstone turned to go, Rob said, 'Thank you Johnstone and...er...I'd be grateful if you'd have another bedroom made ready...for...any guests...we may have.'

'Sir.'

Rob admired the central oak staircase and how it rose and then parted in a fine sweep. The portrait of Anne's mother, like her daughter, gazed down at him from the landing. Her eyes seemed to follow him with some amusement, as he wandered into the library.

The tang of peat and tobacco with the musty scent of old parchment, reminders of the house's former owner, Anne's father, greeted him. An avid reader by the looks of it as bookcases ran from ceiling to floor. Rob grunted his approval.

The view from the window: a golden flourish of the bay and a vast expanse of blue-white surf. He could just make out *Virtuous* on the horizon, white sails puffed out, flags and pennants flying. She headed north.

Rob read the titles of the volumes on the shelves. Perhaps he'd find something of the Lord of Kerbilly and discover more of the daughter, in his taste in literature. Rob discovered an eclectic mix of texts which covered everything from history to mathematics.

The Illiad with its crimson spine and gilt letters, a particular favourite of Rob's. He took it off the shelf and chose a comfortable, stuffed chair which faced the window. On the side table to his right, he found a pair of silver spectacles, a snuff box, a jar of Virginia tobacco and a clay pipe. He sat in what he felt must have been Lord Kerbilly's favourite armchair with the elderly gentleman's necessities to hand. Rob browsed through the book.

'Johnstone told me the scullery weren't my place and to come in 'ere.' Dulcie peered round the door. 'Look at all these books. I didn't know there was so many in the whole world. Where's Lady Anne?'

Damn. He'd forgotten the child, been a bachelor too long and needed to buck up his ideas.

'She's...got other things to do, poppet. Sit and keep me company.'

A light knock at the door disturbed them. 'Yes?'

Johnstone entered carrying a tray. 'Your tea sir, I brought an extra cup for...Miss Dulcie.'

'Who's she?' Dulcie asked and stood beside the butler.

Rob stared at her and Johnstone raised an eyebrow.

'Cook asked whether you'd like some soup,' said Johnstone.

'That would be just the thing, thank you, when Lady...my wife returns.'

'Sir.' Johnstone poured the tea and began to leave.

'A moment.' Rob handed him a watch. 'Must have fallen from your waistcoat.'

Dulcie looked at the ceiling.

'Sir.' Johnstone eyed his watch, Dulcie and then left.

Rob wagged his finger at Dulcie. 'We dinna take things that dinna belong to us. Do you understand?'

'If you says so.' She grabbed a china cup, held it between two hands and slurped as she drank it in one gulp. Then she wiped her sleeve across her mouth, burped and announced, 'That were a funny taste, I prefers ale.'

Rob sighed. He made a mental note to inform Anne she'd have her work cut out to teach Dulcie how things were done. He settled to his book as Dulcie moved from the window, to the shelves and back again. Round and round she walked.

He put down *The Illiad*. 'Come, poppet.' He patted the cushion of a partner chair to his. 'Choose a book, sit and read.'

She went along the shelves and trailed her forefinger across the volumes. A pause. She picked one up, put it down. Repeated the performance again and again. She must have sensed his impatience when she picked a small book and plumped herself beside him. She held the book upside down and looked at it with studied concentration. The pink tip of her tongue slid out of her rosebud mouth as she bent her head from one side and then to the other as if this would help.

Of course he should have known. A waif from the Inverness quay, it was to be expected. Something would indeed have to be done. He made another mental note for Anne.

'Tell you what - why not listen to this story I've found?'

'Oh yes.' She beamed at him and sat, mouth open, as he read.

It wasn't until Dulcie gave a little shriek as the room darkened and the huge window rattled with the incessant beat of rain that he realised a storm raged outside. Thunderous clouds had gathered overhead and the wind howled. Anne would be soaked.

CHAPTER Forty-four

Rob sprang up and looked out of the window towards the church. Dulcie stood beside him and he felt her put her little hand in his. He squeezed her fingers as Anne, with a maid behind her, struggled to open the garden gate. Anne had one hand on her bonnet, whilst the other fought a cloak which threatened to fly away at one moment or wrap itself round her legs at another.

He rang the brass bell on the marble fireplace. The glow from the fire leapt over sculpted vines, figures and Greek urns. Very modern he thought.

'Sir,' said Johnstone.

'Make sure my wife is brought straight here and bring the soup when it's ready,' Rob said.

Anne arrived in a flurry of wet skirts, her face glowed from the wind and rain. She avoided his concerned gaze and headed for the fireplace where she rubbed her hands together as Dulcie clung to her. 'The weather changed so quickly. It's what I love about it. The wind's so strong. Oh Johnstone, you've brought soup, you shouldna.'

Johnstone stopped and looked from one to the other.

'I told him to,' said Rob. 'I thought it would warm you.'

'Leave it.' They both spoke at once.

Anne coloured and looked at her hands.

'If there's nothing else?' Johnstone limped out of the room.

'Eat.' Rob tried to fill the silence. 'No point in letting good food get cold.'

'Is everything an order with you, Captain?' she asked. 'We're not your raw recruits you know.' Nose in the air, she sat beside Dulcie and left Rob to sit at the head.

'Don't yous two like each other?' asked Dulcie.

Anne looked at the ceiling whilst Rob studied the carpet.

He'd never felt less in charge than during this uneasy meal. 'The soup seems salty,' he said and put down his spoon.

'Does it?' said Anne and tasted hers again. 'What salt?'

It didn't seem to affect Dulcie's appetite as she clinked her spoon against her china bowl as she ate. Rob winced and Anne flushed.

'If you'll excuse us,' Anne rose as she said, 'we'll retire now. I've just learned how a member of my...our household has suffered at the hands of redcoats.'

Rob leant forward in his chair. 'Explain yourself, Madam.'

Anne's face paled and she looked at her hands. 'My maid, Joan, was going to be married in June, but her fiancé, Angus, died at Culloden. He was too...young.'

'They were all too young on both sides.'

She flicked a look at him.

Had he surprised her?

'As you say. I need to ensure the...beds are properly aired.'

'I'll be in the guest room.' Rob added, 'until we ken each other a little better.'

'As you wish, Captain,' was all she said as she held Dulcie's hand and swept out.

He breathed a sigh of relief, released his cravat, took off his jacket and eased off his boots. He'd accomplished what he'd set out to do hadn't he? So why did he feel so bloody depressed? He thought of Braedrumie and his family and all that they'd endured. He remembered Culloden, its aftermath and men like Hartlass. Why did they act the way they did? Finally, he dwelt on his marriage and Anne. As a military man he'd sworn not to marry; now his hand had been forced. Though, if he was honest with himself, he knew he'd loved her from their first meeting in Newcastle. Perhaps in time she'd come to love him, for he was tired of being called 'Captain'.

He didn't sleep well that night or any night for a fortnight after that. Every morning, after breakfast Anne would take herself to the churchyard and after a few hours she'd walk back. Then she and Dulcie would attend to household duties and he wouldn't see them till dinner that evening.

He needed advice and sent for Uncle William. After a couple of glasses of brandy, her uncle settled down to listen.

'I've allowed her time to grieve,' said Rob, 'but I sense she's unhappy and nothing I say or do appears to make any difference.' He didn't dare tell him how everything he did seemed to make matters worse, nor tell him of their sleeping arrangements, hard enough to keep it from the servants. Every morning he'd straightened the sheets and plumped up the pillows to make the bed look untouched.

Uncle William put down his glass. 'Hmmph, too much freedom in my opinion; always been headstrong, like her mother. Your marriage...sudden...no time to be alone together. After all you've had to consider your ward, Dulcie, isn't it?

'I...well...'

'If it'll help, send her across to us. My youngest, Florie's about her age. Dulcie can ride our ponies to her heart's content. I'll send Florie tomorrow in the carriage shall I?'

'You do realise Duch...Dulcie is not as you'd expect. She's...had a poor upbringing and Anne has scarcely begun teaching her.'

Uncle William rose. 'I'll send the carriage.' He shook Rob's hand and left.

Dulcie didn't need to be persuaded to visit, not once she met Florie, whose nose scrunched up in humour most of the time. Kerbilly became quieter and at last Rob had Anne to himself.

With Johnstone's help Rob organised a picnic in a sheltered bay on a day with only the odd white cloud which scudded across the blue sky. Rob sent the carriage on ahead with rugs and food when Anne showed him how they could cut across the headland and walk through gorse and long grass to get to it. Her manner remained distant and cold as he unloaded their picnic. He told the driver to return for them in the late afternoon unless the weather turned inclement and waved him away.

Rob spread woollen rugs on the dunes and took off his jacket as she sat prim and proper and as far as possible from him whilst he kept up a commentary on what he did and why.

He knew he'd intrigued her as she watched him tie string round the necks of two bottles of French wine and lower them into an icy burn which fed into the sea.

She intrigued him when she told him the wine had come from a family friend and French privateer. He noted a catch in her voice as if this man meant something to her. He wanted her to sound like that when she talked about him.

Rob suggested a walk along the sand and watched the light breeze burnish her skin and untie stray red-gold curls. A trail of parallel footprints lay behind them in the wet sand. She began to talk of the carefree days of her childhood at Kerbilly and he shared his memories of Braedrumie with her.

She roared with laughter when he regaled her with of some of his exploits. He told her about when he'd told Euan to milk the cow and knew it was a bull. When he Johnnie and Duncan had built a wee dam with tree trunks and pebbles which caused a flash flood to cascade into his mother's scullery and how he and his brothers had sneaked out to camp under the stars one night, like real drovers and scurried home before dawn because of their cold backsides.

By the time she'd confessed she'd climbed trees, cliffs and jumped streams they'd walked miles. He loosened his cravat, rolled up his sleeves.

'Where are we, Anne?' he asked.

'I dinna ken. She said. 'I've never walked so far from Kerbilly before and my feet are hot and sore.' She sat on a rock and pulled off her shoe. Sand poured out of it. Off came the other and more sand sprinkled in a golden stream onto the beach.

She said, 'If you promise not to tell, I intend to walk back barefoot. Would that be terribly unseemly?'

'Terribly,' he said. 'So, I feel, Lady Anne of Kerbilly, I must in all conscience join you. The last one with bare feet is a dried up piece of seaweed!' He threw a brown strand at her and she shrieked in indignation and threw it back. Stockings flew off and they raced to the surf with them in their hands. They jumped in and out of the waves, her dress and petticoats held higher and higher and his breeches wet to the thigh. She waded further and further out. He followed and enjoyed the ice-cold touch of the sea, until he splashed her and she chased him.

She stubbed a toe on a hidden rock, tripped and fell on top of him. They laughed at each other, shocked at being soaked and fell silent. The water plastered her clothes to every curve and he was all too aware of her body next to his.

He put his hand under her chin and drew her closer to him, shoulder to shoulder, breast to breast and thigh to thigh. He breathed in her salt-scent as his lips ignited hers.

Then she scooped water over his head and ran. He raced after her in an instant and when he caught her, his arm went round her shoulders and they joked and laughed as they paddled back to their picnic through the shallows.

Rob thought a simple meal of cheese, bread and wine had never tasted so good. They fed each other as their clothes dried. The sun began to sink. She became quiet as if she remembered she was a lady. She went behind a rock as he packed up and pulled on her stockings, tied her garters and put on shoes.

She tried to harness her hair, but gave up. He enjoyed its glorious disarray. Her cheeks had a fresh bloom and freckles had deepened over her nose, most unfashionable, but so beautiful on her.

His arms had turned dark brown and he hastened to become a gentleman once more. He rolled down his sleeves, tied his cravat and pulled on his jacket.

They rode back in the carriage in silence. No hint of the unrestricted freedom of the hours before.

'Thank you, Captain,' she said when they had dinner that evening and the candles were lit. 'Today made me feel alive again and forget...'

'Rob, call me Rob. And so it should. This last year has been difficult for all of us, no matter which side we've been on.'

'You've hardly eaten.'

'Cook seems heavy-handed with the salt.'

Her brow creased. 'Salt, again? I will mention it.'

'I'm certain of one thing, Anne, life will become better for us both.' He put his hand on hers and she didn't withdraw it as he escorted her to her room as he had every night, kissed her cheek and made to go.

'No,' she whispered and tugged him back.

'No?'

'Dinna go.'

'Not go?'

'No.' She nuzzled his neck.

'But it's quite comfortable in the...'

'No.' She covered his face in kisses.

'I wouldna want to...'

'Damn you, Rob Stewart,' she hissed, then covered his mouth with hers.

He gathered her up and shut the bedroom door behind them.

He settled her on the silk sheets, explored her decolletage, his lips pushed the material further down the valley of her breasts.

One hand moved up a slender, velvet thigh when someone hammered at the front door.

'Hell's teeth. Who wants admittance at this time of night?'

They listened. The door opened downstairs. Johnstone's voice filtered upwards. 'Whose there?' he said.

Rob's heart sank as he heard the answer. 'Urgent orders from Captain Wolfe for Captain Stewart.'

Rob groaned out loud. 'Give me a second,' he said and kissed her. He descended the stairs two at a time and took a packet from tired Private Dunston. 'Wait,' he said. He tore it open and read it. Wolfe needed him to return to Culloden House for an urgent meeting. He had to go.

'Feed him.' He ordered Johnstone and indicated the tired Dunston. 'And tell the stable lad to have my horse saddled.' He raced upstairs to Anne.

'You're leaving.' She looked at him from below her lashes.

'No choice. I've been ordered to go. If I dinna set off now I'll be on a charge.'

She rushed into his arms and nestled her head on his chest. 'What's so important?'

'It might be they've had word...' He looked at her and changed what he was going to say, 'about something...that's of no matter,' he ended. He avoided her eyes. 'I must pack.' She followed him into his bedroom.

'Rob.'

'Yes.'

'Be careful.'

He kissed her then as if for the last time and they clung together.

'I should be back in a few days. Then I promise we'll finish what we started this night.' He gave her one last kiss and she gave him another and another as they descended the stairs. They embraced and then he tore himself away.

Dunston grinned at him and showed his few teeth. Rob mounted and they galloped off. He stopped and turned at the top of a hill before he was out of view. She waved. Rob rode on assured she was his.

CHAPTER Forty-five

Anne couldn't believe it. *I love him, this redcoat, this Rob Stewart. If anyone had told me that he would be as important to me as breathing, I would have called them a fool. If we'd only had a few minutes more...I would have given myself to him like a violin in the hands of a master, each string taut, waiting, to come alive. Drat the British army.*

She chewed at her thumb. *He still hasn't explained about 'M' and didn't tell me why he'd been recalled to duty. What had he said? It might be they've had word...something important. Something important? Lord, it could only be the Prince. They know where he is or how he's going to escape. I've allowed my marriage to get in the way of my duty.*

He's only been away a few days and I've ruined an embroidery, broken a china cup and lost my temper with Dulcie and Joan. All because he had to leave before...we'd settled things. A true Jacobite would have left at once, disappeared and helped the Cause, but I feel tied to Rob Stewart and Dulcie.

The child returned from Uncle William's determined to be difficult. Anne employed a governess, Miss Brown. Straight-backed, dull hair and rigid.

'Dulcie, behaves like a hoyden. She refuses to wear stockings and garters, uses gutter language to the servants and threw a sampler to the floor,' said Miss Brown. 'She threw a vase of flowers at your maid. Joan only called her what everyone thinks 'A guttersnipe no one wants.'

'You will not repeat this,' said Anne and sent for Joan. The maid's shrieks and wails roused the household when Anne ordered her to leave.

'You'd sack me over that Dulcie?' said Joan hands on hips.

'Yes. Johnstone will give you your wages. Think yourself fortunate, you'll have a reference. You'll leave at once.'

'Not till I've had my say.' Joan's face became a pinched patchwork of lines. 'I had my doubts when you married a redcoat, now I ken. We all feel the same, you ask the cook. You're a traitor to my Angus and the Cause, you're nothin'.' She snapped her fingers at Anne and with a swirl of her skirts, strode out of the room.

Johnstone shook his head.

Anne's insides heaved. *Is this what they all think?* She set her jaw. 'Call the servants together, Johnstone,' she said. 'They need to know what is acceptable in this household. We canna change the past, but we need to learn how to live together in the future.'

They lined up in front of her in a hushed silence, the stable hands, boot boys, chamber and parlour maids, the cook, scullery maids and Miss Brown. The cook wrung her hands, the chamber maid twisted a corner of her apron and a boot boy stared at the ceiling. Miss Brown bit her lip.

Anne drew herself up and steeled herself to say what needed to be said. She knew in these troubled times Joan would struggle to find work. 'I've dismissed Joan Chatto.'

A parlour maid gasped with dismay and a stable hand hissed under his breath.

Anne scanned their faces. 'Let her dismissal be a warning to you all. Our ward needs kindness and understanding. She's never known a mother's love or a father's kind hand and I'm determined she will find them here. Understood?'

'Ma'am,' they said in unison.

'Also, Captain Stewart is my husband and master of Braedrumie. I expect the same courtesies that were extended to my father, extended to him. I know what's been going on, Cook. Your continued employment depends solely on keeping my husband well fed.'

An uneasy ripple ran through the line of servants like a wave. Anne gritted her teeth. 'Leave now if you can't comply with my wishes.'

The servants looked at each other, shuffled their feet, but no one moved.

'Good, we're agreed then and can put this unfortunate incident behind us. You may go about your duties.'

They bowed or curtsied and straggled out of the room.

'Well done, Milady,' said Johnstone bowed. 'If I may say so.'

'You may, Johnstone,' she said. *Now, where's Dulcie?* She found the little girl curled up on her bed. She hugged her pillow.

I've tried to be a mother to her, but it's not enough. Anne sat on the silk coverlet beside Dulcie and put a hand on her thin should blade. 'Darling, I've sent the maid packing. Now, tell me what's wrong?'

Dulcie's tiny frame heaved as she sobbed into her pillow.

Anne stroked Dulcie's hair. Shades of golden wheat now framed her oval face. 'You know we love you. Didn't Captain Stewart pick you out and bring you to me?'

Dulcie snuffled into the pillow. 'But he's gone away.'

'He'll be back in a few days.'

'But he didn't say goodbye...was it my fault? Sometimes I think I'm more Duch than Dulcie.' The little girl turned. Her brown eyes, brimmed with tears.

'Oh, sweetheart. He was ordered back by Captain Wolfe late at night. He wouldna have wanted to wake you. I miss him too.'

'Do you?'

'Oh, yes.' Anne meant it and knew the servants weren't the only ones who had to learn to live with Rob Stewart.

'I liked it when he reads to me,' said Dulcie. 'Miss Brown hits my knuckles with a ruler when I get things wrong. She calls me a dimwit.'

Anne closed her eyes. *I'm too consumed with my own thoughts. I promise this child she'd not be hurt again.* Anne hugged Dulcie. 'Miss Brown will also be sent packing. Now, would you like me to read you a story?'

'Yes.'

'Perhaps I could also help you with your letters. We could surprise the captain on his return. What do you think?'

'You won't use a ruler?'

'No. I promise I'll burn any I see.'

'I stole these.' Dulcie put her hand under the pillow and showed Anne two china figurines.

'Why, darling?'

'Because, because…they reminded me of you and the captain. You're not cross are you?'

Anne tucked them behind Dulcie's pillow. 'You keep them here if it makes you feel better.'

Dulcie's top lip quivered. 'I'd like to learn my letters now.' She slipped her hand into Anne's.

Lord, I have to learn to be a mother to this child. She could only try her best. Dulcie needed love and lots of it.

***

As the days passed Dulcie seemed happier. She hummed to herself and learned letter sounds at a fast rate, though Anne still witnessed outbursts of temper.

'Sorry,' said Dulcie after a prolonged screaming fit when Anne had to usher away the servants.

Is she testing me? Anne reassured herself. *It's ridiculous to expect a waif from Inverness quayside to behave according to societies mores when her past life has been full of insecurities. She'll come round, trust me…us. Give her love and time.*

Anne gave up her days to Dulcie and at nights thought of Rob. *Where is he?*

Over breakfast Dulcie said, 'This is an easy life. When I were on the river front I had to thieve for a livin'. Maggie showed me how. She were a bright one was Maggie, till they 'anged her.' She wiped her nose on her sleeve and stopped when Anne shook her head. 'Can't remember me parents, just an old woman, she left me with a black-bearded man on the quay.'

Anne stared at the child and then pulled her into her arms. She dreaded to think what Dulcie's fate would have been if Rob hadn't gone back for her. *How many men would do that? But how many men have secrets they didn't reveal to their wives? Is it because he still loves this 'M'?* The thought made Anne uncomfortable as Dulcie stood swamped by Anne's embrace. Then the child's thin arms reached up to her. *Lord.*

Anne sent a note to Uncle William asking if Florie would like to come to Kerbilly and play with Dulcie. He'd written a kind note in return and agreed.

'Best behaviour,' Anne warned Dulcie.

The two girls played with a doll's house, laid out a tea set and dressed dolls until Dulcie grabbed Florie's hand. The girls chased each other round trees, played hide-and-seek and made castles on the beach.

'Florie's my best friend,' said Dulcie as Anne tucked her in that night. 'She said so.'

Now Dulcie seemed more settled, Anne thought about Rob more and more. Wolfe had recalled him, only for a matter of a few days he'd said, but it had been weeks now and as if light had been driven from the house. She moped around Kerbilly like a bird that had lost its mate. His letters had helped. He'd called her 'My love' and 'dearest wife' and assured her he'd return soon. She'd shared some of his words with Dulcie who'd beamed at her.

Anne decided everything she ever wanted and more lay with this man. She walked the beach and remembered the golden afternoon they'd shared. She thought him handsome, though some might say his nose too long, his lips not full and jaw too strong. She only knew she could drown in his eyes. Nor could anyone dispute his height of six foot four inches in his stocking feet, the breadth of his shoulders and the muscular strength of his arms. His qualities, so many that she counted them off on her fingers: honourable, caring, well-read, interested in the arts and sciences and in everything he said and did a gentleman. Perhaps not everything, he swore, but only in extremis; he liked to have his own way which could be very annoying at times and of course his politics - all wrong. She decided that she disliked perfection so often aligned to vanity and a sense of one's own self-importance. *No. I love him more because of these imperfections and how he treats me with a feigned half-serious manner, which I adore.* It perplexed her how this could be. Of course she'd never let him know.

Those ninnies paraded in front of her as suitors for years had never been interested in what she'd said or thought. Only Rob made her heart career out of control.

It had taken her time to forgive Uncle William, the forced marriage, but how could she hold a grudge now? So when he paid a visit one day and Florie and Dulcie disappeared upstairs hand in hand, she'd said, 'How lovely to see you, Uncle. Do sit down.'

'I take it all is...well between you and Stewart?'

'Very well, thank you, Uncle, why this unexpected visit?'

'Florie requested that Dulcie stay with us for a time,' said Uncle William. 'They'll be schooled together by Mrs. Masham every day and I can assure you no one will raise a hand to either of them. Dulcie will be instructed in reading, writing and mathematics. What do you think?'

'You're very kind, but you must have realised she's a lot to learn. Her language, manner...well, they're no' the best.'

'Florie likes her, that's all I ken. So, what do you say?'

'We'll ask Dulcie. I'll abide with her decision,' said Anne.

Dulcie clapped her hands at the news and Anne couldn't think of a good reason why she shouldn't say yes. *Surely Dulcie's willingness to go means the child feels more secure? After all, if there's a problem I'll be close by.* So, she left Dulcie after lots of hugs and kisses, at Uncle William's and watched her run off with Florie as if she hadn't a care in the world.

Anne, restless, walked along the north cliffs and beach and thought about her future with Rob.

CHAPTER Forty-six

Rob had been ordered to take a group men to patrol the area round Ruthven Barracks. Any Jacobites had left long ago and after a week of fruitless search Rob returned to Inverness. He hungered for Anne, instead he had to report to Wolfe.

Wolfe behaved with his usual charm. 'Pity about Ruthven. Never mind...I heard you married and Lady Anne's a beauty. My congratulations.' He tapped his lip with his forefinger. 'Hard, being the wife of a soldier.'

'Sir.' Rob hoped he'd never discover who she really was.

'Apologies for breaking into your honeymoon, but there's important news. Cumberland wants the Prince, Captain Stewart, he's made that very plain. We need to put a stop to these rebellions once and for all. There's a £30,000 reward, but we've not received a hint of where the Pretender might be from our spies, just names of the blasted women who've been involved.' He shook the list at Rob.

Rob's jaw tensed and his neck muscles tightened. A dull ache began behind his eyes.

'Lady Charlotte Buick, Lady Margaret Ardmore, Lady Jean Pitcalnie I could go on. Those we've caught haven't talked. I heard Jacobite Ann Mckay from Skye had been tortured, but still didn't betray anyone. Not that I agree with those methods of course.'

'May I, sir?' Rob took the list and scanned it for Annie Bryce. He tried not to show his relief when he handed it back.

'They even say the Prince dressed up as some woman called–' Wolfe scrutinised his notes. '–Bessy Burke. These damned Highlanders remain loyal to the last. We've deployed several detachments.' Wolfe pointed at a large map which covered his desk. Rob bent over it to look for familiar landmarks. 'See, we've troops at Moy, Castle Downer, Lord Lovat's seat; Fraser country, Ross, Cromarty, Sutherland and Caithness. Lord Fortrose and the Mackenzies guard the way to the Isles here; Cobham's dragoons are on the east coast and we've militia at highland passes. Stirling's guarded and the Edinburgh regiment is camped on the south side of the Firth of Forth. There's 1,700 militia and 800 Argyleshire men at Lochaber and General Campbell has set sail to secure St. Kilda, Barra and South Uist. We mean to catch Charlie. The net tightens as you can see, but I need information, Captain, and I think you can get it.'

An icy hand squeezed Rob's heart.

Wolfe leant over his desk and stared at him.

Rob broke into a cold sweat, but Wolfe's words calmed him. 'Captain, you were born in the Highlands, you can pass as a Jacobite. I want you to find out where this cursed Pretender is hiding. Head for the west coast first, my gut tells me he's there. The Frenchies know it well and it's where he landed. You'll report directly to Caroline Scott at Fort William.'

Rob stared at him. It meant he wouldn't see Anne for weeks, months even. Hell's teeth.

Well, what do you have to say, man?'

Rob collected himself and came to attention. 'I'll do my best, sir. May I have your permission to collect what I need from my...home?'

Wolfe gave him a wry look. 'You have. Good hunting, Captain.'

'Sir.' He thanked God. Would it always be like this, he thought? Desperate to see Anne, he spurred his horse north all the way to Kerbilly. Rob arrived, his head full of Anne, her face, her scent, her body. How could he have thought they couldn't make a match of it? Though, he had to admit, her ardent support for the Cause nagged at him.

Johnstone greeted him with face like stone and presented Rob with a letter on a silver platter. He noted his name written in black ink in a neat hand as he broke the seal.

Kerbilly
Dear Rob,

Please believe I love you.

The oath I swore at the beginning of all this binds me still. It's a matter of honour. I dare say no more. I'll write as often as I can to let you know I'm safe and well.

Dulcie has become great friends with my niece, Florie, Uncle William's daughter and is staying with them for a time. I told Dulcie you would visit soon. She misses you as much as I.

Do not be too hurt or worried by my departure. I informed the servants and Uncle William that I had been asked to visit a sick relative of yours. It is safer for both of us if you do not know where I am. I should return soon.

I hope I have the long pleasure of being, dear husband, most affectionately yours,

Anne.

Rob crumpled the letter and threw it into the fire. Blast the woman. He'd married her to protect them both and she'd done this. He paced up and down. God almighty, he loved her so much it's as if he'd a missing limb.

There's no doubt she *was* a Jacobite spy, but is she still? Deuced awkward. He called Johnstone. 'Lady Anne may be in trouble, tell her maid, Joan, I want to see her.'

'If I may, sir?' Johnstone placed a full whisky decanter and a tumbler in front of Rob. 'I used to find in times of crisis, the last Lord of Kerbilly found it helped.'

Johnstone's grey eyes gave Rob a shrewd look as his master gulped down two measures one after the other.

'Another,' said Rob. 'And one for yourself.'

Johnstone's eyebrows shot up. He swallowed the golden liquid in one. 'It's fine whisky, our own. If I may be so bold, Lady Anne dismissed Joan over an altercation with Miss Dulcie. I've kenned Lady Anne all her life, Captain, and her mother before her. I saw the Cause for what it was, futile, as did the Master or we'd have had this house burned about our ears. I want no harm to befall Lady Anne.'

'Then help me. Have there been any visitors whilst I've been away?' Rob drummed his fingers on a table.

'Miss Dulcie and Miss Florie visited. Then a few ladies came for tea.' He ran his tongue over his bottom lip.

'Ladies?' Rob gulped as remembered Wolfe's words.

Johnstone poured them another glass. The amber liquid relaxed Rob muscle by muscle.

'They used to come regular before the Rising,' said Johnstone. 'Lady Jean hasna been back. Some had been arrested of course, others...' He shook his head.

'Arrested?' A familiar ache clawed at the back of Rob's head.

'Aye, then freed. ' Johnstone lowered his voice. 'You must have heard of Charlotte Robertson, Lady Buick? She was one of the most ardent, threatened her tenants until they came out for the Cause, lost her fiancé, Archibald Cameron, in the battle. A fine man. Her brother, Lord Alan...well...'

Rob's heart sank, but he tried not to show it.

'All friends of the family you understand, but Lady Anne's uncle calls the ladies, 'Jacobite hoydens'. Years ago, as children, they had the run of the place, acted like boys. Worse when the St. Etiennes visited from France, traded with Lady Anne's father. There's a son, Philippe, Anne had more than a fancy for him I think, if you'll excuse me saying so, sir. He persuaded the girls to climb an oak at the back of the house, must be thirty foot high, and them ladies. The master mostly encouraged 'em. Lady Anne always won.'

'Why doesna that surprise me?'

'Then when they grew up it was tea and politics, tea and politics. Oh they'd go quiet when I entered the room, change the subject to women's fashions. I'd hear them hoot with laughter when I'd gone. But I knew; I'm no' daft. Women are great gossips. News about the Cause flashed from one end of the Highlands to the other before tea leaves left the pot. They'd a nickname for her, Lady Anne I mean - the 'Colonel' that was it. A woman, a colonel. The very notion is nonsensical, if you'll excuse me for saying so, sir.'

Somehow Rob could see how she would suit the role. 'Mmm, any other recent visitors you can think of?'

'When the ladies left, I did see Lady Anne talking to a gentleman by the side gate.'

Rob put down his glass. 'Go on.'

'She'd just returned from a walk along the cliffs on a fine day with a ship on the horizon. I thought it odd she didn't call for her new maid, Gail, when she walked back with him towards the old church. Said he'd brought bad news, told Gail to pack her bags as she had to visit an infirm relative of yours.'

'Had you seen this gentleman before?'

'Too far away. I couldn't be sure. My guess, by his size, Lord Alan, Lady Charlotte's brother. He's badly pockmarked poor devil.'

'Pockmarked?' Hell's teeth. Could Buick be the sutler, Edward Bryce, Anne's supposed dead brother? Lots of the population had pockmarks, but didn't she sometimes call him Alan? Of course she'd had to lie to him in the past, but now when he thought them safe, she'd embroiled herself in a plot that could ensure her execution. He didn't want to imagine her fair neck on the block or his for that matter.

'A visit to Lady Buick mightn't go amiss, though she'll be a Jacobite till her dying day. She threatened to burn out her own people, unless they joined the Cause. ' Johnstone said. 'I did my best, Captain, and ensured Lady Anne took a couple of footmen with her. They headed towards Inverness.'

Thunderation, I must have just missed them. 'Thank you, Johnstone. That will be all.' Rob let him return to his duties and thought about his. As an officer of the king he'd a duty to His Majesty's government, but he'd also a duty to his wife and family. Once again he was pulled in opposing directions.

Anne's friends were active Jacobites. What did they want from her now? He'd thought the Cause was dead, cut off root and branch at Culloden. He paced the room and stopped. Of course, only one person, would be so desperate, the Pretender.
Rob massaged his neck muscles. He'd visit Lady Buick, perhaps she'd know more.

CHAPTER Forty-seven

Buick House stood in its own grounds, one wing blackened by fire. Rob had been shown into the drawing room by an aged servant. 'Captain Stewart to see your ladyship.'

Charlotte Robertson, Lady Buick sat, haughty and proud, her yellow dress spread around her like a dandelion in a green lawn. Rob sat opposite in uniform. Her honour dictated he treat it as if the finest drawing room in the land. He tried to ignore the chipped plaster decorated with roses and buds, symbols of King James and his offspring. At his feet lay ripped furnishings, china shards and shattered glasses.

He studied her. She seemed calm, too calm. He wouldn't have a similar demeanour if soldiers ransacked Braedrumie House.

Lady Buick curled back her lips and squinted at him and as if at a loathsome insect. 'It's only because of your wife and our childhood friendship I've countenanced you in my home, Captain Stewart. I'd be grateful if you'd be quick about your business, I presume this is an official visit?'

She hadn't even acknowledged that, but for his timely arrival, her house would have been about her ears. British troops, led by a Sergeant Griffin in search of Jacobites, had ransacked and looted her home.

Rob had arrived to see the males of the household in the stables lined up in front of a noose slung over a beam. Some in their eighties, incapable of light work. Those from the fields and stables, young boys. The younger men mustn't have returned from Culloden or were in hiding. Rob ascertained that this was one of several visits Griffin had made.

Griffin, a brute, short and squat in size, had a chest and arms that could crush a man to death. He met Rob with polite belligerence. Perhaps the sergeant needed a stronger argument? Rob walked him behind the stables and put all his weight behind two punches in the man's stomach.

Griffin collapsed like a sack of meal. 'Oooff.'

Rob threw whisky from his hip flask over him. 'Corporal,' he shouted. A wiry soldier rushed round the corner to greet him. Rob's hand held Griffin's collar in an attempt to keep him upright. 'Your sergeant seems unwell.'

Griffin groaned.

Rob sniffed at Griffin and wrinkled his nose in disgust. 'Drunk on duty. Put him under arrest.' Rob scribbled on a pad. 'When you get back to Inverness he's to have two weeks in the Black Hole on bread and water.' Rob handed the corporal the signed slip. 'I've made it clear to your commanding officer there's no business for the army here.'

The corporal grinned. 'It'll be a pleasure Sir. Black Hole it is. Privates Jones and Collins, get this drunken man out of the h'officer's sight. By the left...' and they dragged Griffin off.

'Get back to your business,' Rob ordered and they scurried off.

Lady Buick brought him back to the present. 'You're a redcoat.' She spat out the words as if she'd said cockroach.

'I've dealt with the sergeant who did this,' Rob said. 'He'll no' trouble you again.'

'You were at Culloden, took part in the aftermath. Men shot or hanged for no reason, women and bairns molested or killed, but you're also a Highlander by your accent, Captain Stewart. Tell me, just what does it take to fight against your own kin?'

Her words stung. 'About as much as it takes to make kin fight against their will.'

A flame of colour crept up her neck. 'It was their duty, to me and the Cause.'

'So you burned out those who refused?'

'I had no choice.' Two crimson spots flared on her cheeks. 'Did you know redcoats raided Lady Jean of Ardmore's estate. They dishonoured her in her own home. They say she's quite mad. Then they arrested Lady Margaret of Pitcalnie's father, executed him in London and burnt her house around her ears. She refused to leave, you see. They were my friends and your wife's.' She glared at him. 'You'll understand why redcoats are unwelcome, Captain Stewart.'

'I'm here as Lady Anne's husband, no' on official business. Please call me Rob.'

'Stewart...' she gasped. 'Good God, no' *that* Rob Stewart? But you were a Jacobite and jilted her. Did you force her to marry you?'

Rob's eyes narrowed. He could never be a friend to this woman. 'Not your business, but force of circumstance brought about our marriage. I want to keep my wife out of trouble and believe she's up to her graceful neck in it, as are you.'

'Really sir...' she half rose from her chair, but Rob's words pressed her like a weight back into it.

'This is no' a game, Lady Buick, the authorities ken about you and your friends. It only takes one to talk. They could be waiting for her, for the **Colonel**.'

She paled and said with a toss of her head. 'I dinna' ken what you're talking about.'

'Lady Buick-Charlotte, dinna take the British government for dunces. Do you imagine only Jacobites have spies?'

'What?'

'I love my wife and I'd rather have her lovely head on her shoulders, if you ken my meaning.'

'I...'

'If you ken where Anne is, tell me and on my honour, I'll keep the information to myself. I'm only interested in Anne...no one else. You're her only chance.'

There was a long silence. 'You're a redcoat.'

'Dinna let that stop you.' He tore off the jacket, buttons tore from threads and spilled onto her carpet.

'Well.' Her hand went to her throat.

Next he pulled his shirt over his head, rolled it in a ball and threw it on the floor. 'You see only a man, Madam, one who loves his wife with every breath in his being. If I must, I will remove every shred of my clothing, until you tell me where Anne is.'

Her eyes wandered from his chest to his face and then to his torso. A faint blush appeared on her cheeks.

'An interesting proposition Captain, if only all women had men who loved them as much.' She turned her back on him. 'Please clothe yourself. I believe you. Anne is most fortunate in her husband, I havena heard from my fiance since Culloden.' She paused and looked at him out of the corners of her eyes. 'I expect you on your honour, not to betray my trust.'

Rob nodded. 'As I expect you not to betray mine, you have my word.'

'She's on the west coast, in South Morar, Captain, that's all I ken or am willing to say. Anne had no choice, Captain Stewart, it's a debt of honour. Go gently with her. I'll send your buttons to Kerbilly shall I? God knows what the servants will make of them.'

He kissed her cold hand as he left.

CHAPTER Forty-eight

Rob galloped back to Kerbilly in a frenzy of unease. Wolfe had tasked him to find the Prince and he knew if he did so, Anne would be there. He had to find her.

'Johnstone, organise a fresh mount and provisions within the hour.'

'Sir.' Johnstone disappeared for a few minutes and returned. 'May I ask how long you'll be away, Captain?'

'Some time.' Rob stuffed a spare shirt into his saddlebags and saw Johnstone's eyebrow arch in disapproval. 'I've no time for niceties.' A bundle of red and white rags on a chair caught his eye - a rag doll. What about Duch...Dulcie? He threw a pair of breeches at the butler and said, 'Take over the packing, there's a good man. Only essentials. I've a letter to write.' Rob leant over a desk and seized a quill. He dabbed it in an ink pot, grabbed a piece of parchment and wrote like a man possessed.

Kerbilly
Dear Uncle William,

I have been called away and must depart in haste. I'd be most grateful if you'd allow Dulcie to stay with you until my return in a few weeks.

I remain your honourable servant,

Captain Rob Stewart.

'Johnstone, please take this and deliver it into Sir William's hands.' As Rob packed he hoped Anne's uncle would assume he'd rushed to his 'sick relative's' bedside. He stuffed his saddlebags with clean linen, Wolfe's pass, bread and some cheese.

He'd changed out of his officer's uniform and slung a leather bottle of water round his shoulder. He looked like any other traveller on the road as he spurred west with musket, pistol, sword and dirk. If he didn't find Anne, what would he do? His imagination conjured up visions of her captured and mistreated by the worst brutes in the British army. Or wounded without aid or comfort or worse, dead.

As he travelled through the empty countryside, the acrid tang of smoke and decay reminded him again of Cumberland's victory and brutal order of 'No quarter'. His concerns grew as he rode past deserted villages. Croft walls supported seared timbers like black fingers. Fields contained burnt stubble and no livestock. The only sounds his horses hooves, the rush of the wind through the trees and the caw of rooks and crows.

Clouds hung over him like a grey tents. Rain...He pulled off the track behind some firs, to shelter under the branches. Down the track, came the stamp of a horse's hooves.

He tied his mount's reins to a branch, unsheathed the musket from his saddle and waited. The wind rose to a moan, moved the tops of the trees and created shadows which hadn't been there before. He saw danger behind every bough. Horizontal rain interfered with his vision. The pound of hooves came closer. Someone pushed a horse hard and fast, foolhardy on this track, he thought.

Rob brushed his forehead with a sodden sleeve. He squinted through the leaves. A rider broke cover, slight and cloaked. The figure sat low and forward in the saddle. Mud kicked up at every stride. Sweat flecked the horse, it had only to stumble for the rider to be thrown and probably killed.

Some instinct made Rob hold fire. Then he snatched the rider's reins. The horse slowed, snorted and came to a halt.

'Let go,' yelled the rider. 'I'll gut you proper, if you come closer.'

Rob eyed the dirk and grabbed the thin wrist.

'Ow.' The dirk dropped and Rob pulled the horseman to the ground. A familiar face creased up in pain before him.

Dulcie spat white hot rage and shrieked, 'Bastard.' She kicked his left ankle.

Rob hopped up and down. He held up one hand in mock surrender and said, 'Duch...Dulcie, it's me, Captain Stewart, stop fighting before you kill me.'

'You left me. You both...bloody left...me.' She yelled and then broke down in uncontrollable sobs.

Rob held her to him, her face nuzzled against his chest. Oh, God, he thought. 'I'm sorry you're upset, poppet, but I had no choice. Lady Anne is...I have to find out where she is and bring her home.'

'You could have taken me with you.' She stared up at him. 'You're the only folks I got. Nobody cared about me before. I don't even know me parents. All I remembers is dirty streets, heavin' with people. And buildins, bigger than anythin' I've ever seen; 'nd an old woman in a red shawl and red dress pullin' me along; and cobbles, I remembers cobbles, they hurt me feet; and a ship, I remembers a ship and the quayside at Inverness and them men. They was devils, they was. Why don't I remember havin' a mother? Do you think I lost her like you lose a shoe?'

Oh, dear God he'd been thoughtless. He held her shoulders. 'I dinna ken, but what I do ken is you're a brave girl. Dulcie did you, did those men...?'

She looked puzzled and then her face broke into a toothy smile. 'Naw.'

He let out his breath. 'Good, we got that out of the way. Now, poppet, you must go back. It's too dangerous to take you with me.'

'No.'

'You mustna speak of this to anyone. Lady Anne's...involved in something and she's in grave danger and I need to find her.'

'I could go with you...' She clutched at his sleeve.

'No you canna. I need to ken you're safe with Uncle William. Do you understand? Then I can concentrate on Lady Anne and bring her home as soon as possible.'

'You both coming home to Kerbilly?'

'Yes.'

'I thought you was gone for good.' She wrapped her arms round him. 'Promise you'll come back?'

He bowed to her. 'On my honour as a gentleman and an officer in His Majesty's army, but it may be some time.'

Her face beamed. 'I'll go to Uncle William then.'

'There's a good lassie.' He linked the fingers of both hands palms uppermost. She stepped on them and mounted her horse.

He'd have to let her return unescorted. At least she'd only a few miles to travel. He held out the dirk, the thistle handle looked familiar. 'Where did you get this?'

'She looked at her hands. 'Your room. Sorry, I won't do it again.'

He sighed and made a mental note to remind Anne about Dulcie's light fingers. 'Take it.'

She grabbed it.

'I can see you're no' afraid to use it. I wish I could go back with you. Promise you willna stop for anybody or anything till you're safe with Uncle William.' He held up two fingers and crossed them.

'Promise,' she said and crossed her fingers in reply.

He slapped her mare's brown rump and sent it into a trot.

She turned in the saddle and with an impish grin shouted back, 'And don't be bleedin' late.'

He shook his head and made another mental note. Anne needed to improve their ward's vocabulary. He watched Dulcie's horse round a bend and forced himself not to dwell on the dangers that could befall her. He'd already lost an hour. He set off west as fast as he could, his thoughts of Anne.

CHAPTER Forty-nine

The next day Rob watched redcoats trickle like blood over mountain passes, hillsides and glens. He'd been stopped at the point of a bayonet several times, until he'd showed his pass and been allowed on his way. Cumberland had tightened the noose around Prince Charlie, determined he wouldn't escape.

Rob rode under grey firs. Their branches formed cathedrals of green which opened out to great sweeps of purple hills with rocky outcrops. Always, in the distance, sat the sun-kissed mountains with their deep shadows.

The following morning the weather changed. A grey canopy of funereal cloud descended and stayed for the rest of the week. Mist hugged the earth. Rain a constant drizzle, soaked into his bones. He travelled through washed out roads and tracks, round landslides, rock falls and cursed all the time at the delay.

He looked up when he heard a honk and the flutter of numerous wings. Above him, in the bleak sky, the familiar V formation of geese headed south. He envied them their freedom and speed.

On cold, wet nights he stayed at miserable wayside inns or in ramshackle crofts. In fine weather he fell asleep under the stars, with cut boughs for his roof and the scent of pine in the air.

He thought only of Anne as he pushed his horse onward and mountains took on a woman's curves.

He arrived under the sign of the Wild Geese by Borrodale Burn in South Morar, in the middle of a cloud burst. The inn stood on two floors, one overhung the ground floor which sagged towards the ground.

A young hump-backed lad took his horse and the sallow-faced landlord showed him 'the best room in the inn'.

Rob looked at a mouse-infested garret with its lumpy straw mattress. The wind forced itself through a gap in the wooden shutters and whistled round his ankles. 'I'll take it,' he said as exhausted, he dumped his saddlebags on the floorboards.

The landlord seemed surprised. 'Will you be stayin' long?'

'As long as is needed.'

'We dinna have many travellers. Who is it you're visitin' again?

'I didna say. I'm looking for a woman, red hair and green eyes. Have you seen her?'

The landlord's eyes flickered in interest, but he shook his head.

Rob turned his back on him. They'd all be ardent Jacobites here. If they wouldn't hand over the Pretender, they'd say nothing about Anne. The door closed. He took one look at the brown stains on the mattress and settled for a night on the floor. He wrapped his woollen cloak around him and used his saddlebags for a pillow. He thought of Anne.

He woke with morning light on his face. Stiff and sore he stretched, opened the broken shutters and drank in the morning light. The room danced with sun beams and the cries and raucous shriek of the curlew and the gulls rang in his ears. Blue hills and the Atlantic lay ahead in a misty haze.

After a breakfast of warm porridge and a tankard of ale he set off. He spotted a sail on the horizon, but saw little that raised any suspicions of the Prince being near. Redcoats patrolled the glens. He rode up hills and along the coast, before he turned back toward the inn. As night fell he settled himself in the darkest corner. He ate, drank too much and rested his face on the table as if asleep.

CHAPTER Fifty

Anne watched a moth flutter into the croft. It circled a candle and its flame. Lord Alan Buick sat opposite her at a rickety table. In the middle of the room peaty smoke curled up to the rafters and made its way out of a hole in the thatch.

Anne thought about her father, but also what she'd learned from Lord Alan about Charlotte, Margaret and Jean. *We were all so happy once. Now Father's dead and my friends have suffered at the hands of the redcoats. Redcoats, like Rob, my husband. No. Not like him.* She'd reeled at the final dreadful news, Lord Alistair had been executed.

'You've a new hat,' Alan said.

She put down her wooden spoon. The stew would take few more hours. She jumped up from her stool, took the hat and adjusted it. The wide, black brim with a crimson plume sat over one eye. She strutted up and down, with a hand on her hip. 'Suits me don't you think?'

Alan folded his arms. 'I borrowed it from our foreign friend. He's no' happy you've kept him waiting.'

'I dinna suppose he is.'

'You're husband's at the Wild Geese.' Alan's mouth a withered line.

'Ah.' A spark of excitement shot through her. *Rob is so close.* 'I dinna want him harmed. You ken what to do?'

'Aye.' Alan's face loomed closer. The candle highlighted the craters in his face. 'After all we've been through and then Culloden I'd have thought...Did you have to marry that damned redcoat?'

'I love him,' she snapped. Her tone became gentle. 'Take some men and do as I said.'

'If you're sure.'

'I'm sure.'

He put his boot on the stool. 'You've changed, Anne, become more...commanding.'

'Needs must.' She gestured at his boot. 'Do you mind?'

He removed it.

She sat, dipped her wooden spoon into the stew and tasted it. 'Mmm, it's good.'

'Our foreign friend gave me these...'

Anne stretched out her hand and received a sheet of folded parchment and a familiar signet ring made of gold enamel which bore old Queen Mary's arms. Anne scanned the parchment and read the signature. 'He's a fighting cock. Ruffle his feathers a little and then bring him to me.' Anne set the hat at an even more rakish angle on her head. 'Keep a look out just in case.'

With a wry glance and a shake of his head, Alan left and a few minutes later pushed a blindfolded and bound figure into the room.

The man stumbled, 'Merde.'

Anne grinned as the door closed behind Alan. The blindfolded man whirled round.

A little natural light came through the cracks in the door's planks. The man turned his head. *To catch another sound?* Hair, shoulder length and dark as a raven's wing, fell on a clean white linen collar. His crisp, white shirt hung loose on his frame. Brown doe skin boots met black breeches at muscular thighs. Anne had to acknowledge, he'd always had presence. She booted his backside and made him reel round in indignation as she knew he would.

'I protest,' he said in accented English. 'I am...'

'We ken who you are.' She disguised her voice and kicked him again.

'Mademoiselle...'

She cut him off. 'You're the most cold- hearted devil that ever came out of France.'

'This is not true, Mademoiselle, on my honour I swear it. I am a friend. I gave one of your men my Lettre de Marque and my ring.'

She circled him. 'You could have stolen them. You could be a British agent.'

'Non, Mademoiselle...'

She prodded his ribs with the point of her dirk and watched him tense like the enraged tiger she'd seen in one of father's books. His muscles expanded, tried to break the ropes, but they held firm.

'The Lettre de Marque is water damaged, worthless,' she lied. She tapped him on the shoulder with it. He spun round. 'Besides they can be forged.'

'Mon Dieu. I've risked my life, sailors and ships for your Cause and you treat me as if I'm a...'

'Pirate?'

'I'm a privateer, Mademoiselle if you'd just look...'

Anne cut him off. 'Your crimes are many, Monsieur.' She counted them on her fingers as she continued to circle him. 'Lying to a little girl and encouraging her to eat green apples which made her gravely ill; allowing her to take a beating when she was caught riding an untrained stallion you'd put her on despite her protests and the most heinous, leaving her weeping because she'd lost her heart to a French rogue.'

There was a long pause, then he said in a regretful tone, 'Mademoiselle, I am sorry, but...I do not remember...'

Anne dug him in the ribs with her elbow.

'Arrg.'

She grinned.

'Perhaps I remember a little. Anne, my sweet is it you?'

She dug him harder in the ribs again.

'Aargh. You're 'urting me my love.'

'I was never sweet and I was never your love,' she whispered into his ear as she hacked at the ropes which bound him.

He rubbed at the red marks on his wrists and took off his blindfold. He grinned and showed even, white teeth, then bowed with a flourish and kissed her hand.

His lips lingered just a second too long before he jerked upright in surprise. 'You're married?' He fingered her ring. 'I didn't know this.'

Do I detect a note of regret? 'It was...because of the times...done quickly.'

'And your 'usband?'

'Rob Stewart of Braedrumie.'

'Stewart - The man who jilted you?' He stared at her slack-jawed.

'Yes.' She snapped at him and then remembered the day of the picnic. 'He thought better of it.'

'Yet, 'e allows you to be involved in this dangerous business. What sort of man have you married?'

Lord, I canna tell him he's a redcoat. 'An honourable one. Philippe, Father died recently. I had no one except Uncle William. He insisted I marry Rob.'

'Ma petite, I'm so sorry. Mon pere will be distraught, he regarded your father as 'is brother, a man he could trust in business.'

'Thank you, but we must discuss the business that brought us here.' She handed him his Lettre de Marque and ring.

'Of course, Colonel.' He grinned and saluted.

She grinned back. He'd always turned the most serious misdemeanour into an adventure. 'Where and when will you collect the cargo?'

'Was it you that sent Captain Macdonald as a pilot?' he asked.

'Yes.'

'He's a good man. I've two frigates. We'll be at Lochboisdale tomorrow at midnight. Can you have 'im there at that time? What about redcoats?'

'Dinna worry, we've plans to keep them busy. You'll be able to get the cargo safely away.'

'This is dangerous, ma petite.' He held her face in his hands. 'Be very, very careful, the British are not fools. And you are far too beautiful to end your days in gaol or worse.'

I willna tell him I've already been in one.

One hand stroked her hair and his dark eyes bored into hers. She became aware of his masculinity, of his lips spine-tinglingly close to her own. She'd forgotten the effect he'd had on her at sixteen. The sleepless nights she'd longed for him to do just this.

They stayed like that for some seconds, though it felt much longer. The world spun as if they were the only two in it. His lips hovered over hers, and enticed her. *If I just moved, just gave in, succumbed, my craving would end and I'd know what it was like to be kissed by this man, his hand stroking my bare skin. I'd come alive as I did with...*She pulled away. 'I'm married.' *Don't think of 'M'.*

'The forbidden is always the best fruit.' His voice hoarse.

'Not for me.'

'Ah, you love 'im, ma Cherie.' He sounded disappointed.

She lowered her lids. 'You have a wife.'

He looked away. 'A marriage of convenience.' He shrugged his shoulders in regret. 'It's of no matter.' He gave a half smile and raised a dark eyebrow.

The poor woman. 'I'm sorry...' She gathered her wits. 'We must talk business.'

'Of course.'

She shared her plan into the late hours until Philippe rocked back on his chair and crossed his long legs on the table. 'Congratulations, Colonel, it is a good plan, apart from one thing.'

'Really?' He surprised her, she'd covered everything surely?

He leant towards her. 'Come with me, to France. I'll wait an hour. Say yes, Cherie. We'll 'ave such fun. It will be like it was...'

'I canna.' *What's he suggesting?*

'I'll wait.' His brown eyes searched hers.

'No.'

'I'll wait.' He took her hand and kissed it.

So gallant. 'You'd risk all for me?'

'Of course, I've played cat and mouse with the Royal Navy for months whilst delivering men and supplies to Montrose. They 'aven't caught me yet.'

'Dinna wait, promise me.'

'As Madame wishes.' He smiled.

She found it impossible not to smile back. Then she remembered that he might not know about Charlotte, Margaret and Jean.

CHAPTER Fifty-one

September 1746

Rob found nothing for days. News of a lone man who asked questions must have raised suspicions for miles around. Where was she?

After a night of constant rain he wakened from a restless nightmare which involved Anne and redcoats. As the sun rose, he packed his saddlebags with bread and cheese saved from the previous night's meal. He tramped downstairs just as a group of ill-assorted men rode into the courtyard. He sensed a frisson in the air, but rode out unmolested as usual, found no news of Anne or the Prince and returned late into the night.

He strode through the yellow smog of tobacco and peat smoke and settled himself at a table. So, the men had remained. He stayed in the light and ordered drink after drink until his head slumped in a pool of ale. Rain drummed on the thatch. He knew more men had arrived as the cold night air wrapped round him and candles guttered. Rob's hand tightened over the dirk he held under the table.

'We're soaked, bring whisky,' someone with a guttural voice said. They kept their faces hidden, made their way to the fire and turned their backs on him.

Rob strained for hours to hear anything, but learned nought. He forced himself to bed and thought of Anne.

The next morning his mind raged at his impotence. Yesterday he'd seen more sails off shore and increased redcoat patrols. He had to get her away. Where was she?

He needed his musket, pistol and dirk. Before he slept he'd put them on the floor by his right hand. He looked, they weren't there. In two steps he was at his bedroom door, but it wouldn't open. Locked. He thumped repeatedly on the wooden planks and shouted, but no one answered. He strode to the window and wrenched open the shutters. Several Highlanders peered up at the inn as herring gulls squawked and took off from the thatch in a flutter of wings.

'Captain Stewart. Good morning to you, sir. You're an early riser.'

A muscle twitched in Rob's cheek as he recognised Alan's pockmarked face.

'Forget the pleasantries. I ken who you are, Buick. Let me go. I need to ensure my wife's safe.'

'You're a fortunate man, Captain; several of us have volunteered to do that for you.'

Rob put his hands on the windowsill. 'Blast it, she's my wife.'

'There's some would like to make her a widow.' His men laughed at that.

'Your bloody Cause has killed thousands' said Rob.

Mottled purple. The colour emphasised the caverns in Alan Buick's face.

'No captain, your bloody Cumberland did that to the wounded and innocents across the Highlands. You were at Culloden; you've Highland blood on your hands. It'd be easy for us to forget your wife's wishes and make you disappear.'

'I swear, Buick, if anything happens to her, you're a dead man.'

'I'm always at your service, Captain.' He bowed. 'Dinna' try to escape, some of my men lost kin at Culloden and would take great pleasure in killing you. You'll stay here till your wife says you can come out to play.' Hoots of derisive laughter came at that.

Good God, he realised, she's organised this. Made me look a fool again. Rob punched a wall in frustration. He paced the floor, fumed and sweated throughout the day. How to escape? He discarded one plan after another.

The inn keeper, escorted by two burly Highlanders, brought food and drink. Rob took the tray. The door slammed shut and a key turned in the lock.

Rob wanted to hurl the tray at the door, but resisted the temptation. His body needed nourishment for whatever lay ahead. He had to out think these men. The window was too small and the door locked. He kicked the only chair in frustration. It rearranged itself in a tumble of broken legs on the floor. Lady Buick must have warned them, or Anne. She'd know he'd come after her.

He walked backwards and forwards all day. Night fell and as he leant over the fireplace he heard the mutter of voices from the floor below.

'Colonel says it's tonight,' said Sir Alan.

'So it's to be Arisaig?' said a gruff voice.

'Aye,' replied Sir Alan.

'And the French?'

'They'll take him off at midnight,' said Lord Alan. 'And the Captain will sleep through it all. Let's drink to the success of our venture.'

Rob heard the clink of glasses and the voices receded. He had to get out of this accursed inn if he wished to save Anne from harm. His fingers tapped on the wooden mantelpiece. The chimney. He looked inside and saw a square, black tunnel and stars. A narrow space, but he'd slim hips. He stepped into the hearth and bent down. Dark space. He stretched his arms upwards and his fingers clung to an overhang. With a heave he lifted himself amongst a shower of ancient soot. A second heave, a scrabble upwards and he peered out of the chimney. His foot found purchase as his nose twitched. He longed to sneeze.

He waited for the pale moon to go behind a cloud and pulled himself onto the thatch. The sounds of drunken songs and a fiddle filtered out of the windows and doors below. The music would cover his movements across the roof. He couldn't see sentries, but they'd be there in the brush. At least a fine film of soot coated his face and hands.

He scrambled to the back of the inn's thatch. Slid and slithered as he hung. Dropped into the darkness. He landed with a thud and rolled into a ball. He held his breath as his heart pounded. Nothing. The music became louder than ever, the singers drunker. He hugged the inn's walls all the way to the stables. Got there. He patted the restless ponies, found the saddles and bridles slung over one of the horizontal posts. Within minutes he mounted his horse. With the reins of the several ponies in his hand, he trotted out of the stable like any other traveller.

'Halt.'

Rob leant low in the saddle and spurred his horse into a gallop. The other mounts forced to follow as he swerved round low, dark shapes he took to be coarse bracken or heather. Muskets exploded behind him, but he headed for Arisaig.

He urged his horse into the black night, across a beck, up a steep hillside, along a burn and into the cover of trees. Then he pulled up. He listened for the chase, the sound of furious hoof beats, the slap of leather and men's curses. Nothing. This had been too easy: the overheard conversation, his escape, the lack of sentries near the inn and the shots that somehow missed him.

None of them had even come close.

Suspicions aroused, he trotted back the way he'd come. He left his horse and ponies tied at the bottom of the hill. From the top he saw the illuminated inn. A red-bearded man thumped the landlord on the back and laughed as if at some great joke. The humped-back lad even mimed someone who slunk off and rode hell for leather. Then he brought a string of ponies into the courtyard.

Rob watched them mount and set off at a gallop towards the coast, in the opposite direction to the one he'd travelled. Damnation. The joke had been on him.

Grim faced, he followed at a distance. These men would lead him to Anne. He needed to get there before the redcoats, but what about the Prince?

CHAPTER Fifty-two

As Anne told Philippe about her experience of the aftermath of Culloden and their friends' sad stories, he paled. 'Mon dieu, to kill women and children, is barbaric. This Cumberland is a butcher and his redcoats - monsters.'

'They're not all cut from the same cloth.'

Philippe stared at her. 'I never expected you to say such a thing.'

'One redcoat, Colonel Wolfe, refused Cumberland's order to kill one of our wounded, another saved one of our men.' She looked at the glint in Philippe's eyes and his set jaw. 'Perhaps we should change the topic? How's your father?'

Their reminiscences continued until just after dawn when they heard the sound of a hard ridden pony, the pound of feet and the door broke open. Light blinded them.

'Redcoats,' shouted Alan. 'They're a mile off and travelling fast towards us, must have marched through the night. Colonel, the Prince needs to get on his way.'

Philippe put a reassuring hand on her shoulder. 'I'll send him on ahead. I'll stay, 'elp you fight them off.'

'No. We'll stick to my plan. Go. Save the Prince.'

'Anne...'

Muskets fired in the distance. She pushed Philippe out of the door amidst the hubbub and shouted, 'Men, this is Captain Philippe St. Etienne.' She pointed at the men to the right of her. 'You're under his command. Take him to the Prince and the coast. You others stay with me. We'll cover their retreat and guard Shieldaig Pass.'

***

Rob pulled up his horse at the sound of shots ahead of him followed by the cries of men in agony. What the hell? Anne? He knew the Shieldaig Pass with its sheer mountains on each side and narrow track, from his time with the MacDonalds in his youth.

'Halt. Who goes there?' The shout from a redcoat with a raised musket to Rob's left.

Rob shouted above the clash of swords, yells and shrieks. 'Captain Stewart, Wolfe's regiment with special orders.'

'Advance and be recognised.'

He advanced. A ruddy-faced redcoat pulled him off his horse.

'I'm an officer. Get your hands off me, private.'

A hefty sergeant stepped out of the darkness. 'An officer you say, and with a Scots accent. It's difficult to tell friend from foe. You're in civilian clothes and covered in...?'

'Soot. Read my orders damn, you.' Rob snatched them from his waistband and held them out.

The sergeant read them and went pale. 'My apologies, sir, you can't be too careful in these parts.' He stared at Rob, went to ask a question, thought better of it, scanned the orders again and then saluted. 'We've good reason to believe the Prince is in the area. Bet my pay we're close cos as you can see we've been held up by 'ighlanders armed to the teeth. Thought we'd killed the treacherous curs at Culloden.'

'I understand.' Rob thought fast and lied. 'Probably the same ones took my wife prisoner. Have you seen her? I've been following them.'

'Been told the Prince could be dressed as a woman. Your wife's in danger, sir.'

'Newly married, gave in to her pleas to visit relatives. Should have known better, didn't appreciate the dangers.'

The sergeant nodded. 'It's 'er 'onour you'll be worried about then, now she's in the hands of those stinking Jacobites?' A shot whizzed past his right ear and made him duck.

'Yes. Warn your men, the Jacobites have my wife and I want her returned unharmed. *Unharmed* do you hear? I'd be grateful for a sword, they took my weapons.'

***

Anne, Alan and her men had held up the redcoats for a time at the pass, but she'd lost half of her Highlanders. She chewed her thumb. *We'll soon be overwhelmed. What will Rob think? That his wife's disgraced him? We haven't even consummated our marriage. Don't think about 'M'. I'll die not having really lived.*

'I've never run away from a fight in my life,' Philippe's voice whispered in her ear as shots ricocheted off rocks.

'Damn you. What about...?'

'The Prince is with my men, close to the ship. He's in safe hands.'

'And you? Why are you here?'

Musket balls slewed past. He put a protective arm round her as they cowered down. His brown eyes searched her face. Finally he said, 'I told you I like to fight.'

'There are too many. I need a group of us to ride away to the east.'

'A decoy?'

'Yes.'

'Alan and I will buy you time,' Philippe said. 'Go.' He raised his musket and fired.

She recognised the firm line of his mouth.

'Go now,' said Alan. He reached for his ramrod. 'They're getting closer. God speed.'

'God speed,' she said. *Will I ever see them again?* She led half a dozen men behind the lines to their ponies. She mounted, wheeled and spurred along a track which smoked away into the hills to the east. Her men followed.

***

The shout went up along the line of redcoats. 'It's the Prince. He's escaping.'

Rob leapt on his horse. One figure slighter and more slender than the others. Anne. 'Sergeant, get some men and follow me,' he yelled. He didn't look behind him as he galloped towards the roar of battle. With his sword raised he shouted threats into the air and became lost in the melee.

Musket balls flew at him like hail as he thundered between the lines of men which heaved backwards and forwards. A figure flung itself up in front of Rob. His horse reared and threw him at the man's feet. Rob rolled to one side as the man's sword hit empty space. Both men circled each other.

Rob studied his attacker. Dark, tall and light on his feet. Rob parried each thrust and slash and knew he fought a master swordsman. He probed for a gap in his opponent's defence, any weakness and found none. Finally, he threw himself at him and hoped brute strength would win against skill in sword play.

The man didn't seem used to the rough and tumble of a Captain who needed to find his wife. Arms and legs tangled. Rob hit him with the basket of his sword, rewarded to see blood spurt from a gash across his victim's cheek.

'Get Philippe out of here.' Lord Alan of Buick shouted.

Rob knew that name. Philippe. Johnstone had mentioned him. This man, her childhood playmate had enticed Anne away. Rob wanted to kill him. Two fierce Highlanders hauled Rob back as he struggled and cursed them. By rights they should have killed him. He detected Anne's hand in this.

Philippe snarled over his protector's heads, 'We'll meet again Monsieur, and when we do I'll kill you.'

'At your service, sir,' Rob threw off his captors and bowed. 'I suspect you'd like another scar to match the bonny one I gave you? Captain Rob Stewart of Wolfe's 8th and you are...?'

Philippe coiled like a spring and stared hard at Rob. He spat out, 'Philippe St. Etienne and we will meet again. I swear it.'

Hell fire, he was Anne's friend and Rob itched to kill him.

Lord Alan hauled St. Etienne away. Highlanders closed rank as several redcoats, their faces contorted with rage, charged with bayonets at the ready. The air filled with shouts, screams and whimpers as a Highlander used his targe to flick a bayonet aside; a claymore found its redcoat target and a Jacobite fell from a sword thrust to his right side.

Rob parried, hacked and pushed one Jacobite over in his frenzy to mount a rider-less horse. Its eyes rolled, and set off in the direction of the fleeing riders.

***

With relief, Anne saw the redcoats had taken the bait. They'd been hindered by Philippe and Alan, then given chase for mile after mile. She wouldn't let herself think about what had happened to her friends and the men she'd left behind. She needed to lead the redcoats as far away from the Prince as possible.

Their pursuers wouldn't give up. She ordered her men to peel off. They hid under pack-horse bridges, behind hills, rocks and waterfalls. Only she remained. The soldiers must have chased her for half a day. She'd done what she'd set out to do. The Prince had escaped. What happened to her didn't matter. Her lathered pony stumbled, went on and stumbled again. *If I go on I'll kill the poor beast.* She came to a halt beside a burn where the heather and gorse studded the glen and stark mountains surrounded her. The pony drank while she sat and waited for the redcoats to catch up with her. *I won't escape from gaol a second time. Poor Rob, to have such a wife. I bet he thinks 'M' would never have behaved in this manner.*

***

Rob knew this country well. He thought of the time he'd lived with the MacDonald's. His father ordered that as he'd be chief one day, he'd have a hard time of it. Whipped for any transgression, Rob had learnt the Highland code of honour the hard way: to endure without complaint. He'd also learnt which hills could be walked or ridden over and secret paths.

As he galloped by Creag Bhan, he hid behind a fall of rock and allowed the redcoats to carry on their pursuit. He used a shortcut. With luck he'd catch Anne or cut her off.

Anne dabbled her hand in a burn as if she had all the time in the world. The water's babble meant she didn't hear Rob's approach. When he sat down beside her she recoiled, then her brow furrowed. 'You're covered in…'

'Soot,' he said and helped himself to a handful of water. He washed his face.

'I knew you'd come.' Her eyes looked like wells of sadness and turned back to the water. 'Are you very angry?'

Rob's mind raced like a runaway coach. How to explain her actions? Had she any idea of what could happen to her? Imprisonment wasn't the worst of it. They'd executed others for less. Her youth and sex might not save her.

From the distance came the pound of horses' hooves. He had to act. 'Anne, darling, forgive me.' Before she turned her head Rob's fist caught her on the chin and knocked her out. She fell like a cut flower. He put her head on his lap and watched the livid bruise form across her chin. The redcoats found them like that.

'Those Highland bastards mistreated her and left her for dead,' he lied. 'They went that way,' and he pointed towards the north. 'One of you stay and give me a hand. The rest of you, I want those scum dead or alive.' The main group spurred away.

'Help me lift her onto my horse,' he said to a sad-faced private. 'She needs a physician.'

CHAPTER Fifty-three

Rob's forehead creased into a frown. Anne had slept all that day and night on the way to Fort William. Perhaps the first streaks of dawn warmed the cold air? Or she heard the slap of oars plunge in and out of Loch Linnhe or Rob's conversation with the oarsmen?

Her eyes fluttered open. The bruise on her swollen chin no longer bright red and purple, but yellow and green. She groaned.

'What...?'

'Happened?' Rob flicked a look at the boatman, whose face had lines like a cracked plate. 'Highlanders left you for dead,' he lied. 'Why did you ride alone when I told you not to?'

She licked her lips and he gave her a drink of water from his canteen. 'I...,' she began, 'I...canna remember.' She closed her eyes and went back to sleep.

Thank God.

'Poor lady,' said the boatman. 'To be treated so badly. The man that did that should be horsewhipped.'

Rob raised his eyes to Heaven as guilt swept over him. He prayed everyone would believe this tale. It would be the talk of Fort William for weeks.

***

Later that afternoon, Rob paced up and down in front of the fire in the sitting room in the barracks at Fort William. Fifteen minutes earlier, the physician had waddled into the bedroom to examine Anne. Rob whipped round as the door opened. The physician's chest heaved up and down as if he'd just fought ten rounds with a wild cat. The outraged cries and shrieks from behind the bedroom door had certainly sounded like it to Rob.

'How's my wife, sir?' asked Rob.

The physician positioned his fat backside on a chair. 'Your wife you say? She seems...untouched...by this ordeal.'

'We're newly married...an arranged match...' What else could he say?

'Hmph, I understand. She's young with a strong constitution'. The physician rubbed his knee as if to get rid of an ache. 'She should recover, but if you want my advice, you need to take her in hand.' He showed Rob his meaty palm with two sets of teeth marks indented in it. 'In hand I say.' He wheezed himself out of the chair. 'Mind my words,' he said with a parting shot. 'Women need to know who's master.' He left Rob to face his wife.

Rob knocked, then peered round the bedroom door, 'How are...?'

'You hit me,' she yelled.

The sound of china crashed against stout wood. He'd only just shut the door in time. She'd hurled the chamber pot at him. Prudence seemed best, he left her to dwell on her behaviour. He needed a stiff drink.

***

Anne paced her bedroom. Rob had been away for hours. Enough time for her to be demented with worry. Had her friends survived? Had they and the Prince escaped to France? The questions circled inside Anne's head till it ached.

A knock sounded on her door again.

'Oh come in if you must.' Anne jumped into bed and pulled the covers over her.

Rob peeked round the door. 'I thought perhaps you'd run out of china.'

'Insufferable man.' She hoisted the covers higher.

He eased himself into the room. 'It's good to see you're in a better frame of mind.'

'Hmph.'

'Please accept my sincere apologies for hitting you, but the redcoats were too close. At least they believed you'd been kidnapped by Highlanders...'

'Hmph.'

'If you hadn't been such a hoyden and run off to save the Pretender...'

'Prince. Has he been caught?' She lowered the covers.

'No' yet.'

'Good.' She folded her arms. 'And my men?'

'If you mean St. Etienne and Lord Alan, they'll be found. You could have been killed. You should have trusted me, Anne.'

They're alive. 'You're a redcoat officer for goodness sake and you've never told me about...'

'I dinna wish to argue. The matter is closed.'

***

Each wearisome day at Fort William followed another until her head filled with the ring of orders, drums and the clash and clatter of men and horses.

Rob slept under an old blanket on a chair. She'd studied her appearance in a rusty mirror, and could understand why he might want to keep his distance. The ugly bruise covered half her face and had even spread to her nose. Once petite, now a lump of dough wedged on the side of a mountainous discoloured cheek. *I'm not fit to be seen. Does he feel guilty every time he sees my swollen face? Well, he should.*

And what must they think, the redcoats, the women in Fort William, that stupid physician with his intimate prodding and poking? That I'd been raped? If so, I'd definitely not be accepted in society and would be shamed in front of everyone again.

Of course all the ladies at the fort wanted to hear about her 'adventure' first hand and left their cards and little knick-knacks for her edification. She threw out all their gifts of jams and cordials.

Rob had told her about the Victory Ball some days ago.

'But I dinna want to go.' She chewed her thumb. *Did he dance with 'M'?*

He stared at her. 'You must.'

'A lot of my friends died for the Cause. I see no reason to celebrate.' She turned away from him.

His voice became steely. 'I've arranged for a dressmaker to come this afternoon.'

'No.'

'You leave me no choice.' He leant towards her. 'You'll go to the ball in a dress of my style and choosing.'

She stood up. 'You canna force me.'

He dropped his voice to a whisper. 'Anne, we must. For our story to be believed, you have to convince everyone that you're as loyal to the British Crown as they are.'

'I willna, I'd rather die first.' She hurled the words at him and stamped her foot.

'You might well get your wish,' he snapped. 'But I have no wish to die with you. We must go this ball to show face. There must be no suspicion pointed at us. You must do this for the sake of both our families.'

***

Several days later she heard him call through the bedroom door. 'Are you ready, Anne?' She emerged from the bedroom, like a dutiful wife. 'I suppose, if you can call this horse blanket...' She looked at the grim set to his face and continued between tight lips, 'The dress is beautiful.' Low on the shoulders and tight around the waist, the jade silk fitted to perfection. The worst of the bruise, she'd disguised with powder and artful ringlets. Her bruised pride a little more difficult to hide.

He offered his arm. She hesitated, then took it.

'Smile,' he said.

She leant towards him and pressed down on his foot. 'Brute.'

'Thank you, darling,' he said for the ears of the sergeant who'd come to escort them.

She could have hit him.

The ballroom hummed with activity. He left her as the women flocked to offer their condolences and treated her like a freak at the local fair. Rob came to her rescue with a glass of punch that made her eyes run, then whirled her off into a dance.

When the music ended Anne sat whilst Rob offered her sweetmeats and tried to amuse her with his chatter. He turned down invitations from his fellow officers to dance with her. 'My apologies, but I dinna want her overtired.'

As if he cares.

Finally, he decided they should go home.

Anne grateful, tired beyond endurance and determined not to show him, stumbled in the dark. Without a qualm he picked her up, despite her struggles and carried her home.

'Poor darling,' he said.

'Don't you *darling* me,' she said when he set her down. I...I'm going to bed.'

He followed her into the bedroom and shut the door.

'You don't expect, you can't possibly think...?' She stared at him.

'We're married Anne and I'd like for once to sleep in my marriage bed and no' on a chair by a dead fire. Dinna worry I won't disturb you.' With that he turned his back on her and began to strip off his uniform.

She turned her back on him and also undressed. *What else can I do?* She slipped between the covers and ensured no part of her touched him. It was as if 'M' lay like a bolster between them. She cried silent tears, wanted to be at Kerbilly with her Father, for all to be as it was before this dreadful man came into her life. Sleep came. When she woke he'd gone. An indentation in his pillow a reminder where'd he'd slept.

A week went by when she didn't see him from dawn till dusk. At night he just flung himself into bed in an exhausted state. Until one morning as she dressed, she heard him call, 'The horses are saddled. Would you care to ride?'

'I suppose.'

He took her to mauve hills and golden glens. Pointed out crystal clear waterfalls, herds of deer and eagles overhead. She began to love this part of the Highlands and knew she loved him too, but he never touched her. *Lord, how she wished he would.*

CHAPTER Fifty-four

Anne watched Rob shave as his tuneful whistle filled the sitting room. *How can he be so happy, so comfortable with himself, whilst I...long for his touch?* The sun shone in a blue sky. He bent to watch himself in the mirror and drew a razor down his angular chin. The blade gathered soap and stubble as he went. He dipped it in a basin of hot water and started the process again. She'd never seen a man shave before. His height, his size and physicality filled the room. His jacket over a chair and his boots by the door declared him the man of the house.

For over a year she'd made her own decisions, been in charge of men and now she had to contend with Rob Stewart, her husband. She wished they could go back to that carefree day on the beach at Kerbilly, back to her bedroom when she would have given herself to him. Now they were reserved around each other, polite, but not at ease.

'My duty's done, Wolfe's recalled me to Inverness.'
Does this mean the Prince's safe in France?
He dried his face with a towel. 'Thought I'd visit the family in Braedrumie, while there's a break in the weather, would you care to join me?'

'Of course.' Intrigued, Anne remembered the Edinburgh Ball over a year ago and how handsome his brothers appeared. She also remembered the striking woman who stood by their side.

***

Days later, Anne glanced at Rob's face. He looked grim and said little, as if he'd left part of him behind in Braedrumie. What had his family decided? What had been said that had turned Rob in on himself.

And his brother's wife, Morag - the woman at the Prince's ball? Had she imagined the sudden flash of...something, between them? A lapse in his usual manner. No one had remarked on it. 'M'? If he won't speak, how can I help him - us?

Rob took Anne back to Kerbilly through a frozen landscape. They travelled west past dramatic mountain ranges crusted in snow and ice; through glens with frosted trees; along the banks of frozen rivers and lochs which mirrored the crisp, white scenery all round them.

They saw no one, slept in ruined crofts, he against one wall and she another, tucked inside woollen rugs, their heads on saddles. Anne wrestled with the rug and he appeared to do the same.

She remembered his limbs entangled round hers, his masculine scent and skin. His fingers burned, scorched and made her explore his body, in search of release. *This wanting has never left me, but what about him, so close and yet so distant? He's hardly spoken, never touched me and now he lies six feet away making our marriage a mockery. Will I ever bridge the gap between us? And Philippe, Alan and the Prince, what about them?*

She blinked back tears and stared at the embroidered sky through the patchwork of thatch. She needed to love and be loved. *Will we ever consummate our marriage?*

Next day Rob had the same grim expression on his face as they rode through bright sunshine and shadow. *What was it the men had discussed on that last night?*

'It's beautiful isn't it?' she said. Ahead a crystal clear waterfall streamed over tawny rocks in a rainbow of diamond droplets.

'Aye.'

He said nary a word. *What sort of man have I married?*

They arrived late at Kerbilly.

'I'll write to your uncle,' he said as he helped her dismount. 'Thank him for looking after Dulcie.'

'Perhaps ask if he'll bring her back tomorrow?' said Anne.

'Of course.' Rob dashed off to the library.

Anne hoped Dulcie would forgive them. She followed Rob into the house.

'Your relative, my lady? Well I hope?'

'Relative? Oh, very well. Very well indeed,' said Anne. She gave Johnstone her cloak.

'Some mutton, my lady?' asked Johnstone. 'Warm you after your journey.'

'Please,' she said, but had little appetite. Rob seemed to feel the same way as he took one bite and put down his knife and fork.

'I have to deliver my report to Wolfe,' he stated. 'I'll be off to Inverness tomorrow. I've informed Johnstone.'

'Then go.' *Drat him and the British army.*

'It's my duty,' he said by way of explanation.

'Then God damn your duty Rob Stewart.' She banged her cutlery down on the table. Rob looked at her wide-eyed and Johnstone wide-mouthed as she flung her napkin at Rob's head and stormed out of the room.

***

Rob and Johnstone both flinched as she stamped upstairs.

'You'll be needing a wee dram I'm thinking.' Johnstone poured the amber nectar into two glasses. 'Her mother was the same, had a bit of a temper. The auld Master always felt better after a dram.'

'Yes.'

Rob threw it down his throat, enjoyed the fiery taste and the warm sensation in his stomach. Johnstone followed suit.

They both stared at the ceiling as the bedroom door slammed and the chandelier rattled.

'Another dram, sir?'

'Large.'

Johnstone poured two glasses. This time Rob's head swam.

'I'll make up the guest bedroom, shall I, sir?'

'Yes and leave the bottle, there's a good man.'

Rob watched the candle and firelight wink and blink at him. He filled the glass to the brim. Liquid, the colour of rich peat slopped onto the damask tablecloth. He drank deeply again.

He'd been in a foul mood since they'd left Braedrumie. He could understand Euan's reasoning. Hard to give his brother the blessing he craved. Rob, the eldest, had been heir after all. It had been difficult. This decision would change the Stewarts' lives forever. If only there'd been another way. Memories of Duncan came to him at night and he hungered to see Johnnie again. He didn't want to lose those left, but a soldier could be posted to the far ends of the world. He couldn't share any of this with Anne, he'd been an idiot to think she'd forgive him for his treatment of her. Then there was Morag.

He staggered to his feet, took the bottle and glass with him and made his drunken way up the stairs. Paused to toast Anne's mother who smiled lopsidedly at him from her portrait on the wall. Grabbed the oak banister with one hand and crawled up to the top landing. Propped himself against the wall and lurched towards the master bedroom and Anne. Put his hand on the handle, thought better of it and stumbled to the guest bedroom.

It seemed only minutes later when he jerked upright. Some fool had opened the curtains. Light blinded him and a sadist had cooked kippers. His stomach heaved in revolt as he pushed the breakfast tray away and squinted at Johnstone.

'Good morning, sir,' said the butler.

Holding his head in both hands, Rob opened one eye. 'Do you think you could whisper?'

'Of course sir, hair of the dog?' Johnstone offered him a whisky. 'Lady Anne's gone out.'

Rob swept the whisky aside and tried to clear his head. 'Where?' Had she left him? He'd been such a cad, lost in his own misery, with no thought of her.

Johnstone smiled and cocked an eyebrow at the decanter.

'Have a dram,' Rob said. Anne.

'Thank you sir, you're most kind.' Johnstone drank it like water. 'The groom says she's been up since dawn, took the cliff path south. Didna take her maid.'

'What?'

'There's a cove she likes and a rock called the Needle's Eye. You'll ken it when you see it.'

Thunderation, Rob thought, Wolfe's report will have to wait. 'Right get me hot water and lots of it.' Rob leapt out of bed and regretted it. He put a hand to his head, but carried on.

'That's the spirit, sir.' Johnstone grinned at his own pun.

CHAPTER Fifty-five

Rob could see why Anne liked this ride with its views of golden beaches and pewter sea. The wind blew in his face and pushed huge waves to crash in a flurry of white spray on shore. Dark clouds hung like an ebony plume out at sea. In a finger of light on the horizon he caught sight of the white sail of a ship before it disappeared from view. British or French?

A thin needle of rock with a weathered 'eye' appeared in front of him. Anne had tied her horse's reins to a tree stump. She shaded her eyes with one hand as she looked out to sea, oblivious of her loose hair and cloak which flapped in the wind. He dismounted and stood behind her. 'Can you forgive me?' he said.

She started then relaxed. Let him nestle his arms round her waist and put his cheek to hers. He enjoyed their closeness after months of a monk-like existence. She smelt of fresh air. He took her hand. 'Anne?'

'Yes,' she said at last, if you tell me why you left Braedrumie, why you jilted me.'

He released her and looked out to wind-whipped waves for a few moments and then turned 'I loved someone once. She's the reason I left my home and enlisted. You met her...Morag...she's married to Euan now.'

She jerked her hand out of his. 'Morag! You jilted me because of her, your brother's wife?'

'She wasna married at the time. I love you now and after all, you cared for Philippe St. Etienne.'

'How do you know...how dare you, he was a childhood friend...someone I thought I...it was different.'

'Believe me, it was the same for me.'

'So, everything's alright now then? You...you...bastard. You jilted me.'

'I did a foolish thing, Anne, but there's really no reason to call my parentage into doubt.'

'You've no idea, have you, the hurt you caused? I was ostracised, friends and neighbours turned against me. I was a social outcast because of you.'

'Damn. I didna think...'

'No you didna. And what sort of man leaves his family, his ill mother...his home without a word?'

'Don't you think I regret it?'

'You've said little about it.'

'Because I'm tortured by it.' He swept his hand through his hair. 'I canna change any of it and it shames me. I'm so sorry for everything. Can you for forgive me for jilting you, marrying you against your will, for...mistreating you? His eyes held hers as he went down on one knee and took her hand. 'Darling, Anne, I love you with my heart and soul. I'm resolved to spend the rest of my life making you happy. Please say you'll forgive the callow youth and accept the regrets of the man.'

'Oh...I...'

He gave her a wry grin. 'I'll wait.' He kissed her hand and rose to his feet. 'You know we're probably in agreement over one thing?'

'We are?' She looked sceptical.

'We're both pleased Charlie's probably back in France.'

'Oh, he's back in France all right...' she bit her lip.

It was if he'd stumbled into quick-sand. 'I'm no going to ask how you know.' He held her closer. 'I'm just pleased the damned business is over and done with. And if you could find it in your heart to forgive my damned black silences, I'd be eternally grateful. They've gotten me into trouble before, should have been beaten out of me. Of course, if you feel you canna, then I fully understand...'

'I forgive you...for everything.'

'Everything? You do? Really? Oh, Anne. You love me.'

'I've always loved you.' She stood on her toes and kissed him. This left him with no alternative, but to kiss her back.

He forced himself to take a breath. 'What were you thinking about?'

'Now?'

'Before when you looked out to sea.'

'Of...a good friend...who's in danger,' and she turned to the surf again, as it churned over rocks.

'A...man?'

Why did he say that? 'Yes.'

'Do you love him?' He willed her to say no.

She looked at him out of the corner of her eyes and smiled, 'Perhaps.'

'Never say that.' He put his lips to hers, the tip of his tongue traced their outline. He gave her no chance to pull away. Her body tensed, then he sensed her response. His, she'd always be his.

Then she pulled away and her fingers released a sheet of parchment which wafted to the ground.

Their heads bumped as they both went to rescue it from the wind. He trapped it with the sole of boot.

She picked it up. 'It's a letter from another friend, one you know well.'

'Lord Alan?'

'He writes to say he's safe and well.'

'Hmm. It pleases me he is safe and you're no longer concerned about his welfare.'

'Are you? Then you are the most generous of men. Let's walk.' She took his hand and dragged him down the cliff path onto the sand. 'No. Not that way, this.' The tide had turned, and raced in, but not before he'd spotted two sets of footprints, one small and one large. They led in the opposite direction.

'I've been chatting to Joch Mckay,' she said, 'Says the fish are not biting. He lives in one of the fisher crofts behind us.'

'Do you often speak to fishermen?'

'Only if they're eighty and grandfathers.' Her lips curved into a smile.

Reassured, Rob held her close as they walked. He'd tell her one day soon about what had been said at Braedrumie and the decision that had been made. One day when it didn't hurt quite so much.

A gust of wind almost knocked her off her feet. They'd been deep in conversation and failed to notice the storm had been driven inland. The wind rose to a shriek and foam-flecked waves crashed onto rocks. The sea turned an ominous dark grey. The sky lit up like a fractured hand.

'The horses.' She raised her voice so she could be heard above the gusts. 'They'll be frightened.'

They headed back to the cliffs, buffeted by the gale as they went. The horses reared and pulled at their reins.

Anne patted her mount's neck and whispered in her ear. 'It's alright. Sssh.'

'There, there,' said Rob to his mare as the first drops of rain fell.

'We'll be drenched before we get home,' she said, 'Best follow me.' She led him over a hill, down into scrub and under a stone bridge. They tied the horses to a low branch and let them crop in safety as they sheltered from the torrential rain on the banks of a burn. The stone arch of the bridge rose over their heads and soft green ferns lay at their feet. They stood in deep shadow. Thunder rolled above them. Anne jumped and pressed her body closer to his. He put his lips to hers, enjoyed her soft surrender and response when her warm lips sought his. The buds at the tip of her breasts pressed against his chest.

He dropped his cloak on the ground and pulled her down beside him. 'Now where was I when I was so rudely interrupted by that damned redcoat private? Let me see.' His lips played on her neck, her throat and shoulder. He moved to her foot. His fingers fondled, stroked their way up her calf till he massaged her knee, 'I believe I'd just discovered...'Ahah.' He untied her garter and rolled down her stocking. Then he kissed the skin of her naked thigh. Rewarded by a giggle that bubbled from her throat.

She let him unlace her stays, as she threw items of his clothing, one at a time, over her shoulder with careless abandon.

'My favourite waistcoat.' He yelled and watched it float away.

'Too late it'll be in the sea in minutes.' Two dimples appeared either side of her delectable mouth. 'I'm cold.'

'I'm sure I can think of something to cure that.' He gathered her back into his arms and under his cloak

Sometime later when she moved rhythmically beneath him and he thrust ever deeper, she sighed. 'Rob, I dinna want...this moment...to...ever...end.' Her hands clawed his back.

'Dinna fash.' His voice was hoarse as he struggled for control. 'If it's anything to do with me it willna.'

They arrived bedraggled back at Kerbilly late that afternoon.

Rob handed Johnstone their cloaks. 'We're a bit wet I'm afraid.'

'And the twigs and grass sir?' Johnstone brushed the material with his hand.

Rob coughed.

Anne put a hand over her mouth.

'And you seem to have...mislaid your...ahem...waistcoat.'

Rob damned him for being observant. 'Ah, yes well...we took shelter from the storm. Took it off to...to sit on, must have left it. Now fetch some food like the good man you are. I believe my wife and I have developed a hearty appetite.' He held Anne by the waist and twirled her round the hall.

Rob thought he heard Johnstone mutter, 'You'll no' be needing the guest bedroom tonight then?' Then he added, 'Miss Dulcie, Florie and your Uncle William have been here since midday. The girls are tired of waiting and he's just tired.'

Rob and Anne entered the study arm in arm. Uncle William sat with one swollen foot on a stool, whilst Dulcie danced towards them. She shrieked, 'Oh, oh I'm so pleased you're here. We've been waitin' hours and hours. Where've you been? I've decided I like my new name now. Florie says it suits me and dear Uncle William bought me a new dress.' She spun round.

'He said I looked like a princess and should dress like one. He bought Florie one too.' Brown-haired Florie beamed. 'Don't you think I've grown?'

'Let me answer your last question first poppet,' Rob said. 'Without a doubt, but where did you get the hat you minx?'

She'd set it at a jaunty angle on her head and it covered one eye. 'Why, from Lady Anne's bedpost of course. Don't you like it, Captain?' She turned so they could see the wide, black brim and large red plume to best advantage.

'Very much, but it's a man's hat.'

Three pairs of eyes turned to look at Anne whose jaw slackened. 'It...it's...mine,' she said at last. 'It was...a friend's...I thought...I thought Dulcie...would like it...for dressing up and she obviously does.'

'Quite so.' Rob dismissed the hat as raffish. 'And Uncle William - please don't get up - I'm pleased to see you sir, but sorry to see you unwell.'

'It's gout,' said Uncle William. 'And your relative, quite recovered I hope?'

Rob blinked. 'Quite.' He grasped the old man's hand. 'Thank you for looking after Dulcie whilst we were away.'

'Think nought of it Rob,' he beckoned him closer and whispered in his ear. 'Mission accomplished eh?' And dug him in the ribs. 'You've made a match of it and she's glowing, my boy, glowing.' Then he winked.

'What's all this whispering about?' asked Anne and put her arm round Rob's waist.

'Yeah, what's it about?' said Dulcie and squeezed herself between them.

Rob looked at Anne's uncle for help.

'Nothing, my dears, said Uncle William. 'Just explaining about this damn gout.' He eased himself out of his chair and put his foot on the floor. 'I'm away to bed in my own home. Say goodbye, Florie.'

'Goodbye,' said Florie. 'Will Dulcie be able to visit us tomorrow?'

'Of course,' said Anne. She hugged and kissed Florie.

'They're both minxes,' said Uncle William. 'Now give your auld uncle a kiss you two.'

Anne and then Dulcie kissed his ruddy cheek whilst Johnstone brought his hat, cloak and gloves.

Rob stood with his arm round Anne's waist as they waved to Uncle William from the front door. His carriage sped away and they heard him roar at the coachman, 'Slow down you young fool, I'm an auld man and want to live for a few more years.'

Johnstone closed the front door as Rob said, 'I think we'll retire early, still need to recover from the journey. Perhaps you'd like to do the same, Dulcie?'

She closed one eye and wagged a finger at them. 'No bleedin' swiving.'

They ignored her, though Rob made a mental note to tell Anne she really needed to pay attention to Dulcie's choice of language and moral upbringing.

CHAPTER Fifty-six

The next morning Anne woke beside Rob and stretched like a pampered cat. She kissed his ear and said, 'Would you really have put me in an asylum, you know, if I hadna married you?'

Rob pretended to give the question serious thought and then replied, 'No, I'd have shot you first.' A pillow landed on his head. Before he could pull her to him she'd slipped out of bed and looked in the dressing table mirror

'Oh my,' she said. 'The cold doesna suit me. My nose will never recover, it's peeling already.'

'Really? Let me see.' She sat down on the bed beside him and held up her face as he pretended to examine it for damage. 'This does look rather bad I'm afraid, the worst case I've seen in years. I really must investigate further.' To screams of outraged delight he didn't start with her face.

***

'Darling, what are you doing?' asked Rob later that day when he saw Anne scrabble about on her knees in the shrubbery.

'Looking for something.' Her hands searched the soil and under leaves.

He knelt on one leg beside her. 'Can I help?'

'Well.' She flushed. 'Ah, found it.' She held up an oval object covered in soil.

'Was it worth it, darling?'

She chewed her thumb. 'It's a miniature...of you.'

'Oh.'

'I threw it out the window some time ago.'

He looked up and then at her. 'Ah, but all is forgiven now.' He wrapped his arms round her waist and nuzzled her ear.

'Of course...darling.'

'Good, good. I must tell you about my posting. Would you give up all this? Follow the drum to London with me?'

Anne flung herself into his arms. 'I couldna bear not to and Dulcie would come too?'

'Of course.' After many kisses, he extricated himself. 'I must deliver Wolfe's report,' he said. 'It's at least a day late already.'

'If you must.'

He led her out of the garden and upstairs to their bedroom.

'Let me help you dress,' she said and held out his uniform jacket.

He eased his arm into his red coat. 'Ow.' He turned the garment inside out, explored the seams and exclaimed, 'Ahah.' He held up a bright shiny pin. 'It's the strangest thing,' he said. 'This is the second I've found...What?'

Anne's eyes danced as she held a hand over her mouth.

'Anne, what's so amusing?'

'It was me, I forgot the pins. My way of...helping win the war.'

'Win the war? You...'

'I'll find the rest.' She grabbed his jacket.

'The rest? You were going to stab me to death with pins?'

She withdrew several more and offered him his jacket. 'I'm sorry, but you had a fortunate escape, I could have put them in your britches like...'

He shuddered. 'Not Wolfe.'

'No. I liked him. Hartlass.'

Rob's face turned thunderous. 'You put pins in his britches?'

'Yes.'

To her surprise he roared with laughter and wiped his eyes with his sleeve. 'That explains his pained expression.'

He flung his jacket to one side and his right arm caught her round the waist. His lips sought hers. Her hand somehow touched his bare chest, his fingers lingered on her hip and one thing led to another. Some hours later he set off at a mad dash to Inverness and Wolfe as Dulcie wagged her finger at them and Johnstone shook his head.

The End

If you enjoyed this eBook you can read on to find the first two chapters of the third and final story in the *Code of Honour* Trilogy:

It is always helpful to independent publishers and authors to receive feedback about their work. It would be very supportive if you could leave a review on the Amazon page where you bought this book by clicking this link

www.tiny.cc/tynebooks

The Jacobite Affair

Lorna Windham

CHAPTER One
Autumn 1732

Kirsty Lorne knew the moment she loved Johnnie Stewart. At four years old she sat barefoot in the dirt. The weather-beaten sign of *The Salmon* creaked overhead. An ant scrambled over the mountain of her knuckles. Drunken songs and men's low triumphant growls came from the inn.

Kirsty whipped round at a rat-tat-tat on a window pane. Her father stood with his hand on the shoulder of a large, grey bearded man. Her brow creased. Father made an upward movement with his chin. *Not again.* She smiled and revealed her teeth. The man stroked his beard and his thin lips cracked into a smile. Father slapped him on the back and split a pack of cards.

An inner glow spread through Kirsty's spread thin body. Sometimes she'd leave Father's shoes by the fire so they'd warm his feet, or place sprigs of heather on his pillow or save her bannock for him when he came in weary from work in the fields. Occasionally he'd pat her head. She liked that, but more often, the drunken beast rose in him and he'd be unpredictable and snarl at her. Then she'd hide in the byre, beside their calf, clasp her arms round its neck and enjoy the warmth and security it gave her.

Today, another beast held her father in its grasp, the one who smiled and would do anything for anyone, but her. His promise they'd pick flowers, broken when they'd come to the inn. The ant burrowed itself under a grain of soil. Father's laughter crashed over her in waves. *I wish I could make him happy.*

She froze at a sudden roar, turned and saw Father hurl his cards on the table. He lurched up, his face crimson and eyes wild. Kirsty's hand covered her crumpled mouth. *I've nowhere to hide.* She watched the big man shake his fist at him. Father's shoulders slumped and he nodded.

***

Six year old Johnnie Stewart whistled as he strolled along the muddy track towards the inn. He'd an ash pole over one shoulder and a wet gunny sack in his hand. It contained the largest salmon he'd ever caught. Proof for his brothers he could fish with the best of them. The Stewart household would eat well tonight. A child's wail and a low, gruff voice drifted towards him from beyond the bend in the track ahead.

A large, bearded man trudged into sight. He clasped the hand of a small, golden-haired girl. She shrieked and screamed as he dragged her along behind him. 'I want my mammy. Please sir, I want my mammy.'

Johnnie stood, arms on hips and legs astride and blocked the man's path. 'Why, it's wee Kirsty isn't it, Mrs. Lorne's bairn? What you doing, sir?'

The man blew out his weather veined cheeks. 'Mind your own business, you little snot, or I'll be givin' you some of this.' He threatened Johnnie with the large knotted stick he carried in one hand.

'Let Kirsty go.'

'And if I dinna?'

Johnnie bunched his fingers into fists.

'You'd take me on would you, wee man? Well, let me tell you, I'm goin' about my lawful business. Won her in a game of cards from her daddy, didn't I?'

Won her? Johnnie's brain tried to work it out. In a game of cards? You didn't play for bairns. Well, he and his brothers didn't, they played for pebbles, but he'd not tell the man that.

Kirsty wailed, 'I want to go home. I want my mammy.' Tears glistened as they drew lines of dirt down her face.

Johnnie studied the man and tried to remember what his oldest brother Rob always said: 'There's more ways to skin a cat.'

The man held Kirsty in a tighter grip as she clawed at his fist. 'Let me go.'

'I'll trade you,' said Johnnie as his heart sank. His brothers would never see his fine catch.

'Will you now?'

'Yes, this salmon for her.' He held it up in front of him. 'It's fresh from the burn this morning.'

'That tiddler?' The man laughed and showed black stubs for teeth as Kirsty wriggled in his grasp.

Johnnie bunched his fists again.

'Jock Sinclair, return my daughter, this minute,' yelled leather-faced Mrs Lorne as she bowled down the track towards them. She wielded a rolling pin in one fist and reminded Johnnie of an irate sporran.

'Now, Mrs. Lorne, I won her fair and square,' said the man. He backed away with a wary look in his eyes. 'Your Fergus owes me money.'

The sporran drew back her arm and thwacked him across the forehead with her wooden weapon. He dropped like a felled tree.

Kirsty stared at Johnnie and her gaze never left his. The sporran yanked at Kirsty's hand. 'Your Father wouldn't have done it if you'd been a son,' she hissed and hauled her daughter back along the track. Johnnie lost sight of Kirsty as she rounded the bend and headed back to her mother's farm.

CHAPTER Two
Winter 1742

The Lorne's thatched farmhouse squatted on a wide strip of flat, frosted land littered with granite boulders. Loch Linnhe, a rippled pewter sheet, lay a mile to the north.

The wind moaned down the chimney and rain drummed against the windows as Kirsty's mother, dressed in black, sat by the kitchen's meagre fire and eased off her worn boots. 'That churchyard's freezing, I'm wet through.'

Kirsty stood at the kitchen table. The damp shoulders of her patched, black dress reminded her of the steady fall of rain throughout the funeral. *Don't think of Father in the cold ground.* Her hands gripped the scullery table as she steadied herself. Then she took her coarse apron off its hook and put it on. A rabbit hung from an overhead beam. Her nose wrinkled, but she ignored its dead eyes and soft fur, placed it on the table and brought down a cleaver on the animal's leg joints. Thwack. Thwack. Thwack. Thwack.

Mother rubbed her stocking feet. 'When you've made the stew, you can clean these, they're covered in mud. I don't want it trailed round my house. Then fetch some peat.'

Kirsty set her teeth and pulled the rabbit's fur down its silver skin. She'd been fortunate to trap it. She stopped, wiped her eyes with her sleeve and took a deep breath before she gutted the carcase and cut the backbone away from the meat.

'I'm glad it's over.' Mother lifted the pile of bills from the table and waved them at Kirsty. 'He left us nought, but debt.'

'We'll manage, Mother,' Kirsty sniffed.

'How? There's just you and me to work the land and tend the cattle. If only I'd married better and had live sons. Not that anyone cares.'

Kirsty bit her lip. Three sons. They'd have been men now, worked with the black cattle, planted kale, onions and carrots, mended the farmhouse and done hundreds of jobs on their farm. She glanced at the letters on the table. 'Aunt Lizzie cares and your friend...Mrs. Balfour and her daughter Peggy.'

'No one of substance came to his funeral. Just some of his cronies and that Johnnie Stewart.'

'Mother, Aunt Lizzie's in Inverness and the Balfours live in Edinburgh.'

'They knew him for what he was, a spendthrift and drunk. The shame of it.'

'Mother.'

'Now you're fourteen you should understand these things. You'll have to do more to earn your keep, my girl.'

'Course I will.'

'Of course.'

'Of course.' *No matter how hard I try, I'll never speak the way she does.* Kirsty looked at Mother. She'd grey hair scraped back into a bun, a long red nose, deep tracks between eyebrows and ploughed lines which dragged at her mouth. *She looks older than forty and if she's any love inside her, I've never seen it. No kind word ever passes her lips.*

Sometimes Kirsty longed for love. She'd watched the Stewart brothers and how their mother, the Laird's wife, joked with them. She'd a smile for each of her sons and smothered them in embraces and kisses. When little, Rob fought to be free, Johnnie held onto her, Euan wrapped his arms round her and Duncan clung to her legs. *How I wanted one of her kisses.*

Once, when she'd been eight, she and Johnnie had played in the Stewart's orchard. They'd collected the windfalls and gave bruised apples to Johnnie's mother. Mrs. Stewart, had stood arms akimbo, beamed and kissed Johnnie and then Kirsty's cheek. She could feel Mrs. Stewart's soft lips even now.

When Kirsty flung out her arms and clung to her, Mrs. Stewart gave her a puzzled look. 'You can have a hug from me whenever you want,' she said. 'It's nice to have another wee lassie close, there's too many men in this house.'

Johnnie grinned at Kirsty. 'See,' he said. 'You're in our gang.' He'd led her to his three brothers and Morag up to their knees in a burn. 'Let's hunt for its source,' said Rob as Johnnie and Kirsty trailed along behind. The children wandered east until the roar of water made them stop at the bottom of a couple of hanging waterfalls. The water pooled and then raced west and south towards the loch.

Euan, stumbled on the rocks and plunged into the fast flowing stream. Rob and Johnnie raced after him. Kirsty remembered her panic and shouted, 'Help. Help.' But no adult came as Euan disappeared and bobbed up again.

'Swim,' screamed Morag. She whirled her arms round in a frenzy.

'Keep your head up,' shouted Rob.

'Grab something,' yelled Johnnie.

When Euan's head disappeared, Rob dived in and in a few strong strokes grabbed his brother by the scruff of the neck. Euan coughed and spat all the way to the bank. By this time, Kirsty, convinced of the worst, bunched her fists in her eyes.

'Oh stop greeting,' Morag said, hands on her slight hips. 'You're such a cry baby, Kirsty Lorne.'

'No I'm not,' said Kirsty.

'Yes you are. How does your mother put up with you?'

Each word a cut in Kirsty's heart. She stared open-mouthed at Morag.

'That's spiteful, Morag,' said Johnnie and squeezed Kirsty's hand.

'He's right,' said Rob.

'Sorry,' said Morag and looked at the ground.

'Right, no one tells about Euan or the adults will stop us coming here,' said Rob. 'We'll swear a blood oath.' He took out his dirk. 'Euan, you're first.' The children lined up behind him with Kirsty last. She glanced away as a thin red line appeared on each palm.

'Look at me when he does it,' whispered Johnnie.

Her turn came and she stared into Johnnie's grey-blue eyes and lost herself in them.

'Well done,' said Rob. He smiled at her as her palm stung.

'That reminds me,' said Morag. 'Father says we can pet our foal as long as we're gentle. He's let me have my own calf and hen too. Suppose you'll have to get back to your farm, Kirsty?'

'Morag,' said Rob.

'She didna mean it like that,' said Euan.

Johnnie put his arm round Kirsty's shoulder. She drew comfort from that, but Morag's words stung. *Always so sure of herself and with a father who loved her.*

'Let's go to Morag's,' Johnnie said.

Morag and Kirsty wove Rob daisy and clover crowns whilst Johnnie and Euan carried him on their shoulders until they all collapsed in a heap of laughter.

As his brothers and Morag continued their walk east, Johnnie, one finger over his lips, grabbed Kirsty's hand and pulled her up the hillside.

'Won't they miss us?' said Kirsty.

Johnnie shrugged.

A deserted croft with crumbled walls and holed roof stood in front them. Johnnie gathered clumps of heather and laid it inside the croft.

'What you doing?' asked Kirsty.

'You'll see. You gather grass.'

She bent her back to the task and watched him heap the green stalks on top of the heather and fling himself on it with a whoop. She joined him and they lay on it in the cool and stared for hours through the space in the roof's thatch. Johnnie pointed out hawks and eagles whilst Kirsty counted clouds.

'What shall we call it?' asked Johnnie.

Kirsty touched the moss covered walls and wondered who'd lived here. A sense of peace and happiness flooded over her. 'Our place,' she said.

'Ow.' Kirsty put a hand to her ear. Mother's calloused hand brought her back to her senses.

'Stop day dreaming and get on with our dinner.' Mother's words sliced the air like sharp blades. 'Couldn't even pick a nice day to be buried. Husband? Useless, useless man.'

A warm tear rolled down Kirsty's cheek and she brushed it off. *Perhaps if I'd been a lad, they'd have loved me.* She sliced the meat into chunks and swept it into the pot which bubbled over the fire. She looked out of the window. *At least the rain's stopped.*

A knock sounded at the back door. Kirsty turned from her task.

'You carry on, I'll get it,' said Mother.

Kirsty cut a carrot into chunks. The door rattled and a draught circled her ankles. She heard voices and the door slammed shut as she hacked at another carrot.

Mother returned. 'It's that Johnnie Stewart, gave us his condolences, if you please, and asked if you'd walk with him?'

'Can I, Mother?' Joy leapt in her throat as she untied the ribbons of her apron.

'Certainly not. Have you no sense of propriety? We'll be in mourning for months. Why you're interested in him, I don't know. He's only the Laird's third son. The one to set your cap on is the oldest, Rob. Pity he's away. It'll all pass to him you know, the title, the land and the wealth. We just have to wait, he'll come home one day.'

Kirsty hunched her shoulders as she cut more carrots into rounds. 'I like Johnnie and he likes me.'

Mother snorted. 'You're only fourteen, what do you know about men and the ways of the world? Nothing. You need to listen to me, or we'll both end our days in penury. Suppose I'd better do the churning.' She grasped the wooden stick and bent to her task.

Kirsty sliced an onion, poured the vegetables into the cook pot along with the chunks of rabbit and adjusted the heavy chain over the fire. She wiped her hands on her apron. Mother's arms worked in unison as Kirsty slipped past the smoke-blackened wicker fence into the byre as if to answer a call of nature. The cow lowed as Kirsty patted the beast's neck. She paused. Her sharp ears picked out the repetitive beat of cream being churned.

Kirsty headed for the storage room at the end of the croft, rummaged for her shawl on a hook and put her hand on the wooden latch. She listened, then opened the door. It rattled. She grimaced and waited for Mother to miss a beat. Nothing. Sunlight made Kirsty blink and she shaded her eyes with one hand as the other closed the door. An icy breeze wrapped itself round her and she shivered. *Mother will miss me, but it'll be worth the beating.*

Johnnie waved. He'd waited as she knew he would. His cheeky grin lightened her heart. His long, bony wrists stuck out of his shirt sleeves and his breeches seemed short. He held out his hand. She grasped it and loved all the warmth and wiry strength it contained. They raced across the wet pasture towards Loch Linnhe and to where his brothers and Morag huddled together and fished.

Morag cupped her hand to Euan's ear and mouthed something. Only Duncan, eleven years old now, seemed pleased to see her and waved.

Kirsty stopped. 'I dinna think they like me.'

'You're trying too hard,' Johnnie said. 'Give them another chance and pretend it doesna matter.'

Easy for him to say.

Euan's words dragged her into the present. 'What did you bring her for?' he asked as his line jerked.

The breath caught in Kirsty's throat.

'Cos, she's my lassie,' said Johnnie and squeezed Kirsty's hand.

My lassie. Kirsty sensed Johnnie had said something momentous. She raised her head and looked at Euan and Morag. Morag turned away to help Euan reel in the fish.

'Our place?' whispered Johnnie and squeezed Kirsty's hand.

'Our place,' said Kirsty and raced away in front of him.

Printed in Great Britain
by Amazon